Discipleship Training Program

Workbook 5

Third Semester

First Quarter

Classes 53 - 65

Arthur Bailey
Taking The True Gospel Of The Kingdom
To The Whole World

Arthur Bailey Ministries
P.O. Box 1182
Fort Mill, SC 29716
Library Congress Control Number: 2015900605

©2024 Arthur Bailey Ministries www.arthurbaileyministries.com All Rights Reserved.

Welcome to House of Israel Discipleship Training Program

At House Of Israel, it is our goal to reach, to preach, and to teach men and women to become disciples of the Kingdom of YeHoVaH. One method we use to accomplish this goal is through comprehensive and dynamic training classes. We are certain that upon completion of our Discipleship Training Program, you will have a better understanding, and empowered to more effectively study and communicate the Word of YeHoVaH.

If at any time you have questions or concerns about this program, please feel free to contact us by phone, by email through our web sites, or by mail. We invite you and your family and friends to attend and to participate in our services at House Of Israel in Charlotte, at one of our satellites, or through any of our online sites. We provide programs through the internet, in print, and on television stations around the world.

Shalom!

Dr. Arthur Bailey

Mailing Address

Arthur Bailey Ministries
P.O. Box 1182
Fort Mill, SC 29716 - United States

Office Phone
888-899-1479

Website Addresses
http://www.arthurbaileyministries.com/
http://www.discipleship101.tv/

Fellowship Location

House Of Israel
3601 Rose Lake Dr
Charlotte, NC 28217

Live Broadcast

Thursday @ 7 pm ET
Saturday @ 11 am ET

Table Of Contents

Third Semester

First Quarter

Class 53 Principles of Interpretation — Covenantal Principle (part 2) *5*

Class 54 Principles of Interpretation — Covenantal Principle (part 3) *21*

Class 55 Principles of Interpretation — Covenantal Principle (part 4) *37*

Class 56 Principles of Interpretation — Covenantal Principle (part 5) *53*

Class 57 Principles of Interpretation — Covenantal Principle (part 6) *69*

Class 58 Principles of Interpretation — Covenantal Principle (part 7) *85*

Class 59 Ethnic Division Principle (part 1) *101*

Class 60 Ethnic Division Principle (part 2) *117*

Class 61 Ethnic Division Principle (part 3) *133*

Class 62 Ethnic Division Principle (part 4) *151*

Class 63 Ethnic Division Principle (part 5) *167*

Class 64 The Chronometrical Principle (part 1) *185*

Class 65 The Chronometrical Principle (part 2) *205*

Discipleship Training Program

Workbook 5

Third Semester

First Quarter

Classes 53 - 65

Disclaimer: Because of the frankness of the subject matter, some of the content within this educational series may appear critical or possibly offensive to more sensitive persons. Any discussion of ethnicities, cultures, or religious affiliations or their personages are to be considered as personal opinion of the author and are offered for discussion and educational purpose. The author and editor would like readers to feel comfortable with the topics discussed herein. If you have any questions about any of the content in this or any other educational materials either in print or on the ministry's web sites, please contact the ministry with your questions or concerns. We trust that you will enjoy our teachings.

Discipleship Training Class 53

Principles of Interpretation — Covenantal Principle (part 2)

Objectives:

As a Discipleship student, at the end of this class you will be able to:

- Explain the next three covenants: Edenic, Adamic, Noahic; examining the elements and characteristics of each
- Verbally explain a deeper understanding of a covenant as it applies to the Bible
- Verbally explain the place of "covenant" in your life and spiritual walk

We are going to continue on with the covenant principle. As we noted last lesson, the definition of the covenantal principle is that principle by which the interpretation of a verse or group of verses is determined by a consideration of its covenantal setting or the setting of the covenant in which those particular verses are written.

In English, the word "covenant" signifies a mutual understanding between two or more parties; each binding himself to fulfill obligations. In scripture, the Hebrew and Greek words denote a somewhat different meaning. The Old Testament Hebrew word *beriyth*, "to cut, to contract" derives from being made by passing between pieces of flesh. We see that example through Abraham as he is cutting covenant with YeHoVaH or rather, YeHoVaH is cutting covenant with Abraham.

It is a contract or agreement between two parties. The word is derived from a root which means "to cut." Hence a covenant is a "cutting," with reference to the cutting or dividing of an animal into two parts and the contracting parties passing between them as making a covenant. Now, this is a simple definition. People can get very elaborate in defining "covenant." I try to keep things simple. I believe that if you have the basic, simple principle, that all of us can go and search; then you can go as deep and as wide as you like, but you have a base. I believe in establishing a good solid base. People who are not established on a base are out there and are dragging other people out there. They don't have a clue as to what they are talking about.

A Baptist who has been trained will debunk and create havoc in the doctrines of those people who don't have a solid foundation or base. This is how Jehovah's Witnesses got as big as it is; because they visit people's houses who do not have a base. They have knowledge. They have information. They have theology, but they cut to the base and give a scripture. A person who can't define or understand or explain the very basics is now challenged to question everything else they have been taught. They fall prey to these individuals who come knocking upon their door.

It is so important that you have a solid foundation. Once you have the foundation laid, now you just have to be careful how you build upon it.

The corresponding word in the New Testament Greek is *diatheke*, which has been however, rendered "testament," generally in the authorized version. It should be rendered just as the word *beryth* in the Old Testament, as "covenant." When Yeshua said this is the new "testament," that word is actually the new "covenant." This is the New Covenant. You don't find the word "testament" in the entire Old Testament. As a matter of fact, you don't find it in the New Testament. It is not there in its original form.

You have Old Covenant and Renewed Covenant, because the Renewed Covenant or the "New" Covenant is the Old Covenant written upon our hearts.

A covenant is a pack, treaty, alliance or agreement between two parties of equal or unequal authority. The covenant or testament is a central unifying theme in scripture; Elohim's covenants with individuals and the nation Israel finding final fulfillment in the New Covenant in Messiah Yeshua.

The word "covenant" in scripture refers to an agreement or a contract between men or between YeHoVaH and man. As we noted last lesson, there are nine specific divine covenants revealed in scripture; eight of which are progressive expressions of the first. The covenants are:

1. **The Everlasting Covenant**
2. **The Edenic Covenant**
3. **The Adamic Covenant**
4. **The Noahic Covenant**
5. **The Abrahamic Covenant**
6. **The Mosaic Covenant**
7. **The Palestinian Covenant**
8. **The Davidic Covenant**
9. **The New Covenant**

(Don't get thrown off by the term "Palestinian Covenant." The term would be Canaan or Israel Covenant because it concerned the land and the covenant made by YeHoVaH with Jacob, but it actually goes back to Abraham. He said to Abraham, "All this land I am going to give to your descendants." When we get into it, you will see exactly what it is.)

The Edenic Covenant

As we look at the Edenic Covenant, we see from ***Genesis 1:26-30:***

(Genesis 1:26) *"And God said, „Let us make man in our image, after our likeness: and let them have dominion over the fish of the sea, and over the fowl of the air, and over the cattle, and over all the earth, and over every creeping thing that creepeth upon the earth.'"*

Let them. So, Adam and Eve were made in the likeness of whom? YeHoVaH. Who was to have dominion? Adam and Eve or ADAM, which is what YeHoVaH named them. YeHoVaH named them both Adam *(Genesis 5).*

They were both called Adam. They were supposed to have dominion. They were to have dominion over the fish of the sea, over the fowl of the air, over the cattle and over all the earth; over every creeping thing that creepeth upon the earth.

(Genesis 1:27) *"So God created man in his own image, in the image of God created he him; male and female created he them."*

Now what is really interesting is that Father did not go back to the dust of the ground to take Eve out of Adam. He went to Adam to take Eve out of Adam. Eve was already there. The woman was already there. Why? Because Father created the woman and the man.

(Genesis 1:28-30) "And God blessed them, and God said unto them, „Be fruitful, and multiply, and replenish the earth, and subdue it: and have dominion over the fish of the sea, and over the fowl of the air, and over every living thing that moveth upon the earth.' And God said, „Behold, I have given you every herb bearing seed, which is upon the face of all the earth, and every tree, in the which is the fruit of a tree yielding seed; to you it shall be for meat. And to every beast of the earth, and to every fowl of the air, and to every thing that creepeth upon the earth, wherein there is life, I have given every green herb for meat:' and it was so."

When we look at the words of the promises of the Edenic Covenant, we apply the first mention principle remembering that it is often not so much the word, but the definition or idea identifying the principle. There are times when you will find that there is a principle, but the term is not there. The word "covenant" is not specifically used in relation to Eden. Covenantal language though, is evident.

The Edenic Covenant involved the creation of man in the image of Elohim. It was made before the entrance of lawlessness or sin. Adam had only one command. The promise of dominion depended upon obedience. Therefore, this covenant was a conditional covenant.

Remember we talked about the two types of covenants: the conditional covenant and the unconditional covenant. The unconditional covenant is usually prefaced by "I will." YeHoVaH says, "I will" do this. "I will" do that.

But a conditional covenant is always giving man the option. If you do this, then. If you don't do this, then. You will see a "then" typically with an "if." If — then. That is typically the idea that there is a condition involved. The blessings that YeHoVaH talks about — if you keep my commandments, then all these blessings will come upon you. If you don't keep my commandments, then all of these curses will. So, there are conditions.

(Genesis 2:16-17) "And the Lord God commanded the man, saying, „Of every tree of the garden thou mayest freely eat: But of the tree of the knowledge of good and evil, thou shalt not eat of it: for in the day that thou eatest thereof thou shalt surely die.'"

The blood of the Edenic Covenant: Adam was made a living soul. The soul life of man is in the blood.

(Leviticus 17:11-14) "For the life of the flesh is in the blood: and I have given it to you upon the altar to make an atonement for your souls: for it is the blood that maketh an atonement for the soul. Therefore, I said unto the children of Israel, „No soul of you shall eat blood, neither shall any stranger that sojourneth among you eat blood. And whatsoever man there be of the children of Israel, or of the strangers that sojourn among you, which hunteth and catcheth any beast or fowl that may be eaten; he shall even pour out the blood thereof, and cover it with dust. For it is the life of all flesh; the blood of it is for the life thereof: therefore, I said unto the children of Israel, Ye shall eat the blood of no manner of flesh: for the life of all flesh is the blood thereof: whosoever eateth it shall be cut off.'"

Can your soul eat blood? Why can't it? Because obviously it can if Father says don't do it. We are sneaking up on doctrines.

Adam was indeed a type of Messiah who was to come.

(Romans 5:14) *"Nevertheless death reigned from Adam to Moses, even over them that had not sinned after the similitude of Adam's transgression, who is the figure of him that was to come."*

Adam was the figure of him who was to come, according to Sha'ul in chapter 5. And we see from Adam to Moses, even Abraham and even over them who had not sinned, that death reigned. So, the law was important for us because the law exposed what sin is. **Sin is lawlessness. Sin is disobedience to the commandments of YeHoVaH.**

Between Adam and Moses, YeHoVaH spoke to people. He gave them specific instructions, just like he said to Adam, "Don't." He said to Abraham, "Leave. Go." He says to Cain, "Sin lies at your door." He is having these communications. As we look at how to hear the voice of God, we are going to see that YeHoVaH has spoken in many ways at various times. He did not just speak to the prophets, unless Adam was a prophet — and Adam was. Now, the Bible does not refer to Adam as a prophet, but didn't Adam prophesy?

The sign of a prophet is one who prophesies. Here is the deal. When the Holy Spirit has been given to us, we shall do what? We shall prophesy. When Adam said, "This is bone of my bone and flesh of my flesh, for this cause shall a man leave his Father and Mother and cleave to his wife and the two shall become one." Adam knew nothing about a Mother. He knew nothing about a wife. For the first time in human history, these words are coming out of a person who is the first person on earth, so he is speaking futuristically. Today people are still using these terms, "For this cause shall a man leave his Father and Mother and cleave unto his wife and the two shall become one flesh." You could even say that Adam performed his own marriage.

(1 Corinthians 15:21-22) *"For since by man came death, by man came also the resurrection of the dead. For as in Adam all die, even so in Christ shall all be made alive."*

What man did death come through? Adam. Through Adam, all died. And through Messiah all are made alive. If we think about it, every human being on the planet can take their bloodline all the way back to Noah. In essence, Ham, Shem and Japheth are the fathers of all mankind (if you would). Noah was their Father.

Regardless of what your nationality is, regardless of where you were born, regardless of what country of origin, regardless of what you call yourself; we are all (according to the Bible) first cousins (that is biologically).

The children of Japheth were the cousins of the children of Ham. They were first cousins. The children of Shem were the first cousins of the children of Ham. Ham's children, Shem's children and Japheth's children all claim Noah as their grandfather. Noah traces his lineage all the way back to Adam. Thus, all of us go back to Adam. Therefore, all were born according to and under the sin of Adam.

Messiah comes along and reverses or undoes what Adam did. Now, this is critical because when we begin to talk about the covenant, this is a powerful covenant here. The bottom line is that every human being on the planet is biologically related.

(1 Corinthians 15:45) *"And so it is written, The first man Adam was made a living soul; the last Adam was made a quickening spirit."*

The seal of the Edenic Covenant is according to *Genesis* chapter 2. Read this. I want to get you into reading your Bible. I know that you already do, but I want you to practice. You can mark it and asterisk it and now it is in your book.

(Genesis 2:8-17) "*And the L*ORD *God planted a garden eastward in Eden; and there he put the man whom he had formed. And out of the ground made the L*ORD *God to grow every tree that is pleasant to the sight, and good for food; the tree of life also in the midst of the garden, and the tree of knowledge of good and evil. And a river went out of Eden to water the garden; and from thence it was parted, and became into four heads. The name of the first is Pison: that is it which compasseth the whole land of Havilah, where there is gold; And the gold of that land is good: there is bdellium and the onyx stone. And the name of the second river is Gihon: the same is it that compasseth the whole land of Ethiopia. And the name of the third river is Hiddekel: that is it which goeth toward the east of Assyria. And the fourth river is Euphrates. And the L*ORD *God took the man, and put him into the garden of Eden to dress it and to keep it. And the L*ORD *God commanded the man, saying, „Of every tree of the garden thou mayest freely eat: But of the tree of the knowledge of good and evil, thou shalt not eat of it: for in the day that thou eatest thereof thou shalt surely die.'"*

Don't eat of the tree. If you eat of the tree, here are the consequences.

(Genesis 3:22-24) "*And the Lord God said, „Behold, the man is become as one of us, to know good and evil: and now, lest he put forth his hand, and take also of the tree of life, and eat, and live for ever:' Therefore the Lord God sent him forth from the garden of Eden, to till the ground from whence he was taken. So, he drove out the man; and he placed at the east of the garden of Eden Cherubims, and a flaming sword which turned every way, to keep the way of the tree of life.*"

Here we see that YeHoVaH now follows through on what He said. He is not putting man out. Man now has to work by the sweat of his brow because man has disobeyed the covenant. He has broken the covenant.

The tree of eternal life was the sign or seal of the Edenic Covenant. It was forfeited through sin and man was cast out of the paradise of God. The tree of life was what Father was now protecting man from. The tree of life is restored in and through Messiah.

(Revelation 2:7) "*He that hath an ear, let him hear what the Spirit saith unto the churches; „To him that overcometh will I give to eat of the tree of life, which is in the midst of the paradise of God.'*"

What is interesting is that this is the very tree of life from which YeHoVaH barred Adam and Eve from eating. Yeshua restored that relationship. Yeshua gave us access back to the tree of life. In a spiritually symbolic, but also a natural reality, Yeshua has granted us life. Those who believe in him shall never die. Those who believe in Yeshua shall have everlasting life. When does that life start? It doesn't start in the good ol' by and by. It starts right now. Once we have been regenerated by his Spirit, the life of YeHoVaH lives in us. We are to walk in the light because in him is no darkness. He who is light dwells in us. We are not to walk in darkness. We have come to the light.

(Revelation 22:2) "*In the midst of the street of it, and on either side of the river, was there the tree of life, which bare twelve manner of fruits, and yielded her fruit every month: and the leaves of the tree were for the healing of the nations.*"

The time is going to come when the nations are going to come up. The nations are going to eat. But right now, you and I bring forth the leaves of the tree. The leaves of the tree bring forth the healing of the nations. We have been given the gift of healing, the ability to heal, the manifestation of healing. We now lay hands upon the sick and they are to recover. We are like the tree of life. We are the life. We are the light of the world.

Because of us in the earth, the grace of YeHoVaH is not destroying this earth. The Father has called us to take the good news to the ends of the earth in every nation. We have to preach this good news, this gospel of the kingdom to the entire world. We are the preservative. We are the salt. We are those who preserve this world from the wrath of Almighty YeHoVaH.

> ***(Revelation 22:14)*** *"Blessed are they that do his commandments, that they may have right to the tree of life, and may enter in through the gates into the city."*

Who does his commandment? That's us. Now of course this is speaking of that which is to come, but the Kingdom of YeHoVaH has come to us. The Kingdom is not established in the earth. It is established in you and me. The Kingdom of YeHoVaH is within us.

The Adamic Covenant

We are going to do some more reading. We read part of *Genesis 3*, but I want us to read ***Genesis 3:1-24***. Read that in your Bible.

When we look at this Adamic Covenant, we see the words of the promise of the covenant, even though the word "covenant" is not specifically mentioned. The covenantal language is evident. The Adamic Covenant was made after the entrance of sin.

The Adamic Covenant is the most comprehensive covenant of all. It is important that you see this. If you don't, you will miss it. It is an unconditional covenant. It was founded upon the grace of YeHoVaH. **Grace existed before the law.** The Adamic Covenant was an unconditional covenant. It involved the promises of redemption for man and the ultimate bruising of the head of Satan.

Theologians say it is the first Messianic prophecy. It is a covenant, an unconditional covenant. Yes it prophesied Messiah, but what did it prophesy? It prophesied that Messiah was going to destroy Satan's hold on those whom Adam brought into bondage and it is unconditional. YeHoVaH promised to save us. He promised to deliver his people and he delivers on this promise over and over and over again.

This is what I remind people. **You don't keep the law to be saved. You keep the law because you are saved.** YeHoVaH did not tell the children of Israel, "Well, if you all keep all of these 613, I will come in there and deliver you." That is not what he did. He delivered them first. He saves us first.

Then he says, "Here you are. I am bringing you out of darkness into light. I am bringing you from death to life. I am taking you out of the world and bringing you into my Kingdom. Now, here is how you conduct yourself in my Kingdom. Here are my rules. Here are my commands. If you keep these commands, you shall live long in the Kingdom. If you don't, you are going to live someplace else. Ultimately it is going to be in the lowest part of the Kingdom where I put people who are disobedient.

I have to remind people because they think that hell and the Lake of Fire is on some planet outside of the Kingdom of God. You ask people, "Where is the Lake of Fire?" or "Where is hell?" Some of us reply (and I am one of them). I used to arrogantly and boldly proclaim, like Yeshua says, "Whosoever teaches these commands and whoever does these commands and teaches others will be called "great" in the Kingdom. But whoever breaks one of these commands and teaches others shall be called "least" in the Kingdom. I used to say, "At least I am in the Kingdom." So is hell. So is the Lake of Fire.

Until you can identify where it is; if he made it, it is somewhere he created. And if he created it, it belongs to him. Hello? I don't know where we get the idea that hell and the Lake of Fire are somewhere outside of the Kingdom.

So yeah, you will be least in the Kingdom — in the lake. It is the least part of the Kingdom. That was designed for Satan, the dragon and all those who follow him. It wasn't designed for YeHoVaH's people. You have to work like hell to get there. It is not easy to go there.

To go to the Lake of Fire is a hard way to go. **You have to ignore the voice.** You have to turn off all manner of prompting of his Spirit. You have to ignore every believer on the planet. You have to disregard every sermon, whether it be street preachers or some zealous person on the job. There are a lot of people on the job. You have Bible thumpers, Bible bashers, *Facebook* bashers. You can't get away from some form of the gospel. Whether it is the true gospel or not, you literally have to work hard to go to the Lake. Father says, "No, that is not for you."

The good news is that the Lake is not for you!

Yeshua made it possible and literally blocked all access to the Lake of Fire. In order to get to the Lake of Fire, you have to move Yeshua out of the way. Father has made it unconditional. I don't know how much harder to preach here. Salvation is a gift. Deliverance is a gift. *It is not based upon whether or not you keep the law.*

However, you can accept it or you can reject it. Why? Because YeHoVaH gave you that ability from creation.

Adam was made in the image and likeness of YeHoVaH. He was perfect in the day he created him, yet he was created with the ability to disobey. He had the choice to eat or not to eat just like you have the choice today to obey or disobey. Here is the option: life or death, Lake of Fire or eternal life, blessing or curses. The choice is yours.

This is why Yeshua says when you go into a town and they don't receive you — it wasn't like it says, "Oh man, I don't want to hear that." That's not what he is talking about. He says you are going into a town and they don't want to hear you. You can see when Paul went into these towns and they did not want to hear him. They did not just say, "Hey, man, we don't want to hear that." They threw rocks. They literally chased them out of town. They beat them. They had to hide. Sometimes they had to sneak out.

*(Genesis 3:15) "And **I will** put enmity between thee and the woman, and between thy seed and her seed; it shall bruise thy head, and thou shalt bruise his heel."*

You see the "I will." That is the unconditional. He says, "I am going to do this." This has absolutely nothing to do with what man does. This is what Yeshua did on the stake when he said, "It is finished," according to John who wrote it. In *1 John* he says:

(1 John 3:8) "He that committeth sin is of the devil; for the devil sinneth from the beginning. For this purpose, the Son of God was manifested, that he might destroy the works of the devil."

He who practices lawlessness is of the devil. Yeshua was manifested to undo what Satan (through the serpent) had done. What had he done? He had come and deceived the woman, tempted the man, caused the man to disobey and therefore brought them into bondage. This is why Yeshua could say to the religious leaders, "You are like your Father, the devil." Either YeHoVaH is your Father, or the devil is your Father, period.

We are born children of the devil, even though we are born sometimes into Torah-centered, Spirit-filled homes. You talk about innocent children. **There is no child that is innocent.** Don't get angry at me. **All have sinned.** Every child born — yes, even your saved, born-again, filled- with-the-Holy-Spirit-speaking-in-tongues self. Your child is born of the devil, which is why your child must be born again.

Now the good news is that because that child is in your household, you cover. Because as a believing (and here is the power) — if you have an unbelieving man in your house, who is the cover? That believing wife. She is the spiritual covering in that house, not that man. This is why YeHoVaH said, "You, believing wife, don't divorce that unbelieving man." If you are a believer and some unbeliever wants to make you his wife, you better run. You can run now or try to run later. But running later is going to be a lot more difficult because you have already been had.

Too many believing wives trying to get out of a relationship with unbelieving husbands who were unbelievers when they met them. And they say, "You knew what I was when you met me." They come out of the closet once you say, "I do," because they don't have to pretend any more. "I was a snake when you met me." Just calling it as it is. The glossiness comes over people's eyes because they fall in love. Love doesn't have anything to do with it. "What has love got to do with it?"

Love doesn't have anything to do with it. It is a covenant. You come into agreement. You make a covenant. That's what a marriage contract is. That's what the marriage license is. It is a contract. Once you sign, once you say, "I do" and sign, it has nothing to do with how you feel. You cut a covenant. People are talking about how "I don't love him anymore" or "I don't love her anymore." It never had anything to do with love. That's why you have to know who you are getting into covenant with. Be not unequally yoked. What fellowship is light and darkness?

Yeshua came to set us free. Even though he came to set us free, some silly women and silly men — some of you silly men marry some woman because of what her butt looks like. I'll just call it out. You are looking at the wrong end and thinking with the wrong head.

It is too many times I counsel too many people who are trying to get out of relationships that they wide-open-eyes walked right into it. You better know what you are getting into because once you cut the covenant; the Bible says that you have made a vow. Once you have made that vow, that vow is till death do you part. I am not going to get into marriage counseling right now, but many of you know exactly what I am talking about. You can't wait? You better wait.

The Blood of the Adamic Covenant

(Genesis 3:21) *"Unto Adam also and to his wife did Elohim make **coats of skins**, and clothed them."*

Notice it says that he did not make coats of fur or coats of wool, but coats of skin which meant that the animal died. You don't skin an animal and leave the animal alive because that is cruel. It won't survive. Adam and Eve witnessed the first substitutionary death and the shedding of sacrificial animal blood. YeHoVaH was the first one to shed blood.

I could not imagine. Here it is. I think sometimes we read the Bible and look at it and do not get the picture. Imagine. Here it is. There is a forest, a beautiful wood. There are animals everywhere. I could imagine that while YeHoVaH is walking through the garden, every animal on the planet knows that he is present. The birds stop chirping. The lions aren't roaring. The frogs aren't croaking. The crickets aren't chirping. There is silence.

I can imagine the animals saying, "Uh-oh! Somebody is in trouble." They had heard him walking through the garden before, but that is a different kind of walk. "Adam!"

You know that sound your parent makes when you are in trouble? It is different from the sound they make when they brought you a gift. You can feel it. Oh, yeah. You know you are in trouble. This was not the first time YeHoVaH, Adam and his wife had relationship, conversation or fellowship. Every other time they were out there walking in the cool of the day. This particular time, they hear his voice and they hide. They know something is up and every animal knows something is up.

YeHoVaH is now coming and he is not happy. The animals know. And I can imagine the animals talking to themselves, "Somebody's about to die. I don't know who it is, but I gotta bad feeling about this." So, Father himself, in the midst of Adam and Eve, takes an animal. Get the picture? He did not just magically wave a coat. There was something that was selected. I can't prove this, but I would think it was a sheep. I would think that it was probably a one-year-old. I would think that it would probably be the lamb that takes away the sin of Adam and Eve. It obviously was a sacrifice on their behalf, an atoning sacrifice.

The Father is the first one to shed blood. The innocent died for the guilty. It foreshadowed the plan of redemption and the broken body and shed blood of the Lamb of God. It was covenant blood.

The seal of the Adamic Covenant, same verse:

*(Genesis 3:21) "Unto Adam also and to his wife did Elohim make **coats of skins**, and clothed them."*

The seal of the covenant to Adam and Eve were the coats of skins. They had sewed on fig leaves. Now here is an act of faith. They discarded the fig leaf covering and accepted the coats of skin; a covering acceptable to God and provided through the death of a victim. These coats of skin shadowed forth the seal of a faith-righteousness that would come through Messiah.

They accept the sacrifice. It is because of this acceptance of the sacrifice that they did not get angry and bitter. They could decide and say, "YeHoVaH has given me a man." Eve was fully aware of what she had done. Adam was fully aware of what he had done. And yet we don't see them — they pass the blame initially, but they realize that passing the blame was not going to alleviate or pardon them from the consequences of their own individual action.

Every person from the beginning of time and the serpent had to pay for his action. Eve had to pay for her action. Adam had to pay for his action. Get this. The ground suffered and the animals suffered because of their action. They had not done anything. The ground had not done anything. The entire earth is groaning, travailing, waiting for the redemption, for the sons of YeHoVaH; for you and me to stand and proclaim and declare that YeHoVaH is not holding the sins of the world against it. If they would repent and accept the atoning sacrifice of Yeshua, then the reconciliation which YeHoVaH desires to have with his creation is certain.

It is not about a lot of this other stuff that we want to add to it.

Now, when a person comes into right relationship with the Father by faith, here is the covenant language, the Kingdom language. How do we live in YeHoVaH's Kingdom without destroying one another? How do we honor him? How do we love our neighbor? How do we treat our wives and children? How do we administer justice when wrong has been done? It would be nice if every human being on the planet of the earth accepted the atoning sacrifice of the blood of Yeshua. But the fact of the matter is that there are people all over on earth who are predestined to burn in the Lake of Fire.

They are the tares. There will be tares as long as there is wheat. As long as there is righteousness, there is unrighteousness. As long as there is Godliness, there is ungodliness.

(John 1:29) *"The next day John seeth Jesus coming unto him, and saith, „Behold the Lamb of God, which taketh away the sin of the world.'"*

The Lamb that YeHoVaH chose took away Adam and Eve's sin. Yeshua, the Lamb of God takes away the sins of the world, but think about it. The Lamb that was sacrificed on Adam's and Eve's behalf took away the sins of the world. They were the only ones in it. Lawlessness came to the garden long before Adam or Eve ate from the tree.

When we read the book of *Revelation*, the bottom line is that Satan (that serpent), that great dragon, was hurled down from the heavens. Where did he land? He landed in the garden. That great serpent, which is the devil, was in the garden of YeHoVaH.

The Noahic Covenant

🔍 Read *Genesis 8 and 9*. These chapters explain the covenant. The words or promises of the covenant are *Genesis 9:1-17*. This is so powerful. It is extremely powerful.

It is the same command he gave to Adam and Eve. We see that all creatures of the earth are delivered into Noah's and his wife's hands. They cared for these lions and tigers and bears and scorpions and serpents and snakes and all of these dangerous, poisonous critters. They had been in the Ark for over a year with Noah and his family. And from what I can tell, there was not one incident.

(Genesis 9:9-11) *"And I, behold, I establish my covenant with you, and with your seed after you; And with every living creature that is with you, of the fowl, of the cattle, and of every beast of the earth with you; from all that go out of the ark, to every beast of the earth. And I will establish my covenant with you, neither shall all flesh be cut off any more by the waters of a flood; neither shall there any more be a flood to destroy the earth."*

Who is this covenant established with? Noah, his seed, and all the seeds beyond him; and every living creature. Do you see that? This is the first time the word "covenant" is being used. You have to understand. YeHoVaH established a covenant with everything that was in the ark. There was nothing on the earth because everything had been destroyed. So, he established a covenant with every creature.

(Genesis 9:12-17) *"And God said, „This is the token of the covenant which I make between me and you and every living creature that is with you, for perpetual generations: I do set my bow in the cloud, and it shall be for a token of a covenant between me and the earth. And it shall come to pass, when I bring a cloud over the earth, that the bow shall be seen in the cloud: And I will remember my covenant, which is between me and you and every living creature of all flesh; and the waters shall no more become a flood to destroy all flesh. And the bow shall be in the cloud; and I will look upon it, that I may remember the everlasting covenant between God and every living creature of all flesh that is upon the earth.' And God said unto Noah, „This is the token of the covenant, which I have established between me and all flesh that is upon the earth.'"*

So, there is a sign. Notice something that he said. YeHoVaH established a covenant with everything, with every seed. He says, "I am establishing a covenant with you Noah. I am going to establish a covenant with your seeds (which are his sons). I am going to establish a covenant with their seed." Notice what he is doing. He is establishing a covenant with all mankind, both good and evil. Nobody is left out of this covenant.

This is why the Bible can say that when YeHoVaH makes it rain, he makes it rain on the just and the unjust. He said let the wheat grow up with the tares. In the end, I will do the separation because we don't know. All we know is the fruit that people bare. Because we are personable, we oftentimes ignore what is right there in front of us.

I remember one day somebody prophesied to me about my son. We rejected that prophecy, but they were right on. I know people who you say their children did something and they think their children's poop doesn't stink. They think their children do no wrong. They think their children are angels. You are deceived if you think your child is an angel. You are about as deceived as they are.

There are no baby angels. If you see baby angels, you have a problem. I don't think angels have babies, so where do baby angels come from? They are a creation, the figment of somebody's imagination that has been sold in a Catholic store near you. I am not mocking Catholics, but they are the ones who have the baby angels and so do some people who come out of Catholicism.

When you think about it, your child needs correction, instruction and discipline. It is amazing. Sometimes I watch and the television is filled with court TV. There are all these court programs where people show up in court. And you watch these parents who come in to defend their children. Listen. I know that my child is no more of an angel than your child. And I know that when I get on the subject of children, people get defensive. "How dare you talk about my little angel?" And they will say, "Oh, he is a cute little devil." You called him a devil yourself. All of our children are little devils. Some of them are cute and some of them aren't.

I am stepping way out there. Sometimes you have to drive points home. YeHoVaH made a covenant with all of creation; everything that lives, everything that moves and everything that breathes. He made a covenant with them (with us).

My wife and I had the revelation that our children don't belong to us. The moment you take ownership of your children is the moment you get between them and God. And the moment you get between them and God is the moment you shield them from his correction and from his discipline. That is why they are a pain in your "tookus" until they are dead. We have grown-up rebels.

I'll tell you. You talk about how hell has no fury like a woman scorned? Try to get to her baby. Mom, get out of the way of God. Let God at them, because if God can't get to them, you have problems.

The word of the covenant according to *Genesis* deals with the rainbow. It is here that we have the first specific mention of the word "covenant." This covenant was made with Noah and every living creature after the flood — every living creature.

That includes the homosexual, the adulterer, the lesbian, the bisexual, the transgender, the murderer. Every living creature has a covenant with the Almighty and that covenant is unconditional. YeHoVaH made it. We don't judge. We can't determine who is going to go to hell or who is not. This is why Paul says you don't know. You can't say who is going to sin. You cannot do it.

The Covenant is between YeHoVaH and his creation.

The language of the covenant is very similar to the language of the covenant made with Adam. (Compare *Genesis 1:26-30* with *Genesis 9:1-12*). This is an unconditional covenant.

The promises of God concerning the earth never being destroyed with a flood again were made to all generations. It was not made to the Jewish people or to the Hebrew people or to Israel. It was made to all people — all generations. It is all.

We have to understand this covenant in light of the passage and the covenantal principle. If we don't understand this covenant, we will get misguided. We will end up on the path of religion. Then we will start passing judgment in situations where we have no authority to pass judgment.

We will know a tree by its fruit. We do have a right and an authority to speak out against injustices and lawlessness, but our role is simply to preach, to proclaim. You can't force people. You can't make people. You can't beat up on people. Yeshua says if they don't want to hear what you say, to shake the dust off your feet and keep on moving. He will deal with them.

The blood of the covenant:

(Genesis 8:20-21) *"And Noah builded an altar unto Elohim; and took of every clean beast, and of every clean fowl, and offered burnt offerings on the altar. And YeHoVaH smelled a sweet savour; and the Lord said in his heart, „I will not again curse the ground any more for man's sake; for the imagination of man's heart is evil from his youth; neither will I again smite any more every thing living, as I have done.'"*

The imagination of a man's heart is evil, but that did not stop YeHoVaH from making a covenant with him.

(Jeremiah 17:9-10) *"The heart is deceitful above all things, and desperately wicked: who can know it? I, YeHoVaH, search the heart, I try the reins, even to give every man according to his ways, and according to the fruit of his doings."*

You don't know what is in a person's heart. All you know is what they tell you. Oftentimes we ignore what we discern because we want to believe what somebody said. Men are liars. Even born-again men are liars because there is nothing good in the flesh. Only the spirit of man which the Spirit of YeHoVaH communes with — we are to be led by the Spirit of YeHoVaH and not by our spirit. When we are led by his Spirit, then and only then are we in a state of goodness because there is nothing good in man.

We have to die constantly, daily, moment-by-moment. Every individual will be responsible for his or her actions. Noah sacrificed to YeHoVaH and burnt offerings of every clean beast and fowl. Here faith is substitutionary. Blood is evidenced *(Hebrews 11:6-7)*. Life is forfeited and covenant blood becomes the evidence of death.

(Hebrews 11:6-7) *"But without faith it is impossible to please him: for he that cometh to God must believe that he is, and that he is a rewarder of them that diligently seek him. By faith Noah, being warned of God of things not seen as yet, moved with fear, prepared an ark to the saving of his house; by the which he condemned the world, and became heir of the righteousness which is by faith."*

Do you think after that YeHoVaH stopped talking to Noah? YeHoVaH told him when to come out of the ark. YeHoVaH could have very easily told him what to sacrifice.

The sign, seal or token of the Noahic Covenant was the rainbow. It is still the seal of that covenant to all of the world; to the wicked and the just. Any reference to the rainbow in scriptures attests to the fact that God is a covenant-keeping God.

(Revelation 4:3) *"And he that sat was to look upon like jasper and a sardine stone: and there was a rainbow round about the throne, in sight like unto an emerald."*

That rainbow in heaven reminded YeHoVaH of the covenant that he made. It was not just a sign to us, but a reminder to him. And it is this rainbow that causes the Father to be long- suffering. He is waiting on us. He is waiting on us to get the gospel to the whole world. He said this gospel must be preached to the whole world as a witness. YeHoVaH cannot judge man unless man knows.

(Revelation 10:1-2) *"And I saw another mighty angel come down from heaven, clothed with a cloud: and a rainbow was upon his head, and his face was as it were the sun, and his feet as pillars of fire: And he had in his hand a little book open: and he set his right foot upon the sea, and his left foot on the earth,"*

The angel came. Even the angel with a rainbow on his head was a sign of the covenant. This is the end times. Father made a covenant in the book of *Genesis* and because of the covenant that he made; we see it even being adhered to in the book of *Revelation*.

In the next lesson we will take up the **Abrahamic Covenant**.

Class 53 Study Summary

Key Points

1. The covenantal principle is that principle by which the interpretation of a verse or group of verses is determined by a consideration of its covenantal setting or the setting of the covenant in which those particular verses are written.
2. A covenant is a contract, pack, treaty, alliance or agreement between two parties. The word "covenant" is from a root word that means "to cut."
3. The term "Palestinian Covenant" is really the Canaan or Israel Covenant. It concerns the land.
4. Adam and Eve were made in the likeness of YeHoVaH. They have coequal dominion.
5. The Edenic Covenant involved the creation of man in the image of Elohim. It was made before sin or lawlessness entered.
6. There are two types of covenants: Conditional (I will) and Unconditional (if/then).
7. Sin is disobedience to the commandments of YeHoVaH.
8. The sign or seal of the Edenic covenant was the tree of eternal life.
9. The Adamic Covenant is unconditional.
10. Grace existed before the law.
11. You don't keep the law to be saved. You keep the law because you are saved.
12. To go to the Lake of Fire is a hard way to go. You have to ignore the voice of YeHoVaH.
13. The seal of the Adamic Covenant was the coats of skin.
14. That great serpent which is the devil was hurled down from the heavens into the garden.
15. The Noahic Covenant was between YeHoVaH and his creation.
16. There are no baby angels (cherubs). That is an invention of Catholicism.
17. The sign, seal or token of the Noahic Covenant was the rainbow.

Divine Covenants in Scripture

There are nine divine covenants revealed in Scripture; eight of which are progressive expressions of the first. They are:

1. The Everlasting Covenant
2. The Edenic Covenant
3. The Adamic Covenant
4. The Noahic Covenant
5. The Abrahamic Covenant
6. The Mosaic Covenant
7. The Palestinian Covenant
8. The Davidic Covenant
9. The New Covenant

Review Exercise

1. Compare our definition of a "covenant" with this definition and origin of "testament" *(http://www.merriam-webster.com/dictionary/testament)*. Do you think "testament" as it is now delineating the divisions of the Bible is accurate or acceptable? Why or why not?

   1a. archaic: a covenant between God and the human race; b. capitalized: either of the two main divisions of the Bible. 2 a: a tangible proof or tribute; b: an expression of conviction: creed. 3 a: an act by which a person determines the disposition of his or her property after death; b: (a) will

   From: Middle English, from Anglo-French, from Late Latin & Latin; Late Latin testamentum covenant with God, holy scripture, from Latin, last will, from testari to be a witness, call to witness, make a will, from testis witness; akin to Latin (tres) three and to Latin stare to stand; from the witness's standing by as a third party in a litigation. First Known Use: 14th century.

2. Compare and contrast the three covenants covered in this lesson by summarizing the three must-have elements of each. Place a check or "X" as to which applies, either unconditional or conditional.

Covenant	Word or Promise	Blood	Seal
Edenic Unconditional____ Conditional____			
Adamic Unconditional____ Conditional____			
Noahic Unconditional____ Conditional____			

3. The covenants we are talking about are made between YeHoVaH, the Almighty, Creator of the universe and his people. Reflect on your reactions to that truth, that concept. What exactly does that mean for YOU?

   _____
   _____
   _____
   _____
   _____
   _____
   _____
   _____

Rate the following statements
by filling in the most appropriate number.

(1 = I do not agree 10 = I agree completely)

Objectives:

1. I can explain the next three covenants: Edenic, Adamic, Noahic; examining the elements and characteristics of each.

   1. ○   2. ○   3. ○   4. ○   5. ○   6. ○   7. ○   8. ○   9. ○   10. ○

2. I can explain a deeper understanding of a covenant as it applies to the Bible.

   1. ○   2. ○   3. ○   4. ○   5. ○   6. ○   7. ○   8. ○   9. ○   10. ○

3. I can verbally explain the place of "covenant" in my life and spiritual walk.

   1. ○   2. ○   3. ○   4. ○   5. ○   6. ○   7. ○   8. ○   9. ○   10. ○

My Journal

What I learned from this class:

_____
_____
_____
_____
_____
_____
_____
_____
_____
_____
_____
_____
_____
_____
_____

Discipleship Training Class 54

Principles of Interpretation — Covenantal Principle (part 3)

Objectives:

As a Discipleship student, at the end of this class you will be able to:

- Explain the Abrahamic Covenant by identifying its critical elements and specifications
- Explain your understanding of the covenant made with Abraham considering all his progeny as it compares with popular understanding

In this lesson we are moving forward through the covenantal principle. Just to review the definition: That principle by which the interpretation of a verse or group of verses is determined by a consideration of its covenantal setting. We have been looking at the various covenantal settings: the Everlasting Covenant, the Edenic Covenant, the Adamic Covenant and the Noahic Covenant.

The English word "covenant" signifies a mutual understanding between two or more parties; each binding himself to fulfill obligations. In scripture, the Hebrew and Greek words as we have seen denote a somewhat different meaning.

The Old Testament[1] meaning "to cut, to contract" derives from the practice of passing between two pieces of animal flesh. A contract or agreement between two parties was made with reference to the cutting or dividing of animals into two parts and the contracting parties passing between them making a covenant. The Hebrew *beriyth* conveys this meaning.

The corresponding word in the New Testament Greek is *diatheke,* which is rendered "testament" although it ought to be rendered "covenant." That is to say that when we see the word "testament," it is Greek for a similar, although not same idea. We are going to be looking at some of the attempts of translators and others to infuse a belief system into the Bible. We are just going to look at it. I leave the searching up to you.

A covenant is a pact, treaty, alliance or agreement between two parties of equal or unequal standing. The covenant (or testament) is a central unifying theme in scripture, Elohim's covenants with individuals and the nation Israel finding final fulfillment in the New Covenant in Messiah Yeshua. The word "covenant" refers in scripture to an agreement or contract between men or between YeHoVaH and man.

The Abrahamic Covenant

We find the focus of the Abrahamic Covenant in **Genesis 12:1-3** and *Genesis 22*. This is where Father begins to speak.

*(**Genesis 12:1-3**) "Now YeHoVaH had said unto Abram, ,,Get thee out of thy country, and from thy kindred, and from thy father's house, unto a land that I will show thee: And I will make of thee a great nation, and I will bless thee, and make thy name great; and thou shalt be a blessing: And I*

---

[1] The word "testament" actually never occurs in the Old "Testament." It is always "covenant."

will bless them that bless thee, and curse him that curseth thee: and in thee shall all families of the earth be blessed.""

I want you to see something right here in verse 3. Father makes this statement one time to one person, but there are people who claim this as their own. There are folks who will say that whoever blesses Israel, God is going to bless and whoever curses Israel, God will curse. But Father did not make that statement to Israel.

Now sure, he made it to Abraham. When he made this statement to Abraham, Abraham had no children. What you will find are theologians and history buffs and those who consider themselves to be those who have correctly kept history in the correct context. Historians will try to direct us through a lineage. What happens at the end of that directing? We are going to see Paul doing some of that same thing because Paul has a tendency to say things in the context that it is written. But when we research some of that "it is written" that he refers to, it is simply not there.

Oftentimes what people do is say that Paul said something. But you have to understand that **when we get the Bible, we get the Bible that has been translated.** This means that there are people who, in the process of translation, just as you have preachers; you have to see this for what it is. You have preachers who cut and paste verses of scripture together to create a doctrine, to create a belief system. People who buy into that doctrine and buy into that belief system will swear and argue and be ready to fight to defend that doctrine when in essence it is not defendable.

Those of us who have come out of Christian circles understand that we were as zealous as many individuals in those environments. People had taken the Bible, put a spin on it, and caused us to buy into the spin. Translators did this. If I am of a certain mindset, if I am of a certain bent, if I am of a certain belief system and I decide that I am going to translate the Bible or retranslate the Bible or write my own version of the Bible; it is going to be written from the mindset that I am grounded in. I am going to see it from that perspective. So, a Baptist sees it from that perspective. A Pentecostal sees it from a different perspective. A Jehovah's Witness sees it from a perspective. A Seventh Day Adventist sees it from a perspective. A Greek sees it from a perspective. A Hebrew or Jew sees it from a perspective. Everybody is going to look at it from a perspective in which they were brought up.

Even in the Hebrew community you have people who practice Judaism, but who do not know the Torah. You have Catholics who practice Catholicism, but they do not know the Bible and they will argue with you.

They will argue from a theological perspective and not from a biblical perspective. They will use the Bible to back a theology. This is what people do with this book. **They use this book to justify a belief system.**

YeHoVaH says he is going to bless Abraham. He did not say this to Isaac. He did not say this to Jacob. He did not say this to Israel. He said this to Abraham. When you have a nation Israel who takes this blessing — and they make the statement that whoever blesses Israel, and whoever curses Israel will be cursed because they are of the lineage of Abraham — BUT...

Ishmael can make the same claim. Not just Ishmael, but all of Keturah's children. They could make the same statement. Well, we are who Abraham was talking about. He was talking to Abraham. And if he was talking to Abraham's seed, he was talking to <u>all</u> of Abraham's seed. You can't separate the seed. That is just like taking your children from a Mother and a Father who are biologically the same. He did not make this statement to Sarah.[2]

---

[2] We know that in this particular situation, Abraham had Ishmael and Abraham had Isaac. I understand that concept, but they both came from Abraham. YeHoVaH did not make this with Sarai/Sarah. He said this to Abraham.

Sarah was the mother of Isaac. Isaac was the son of Abraham, as was Ishmael the son of Abraham and so were the children of Keturah.

As a matter of fact, this would be a good place to go on a quick rabbit trail.

(Genesis 25:1-6) *"Then again Abraham took a wife, and her name was Keturah. And she bare him Zimran and Joksham, and Medan, and Midian, and Ishback, and Shuah. And Joksham begot Sheba and Dedan. And the sons of Dedan were Asshurim, and Letushim, and Leummim. And the sons of Midian: Ephah, and Epher, and Hanoch, and Abidah, and Eldaah. All these were the children of Keturah. And Abraham gave all that he had unto Isaac. But unto the sons of the concubines, which Abraham had, Abraham gave gifts, and sent them away from Isaac his son, while he yet lived, eastward, unto the east country."*

Now we see that YeHoVaH had made some revelation to Sarai, who wanted Abraham to send Ishmael away. YeHoVaH says, "Abraham, listen to your wife." Well, Sarah is dead. Abraham has more children and what does he do? He sends them away, too. Now, we don't see where YeHoVaH tells him to do that, but he is still in a place, in a mindset as far as what the last thing was that YeHoVaH told him about Isaac.

Understand something, because what I am trying to get you to see and understand is that YeHoVaH made promises to Abraham. And if someone today can claim the promises of Abraham while not being natural children, how much more can his biological children claim those promises?

Let's keep reading. Let's first look at:

(Genesis 12:3) *"And I will bless them that bless thee, and curse him that curseth thee: and **in thee shall all families of the earth be blessed**."*

(Genesis 22:1-2) *"And it came to pass after these things, that God did tempt Abraham, and said unto him, „Abraham:" and he said, „Behold, here I am." And he said, „Take now they son, thy only son Isaac, who thou lovest, and get these into the land of Moriah: and offer him there for a burnt offering upon one of the mountains which I will you of.""*

This idea of "whom you love" is the indication that Abraham truly loved his son. He really loved his son. The idea here when he is saying "whom you love" is that he is (as you know), about to test Abraham as to whom he loves more. Do you love your son more than me?

Now, Yeshua comes along and says to us, "Who is my Mother? Who are my brothers except those who do the will of my Father?" He says except you love your Father more, except you hate your Mother and hate your sisters and hate your brothers. He is not saying to hate them. What he is saying is except that you love your Father *more*.

What YeHoVaH is doing to all of us (and he uses Abraham as the model), is that he uses Abraham and tests Abraham to show us that we too will be tested to the point where we have to make a decision as to whom we love more. We will be asked whether we love our Father and our earthly Mother and our earthly sisters and our earthly brothers more than we love our heavenly Father. We will always be tested in that area.

Father is constantly testing his people. Why?

As we look in *Genesis*, as we look in *Exodus, Numbers* and *Deuteronomy*, what we find is that the Father tests us to show us what is in our hearts to prove us. He comes to prove what is in you; to see what you love more than him. And what you love more than him is what you will put before him. It is those things that will cause us to disobey his commands; the things that we love more than him.

When we love him more than anything else, then his commands become preeminent in our lives. His commands are what govern us. His commands are what cause us to live. And we live in a way where we are obedient to what he says, even when it means separating from the people that we love — less.

If we are not willing to separate from the people whom we love less, then what we are saying is that we love them more.

Now read further along in *Genesis 3:2-12*. Don't skip over that because you know the story. What he is saying here is that Abraham loved Isaac. He loved him more than anything other than Elohim himself.

🔍**Read *Genesis 3:13-18***. See in verse 18 where it says,

"In your seed shall all the nations of the earth be blessed because you have obeyed my voice."

🔍 **Read *Genesis 3:19-20***. I want you to see something here because I know that a lot of times people will (when they get into genealogies) miss certain things. But notice what the writer here does for us.

(Genesis 22:19) "So Abraham returned unto his young men, and they rose up and went together to Beersheba; and Abraham dwelt at Beersheba."

We see that Abraham is back dwelling in Beersheba. We don't know how many years he is dwelling there.

(Genesis 22:20) "And it came to pass after these things, that it was told Abraham, saying, „Behold, Milcah, she hath also born children unto thy brother Nahor;""

There is communication between Abraham and Nahor, but there is someone who brings a message saying, "Hey, Milcah has born children unto your brother." Who is Milcah? Nahor's wife.

(Genesis 22:21) "Huz his firstborn, and Buz his brother, and Kemuel the father of Aram,"

Huz and Buz may have been twins. We know there are twins in this family gene because of Esau and Jacob. Now Nahor has children. One of his sons has a child named Aram.

(Genesis 22:22-23) "And Chesed, and Hazo, and Pildash, and Jidlaph, and Bethuel. And Bethuel begat Rebekah: these eight Milcah did bear to Nahor, Abraham's brother."

Now we see Rebekah is Abraham's great-niece.

(Genesis 22:24) "And his concubine, whose name was Reumah, she bare also Tebah, and Gaham, and Thahash, and Maachah."

Whenever you see genealogies, whenever you see names in the Bible, they are there for a reason. They are always there for a reason. But one of the least read passages of scripture are genealogies. The genealogy will reveal things to us that if we did not pay attention to it, it wouldn't even make sense. It is like, "Why are all of these genealogies in here?"

Well, if you look at the genealogy, you can actually trace bloodlines. You can actually trace information. The genealogy is a dot, if you would. The Bible is like this puzzle. It is like one of those connect-the-dot puzzles. And if you look at the genealogy as dots, you will be able to see how to connect the dots together to see some things that Father may be trying to communicate to us.

The words or promises of the Abrahamic Covenant: Abraham is the Father of all who believe.

(Romans 4:16-17) *"Therefore it is of faith, that it might be by grace; to the end the promise might be sure to all the seed; not to that only which is of the law, but to that also which is of the faith of Abraham, who is the father of us all, (As it is written, I have made thee a father of many nations,) before him whom he believed, even God, who quickeneth the dead, and calleth those things which be not as though they were."*

Notice "As it is written." Who is he talking to? Abraham. The promises of God involved in the Abrahamic Covenant touch the natural and the spiritual, the temporal and the eternal. The major promise was the promise of salvation through Messiah, the seed of Abraham.

(Matthew 1:1) *"The book of the generation of Jesus Christ, the son of David, the son of Abraham."*

Here we see that Yeshua is called the son of David. We see that in the Bible, but he is also the seed of Abraham. So, if Yeshua is the seed of Abraham, then also David all the more because David came before Yeshua. Who was the actual seed of Abraham? Isaac. Isaac and Ishmael were the physical, biological seeds of Abraham.

Now you have the natural, but you also have a spiritual. There is a promise that is associated with the seed of Abraham. Oftentimes when you see "seed," you can look at it from a natural and from a spiritual perspective. We know the parable that Yeshua told about the sower who sowed seed. Some seed fell in various places. And it talked about how the sower was sowing the word. The seed was the word of YeHoVaH.

We know that there is a natural, physical seed. That is where a person is born through or from the seed.

(Galatians 3:16) *"Now to Abraham and his seed were the promises made. He saith not, „And to seeds, as of many; but as of one, And to thy seed, which is Christ.""*

This is where Paul gets a little tricky. We have to ask ourselves if this is Paul's doing or is this translation? Oftentimes Paul is confused in things that may be caused by translators. The assumption is that translators accurately translated everything that was written from the Hebrew to the Greek to the Latin to the English. This is why the Torah becomes so vital. If we look at the New Testament only and apart from the Torah, we don't necessarily have a foundation whereby we can compare or ascertain where these things are coming from.

Whenever the Bible refers to something that is "written" and you don't see where it is written, the assumption is that it is written somewhere. That is just the natural assumption. If it is in the Bible and Paul said it, then you would assume it.

Paul writes, *"He saith not, „And to seeds, as of many; but as of one..."* We look at *Galatians* and see *"And to thy seed, **which is Messiah**."* I don't think when Abraham heard this that the idea of Messiah came to mind. What do you think? Abraham wanted a son. YeHoVaH says, *"I am going to give you a son."* He referred to that son as a seed.

Now we see some spiritual connotation here. What the writer is saying, what the translators are saying, is to disregard all of the seed. Disregard the natural seeds of Abraham: Ishmael, Isaac and the sons of Keturah. Ignore the genealogy of Isaac, Jacob and all the way to David and to Messiah. What YeHoVaH was saying to Abraham was:

"Abraham, I am going to give you a seed and his name is going to be Yeshua."

This is what this verse is saying. This is what the translators said. Look at it again. How does a translator get Messiah from Abraham and the conversation YeHoVaH is having with Abraham? Do you see the spiritualization taking place here?

The assumption is that because it is written in the book of *Galatians* that YeHoVaH said to Abraham, "I am going to give you a seed and this seed is going to be the Savior of the world. And just so you know, his name is Yeshua." Abraham makes no reference to that.

It was to be through Messiah that all nations would be blessed. This covenant was confirmed to Isaac. We know that in the long haul, what YeHoVaH was saying to Abraham basically was what he established with Adam and Eve when he told Eve "and your seed." It would be more appropriate to associate this with Eve than with Abraham, because he said that the seed of the woman is going to crush the head of the serpent.

Now you can put a spiritual connotation on that because it specifically says that the seed of the woman is going to crush the seed of the serpent. The serpent's seed will bruise his heel, but the woman's seed is going to crush his head.

(Genesis 26:2-4) *"And the Lord appeared unto him (Isaac), and said, „Go not down into Egypt; dwell in the land which I shall tell thee of: Sojourn in this land, and I will be with thee, and will bless thee; for unto thee, and unto thy seed, I will give all these countries, and I will perform the oath which I sware unto Abraham thy father; And I will make thy seed to multiply as the stars of heaven, and will give unto thy seed all these countries; and in thy seed shall all the nations of the earth be blessed;""*

Now the seed continues. He is speaking to Isaac. So, when you see "unto your seed all these countries," what you are seeing is a Land Covenant. That is what we are going to be looking at later under the Palestinian Covenant.

This covenant was confirmed to Jacob.

(Genesis 28:3-5) *"„And God Almighty bless thee, and make thee fruitful, and multiply thee, that thou mayest be a multitude of people; And give thee the blessing of Abraham, to thee, and to thy seed with thee; that thou mayest inherit the land wherein thou art a stranger, which God gave unto Abraham." And Isaac sent away Jacob: and he went to Padanaram unto Laban, son of Bethuel the Syrian, the brother of Rebekah, Jacob's and Esau's mother."*

Isaac is now doing what? He is giving Jacob a blessing. In verse 1: *"And Isaac called Jacob, and blessed him..."* Do you see this?

Here is something. If you wanted to get spiritual, here is a good place to get really, really spiritual. When Isaac pronounces the blessing upon Jacob his son, now Father has been given permission to bless Jacob. He released the blessing. Parents, you can release the blessing or curses. It is all about what you allow to come out of your mouth over your seed.

Isaac blessed Jacob. When Isaac blessed Jacob, what Isaac was doing is very similar to what YeHoVaH told Aaron to do to Israel. "I want you to pronounce the blessing over my people and when you do that, you are putting my name upon them."

When you open your mouth, either blessings are going to come out or curses are going to come out. You have to be very careful because whatever you release is going to give something authority in the spirit realm. You are releasing either a blessing that is going to give the angels of YeHoVaH authority, YeHoVaH himself authority or you are pronouncing curses that are going to give the forces of evil (HaSatan) authority.

Death and life are in the power of the tongue. This means blessings and curses. A spring cannot bring up pure, clean water, sweet water and bitter water. You can't pronounce blessings and curses. Yeshua says we are to bless them that curse us. We should not be a people that are pronouncing curses. We have to practice pronouncing blessings. When we release blessings — one, it shows us whose side we are on; and two, who we are giving permission to operate according to our words.

We see that Isaac calls Jacob and he blessed him.

(Genesis 28:5) *"And Isaac sent away Jacob: and he went to Padanaram unto Laban, son of Bethuel the Syrian, the brother of Rebekah, Jacob's and Esau's mother."*

Bethuel has a daughter Rivka (Rebekah), but he also has a son. So, now we see that Abraham was a Syrian. You did know that, right? When we look at that, people want to say that Abraham was Hebrew. He was Jewish. No, Abraham was from Syria. He was a wandering Aramean. Can any good thing come from Syria? Absolutely. Abraham did.

(Genesis 28:6-9) *"When Esau saw that Isaac had blessed Jacob, and sent him away to Padanaram, to take him a wife from thence; and that as he blessed him he gave him a charge, saying, „Thou shalt not take a wife of the daughters of Canaan;" And that Jacob obeyed his father and his mother, and was gone to Padanaram; And Esau seeing that the daughters of Canaan pleased not Isaac his father; Then went Esau unto Ishmael, and took unto the wives which he had Mahalath the daughter of Ishmael Abraham's son, the sister of Nebajoth, to be his wife."*

What does this tell us? It tells us that Abraham and Ishmael and Jacob and Isaac and Esau all lived in close proximity. Even though Abraham sent Ishmael away, they were still in proximity to one another. I think we get the impression that he sent them hundreds and hundreds of miles away. I just find it strange that shortly after his encounter with his Dad who pronounces the blessing and calls upon the name of YeHoVaH upon his son, that now the Almighty appears to this young man and says, "Yes, I am the one whom your Father called upon when he blessed you."

The blood of the Abrahamic Covenant, going back in *Genesis*:

(Genesis 15:1-2) *"After these things the word of the Lord came unto Abram in a vision, saying, „Fear not, Abram: I am thy shield, and thy exceeding great reward. And Abram said, Lord God, what wilt thou give me, seeing I go childless, and the steward of my house is this Eliezer of Damascus?""*

Where is Damascus? Syria. Abraham and Eliezer left Syria together. Eliezer was a servant.

Read *Genesis 15:3-13*. Notice verse 13:

"And he said unto Abram, „Know of a surety that <u>thy seed shall be a stranger in a land that is not theirs</u>, and shall serve them; and they shall afflict them four hundred years;"'"

Oftentimes "seed" is plural.

🔍 **Read the rest of *Genesis 15*.** He is saying, "I am going to give you all this land and here are the people who are on this land now." They occupied the land, but the land belongs to whom? The land belongs to YeHoVaH. "The earth is His; the fullness thereof". So, you have people who occupy land that YeHoVaH has assigned to someone else.

Sometimes we are living our lives based upon the limitations that we have established in our own minds. Father may have land just like he had for them that was being occupied by someone else.

The covenant blood was shed in the offering of the God-appointed five sacrifices mentioned in ***Genesis 15:9***. We see a three-year old heifer, a three-year old ram, a three-year old she-goat, a pigeon and a turtledove. God passed between the pieces of those sacrifices as he covenanted with Abraham.

The seal of the Abrahamic Covenant is where this gets really interesting. The seal of the covenant — **Read *Genesis 17:1-13*.** I want you to pay attention to what he is saying. He is saying,

"Abraham, this is the covenant. You, all of your seed; all that is born in your house shall be circumcised. Every male child: those who are bought with money or any stranger which is not of your seed."

Let's keep going.

(Genesis 17:14) *"And the uncircumcised man child whose flesh of his foreskin is not circumcised, that soul shall be cut off from his people; he hath broken my covenant."*

With whom is the covenant being made? I want you to see that the covenant is made with Abraham, but not just with Abraham. Anyone that does not get circumcised has broken the covenant that YeHoVaH made with Abraham. So, through circumcision they are part of the covenant of Abraham.

Father could have made this covenant with Abraham and no one else had to be circumcised. Isn't that right? I am pointing this out to you because the New Testament is going to say something that seems to contradict this. This is where the Christians are.

Again, **verse 14**:

"And the uncircumcised man child whose flesh of his foreskin is not circumcised, that soul shall be cut off from his people; he hath broken my covenant."

Who is the covenant with? Abraham and all those who enter into the Abrahamic Covenant.

(Genesis 17:15-16) *"And God said unto Abraham, „As for Sarai thy wife, thou shalt not call her name Sarai, but Sarah shall her name be. And I will bless her, and give thee a son also of her: yea, I will bless her, and she shall be a mother of nations; kings of people shall be of her."'"*

So, he is talking about Isaac and Isaac's offspring. **Now read *Genesis 17:17-23*.** Did he miss the message? Did he misinterpret the message? No. Abraham took Ishmael and all that were born in his house and all that were bought with his money, every male among the men of Abraham's house.

(Genesis 17:24) *"And Abraham was ninety years old and nine, when he was circumcised in the flesh of his foreskin."*

For those of you who did not get circumcised on the eighth day, there is still hope.

(Genesis 17:25-27) *"And Ishmael his son was thirteen years old, when he was circumcised in the flesh of his foreskin. In the selfsame day was Abraham circumcised, and Ishmael his son. And all the men of his house, born in the house, and bought with money of the stranger, were circumcised with him."*

The sign, seal or token of the covenant was circumcision. The covenant is distinctly called the "**seal of the covenant**."

(Romans 4:11 with Acts 7:8) *"And he received the sign of circumcision, a seal of the righteousness of the faith which he had yet being uncircumcised: that he might be the father of all them that believe, though they be not circumcised; that righteousness might be imputed unto them also:"*

Notice this. Here is where it gets tricky. "Though they be not circumcised." What is he saying here and is he saying it? "Look, Abraham received the sign of circumcision, a seal of the righteousness of the faith, which he had yet being uncircumcised."

Wait a minute. The sign of the circumcision was the seal. He received the word, but when he obeyed it, he entered into the covenant. Had he not been circumcised, what would have happened? He would have been cut off and also all of the people in his house. So, now the book of *Romans* comes along. I really questioned this because I know that there were those who accused Paul of teaching that the people of YeHoVaH no longer needed to be circumcised.

That causes one to ask was Paul really teaching the Torah or are these actually the words of Paul? You see, there are certain things that become questionable because if Paul is changing something YeHoVaH said, does he have the authority or the right to do that? I don't think so.

(Acts 7:8) *"And he gave him the covenant of circumcision: and so, Abraham begat Isaac, and circumcised him the eighth day; and Isaac begat Jacob; and Jacob begat the twelve patriarchs."*

Notice here that what the book of *Acts* is saying is actually the historical event. Paul writes *Romans* and this is what we are instructed. We are told that Paul wrote it. We assume that Paul wrote every word in the book of *Romans*. That is the assumption. What he is saying here in the book of *Romans* is that Abraham received the sign of circumcision, although he had not been circumcised.

Now, does this make sense to you? It is twisted. So, a twisted mind would say, "See here! Here it is!" If you throw away the Torah and you throw away the book of *Acts* (because *Acts* accurately says what Abraham did). If you look at this, you would get the impression that Abraham did not need to be circumcised in order to receive the promise. You would think that none of his household needed to be circumcised and that none of us need to be circumcised. All we have to do is believe.

Abraham believed and it was accounted unto him as righteousness. But Abraham's action was the indication that he believed, because Abraham did what God said.

When you separate the New Testament out from the Tanakh, now you can begin to play with words. This is because ***Romans 4:11*** seems a little bit confusing and contradictory to what the Torah actually teaches.

You will find the same thing in the book of *Galatians* as well, so we have to compare spiritual with spiritual. We have to compare the word. This book points to circumcision of the heart that is of the Spirit, not of the letter or of the flesh.

(Romans 2:28-29) *"For he is not a Jew, which is one outwardly; neither is that circumcision, which is outward in the flesh: But he is a Jew, which is one inwardly; and circumcision is that of the heart, in the spirit, and not in the letter; whose praise is not of men, but of God."*

If you look at this at face value, you will pass right over it. But if you look at it from a mind of okay, I really want to understand what Paul is saying; what Paul is saying here is that the circumcision is not what makes you a Jewish person. Understand that Paul came out of what faith? Judaism. In order to convert to Judaism, if you were a man and you converted to Judaism, you have to be circumcised. That is a conversion. That is where you have a proselyte, one who converts to Judaism.

When we look at the book of *Acts*, we found that there were proselytes from Rome. The word "proselyte" means a convert; one who came up to the feast as a proselyte, one who had converted to Judaism. There were many proselytes. That is what the Pharisees taught. So, you get to *Acts 15* and the Pharisees come along.

Some people want to think that the circumcision of the heart just miraculously shows up in the book of *Romans*. It is throughout the Bible. But folks say, "You don't need a physical circumcision. You just need a heart circumcision." Listen, who circumcises the heart?

(Deuteronomy 10:15-16) *"Only the Lord had a delight in thy fathers to love them, and he chose their seed after them, even you above all people, as it is this day. Circumcise therefore the foreskin of your heart, and be no more stiffnecked."*

(Deuteronomy 30:6) *"And the Lord thy God will circumcise thine heart, and the heart of thy seed, to love the Lord thy God with all thine heart, and with all thy soul, that thou mayest live."*

So, before YeHoVaH does it, you have to do it. He is asking you to circumcise your heart. How do you circumcise your heart? The key is, don't be stiff-necked. When you are hard-hearted, sniff-necked, rebellious and anti-law, you have taken a position that you are not going to obey the commands of YeHoVaH, which is exactly what the children of Israel did.

He says that you circumcise your heart. I have given you the instructions to circumcise your foreskin. That is a given. If you don't do that, you are automatically cut off. Anybody who does not circumcise their foreskin; how in the world are they going to circumcise their heart? What is the point in circumcising your heart if you are not even in covenant?

Back to Paul:

(Romans 2:29) *"But he is a Jew, which is one inwardly; and circumcision is that of the heart, in the spirit, and not in the letter; whose praise is not of men, but of God."*

It is not what you do outside. What is going on inside is what is going to manifest outside. This is how you are going to know a tree. You are going to know the tree by its fruit. What is in your heart is what is going to come out. Out of the abundance of the heart is what people speak. What is in you is going to come out. It is not what goes into you that makes you unclean. It is what comes out.

That has nothing to do with food. But in a sense, people call things that are not food, "food." How can you call something food that Father says is an abomination? He said it is not food. "Oh, but we sanctified it." Well, it doesn't matter. You can sanctify skunk. But people eat what they want to eat.

I was at *Best Buy* and it was around seven o'clock. It was dark out. I saw this raccoon. I remembered growing up how there were people who used to sell possums, raccoon and rabbit. My parents bought some of that stuff and we ate it. It was some of the stinkiest stuff. One of the most disgusting smells I have ever smelled in my entire life was a hog being slaughtered. Then they had to burn the hair off of this thing because you just couldn't pluck it out. They burned the hair because you want to eat all of that pig. It is so disgusting. Smelling it fried and cooked — and anybody who fries bacon today, right when it first starts to fry, you can smell the stench.

After a while you don't smell it anymore. But when it first starts, you can smell it and hear those parasites popping. That is not food.

When you come down to the commands of YeHoVaH, if a person has not circumcised their foreskin, they are not going to circumcise their heart. To circumcise one's heart is to come to the point that YeHoVaH's law is what governs. If you have not come to that point, why are you going to — what's the need? All you have to do is believe in Jesus now.

Then he wants you to circumcise your heart, but he wants to give you a new one. He wants to remove the old one, the stony one; but one has to recognize the need for it.

Paul's argument with the Pharisees in *Acts 15* had nothing to do with the **Torah**. It had everything to do with **Judaism**, which he came out of.

(Romans 3:1-2) *"What advantage then hath the Jew? or what profit is there of circumcision? Much every way: chiefly, because that unto them were committed the oracles of God."*

He asks a question and answers it. What is the advantage to being a Jew? There is an advantage to being a Jew. What is the advantage of being circumcised? There is an advantage to being circumcised. The word there is actually "Judean." Paul says much in every way. Why? The main reason is because unto them were committed the oracles of YeHoVaH.

What were the oracles?

The commandments!

That is what profited them. No other nation was given them — no other nation. No other nation had YeHoVaH as their Elohim and the promise that he was going to raise them high above all nations. That is the profit. That is the advantage.

Those who enter into the commonwealth of Israel are those who come in by faith in Messiah. It is not based upon keeping the commands.

I will be the first to say that we are not saved *because we keep the commands*. We keep the commands *because we are saved*.

In the next lesson we will get into the **Mosaic Covenant**.

Class 54 Study Summary

Key Points

1. The word for "covenant" in the New Testament is *diatheke,* which is rendered as "testament."
2. When we read the Bible, we are reading what has been translated. That is why we must search the scriptures using every available tool.
3. Most people in religions do not know the Torah or the Bible. They are arguing doctrine. They are arguing a theological perspective. They use the Bible to justify a belief system.
4. YeHoVaH said he was going to bless Abraham. He didn't say this to Isaac, Jacob or Israel.
5. We are to love our Father more than anyone and anything else. That means that his commandments will govern us.
6. If we are unwilling to separate from people whom we are to love less than YeHoVaH, then what we are saying is that we love them more than him.
7. Abraham is the Father of faith. He is the Father of all those who believe.
8. The promises of God involved in the Abrahamic Covenant touch the natural, spiritual, temporal and eternal. The major promise was that of salvation through Messiah, the seed of Abraham.
9. Yeshua is called the son of David, but he is also the seed of Abraham.
10. The seed from the parable of the sower was the word of YeHoVaH.
11. The assumption is that the Bible's translators accurately translated everything from Hebrew to Greek to Latin and then to English. That is why the Torah is so vital. We can't look at the New Testament apart from the Torah, which is the foundation.
12. When the Bible refers to something that is "written" and you don't see where it is written, you should go and see where it is written.
13. It was through Messiah that all nations would be blessed.
14. Death and life are in the power of the tongue. This means blessings and curses.
15. Yeshua says that we are to bless them that curse us. We should not be pronouncing curses.
16. Abraham, Ishmael, Jacob, Isaac and Esau all lived in close proximity.
17. Sometimes we live our lives based on the limitations that we have established in our own minds.
18. Circumcision is a requirement in order to be in covenant with YeHoVaH.
19. The sign, seal or token of the Abrahamic Covenant is circumcision.
20. Abraham believed God and it was accounted unto him as righteousness. His actions were the indication that he believed what God had said.
21. In order to circumcise our heart, we must not be hardhearted or stiff-necked, rebellious or anti-law. We must obey the commandments of YeHoVaH. We must allow him to give us a new heart.
22. The oracles that were given to the Jewish people (Judeans) were the commandments. They were not given to people to become part of Judaism (the religion).

Review Exercise

1. This entire lesson focused on one covenant: the Abrahamic. How are the covenantal elements of word or promise, blood and seal described pertaining to the Abrahamic Covenant?

   Word or Promise:

   Blood:

   Seal:

2. It is said that history is written by the winners. How does that saying apply when it comes to the Abrahamic Covenant as it is sort of popularly understood relating to the modern state of Israel?

3. In the Abrahamic Covenant, YeHoVaH required for Abraham to be circumcised and to circumcise males in his household. In Judaism, a *bris* (see the resemblance to the word *beriyth* in Hebrew) is the ceremony of circumcision of eight-day old male infants. Presumably, the baby has no say in the matter (except for angry crying immediately afterward maybe!). What does the eighth-day requirement in **Genesis 17:12** really mean then in terms of who is participating and how?

   Parents:

   Baby:

   Community:

4. What is wrong with this picture? *Google* "Abraham's family tree." Most of the results have been prepared or at least overseen or authorized by theologians and Bible scholars. But what do you notice that is wrong with probably 98% of them? Use this space to work out your own family tree for Abraham. Start at the bottom of the space below or the top, whichever makes more sense to you.

5. See if you can build "the short course" about the Abrahamic Covenant as though you were going to tell it to someone. Using the framework of the three main elements, expand it just enough to explain but not overburden your hearer. You want something left for them to study.

Rate the following statements
by filling in the most appropriate number.

(1 = I do not agree 10 = I agree completely)

Objectives:

1. I can explain the Abrahamic Covenant by identifying its critical elements and specifications.

   1. ○   2. ○   3. ○   4. ○   5. ○   6. ○   7. ○   8. ○   9. ○   10. ○

2. I can explain my understanding of the covenant made with Abraham considering all of his progeny as it compares with popular understanding.

   1. ○   2. ○   3. ○   4. ○   5. ○   6. ○   7. ○   8. ○   9. ○   10. ○

My Journal

What I learned from this class:

Discipleship Training Class 55

Principles of Interpretation — Covenantal Principle (part 4)

Objectives:

As a Discipleship student, at the end of this class you will be able to:

- Explain what the Mosaic Covenant's critical elements and implications are
- Explain how the Mosaic Covenant relates to Yeshua
- Explain who the Mosaic Covenant was made between

Of all of the teachings that I do, these discipleship classes are probably the most informational. This is where individuals will learn how to apply tools for studying the scriptures. We should all be disciples. We should all be disciplined in our study and searching the scriptures ourselves to make sure that, what I am teaching and what others are teaching is actually biblical.

There is a lot of teaching that is going on out there with the tags of –Hebrew Roots, –Messianic and others that are not necessarily grounded in the scriptures. The only way you will know that is to be able to research the scriptures for yourself. You must study and search, like Paul told us concerning the Bereans. They were of more noble character because they searched the scriptures daily to see if the things that Paul was preaching were actually for real. They searched to see if what he was saying was true.

Notice that what they were searching was the scriptures. When Paul wrote that, there was no *Matthew, Mark, Luke* and *John*. There were no letters to any of the congregations, so they were searching the scriptures (which is the Tanakh) to make sure that the things that Paul taught were actually so.

Make sure that you do that.

The Mosaic Covenant

We are going to be taking a journey through the Mosaic Covenant. There is a lot of ground we are going to cover because I believe that this is one of the critical covenants in the Bible. Unfortunately, the Mosaic Covenant has been identified with the commands that were given on Mount Sinai. However, I want to say to you that when we look at who is given the credit for writing the Torah, who is given that credit? Who do most scholars believe wrote the Torah? Moses.

So, it is believed that Moses wrote the Torah. The question now becomes, when does the Torah begin? Does it begin at *Exodus 20* or does it begin in *Genesis 1?* There are terms that are given to principles and covenants that may not necessarily always be applicable. It is the language that most people in the biblical theological environment recognize that you can communicate and they understand what you are saying.

For the sake of our study of the Mosaic Covenant, let's begin in the book of *Exodus* here at chapters 12-40 (although we know that the Mosaic Covenant covered from the book of *Genesis* to the book of *Deuteronomy*).

Within all of these covenants is the **Everlasting Covenant**, which was the covenant that Father made with his creation and with himself from the very foundation before the world was formed. We look at the Edenic Covenant and the Adamic Covenant. We looked at the Noahic Covenant. We looked the Abrahamic Covenant.

When most people today think of the Middle East, the term that comes to mind is –Palestine. We are going to help define some of that, because again, language that is being used is universal language where you communicate with people across all denominational and theological lines that they identify. We are using a common language that may not necessarily be acceptable to many people. But for the sake of study so that we are all on the same page, we will use it and we will bring clarity to that later.

This covenant (the Mosaic Covenant) was expressly made with the chosen nation, Israel and the mixed multitude that would join with Israel. *(Exodus 12; Deuteronomy 4:10-13; 5:1-33)* This mixed multitude is not just those who came out of Egypt with Israel, but is even unto this day.

(Exodus 12:37-38) *"And the children of Israel journeyed from Rameses to Succoth, about six hundred thousand on foot that were men, beside children. And a mixed multitude went up also with them; and flocks, and herds, even very much cattle."*

You have 600,000 men (besides children). Here is one of those situations where the word –men is distinguished from women and children. It is not –mankind. Oftentimes I think that people look at the scriptures and they look at them through a narrow lens, but let's keep reading.

Unfortunately, here in this particular passage it only counts the men of Israel. It does not count the children. It does not seem to count the women and it does not seem to number the mixed multitude, so we don't know how many per se that were non-Israelite-born that came up from Egypt into covenant with Father (with Israel).

(Exodus 12:43-44) *"And the Lord said unto Moses and Aaron, ,,This is the ordinance of the Passover: There shall no stranger eat thereof: But every man's servant that is bought for money, when thou hast circumcised him, then shall he eat thereof. A foreigner and an hired servant shall not eat thereof.""*

We skipped from verse 38, but do read that. I am just trying to get to the language. In the last lesson we talked about circumcision. Let's move beyond that. We see as we looked at the Abrahamic Covenant, even here in the Mosaic Covenant, that no stranger could eat. No Israelite could eat of the Passover unless they were circumcised.

(Exodus 12:47-48) *"All the congregation of Israel shall keep it. And when a stranger shall sojourn with thee, and will keep the Passover to the Lord, let all his males be circumcised, and then let him come near and keep it; and he shall be as one that is born in the land: for no uncircumcised person shall eat thereof."*

When you look at the congregation of Israel, those who came up out of Egypt were the congregation of Israel. Verse 48 speaks futuristically. What you have here is an individual who is coming into covenant with Israel. Over the course of time the Pharisees and the Sadducees took this particular instruction and added rituals to it. These rituals are now known today as one who becomes a proselyte, although the term –proselyte is not used here.

According to Greek terminology, a proselyte is one who converts to Judaism. The process of conversion is through a term known as *Brit milah*. Brit milah is the issue that is being used in *Acts 15* that Paul has an issue with, because this is now a conversion. When they say that a person must be circumcised according to the Law of Moses — no, it is not according to the Law of Moses, but after the manner of Moses. Moses did not have a process by which a person was circumcised. They just needed to be circumcised.

That issue in *Acts 15* has nothing to do per sé with a person being circumcised as much as it has to do with the person converting to Judaism in order to be saved or to receive the Jewish Messiah.

Concerning the Passover, strict rules were given that a person had to come through the process of circumcision before they could eat. Here is the key:

(Exodus 12:49-50) "One law shall be to him that is home born, and unto the stranger that sojourneth among you. Thus did all the children of Israel; as the Lord commanded Moses and Aaron, so did they."

In Babylon the creation of religion and religious traditions that evolved into Phariseeism and Sadduceeism in the days of Yeshua is called –Orthodox Judaism. Today Conservative Judaism, Reformed Judaism, even secular Judaism and Ultra-Orthodox Judaism come to the conclusion that only a Jew has to keep these commands. They have created what is known in Messianic circles and in Jewish circles as the *"Noahide Law."*

There is NO Noahide Law. This is religion cutting and pasting laws specifically geared toward the Gentile population that wants to become part of Israel. So, they have created a second- class citizenship by cutting and pasting laws from the Bible, from *Genesis* to *Deuteronomy*. But YeHoVaH says that **there is only one law**. There are not two. There are not laws for the Jews and laws for the Gentiles. There is one law that shall be unto him who is home born and unto the stranger that sojourns among you.

This is the Mosaic Covenant. It is any stranger, any foreigner, any person that comes into the commonwealth of Israel which Paul talks about in *Ephesians 2* and *Ephesians 4*.

We who were afar off (Gentiles by birth) have now been brought near. We are now part of the commonwealth of Israel. That is the meaning of –Gentiles. (By the way, Gentiles are oftentimes referred to as the lost ten tribes and at times are referred to as –Jews and –Israel or –Judah).

The term –Gentile is not just a person who is not part of the twelve tribes. The word is *gowy*, (go-ee) which is the word –nation. Oftentimes Israel, Judah and the House of Israel were referred to as the nation, as *gowy*, as Gentiles.[3]

(Deuteronomy 4:10) "Specially the day that thou stoodest before the Lord thy God in Horeb, when the Lord said unto me, ,, Gather me the people together, and I will make them hear my words, that they may learn to fear me all the days that they shall live upon the earth, and that they may teach their children.""

Some of this stuff I want to highlight for you because we have to stop reading the Bible with our Messianic glasses. In addition to all of the glasses of denominations, there are Messianic glasses. There are Hebrew Roots glasses and people will read the Bible through those lenses.

Often when we put on those glasses with those lenses, we miss a lot that is right there in front of us. For instance,

---

[3] This concept is expanded in Lessons 59 and 60.

"...Gather me the people together, and I will make them hear my <u>words</u>..."

YeHoVaH's desire in the Mosaic Covenant as we know was to establish what a lot of Christians preach today — a –personal relationship with the Almighty. That is what YeHoVaH desired. He did not want a mediator. He wanted them to hear his voice. He wanted them to know his voice. He wanted them to establish relationship with him as he desired to establish relationship with them.

He said,

"...that they may learn to fear me all the days that they shall live upon the earth and that they may teach their children..."

So now you see from generation to generation. You see the generational blessing being spoken here. We learn to fear him all of our days upon the earth and we teach our children and they teach their children and those children teach their children. You will see the blessing of YeHoVaH, the love where he says in *Exodus 20*,

"...showing love to the thousandth generation of them that love me AND KEEP MY COMMANDMENTS."

When you look at a thousand generations, you have to ask yourself, —Has mankind been on the earth a thousand generations? That is a lot of generations!

Now what you are seeing is that it is not just a thousand, but to the thousandth. It just continues as long as there is man on the earth. These words should ring true.

Notice this:

(Deuteronomy 4:11-12) *"And ye came near and stood under the mountain; and the mountain burned with fire unto the midst of heaven, with darkness, clouds, and thick darkness. And* **the LORD spake unto you** *out of the midst of the fire: ye heard the voice of the words, but saw no similitude; only ye heard a voice."*

Long before he gave Moses tablets and long before there was the written word given to the people, there was the spoken word. That was YeHoVaH's desire. **The Mosaic Covenant was to establish the relationship with YeHoVaH and his people.**

It was not just about a bunch of laws that people today want to discard. Man chose that. That was not YeHoVaH's plan. YeHoVaH spoke unto them. You heard the voice of the word, only a voice. You heard the voice.

At this point in human history, every person whom YeHoVaH called; every stranger, every man, every woman, every child, every animal — all heard the voice of YeHoVaH. Do you see this?

(Deuteronomy 4:13) *–And he declared unto you his covenant, which he commanded you to perform, even ten commandments; and he wrote them upon two tables of stone."*

He <u>declared</u> his covenant which he commanded to be performed. Now this is progressive because when he called upon them and declared his covenant, he had not given them stones. That came afterward. You see, the stone tablets were the result of –We don't want to hear your voice.

It held promises out to Israel and the mixed multitude that would join Israel specifically and this also was a conditional covenant. The words were spoken in the Ten Commandments and given in entirety to Moses. The words that he spoke were the only ones they could handle. The Ten Commandments were as far as they got and they said, ―We can't take any more.

It must be noted that YeHoVaH would have spoken the entire commandments to the people had they been willing to hear. When we hear the words, -Let they that have ears, hear, we see from the very beginning that people were not willing to hear the voice of YeHoVaH. Instead, it was, ―Give it to us in a book. Give it to us upon stone tablets. Don't speak to us. Write to us. -It is written.

You have people who want to talk about arguing with the devil. -Whenever the devil comes, just tell the devil just like Yeshua said: -It is written.' No, you have to do what Yeshua did, not just say what he did. There are many people who are spouting off what Yeshua said and it is not working for them. Devils are not leaving. People are not getting healed. Words are not coming to pass because this is not about words. This is a <u>lifestyle</u>.

It is amazing to me. Let me just set this up right now. Some people wonder why I answer questions the way I answer them. Oftentimes when I hear questions being read, I hear the spirit behind the questions. It seems like I am just going on and on and on and not even answering the question. But I am answering the question.

We are dealing with people. I know you from what you tell me. The Bible says that we are to know no man by the flesh, but by the spirit. Oftentimes the words that I speak are not for people's flesh to revel in. I am speaking to people's spirit. This is why it doesn't matter if a person is sleeping. The body is sleeping. Their spirit is very much attentive.

Your spirit man does not sleep. Even while you sleep, your flesh sleeps. Your body gets tired, but your spirit man is always aware of what is going on — always. Even when your body expires, your spirit leaves it. -Can't stay here anymore.

We have to learn Spirit things. When we speak Spirit things — and here is the challenge. The Spirit is (most of the time if not all of the time) going to confront and oppose our natural mind. It is not going to make sense to our natural mind. It is in that place that our emotions and our pride and all of the stuff that responds naturally to words that are Spirit that causes people to respond.

You have to understand that you are not a human being. You are a spirit being. You are not a person with a spirit. You are a spirit in a person. Your spirit man is the one who is supposed to dominate your flesh man. And unless your spirit man dominates your flesh, your flesh will always get your spirit into trouble. Your flesh will sabotage the purpose and plan of the Almighty because your flesh only wants ministry to the flesh. That is what it wants.

-Talk to me. My ears are itching. Tell me what I want to hear. No, I don't want to hear that. You might not want to hear it, but that is what you need to hear. Then people get mad and angry. Now they want to fight and cuss and send nasty emails.

You better wake up. I am going to tell you it (as they say where I come from) like it is. I want to do it in a way that people can get it, but sometimes that is just not the way it is.

Father just called it like it is to the children of Israel — hardhearted, stiff-necked, stubborn.

–I can't talk to you. You don't want to hear me. You want me to put it in an email, in a letter. For myself, I spend all of this time teaching just to have people who have been on-screen chatting ask questions about what I just spent twenty minutes teaching.

Remember when the word is sown, the enemy immediately comes to steal it. He will do it through distraction. That is the number one tool that the enemy uses. He has you miss the very thing you have been praying for, fasting for — you are on a hundred people's prayer lists. And the word is coming forth just for you, but you are too busy talking to somebody else that may not necessarily be operating by the power of the Spirit. They are used to distract you from receiving what you are supposed to be receiving at that very time.

I hope that this is provoking you enough to say, –Enough is enough. This is the day.

(Exodus 20:1) *–And God spake all these words, saying,"*

You have to look at this. This does not seem like much to people, but what people are more familiar with is *The Ten Commandments* and Cecil B. DeMille. That is what they are familiar with. Do you know why? Well, not just because it's visual, but Cecil B. DeMille put the voice of YeHoVaH in the mountain with Moses. And the words coming out of his mouth are etching the tablets. Cecil B. DeMille did not put you at the foot of the mountain where YeHoVaH is speaking to the people.

http://www.classicmoviestills.com

So, people's familiarity with the Ten Commandments is first of all, Cecil B. DeMille's *Ten Commandments* movie version of the Bible. The moment a person thinks of the Ten Commandments, what are they thinking about? They are thinking about stone tablets. Then you have denominations out there that are only concerned about the Ten Commandments because those are the words that God wrote upon tablets.

(Exodus 20:18) *"And all the people saw the thunderings, and the lightnings, and the noise of the trumpet, and the mountain smoking: and when the people saw it, they removed, and stood afar off."*

I jumped to <u>verse 18</u> because that is where everything changes — everything. YeHoVaH's relationship with his people changes at this very moment. If you remember in *Exodus 19*, YeHoVaH told Moses to prepare the people. –Tell the people to get themselves ready. Don't touch your wife. Don't have relationship. Wash your garments. Purify yourselves. I, your Elohim, who brought you out of Egypt, out from the land of bondage, am going to introduce myself to my people. I want you all to know who I am. So, He says, –I am YeHoVaH your Elohim, who brought you out of the land of bondage and out of the land of Egypt. You are to put no other one before my face. Have no other Elohim. He is talking to his people.

Up until this point, he only talked to Moses and Aaron. Now he is talking to everybody. This is what he is doing. When the people saw the thundering and the lightning and the noise of the trumpet and the mountain smoking, <u>they removed</u>. They <u>stood afar off</u>. That is the King James. They scattered! They got out of Dodge. They were close and now they are far off.

They were close, but when they saw all of this, you have to understand something. Notice something please. They had seen Moses go in and out of this for I don't know how many times.

Moses went up into the mountain of fire and thunder and lightning and quaking and shaking. Moses goes up and Moses comes down.

YeHoVaH says to Moses to put a rope around the mountain so the people won't rush me. Yeah, right. Make sure nobody rushes me because I am not in the killing mood today. I don't want to kill anybody.

Instead, what happens? Oftentimes just like Adam, when the fear of YeHoVaH — that is the wrong kind of fear begins to make people afraid to the point of being scared. Instead of creating fear that brings reverence and humility, the kind of fear that would cause one to fall upon one's face and bow and lie prostrate; the opposite of that fear is the fear that causes one to repel, to remove, to run and to hide.

The people removed themselves and got far away. That word there is the word *nuwa* (noo-ah), meaning to waver, scatter. They scattered. It was like –See ya, Moses! We are out of here. We can't take anymore.

(Exodus 20:19) "And they said unto Moses, „Speak thou with us, and we will hear: but let not God speak with us, lest we die."

Where did they get that impression that if he speaks to us that we will die? It is these kinds of words in sermons that preachers who want to lord over people have preached. –Touch not my anointing. Do my prophets no harm. They put the fear of man into the hearts of the people instead of the fear of YeHoVaH. So, peoples' relationships and their reverence are toward their pastor, their bishop, their apostle or their –Reverend Doctor instead of having the fear of YeHoVaH.

People become more concerned about what man sees. They are totally ignorant of the fact that YeHoVaH sees all things, so they are hiding.

(Exodus 20:20-21) "And Moses said unto the people, „Fear not: for God is come to prove you, and that his fear may be before your faces, that ye sin not." And the people stood afar off, and Moses drew near unto the thick darkness where God was."

Remember that they were close until YeHoVaH spoke. Once he spoke, they got out of there. They were once near. Now they are far off. James says that if you draw near to him, he will draw near to you. What happens if you draw back? Yeshua says that whoever puts their hand to the plow and draws back is not even worthy. You can't start this thing and stop it. You can't start it and then decide okay, –Well, I am not sure if this is the direction. This is why one must count the cost.

This is why those people who are quick to make a decision are probably one of the first ones to fall back. Those people who take time — you have to give them the right information. You have to spend some time with them. You have to share with them. You have to answer their questions (and they have lots of them). Once their questions are answered, they can make an informed decision.

Now they can have a place to have their wedding or funeral. The church pastor will say my eulogy. I want to be on the church rolls. Let me tell you something. The church roll is not the roll to be on. It's the roll that is called the Book of Life. That roll you can't join. You are either added to it by faith in Messiah (or not).

> *This is why the gospel of Jesus Christ that the churches preach doesn't work. People don't have enough information to make a decision. They make an emotional decision based upon a gospel that is designed to tug on their heart and cause them to fear going to hell for eternity. They don't want to go to hell. The alternative is to ask Jesus to come into your life. Okay, Jesus come into my life so I don't go to hell. It is not about serving him or being a disciple. That is not what it is about.*
>
> It is the fear of hell.

You can join a church. You can get baptized in –Father, Son, Holy Spirit. You can get baptized in the name of Jesus. In one of the churches, I went to just to be saved, this is how they did it. –I now baptize you in the name of the Father, in the name of the Son, in the name of the Holy Ghost and in Jesus' name. All righty. That way everybody is covered, just in case.

(Exodus 20:21) *"And the people stood afar off, and Moses drew near unto the thick darkness where God was."*

If I am seeing this, then think about this. If the Father was going to kill somebody for being too close to him, who do you think would have died first? Who do you think he would have killed first? Moses. If Moses' carcass rolled down the mountain burnt to a crisp, then I could understand, okay, –See ya. I wasn't coming to any barbecue today. Thank you.

Here it is and the people are scared. Then in their fear, Moses just walks up the mountain. I would be standing there saying, –Well, wait a minute. If Moses is not afraid, why should we be? Joshua is watching this and Caleb is watching this. —What are we afraid of, folks?

This is he who destroyed Pharaoh. This is he who destroyed Pharaoh's army. He delivered us out of the land of bondage. He led us to the foot of this mountain. He provided us with manna and quail. He sustained us in the wilderness. He kept us warm at night and cool in the daytime. He has introduced himself to us because he wants us to know him. He said prepare yourself because I am coming down and I want to talk to you and introduce myself to you. It is obvious that he did not bring us here to kill us, because if murder was on his mind, we would be dead already. He could have starved us and not sent us manna; not fed us in the wilderness. We could have frozen to death in the desert night, or burnt to a crisp in the desert day.

But instead…

These are the things that would be going on in my mind. And as people are running, it's like now the same people want to question Moses' authority. –We can hear his voice just like you. Yeah, but when he spoke to you, you ran. Now you want to challenge Moses. He went up the mountain. Did you?

The Mosaic Covenant involved how the people would conduct themselves in the Kingdom of YeHoVaH, how they would approach YeHoVaH, how to love him and their neighbors and how to treat their wives and children. The covenant made distinctions of clean and unclean, the holy and the profane. It defined food, keeping of Sabbaths and festival days. It pointed to the coming of the Prophet.

(Deuteronomy 18:15-16) "The Lord thy God will raise up unto thee a Prophet from the midst of thee, of thy brethren, like unto me; unto him ye shall hearken; According to all that thou desiredst of the Lord thy God in Horeb in the day of the assembly, saying, „Let me not hear again the voice of the Lord my God, neither let me see this great fire any more, that I die not.""

The people had said, –We don't want to hear his voice ever again. Can you imagine being in with that kind of people, who don't want to hear His voice? They not only did not want to hear Him, they did not even want to see Him. –We don't want to see this great fire. People were afraid that they would die.

(Deuteronomy 18:17-18) "And the Lord said unto me, „They have well spoken that which they have spoken. I will raise them up a Prophet from among their brethren, like unto thee, and will put my words in his mouth; and he shall speak unto them all that I shall command him.""

This is Yeshua.

(Deuteronomy 18:19) "And it shall come to pass, that whosoever will not hearken unto my words which he shall speak in my name, I will require it of him."

That leads me to a thought concerning prayer, because in the Christian Churches that I was in, it became common for people to pray to Yeshua. Have you heard these prayers?

–Dear Lord Jesus…

–I come to you, Lord Jesus…

–I pray Lord that you will hear my prayer.

–I ask you Lord to…

–Thank you, Lord Jesus.

–In Jesus' name I pray.

When the people came to Yeshua, his disciples said, –Teach us how to pray. He pointed people to his Father. When you pray, this is how you pray, –Our Father. **YeHoVaH was the purpose for Yeshua coming; that he might reconcile people to YeHoVaH.**

This is what YeHoVaH spoke to Moses. He says,

"Moses, I am going to raise up a Prophet like you, from among the brethren. I will put my words into his mouth. And whoever will not hearken unto my words…"

Yeshua said it very clearly.

"The words I speak are not my own. I only say what the Father gives me to say. I only do what he says do."

He came to represent the Father and to reconcile people to Father. **But instead, people want to be reconciled to Jesus.** I personally believe that this is one of the reasons He got up out of here. His disciples wanted to make him king. They wanted to sit on the right and they wanted to sit on the left. Yeshua said,

"It is not for me to know. I don't know the time."

"When are you coming back?"

"That is up to the Father. I'll come when he says to come."

Christianity has taken the focus off of the Father and put it onto Jesus. Because Jesus came and – delivered us from the Father, we don't have to be concerned with this covenant. Let me tell you something. It was this covenant that proclaimed that he would come in the name of the Father and that he would speak the word of the Father. Whoever did not listen to him was not listening to the Father.

This is why the disciples said, *"Show us the Father."* He said, *"If you have seen me, you have seen the Father."*

The blood of the Mosaic Covenant is found in *Exodus 24:3-8* and *Hebrews 9:18-20*.

(Exodus 24:3-4) *"And Moses came and told the people all the words of the Lord, and all the judgments: and all the people answered with one voice, and said, „All the words which the Lord hath said will we do. And Moses wrote all the words of the Lord, and rose up early in the morning, and builded an altar under the hill, and twelve pillars, according to the twelve tribes of Israel.""*

We now see that Moses is building an altar.

(Exodus 24:5-6) *"And he sent young men of the children of Israel, which offered burnt offerings, and sacrificed peace offerings of oxen unto the Lord. And Moses took half of the blood, and put it in basins; and half of the blood he sprinkled on the altar."*

Notice something. Please notice this. He sent young men of the children of Israel which offered burnt offerings and sacrificed peace offerings of oxen. This is what is going on here. We don't see how much blood is here, do we? But I will tell you. There is a lot of blood.

(Exodus 24:7-8) *"And he took the book of the covenant, and read in the audience of the people: and they said, „All that the LORD hath said will we do, and be obedient." **And Moses took the blood, and sprinkled it on the people**, and said, „Behold **the blood of the covenant**, which the LORD hath made with you concerning all these words.""*

Do you see this? How many men were there? **600,000**. Those were men of Israel. That did not count the women and children or the strangers. Can you imagine how much blood it would take to sprinkle on probably over a million people? That is a lot of blood and it would take a long time.

(Hebrews 9:18-20) *"Whereupon neither the first testament was dedicated without blood. For when Moses had spoken every precept to all the people according to the law, he took the blood of calves and of goats, with water, and scarlet wool, and hyssop, and sprinkled both the book, and all the people, Saying, „This is the blood of the covenant""* [not —testament – my note] *"„which God hath enjoined unto you.""*

Here you have individuals who are trying to validate the New –Testament and separate it from the Old Testament, when it is actually a covenant. This is the blood of the covenant.

We see this blood of the covenant when Yeshua has the last supper (if you would). He takes the wine and proclaims it as the blood of the covenant. This is the covenant that was made that Father said he was going to make as a New Covenant — with whom?

Replacement theology and all of Christendom is trying to separate the people today from the Hebrews, from the Israelites. They believe that they have effectively done that through Jesus Christ. Like Marcionian doctrine, if we can get people to focus on Jesus Christ; take their focus off of God the Father, the Creator, the maker of heaven and earth, the giver and sustainer of life. What we can now do is put this wedge, this little blank page in between the New Testament and the Old Testament in our Bibles.

If you have that blank page in your Bible between the Old Testament and the New, please tear it out. If it is one of the newer translations, I am sure it is there. It is amazing how they put that page in there. They have done these tests with these sharks. They put them in a tank and they put fish that sharks eat on one side and the sharks on the other side. They put this glass in between them. The sharks would go after the fish and what happens? They hit the glass. Eventually it convinces the sharks that the fish are not accessible. After the sharks gave up, they removed the glass. The fish swam around the sharks and the sharks were convinced they could not eat the fish.

What does that have to do with it? That barrier, that blank page that has been in the Bible on the table; the big white Bible many of us grew up with on the coffee table in the front room that was hardly ever opened, that blank page is like that glass in the tank. After a while you think, okay. This piece of paper separates. This one piece of paper here separates this part of the Bible from this part. This is the –Old. This is the –New. Which one do you want, the old or the new? I don't want the old. I want the new. Now we have the New Testament which is a –Renewed Covenant. Actually, the New Testament is a compilation of gospel narratives and letters.

(Hebrews 9:20) *"Saying, ,,This is the blood of **the testament** which God hath enjoined unto you.""*
The word –testament is not found in the Hebrew Scriptures (commonly referred to as the Old Testament). The Mosaic Covenant was established upon sacrificial blood. It was called the blood of the covenant, and it was sprinkled upon the people and the book of the covenant. That blood was what tied the people to the book.

Today people are trained to be under the blood, but they are disconnected to the book. The book that they are connected to is the New Testament. That does not give them instructions on how, but commands to: –Husbands, love your wife like Christ loved the church. Well, how did he do that? He died.

–So, if I die right now for my wife… Well, you have to die to self. Yeshua did not die to self. He died. He gave his life upon a stake. Is that how I love my wife? I go up onto the cross and die? Well, now who is going to provide for her? Who is going to take care of her? That is not what he is talking about when he says –husbands love your wife. The New Testament tells us to do it, but it does not tell us how.

That is why a lot of New Testament Christian marriages are in trouble, because they don't know how. They have disconnected themselves. That page has separated them from the instructions of YeHoVaH, which gives us the how-to. If you don't have the how-to, you won't know what to do, so you will make it up. By the time you figure it out, it is too late.

The blood of the covenant was sprinkled upon the people and upon the book. It was not just a person being –under the blood. People want to say that you are covered by the blood. –I just plead the blood of Jesus. How can you minimize the sacrificial blood of the Messiah?

Understand something here. It was the blood of the bulls, rams and goats that was sprinkled upon the people. Yeshua's blood was sprinkled upon the Ark of heaven, not upon the people. Yeshua's blood was sprinkled upon the covering. It was sprinkled upon the Ark that covered, the Ark of the Covenant that contained the book. The people now have to come through the book.

How can they come through the book if they are hearing a gospel that is disconnected from the book?

This is why he said to make disciples. If the disciples were going to go and make disciples, guess what they would be using in their discipleship process? The books of *Matthew, Mark, Luke* and *John* were not written yet. They would be using the scriptures!

That is how they made disciples and guess what? The disciples of Yeshua and the disciples of the apostles of Yeshua were filled with power. Peter's shadow fell upon people and they were healed. They were casting out devils, raising the dead, healing the sick, confronting nations and all they had was the Tanakh and the Holy Spirit. They had the word of YeHoVaH.

Today we have the Bible. We have that blank page in between the Old Testament and the New Testament. We have two billion people on the planet who call themselves Catholics and Christians and there is no power. There is a form of Godliness, but no power. The best excuse is that stuff has been done away with because we don't need it anymore.

We find the seal of the covenant in *Exodus 31*. The Mosaic Covenant had the seal of the Sabbath day upon it, which Paul reaffirms.

(Exodus 31:12-13) *"And the LORD spake unto Moses, saying, "Speak thou also unto the children of Israel, saying, Verily my sabbaths ye shall keep: for it is a sign between me and you throughout your generations; that ye may know that I am the LORD that doth sanctify you.""*

How does he sanctify his people? He gave his sanctified, set apart people his set apart days. His set apart people are keeping the set apart days that YeHoVaH set apart for the set apart people. He sanctified the people and gave them days that he sanctified. He sanctified (which means to make holy) his Sabbath day. He said to remember and to keep it holy. He sanctified high Sabbaths with Passover, Unleavened Bread, Shavuot, Trumpets, Yom Kippur and Tabernacles. He sanctified, set apart and made holy days for this sanctified, set apart, holy people. And by these holy people keeping these holy days, it sent a message to an unholy world that these are a holy people who have holy days given by a holy Elohim.

Instead, you have people saying, –Well, you know, we will make our own day holy. Okay, so now you have become God. You have become the creator.

(Exodus 31:14) *"Ye shall keep the sabbath therefore; for it is holy unto you: every one that defileth it shall surely be put to death: for whosoever doeth any work therein, that soul shall be cut off from among his people."*

Do you know that there is no other day that YeHoVaH made holy? He did not make the first day holy, second day holy, third, fourth, fifth, sixth days — none of them holy. He only made the seventh day holy. Did he ever make it unholy? That is the way the church wants to put it; that whoever keeps that day is – under the law. Under what law? Under the Law of YeHoVaH.

I tell you this. I would much rather be under the Law of YeHoVaH than not being under the Law of YeHoVaH. I say this because those who are not under the Law of YeHoVaH are called –lawless. They are without law and they will fall under the same condemnation of the lawless one, a.k.a. HaSatan; better known in the modern vernacular as Satan.

(Exodus 31:15-16) *"Six days may work be done; but in the seventh is the sabbath of rest, holy to the LORD: whosoever doeth any work in the sabbath day, he shall surely be put to death. Wherefore the children of Israel shall keep the sabbath, to observe the sabbath throughout their generations, for a perpetual covenant."*

That is a covenant without end.

(Exodus 31:17) *"It is a sign between me and the children of Israel for ever: for in six days the LORD made heaven and earth, and on the seventh day he rested, and was refreshed."*

Here he connects *Genesis*.

(Exodus 31:18) *"And he gave unto Moses, when he had made an end of communing with him upon Mount Sinai, two tables of testimony, tables of stone, written with the finger of God."*

You see what YeHoVaH did. He connects *Genesis* to *Exodus*. That is what He does. He says, *"This Sabbath day I am giving you to remember is the one I established in Genesis."* But people want to say, – Well, that is the law of Moses. Yeah, creation is in the law of Moses.

The **Mosaic Covenant** had the seal of the Sabbath day upon it. Paul says:

(Colossians 2:16-17) *"Let no man therefore judge you in meat, or in drink, or in respect of an holyday, or of the new moon, or of the Sabbath days: Which are a shadow of things to come; but the body is of Messiah."*

Take off your Christian glasses or your Messianic glasses. They are the shadow of things to come. They are not done away with.

The Christian Wants to Argue

See what Paul wrote? Paul says don't let anybody judge because you don't keep a new moon or a Sabbath or eating swine. They say that you are covered under the blood of Jesus. You can eat whatever you want. You don't have to keep the Sabbath. As a matter of fact, you can do whatever you want because Jesus Christ has paid the price and you don't have to do anything except accept his atoning sacrifice. You can live like the devil. You can live like a sinner. You can live like a heathen. You can go, do and eat whatever. You can have as many wives as you want. You can commit adultery. You can lie, cheat, steal, cuss out your Mama and disrespect your Daddy because it's all under the blood. Jesus Christ has paid the price and it doesn't require anything from you. –You are saved by grace. Just ask Jesus to come into your life.

These things are shadows of things to come, not things past. Paul here is thinking *future*, not past tense — things to come.
"...but the body is of Messiah."

We belong to Messiah. We keep the commands. We have the testimony of Yeshua and we keep the commands of YeHoVaH. Yeshua came to show us how to do it.

Class 55 Study Summary
Key Points

1. The Bereans were of noble character because they searched the scriptures daily to see if the things that were preached were real.
2. Most scholars believe that Moses wrote the Torah.
3. The Everlasting Covenant is the covenant that Father made with his creation from the foundation before the world was formed.
4. The Mosaic Covenant was made with the chosen nation Israel and the mixed multitude that would join with Israel.
5. According to Greek terminology, a proselyte is one who converts to Judaism through Brit milah (circumcision).
6. There is no such thing as Noahide Laws. That is a religious invention.
7. There is only one Law of YeHoVaH. There are not two laws. There is not a law for the Jews and another law for the Gentiles.
8. In additional to denominational glasses, there are Hebrew Roots or Messianic glasses that we should be careful not to wear.
9. The Mosaic Covenant was to establish a relationship between YeHoVaH and his people.
10. When the word is sown, the enemy immediately comes to steal it.
11. Yeshua says that whoever puts their hand to the plow and draws back is not worthy.
12. The purpose for Yeshua's coming was that he might reconcile people to YeHoVaH.
13. Christianity has taken the focus off of the Father and put it onto Jesus.
14. Replacement theology and all of Christendom is trying to separate the people today from the Hebrews, from the Israelites. They believe they have done this through Jesus Christ. That is a Marcionian doctrine.
15. The Mosaic Covenant was established upon sacrificial blood.
16. The seal of the Mosaic Covenant is the Sabbath day. It is a covenant without end.
17. We belong to Messiah. We keep the commands and have the testimony of Yeshua. He came and demonstrated how we are to live them.

Review Exercise

1. In terms of the three elements that we have found to be essential to a covenant, in the Mosaic Covenant we find these below. Elaborate upon them.

   Words or Promise:_____

   Blood: _____

   Seal: _____

2. If you overlook one key specific about both the Abrahamic and Mosaic Covenants, you will likely fall into a certain and too common pitfall. What is that one thing that is easily to be overlooked? And what pitfall does overlooking that set you up for?

   _____
   _____
   _____
   _____

3. What crucial thing are –Sunday Churches overlooking with regard to the Mosaic Covenant?

   _____
   _____
   _____
   _____

4. What is one vital link between the Abrahamic and Mosaic Covenants with respect to Passover?

   _____
   _____
   _____
   _____

5. Modern Christianity has pushed the idea of –a personal relationship with Jesus Christ. Discuss the danger of that emphasis.

   _____
   _____
   _____
   _____

Rate the following statements by filling in the most appropriate number.

(1 = I do not agree 10 = I agree completely)

1. I can explain what the Mosaic Covenant's critical elements and implications are.

   1.○ 2.○ 3.○ 4.○ 5.○ 6.○ 7.○ 8.○ 9.○ 10.○

2. I can explain how the Mosaic Covenant relates to Yeshua.

   1.○ 2.○ 3.○ 4.○ 5.○ 6.○ 7.○ 8.○ 9.○ 10.○

3. I can explain who the Mosaic Covenant was made between.

   1.○ 2.○ 3.○ 4.○ 5.○ 6.○ 7.○ 8.○ 9.○ 10.○

My Journal

What I learned from this class:

_____
_____
_____
_____
_____
_____
_____
_____
_____
_____
_____
_____
_____
_____
_____
_____
_____
_____
_____
_____

Discipleship Training Class 56

Principles of Interpretation — Covenantal Principle (part 5)

Objectives:

As a Discipleship student, at the end of this class you will be able to:

- Define the Palestinian (Canaan, Land) Covenant, especially in relation to the Abrahamic and Mosaic Covenants
- Describe how the actions of obedience or disobedience have directly impacted the physical land, the natural environment

---

Today's teaching deals with the Palestinian Covenant. This is the theological term that is recognized by most Seminaries and Bible Colleges. The other term that I think is more appropriate and more simple is the Land Covenant. More specifically, the Land Covenant is referred to as the Canaan Covenant or Israel Covenant.

As we continue on, I want to point us to some particular scriptures. In dealing with the Land Covenant, the land that the Father gave the children of Israel was actually what is considered to be the land of Canaan. And so, the more proper term would probably be the Canaan Covenant or the Land Covenant.

As we are dealing with the Land Covenant, it specifically deals with the covenant the Father made with the children of Israel. It actually deals with a covenant made way back when he told Abraham that he was going to give him this land. When he made that promise to Abraham; of course, we know that when he brought the children of Israel out of the land of Egypt that he actually gave them that land. So that is what we are going to be talking about — the covenant between the Father and the people concerning the land.

We are going to be looking at the book of *Deuteronomy*. The Land Covenant deals with *Deuteronomy chapters 27-30*. It also deals with some additional scriptures. As we consider covenants, remember that we talked about the blood or the words of the promise.

The Abrahamic, Mosaic and the Land Covenants are all connected. It really (as most would say) is not recognized as a covenant. However, when we look at *Deuteronomy 29,* we see these words:

(Deuteronomy 29:1) *"These are the words of the covenant..."*

The question is what covenant is he talking about? Well, it goes on:

(Deuteronomy 29:1) *"These are the words of the covenant, which the* LORD *commanded Moses to make with the children of Israel in the land of Moab, beside the covenant which he made with them in Horeb."*

If you look at the covenant that he made with them in the land of Moab, you will know exactly what he is talking about. It is beside the covenant which he made with them in Horeb. Now we see that there was the covenant that he made in Horeb and there was a covenant that was made in the land of Moab.

As we continue, it was made with the generation that were about to enter the land. It was a conditional covenant. **Its promise concerned the blessings and/or cursing on Palestine/Canaan or the Promised Land.** When we think about the land, we think of the Promised Land. We think of the land of Israel. We think of the land that Father gave to the children of Israel (which are actually the children, the offspring of Abraham). And we talk about the Promised Land, but we also note that it is a covenant.

That land was given to Israel in a covenant that YeHoVaH made.

(Deuteronomy 32:49) *"Get thee up into this mountain Abarim, unto mount Nebo, which is in the land of Moab, that is over against Jericho; and behold the land of Canaan, which I give unto the children of Israel for a possession:"*

We see here in *Deuteronomy 32* that this is actually the land of Canaan. Most people don't know or get the fact that the land of Israel was not always the land of Israel. Father took this land because he has a right to take the land and give it to whomever he chooses. Now, no man can take the land, because Father knows how to put one up and take one down. And yet people have a tendency to put a power into the hands of men, talking about dividing Jerusalem. Man can't do anything that the Father does not allow him to do. If Father allowed the land to be divided by the hand of men, he certainly knows how to unify the land again.

Oftentimes what we have seen in the history of scripture is that it has literally been the Father bringing his master plan together. We know that the Father works all things for the good for those who love him, who walk not according to their flesh, but who walk according to his Spirit. Father works these things out.

We see that Father said, "Look at this land. Behold the land." The Father displaced the Canaanites. He gave this land to the Israelites. The challenge is that the Israelites had to go in and possess the land. This was not a cake walk.

Christianity for sure teaches that once you come to "Jesus," it is going to be a walk in the park. All of your problems are going to be resolved. It is going to be like, "Hey. The heavens are opened and the angels are singing and everything is fine." It is not that way.

Oftentimes Father will send you into a place. Where he is sending you — if he is sending you in, he has given you that, but you have to stand firm and let him go forth and fight the battle. You have to follow his instructions. Then he makes you ruler over that which he has caused you to possess.

This is the thing that I have had to really embrace. **What Father has for you, no one can take. What he has for you is yours.** Now, you may not go in to possess it. Oftentimes Father has things that he has set aside for you, but he is trying to get you and I to the place where we walk in and possess that which he has already ordained for us. There are things Father has hidden from you. The only way he is going to reveal them to you is if you seek him out and if you search him.

In the process of seeking him, in the process of searching him out, he now reveals things, but in the process he oftentimes will test. So, before he brought the children of Israel out of Egypt, they knew there was a "land of promise." They knew that there was a land that Father had promised Abraham and that he had a land flowing with milk and honey. Even though they knew that was their possession, many of them never possessed it.

They died wandering, murmuring, complaining and challenging the established leadership that Father had placed. As a result, they never saw the very promise the Father promised them.

He says, "I am going to give this land unto the children of Israel as a possession." Israel's dwelling in the land was conditional. If these conditions were not met, they would be expelled. *(Leviticus 26; Deuteronomy 28 and 29)*

(Leviticus 26:14-15) "But if ye will not hearken unto me, and will not do all these commandments; And if ye shall despise my statutes, or if your soul abhor my judgments, so that ye will not do all my commandments, but that ye break my covenant:"

Remember an unconditional covenant was a covenant that was preceded with "I will." Father says, "I will do this." "I will do that." A conditional covenant is always "if then," so if there is an "if," then there is a "but."

(Leviticus 26:16) "I also will do this unto you; I will even appoint over you terror, consumption, and the burning ague, that shall consume the eyes, and cause sorrow of heart: and ye shall sow your seed in vain, for your enemies shall eat it."

I want to pick up on this. In verse 15 it says, *"If you will despise my statutes."* Do you know what is really sad today? It is that most of the world that calls themselves "Christian" despise the statutes. They despise the law. They despise the covenant. Surely what we are talking about is the land of promise and we are talking about the Promised Land. But the covenant that Father made with Abraham, with Isaac and with Jacob is for those who come into covenant relationship with him. It is for those who come into the commonwealth of Israel.

What is really interesting is that as believers in Messiah, legally according to scripture and according to Kingdom law, every believer in Messiah should be able to make aliyah to the land of promise because we enter into the covenant promises. Now, unfortunately because of the control and people who have taken power and have made laws as to who can make aliyah, they have now established a system where people have to convert to religious Judaism and denounce Messiah. Think about this. **The people who are in charge of the land require those who make aliyah to the land to reject and to denounce the Messiah that we are supposed to confess.**

Just let that sink in for a minute.

As believers, we should have an issue with that. That land belongs to the children of YeHoVaH; those who come into covenant relationship. And yet there are a select group of individuals who say that no, this land belongs to the Jews.

Our Messiah was of the tribe of Judah. Those of us who come in through the blood of Messiah become Judeans. We become part of the tribe of Judah. We are engrafted into the commonwealth of Israel and by faith in Messiah we should be able to make aliyah if we choose to go to the land of promise.

This is what happens when the hand of man gets involved in the things of YeHoVaH. Because of perverted Christianity and religion, individuals are aligned with the system that is not necessarily biblical.

The other part is that even if we look in the book of *Deuteronomy*; the Bible makes it very clear for those who add to the law or those who diminish the law. It says that plagues will also be added to them. Judaism is manmade religion.

He says he will if you don't appoint over you terror, consumption and the burning ague.

(Leviticus 26:17) *"And I will set my face against you, and ye shall be slain before your enemies: they that hate you shall reign over you; and ye shall flee when none pursueth you."*

We have to decide whether or not we believe the Bible. The question is if we believe the Bible, then we have to stand upon what the Bible teaches. But I think that there are times when our allegiance, our alliance, is somewhat not according to scripture. It is like having to deal with family members who don't walk in the Torah. It is like having to work with people who could care less about YeHoVaH's law. And yet because we are blood tied in relationship, those blood ties have a tendency sometimes to cause us not to see things biblically correctly, but emotionally.

We have to be very careful that our emotions don't override our spiritual responsibility to the word of YeHoVaH. What am I saying? I am trying (in the most delicate way I know how) to say that any people who rise up and despise or who deviate or who add to or diminish from the Torah of YeHoVaH, regardless of what they call themselves, will have to pay the price.

YeHoVaH and his word are one. Every time Israel decided that they were not going to do what the commands said, they added to or diminished from it. It created problems. I believe very, very candidly that I know that the land that Father ordained for the chosen people, no man can take. It is always going to be because it is an Everlasting Covenant. That land will always belong to the Hebrew people, to the children of Israel — to all of the children of Israel.

Interestingly enough before the Knesset and before the state of Israel was established and all of that, there were these citizenship issues that exist in countries today. Now you have people who put up fences and borders and have drawn lines upon the property that Father has ordained. They put people into concentration camps and reservations. Furthermore, they isolate them into certain communities by color and ethnic groups and by red lining and redistricting. This is the work of man.

It just continues on the least to the greatest levels. They are marginalizing individuals, the haves and have-nots. They are controlling the land that Father created. No man can control the land that Father created. That is where the rules are. Father established his rules that we may be able to get along with one another. But whenever a nation — blessed is the nation whose Elohim is YeHoVaH.

It really grieves my heart. I am watching things and seeing things and it really hurts to watch our nation; to watch the Father's earth, his planet, continue to be destroyed in the hands of men who could care less about the Almighty.

That is why our responsibility and our job is so vital. We have been so enamored with coming into the Hebrew Roots and understanding the Torah and learning how to live according to the Torah and keeping the Feasts. Yet the commission that Father has given to us goes neglected. We have to learn. We have to get homes together. We have to get husbands loving their wives and wives loving their husbands and children honoring their parents. The thing that Father has really impressed upon me in the last little while is something that when I was a Christian, it used to always be in my heart. That is the fact that **judgment begins in the House of YeHoVaH.**

If I interpret that correctly, I used to think that judgment began in the church, but judgment begins in the House of YeHoVaH. It begins in the true community of believers. That is all of those who call upon the name of Yeshua and who keep the commandments of YeHoVaH. We have to get our act together.

We start by understanding the covenants that Father has made to us so we can enter into the covenant promises. We are supposed to be the most blessed people on the planet. No people are supposed to be more blessed than YeHoVaH's people. We are supposed to be so blessed that the nations of the world envy and want to know about our Elohim.

Instead, for the most part we are being despised and turned on.

(Leviticus 26:31) *"And I will make your cities waste, and bring your sanctuaries unto desolation, and I will not smell the savour of your sweet odours."*

What is he saying here? If you look at it, he says that if you will not hearken unto me and will not do all of these commandments, then. What does it go back to? It goes back to the commands.

Unfortunately, we live in a society today where there are two billion people on the planet who call themselves Christians. They believe that there is another set of commands for them than there is for the children of YeHoVaH. You hear it like this: "Well, those laws are for the Jewish people."

That is the way it comes out, so now Father has another set of laws for the Christians, which is really that there are no laws at all. That is lawlessness. So, he is saying all of this is because you will not.

He says, *"I will make your cities waste."* What is the savour? You are offering sacrifices, but they mean absolutely nothing. "I have turned my nose up. I close my nose. I don't want to smell it, because even though it may be something sweet to you, it is a stench to me. How dare you offer up sacrifices and yet you do not obey my commands?" **Obedience is better than sacrifice.**

(Leviticus 26:32) *"And I will bring the land into desolation: and your enemies which dwell therein shall be astonished at it."*

Who is bringing the land to desolation? YeHoVaH is bringing the land into desolation, but why? Who in essence is bringing the land into desolation? The people are. **When you rebel against the covenant of YeHoVaH, you bring your land into desolation. You bring trouble upon yourself.** It is not somebody bringing trouble upon you. You bring trouble upon yourself through acts of disobedience and through acts of rebellion.

Your enemies are going to look and say, "Oh! I feel sorry for those people." These are the people of YeHoVaH. But look at this:

(Leviticus 26:33) *"And I will scatter you among the heathen, and will draw out a sword after you: and your land shall be desolate, and your cities waste."*

Now, you know this has happened several times. The walls are torn down. The gates are destroyed and the temple burned. The people are carried into captivity. Other rulers have come in — the Greeks, the Romans, the Syrians, the Babylonians.

(Leviticus 26:34) *"Then shall the land enjoy her sabbaths, as long as it lieth desolate, and ye be in your enemies" land; even then shall the land rest, and enjoy her sabbaths."*

In other words, Father says that the only way the land is going to be at rest and at peace is if I kick you all out of it. Notice here what is going on. What you see happening in these passages of scripture is that this is not the first time. Remember that Adam was in the land of milk and honey, if you would. They did not have to do anything until they disobeyed the commands and Father spewed them out of the land. It was the same thing. You who were supposed to be a blessing to the land are literally destroying the land. The only way that I can restore the land is to get those of you who destroy the land, out of it.

This should cause us to have second thoughts. For those of us who have issues with people who are trying to preserve the planet, I don't know where you are on global warming and I don't understand it, but I do know this. It is cold in places where it is supposed to be hot. It is hot in places it is supposed to be cold. It is snowing in places it typically does not snow. There is something going on in the earth. I can't explain it. I am not a scientist. I don't know how it works, but I know something is not right.

I know that even with what is being done in the land called the United States of America and other countries, that things are going into the ground. There are chemicals that are not being properly disposed of. We live surrounded by nuclear waste or nuclear plants and cell phone towers. We have all types of greenhouse gases. There is a lot going on that we are smelling and sniffing. I was watching the news. In China they call it smog because you can't see through it. It is almost like fog, but it is not fog at all. It is the hand of man. It is pollution.

Can you imagine we have gone from a land where you could see to the bottom of the lake, to where you can't see into the lake? We have gone from a place where the air was so fresh, to where you now have people having to wear masks every day.

All kinds of things are happening. People are dying and sickness is running rampant and there are diseases that there is no cure for and hospitals and cancer centers. I mean, something is terribly, terribly wrong. Man is destroying the planet that we are supposed to preserve. It is not going to get any better.

(Leviticus 26:35) *"As long as it lieth desolate it shall rest; because it did not rest in your sabbaths, when ye dwelt upon it."*

Because you did not keep a Sabbath, the land never had a Sabbath. When we violate the Sabbath, it is like a domino effect. Everything is affected when man does not honor YeHoVaH. This is what I believe that Paul meant when he said that all creation groans. The entire creation is groaning. The animals know that things are out of sync — the fowl. You have whales being beached and dolphins losing their sense of direction. We have a real mess on our hands and we are acting like it doesn't exist.

We could be thinking so much about the economy. You can focus upon what you choose to focus upon. But when I read the Bible, it breaks my heart to see what is actually going on. So, Father is saying, "Listen. You guys can ignore these commands if you want. You can ignore my covenant if you want, but you need to understand that within the word, within the covenant, there are some built-in mechanisms that automatically release based upon your actions." How you approach this word will determine your outcome.

It is not the word that is determining the outcome. It is how you approach the word. You can have the truth, but if you don't apply the truth, then what good is it? You can be a hearer, but if you don't do it, what good is it? You are deceived. People get deceived. Before we can do it, we have to know what it says and what it means. We have to learn how to get into it for ourselves so we are not dependent upon people.

Let me tell you something and please listen to me. There are people who are pulling stuff out of the air and throwing stuff together and mesmerizing you with their ability to speak. Yet if you go to the word and research it and study it, you don't come anywhere near the conclusions they have come to.

Something is wrong.

I am always leery if you are coming away with something from the word that I study, when I try to put your pieces together and it doesn't line up. Unfortunately, the majority of the faith world is so awed and mesmerized by it. They have information without the ability to apply it. Information without application only leads to inflation.

All you have is a puffed-up head with information you can't use. Wow! Okay, what do I do with that? What do I do with this that you just taught me? How do I apply this that you just taught me in my life today to see the hand of the Almighty? Or is it just heady, puffed-up information that you have whipped up in your spiritual kitchen that doesn't do anything, but give me a puffy head?

Let's look at the blood of the Palestinian Covenant, the Land Covenant and the covenant that Father made concerning the land. When you look at the Land Covenant, you have to see with whom he made the covenant. Did he make the covenant with the Jewish people? He made the covenant with Israel — with all of Israel.

All Israelites are not Jews. I don't care what Jewish people tell you. Don't think for a moment and try to pass that "anti-Semitic" stuff on me, because that is not the case. I will not bow down to some anti-Semitic threat. I am not going there. The bottom line is that the people of YeHoVaH have a right to the land of YeHoVaH. And every believer has a right to that land. There are those out there who want to tell you that all the Jewish people are now of the same — that Dan is Jewish, Naphtali is Jewish, Simeon is Jewish. No, Simeon is Simeonite. Dan is Danite.[4] The bottom line is when we look at all of the tribes of Israel, they don't just miraculously become Jews because you say so.

The Jews come from the tribe of Judah, period. Let me tell you something. In Messiah, get this. If my Master is Jewish and he bought me with his blood, then that makes me a Jew. I have as much right to claim myself as a Jew. But what is a Jew? A Jew is one who supposedly practices Judaism. That is what a Jew is, so we don't practice Judaism.

Yeshua was Judean. He was of the tribe of Judah. I don't have a problem being of the tribe of Judah. I am just trying to help you understand. You don't have to get it twisted. People hear the term "Jew" and they think of Judaism. Why wouldn't I want to be a Jew? My Master is Jewish. Why wouldn't I want to be like my Master?

But Christianity has given Judaism or the term "Jew" (based upon Judaism) such a bad name. It is at a point where people now want to bash. They want to destroy and to alienate and isolate. They do not want anything to do with it. I don't have a problem with it. I am not Jewish, but my Master is. Yeshua is from the tribe of Judah and according to the terminology, that would make him Jewish.

But according to *religious* terminology, a Jew is one who practices Judaism.

(Deuteronomy 27:1-3) "And Moses with the elders of Israel commanded the people, saying, „Keep all the commandments which I command you this day. And it shall be on the day when ye shall pass over Jordan unto the land which the LORD thy God giveth thee, that thou shalt set thee up great stones, and plaister them with plaister: And thou shalt write upon them all the words of this law, when thou art passed over, that thou mayest go in unto the land which the LORD thy God giveth thee, a land that floweth with milk and honey; as the LORD God of thy fathers hath promised thee.""

---
[4] I am not getting into *Revelation*. That was John's vision and I understand where you are coming from there.

This promise was promised to the Fathers. It was promised to Abraham, to Isaac and then to Jacob whose name was changed to Israel. Jacob's name was not changed to Judah. Jacob had a son named Judah. Jacob's name was changed to Israel. YeHoVaH gave the land to Jacob which is Israel. Therefore, it was given to all of his sons, even the strangers who joined themselves.

I just wonder. Think about this for a moment. Let me mess with your head a little bit. The strangers who joined themselves with Israel, what were they called? They were Israelites. What tribe? Any one they joined. They were connected to whatever household they were connected to.

(Deuteronomy 27:4-7) "Therefore it shall be when ye be gone over Jordan, that ye shall set up these stones, which I command you this day, in mount Ebal, and thou shalt plaister them with plaister. And there shalt thou build an altar unto the LORD thy God, an altar of stones: thou shalt not lift up any iron tool upon them. Thou shalt build the altar of the LORD thy God of whole stones: and thou shalt offer burnt offerings thereon unto the LORD thy God: And thou shalt offer peace offerings, and shalt eat there, and rejoice before the LORD thy God."

Father is saying, "We are going to have a party! I am going to bring you into the land and then we are going to party. I am giving you some specific instructions. This is not to be hard. This is not to be a lot of work. You don't have to try to cut stones into sizes. Take whole stones; plaster over them, write these laws upon them and you are good to go. Then we are going to rejoice together."

(Deuteronomy 27:8) "And thou shalt write upon the stones all the words of this law very plainly."

The day that the new generation of Israel entered Canaan land, an altar of stones was built to YeHoVaH and sacrificial offerings were made. **It signified the cleansing of the land by atoning covenant blood (the blood of the covenant).**

Notice that before the people took the land, there were what you would consider to be heathens in the land. Chances are that these heathens practiced heathenism. They certainly had idolatrous worship going on. YeHoVaH did not want his people doing what they did or worshipping him the way they worshipped their idols.

What is the **seal of the Palestinian Covenant**? *(Deuteronomy 11; 28* and *29)*

(Deuteronomy 11:11) "But the land, whither ye go to possess it, is a land of hills and valleys, and drinketh water of the rain of heaven:"

(Deuteronomy 11:14) "That I will give you the rain of your land in his due season, the first rain and the latter rain, that thou mayest gather in thy corn, and thy wine, and thine oil."

Now this (whether you know it or not) is a seal.

(Deuteronomy 11:17) "And then the LORD"s wrath be kindled against you, and he shut up the heaven, that there be no rain, and that the land yield not her fruit; and lest ye perish quickly from off the good land which the LORD giveth you."

(Deuteronomy 28:12) "The LORD shall open unto thee his good treasure, the heaven to give the rain unto thy land in his season, and to bless all the work of thine hand: and thou shalt lend unto many nations, and thou shalt not borrow."

Let me tell you something. I did a teaching called *The Most Coveted Blessing*. It actually deals with this covenant. Too much rain is considered to be a flood. If you don't get enough rain, what do you have? You have a drought. Now, it is important that it doesn't rain during the winter, because if it rains during the winter, you get ice all over and you certainly can't move around. And it is important that it doesn't snow in the summer. In the spring you have seen places like California and Florida when they had a frost after the citrus budded. When you have a frost and the buds are on the trees, the crops are going to be destroyed. Whether you work the land or not you pay for it. If the oranges and the lemons and the cherries and all of these crops that people are dependent upon; if these things don't bud properly, if there is a frost that destroys the buds, then the tree is not going to produce.

It is not only important to get rain. It is important to get rain at the right time, in season. It is the Father who controls the heavens. So, whether you are a farmer or not, if there is a drought, you are going to pay for it. If there is a drought like we have had in different places, you will see the price of produce go up. A thunderstorm or a tornado or a hurricane can come in and just wipe out an entire crop.

This is one of the things in Malachi. Malachi says to "bring all of the tithes into the storehouse that there may be meat in my house. Try me herewith to see if I won't open the windows of heaven and pour out blessings." People start spiritualizing the word of YeHoVaH like they try to spiritualize this former and latter rain to associate it with the Holy Spirit. You take it out of the natural realm in which Father speaks it in. Then you put it into the spirit realm Now the former rain and the latter rain is the outpouring of the Holy Spirit.

Now it is totally disconnected. The word that is associated with the land and with the rain and with heaven is put into a spiritual realm where now you are the land. The rain is the Holy Spirit and the latter rain is going to be greater than the former rain. That means that the latter outpouring of the Holy Spirit is going to be greater than the former outpouring of the Holy Spirit. Now you start associating prophecy with it and you talk about this great end-time harvest. Oh man, people have just taken the word way out of context. They have put it so far into the spirit realm. Give it to people with a nice spin to it. Get people all worked up on some superficial message that is totally disconnected from the word.

I hate to be the one to have to tell you this. I have been through all of that and I have seen it. I have seen how people twist the word. They take it into the spirit and make it something spiritual. For some reason people buy this stuff hook, line and sinker. That is because it doesn't require anything from them as an individual to line themselves up responsibly with what the word says about how they are supposed to live their lives. That is greasy grace in the spirit.

When Father says you will lend to many nations and not borrow, that is exactly what he meant. When he said he will give rain in your land in season, that is exactly what he meant. So how in the world did the former rain and the latter rain become the outpouring of the Holy Spirit? He spoke very specifically about the outpouring of the Holy Spirit. He did not speak to it in allegorical terms associated with rain. He said, "I am going to pour out my Spirit," not that he would pour out the latter rain. "I'm going to pour out my Spirit on all flesh." People associate the baptism of the Spirit to being immersed in the Spirit; meaning just what he said. You will be immersed in the Spirit. That does not transform the former rain and the latter rain because the former rain and the latter rain have to do with rain in season in the land upon the crops.

Ask any farmer. A farmer would much rather have the former rain and the latter rain that is associated with scripture than the Holy Spirit being poured upon his crops. I guess the corn is going to prophesy now. The beans and the cotton are going to speak in tongues.

Search the scriptures and see if what I am saying to you is true. Get your head out of the clouds and out of the spirit realm and see that this is actually talking about literal rain. Look it up.

> The blessings of YeHoVaH make one rich and He adds no sorrow to it.

You need the avocados and the pomegranates. You need the mangoes. You need all of the apples. That is what your treasures are because once you have a good treasure; that good treasure is taken to market and guess what? You have a pocket full of money. Father is not pouring out pennies from heaven, quarters from heaven, nickels from heaven, dimes from heaven, half dollars, silver dollars or paper money. You have not seen it. It is not coming out. And it doesn't grow on trees.

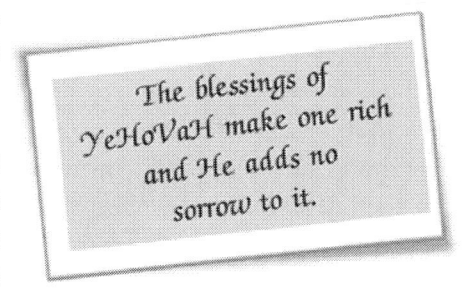

"I'm just waiting for Father to open up the heavens and pour out my blessings." Well, I'll tell you what. If you are waiting for the heavens to open and pour out your blessings, then you make sure you have an umbrella, because it is going to be wet.

Now, there are the manifestations of things that Father has released that are going to come in a natural realm. They are going to manifest themselves in the natural realm. Father is not getting spiritual money to you. If he gave you spiritual money, you would need a spiritual bank to cash it in. And you would need spiritual businesses to take your spiritual currency in the Spirit.

It is time that we came back down to earth. "Scotty, beam me down" (for those of you Trekkies out there). Let me tell you something. There is just so much foolishness out there. This is why people don't know which way is up. They are confused. There is way too much confusion out there. People are trying to associate natural reality according to the scriptures in spiritual terms. They are trying to manifest spiritual blessings.

Listen. The blessings that the Father gives make one rich. The blessings of YeHoVaH makes one rich and that is not spiritual richness. You can be rich in the spirit, but that means you are happy regardless of your external circumstances. The blessing that he is talking about is not spiritual riches. He said that the blessings of YeHoVaH makes one rich and he adds no sorrow to it.

It is unfortunate that people who are rich in the Spirit are sorrowful because they don't have money to pay their bills. When you don't have money to pay your bills, I don't know about you, but it makes me sorrowful. I don't like having to tell people that I don't have their money. Fortunately for me, I have not had to do that in thirty years. I don't plan on it today. I don't like not answering the phone because there is a debt collector. Caller ID has allowed people to get around paying their responsibilities.

The blessings of YeHoVaH makes one rich and he adds no sorrow to it. The people of YeHoVaH are supposed to be doing well, not struggling. If that be the case, then it is not the Father's fault. Everything that we have need of is in the earth.

I was sharing with someone who called. I spend a lot of time in front of the computer when I am at home in my office putting together plans and messages. A lot of the stuff you all see is me behind the scenes. I spend a lot of time on the phone. I spend a lot of time counseling and ministering to people in various ways.

We have a teaching called *Maximizing Your Talents*. I am not saying this because I did it, but that is a true blessing to understand what talent is. It is amazing how the church world turned talents into abilities and gifts.

That is the problem with Christianity. It is always trying to spiritualize the word. It takes it out of the natural and puts it into the spiritual where you can't grasp it. Therefore, you don't see the manifestation of what Father said you are supposed to see.

"I'm blessed in my mess." No, you are not!

"I'm going to fake it till I make it." Why are you faking it? That is the problem. You are a fake.

We try to put things into practical terms so that everyday people can grab hold of it and see the reality of the Father's blessings on their lives. You are going to have to get your head out of the clouds. You have to put some feet to this book and stop trying to spiritualize it. See it for what it is. Apply it for what it is and you will see the blessing of the Almighty.

There are things we are trying to do. I am always trying to figure out Father, where is your blessing? I need to know. I don't want to be wandering around trying to figure this thing out because I shouldn't have to figure out how to do your business. I shouldn't have to figure this out at all. I am sold out to you. You tell me who am I supposed to be connected to. That requires patience.

I got up this morning trying to get the mind of YeHoVaH. Just today I am sitting negotiating with this person. I am negotiating over here, trying to make things happen. Father blesses my work. He does. He just blesses it and it is not because I'm me. It is because I am trying to get his mind. I am taking the time to get into his presence, to get in his face, to get quiet, to turn off all of the noise. I feel sorry sometimes for my household because my son comes home. We have a TV upstairs and we have a TV downstairs. My office is behind the wall. Then there is the living room where children come in to watch the TV. When I am in my office working, the TV can't be on. You all go upstairs. I don't need the noise. I cannot listen to the little squealy cartoon noises and faint noises that you can't make out. The way my mind works, I need to have quiet so I can hear and think.

I have seven children and a wife who live in our house. When I try to get my things done, there are times when I need that quiet (and so do you). But we have too much stuff coming at us. We need that quiet time so Father can speak to us and show us and instruct us. I was about to make some serious errors. When we don't take time to listen to the Father, we make financial decisions. Then we end up with buyer's remorse. We have that because we made a decision, sometimes paying more and sometimes three times more than what we should have paid because we were anxious and in a hurry and won't wait.

There was a time when I thought my waiting was procrastination. I don't procrastinate. I wait, but let me tell you something. Waiting can sometimes be viewed as procrastination. And when the time is right, now it is time to move. I have clear instructions. If I don't have clear instructions, then I am going to wait. To others, it may look like procrastination.

You have people who want you to make a decision. This is going to be over or you are going to miss this deal. Now you are under this pressure. You don't make decisions under pressure. If you make decisions under pressure, you will live to regret it.

Don't try to spiritualize the word. He has given us some very clear-cut instructions that he is going to do this. We have to do that. If we don't do this, he is going to do that and that is simple, so we should not be surprised.

(Deuteronomy 28:24) *"The LORD shall make the rain of thy land powder and dust: from heaven shall it come down upon thee, until thou be destroyed."*

Now, is that the Holy Spirit?

We were in the building putting some equipment together and the rain was coming down. I looked outside and it was just blowing. It felt like the building was shaking. Had we walked outside at a certain time, we probably would have been blown away.

Father says he will make the rain of the land powder and dust. He will use the very thing that is supposed to be a blessing to us, to destroy us. The very thing that is supposed to bless us will destroy us.

The seal of YeHoVaH upon the land was to be evidenced in the early and latter rains. Blessings and fruitfulness by the rains was God's seal to Israel upon their obedience to the laws of his land. When God withheld the rains, it was the evidence of his withholding the seal of his blessing.

The blessing of YeHoVaH to the land of Israel was rain in season. If you have rain in season, you have prosperity. The last time I went to Israel, you could go into certain places and it was just flush. There was greenery and some of the most beautiful flowers you will see on the planet. Certain areas are just greenery. The garden of Gethsemane has several hundred- or thousand-year-old olive trees.

Some say that this seal foreshadowed the coming of the early/former and latter rains in the outpouring of the Holy Spirit. I will tell you something. I have serious questions about that, because people always want to associate everything with the Holy Spirit. If you are in Children's Church," the answer to every question is "Jesus."

I want to show you something. I really think that people need to understand. Some of you who are still in church need to look at what it says:

(Malachi 3:8-9) *"Will a man rob God? Yet ye have robbed me. But ye say, Wherein have we robbed thee? In tithes and offerings. Ye are cursed with a curse: for ye have robbed me, even this whole nation."*

What are they cursed with? It is the same curse in *Deuteronomy 28*. Father will withhold the rain. We looked at that. He is going to make the heavens like brass. The ground is going to be like iron. Nothing is coming down and nothing is coming up. You will not get rain and there will be no crop. No buds are going to break through the ground. The land is going to be desolate.

You have to understand this. If there is no rain, here are the dominoes. No rain and you have drought. No rain, no crops. No crops and what happens to the animals? What happens to the human beings? No rain will bring death.

Father says, "Okay, no problem. I will show you no rain and let me see you work your miracles now." If you don't get rain on those crops, the crops are not going to grow.

The cows, the animals are not going to have any vegetation to eat. They are not going to produce milk. They are not going to produce the eggs. You will starve. Eventually folks are just going to die.

(Malachi 3:10) *"Bring ye all the tithes into the storehouse, that there may be meat in mine house, and prove me now herewith, saith the LORD of hosts, if I will not open you the windows of heaven, and pour you out a blessing, that there shall not be room enough to receive it."*

Notice these words.

(Malachi 3:11) *"And I will rebuke the devourer for your sakes, and he shall not destroy the fruits of your ground; neither shall your vine cast her fruit before the time in the field, saith the LORD of hosts."*

What is the devourer? The church wants to tell us that it is the devil. You can look this up and it is not dealing with the devil. *The devourer is the locusts. The devourer is the pestilence.* It is not going to destroy the fruits of your ground. He is not going to eat your buds. He is not going to eat your fruit. He is not going to destroy your crops. All you need is locusts to come in and they will eat up everything in sight and leave you with nothing. That is the devourer.

The church wants to tell us that the devourer is the devil. He is going to rebuke the devil. He is going to rebuke the devil and you will have all of these blessings. You are going to get a new car. He is going to get you a new house. He is going to give you money. He is going to cause debt cancellation. He is going to do all of these supernatural things.

No. He is talking about — RAIN!

(Malachi 3:11b-12) *"…neither shall your vine cast her fruit before the time in the field, saith the LORD of hosts. And all nations shall call you blessed: for ye shall be a delightsome land, saith the LORD of hosts."*

They are going to look at your land and they are going to see plush crops. They are going to see fruit galore. They are going to see dates. They are going to see all kinds of olives and all kinds of exotic fruit growing on your vines. Your plants are just going to produce hundred-fold return. And while there is a famine in the lands all around you, these people in those lands are going to look at your land and they are going to see that your land is a delightsome land — a land flowing with milk and honey.

But why do people want to take that into the spirit realm and take it out of the natural realm? Because then they can twist it and you get a twisted doctrine and a twisted interpretation.

You now think that all you have to do is give your money to the church and God is just going to bless you overwhelmingly, whether you keep his commandments or not. That is not what it is saying here.

How can Father bless people who reject his commandments? That has been our issue. We have had situations where our homes have fallen apart. Our bodies have fallen apart. Our businesses have fallen apart and our finances have fallen apart. We keep giving and giving and giving. We keep searching our lives to see where the sin is. What is the problem? What am I not doing right? What am I doing wrong? Am I hanging around with the wrong people? Are people bringing a curse into my life? Am I cursed?

I have good news for you. Repent. Turn back toward the commands of the Almighty. When you honor the commands of the Almighty, you enter into the covenant and all of his commands. You enter into the true covenant. When you enter into the true covenant, he says if you keep my commands, all of these blessings will come upon you. That is something I can personally guarantee. Why? It's because Father doesn't lie.

When he sends out his word, it accomplishes what it was sent out to accomplish. It will not return to him empty. You keep his commands. He is obligated to bless you. That is a promise. That is a covenant promise.

Class 56 Study Summary
Key Points

1. The Palestinian Covenant is more simply called the Land Covenant.
2. The Palestinian Covenant's promise concerned the blessings and/or cursing on Palestine/Canaan or the Promised Land.
3. If YeHoVaH is sending you to a place, you have to stand firm and let him go forth and fight the battle. But what Father has for you, no one else can take. What he has for you is yours.
4. An unconditional covenant is a covenant that is preceded with "I will."
5. Today in order to make aliyah to the land of promise in Israel, people must convert to Judaism and denounce Messiah Yeshua.
6. We have to decide whether or not we believe the Bible. We have to stand on what the Bible teaches.
7. Judgment begins in the House of YeHoVaH.
8. Those who call themselves Christians believe that there is another set of commands for them than there are for the children of YeHoVaH. You may hear "Those laws are for the Jewish people," but that is no laws at all or lawlessness.
9. When you rebel against the covenant of YeHoVaH, you bring your land into desolation. You bring trouble upon yourself.
10. YeHoVaH made the Palestinian Covenant concerning the land with all of Israel.
11. The "Jews" come from the tribe of Judah, period. Yeshua was Judean.
12. The altar of stones that was built when Israel entered the land of Canaan signified the cleansing of the land by atoning covenant blood (the blood of the covenant).
13. The seal of the Palestinian Covenant is rain in due season.
14. The Father says that we will lend to many nations and not borrow.
15. The blessings of YeHoVaH make one rich and He adds no sorrow to it.
16. According to the Bible, talents are funds or money. The church has turned that into abilities and gifts.
17. Don't try to spiritualize the word.
18. The devourer in the Bible is the locusts or other insects that eat our crops, our produce. The church wants to say that the devil (Satan) is the devourer.
19. We must repent and turn back toward the commands of the Almighty. When we honor the commands of the Almighty, we enter into the covenant. He says that if we keep his commands, all of these blessings will come upon us. If we reject his commands, all of these curses will come upon us. That is a covenant promise.

Review Exercise

1. The Palestinian Covenant is a conditional covenant, meaning there was an "if...then" construction involved in it. What was the "if?" What was the "then?" Finish the sentence:

    If _____

    Then _____.

2. YeHoVaH called Abraham out from Ur and told him he would give him the land where his footsteps fell. The children of Israel were told they would receive a land of milk and honey. Now the Palestinian Covenant lays out the specific land and terms. This intersection of the land of the Palestinian Covenant with the Abrahamic and Mosaic also gives rise to one huge threat prevalent in the latter two. What is that and how is it playing out today?

    _____
    _____
    _____
    _____
    _____
    _____
    _____

3. What are the relationships of the Palestinian Covenant with modern day environmentalism?

    _____
    _____
    _____
    _____
    _____
    _____
    _____

4. In this lesson the question was asked about which tribe the "strangers" who had chosen to align with Israel belonged to. How were they going to know where they would live? The answer was that they were with any tribe they wanted to be with, so they could live pretty much anywhere.

    Just for fun, read again the descriptions of the tribes as presented in *Genesis 49* along with the land assignments in ***Joshua 13:1-14:5***. Figure out what tribe you want to be in, assuming you can join any of them. You might also consult a map of the allotments to inform your choice.

    What tribe did you join, stranger? _____

    Why? _____

Rate the following statements by filling in the most appropriate number.

(1 = I do not agree 10 = I agree completely)

Objectives:

1. I can define the Palestinian (Canaan, Land) Covenant, especially in relation to the Abrahamic and Mosaic Covenants.

   1. ○ 2. ○ 3. ○ 4. ○ 5. ○ 6. ○ 7. ○ 8. ○ 9. ○ 10. ○

2. I can describe how the actions of obedience or disobedience have directly impacted the physical land, the natural environment.

   1. ○ 2. ○ 3. ○ 4. ○ 5. ○ 6. ○ 7. ○ 8. ○ 9. ○ 10. ○

My Journal

What I learned from this class:

_____
_____
_____
_____
_____
_____
_____
_____
_____
_____
_____
_____
_____
_____
_____
_____
_____
_____
_____
_____

Discipleship Training Class 57

Principles of Interpretation — Covenantal Principle (part 6)

Objectives:

As a Discipleship student, at the end of this class you will be able to:

- Define the Davidic Covenant and its significance toward faith and salvation
- Compose an overview of the New/Renewed Covenant

We are going to pick up today in looking at the Davidic Covenant. The Davidic Covenant is that covenant by which we have our salvation and faith in the Messiah. You will see that as we continue on. He came to establish the New Covenant based upon the promises the Father made to Abraham and to David.

We are going to spend a lot of time in our Bible today. It is important that we familiarize ourselves with the Bible in these particular discussions. Make sure and don't be afraid to mark your Bible. Take notes, but make some marks if you have to.

The Davidic Covenant

(2 Samuel 7:4-8) *"And it came to pass that night, that the word of the Lord came unto Nathan, saying, ,,Go and tell my servant David, Thus saith the Lord, Shalt thou build me an house for me to dwell in? Whereas I have not dwelt in any house since the time that I brought up the children of Israel out of Egypt, even to this day, but have walked in a tent and in a tabernacle. In all the places wherein I have walked with all the children of Israel spake I a word with any of the tribes of Israel, whom I commanded to feed my people Israel, saying, Why build ye not me an house of cedar? Now therefore so shalt thou say unto my servant David, Thus saith the Lord of hosts, I took thee from the sheepcote, from following the sheep, to be ruler over my people, over Israel:"*

So, we see that Father here makes it very clear who his people are (his people Israel).

(2 Samuel 7:9-12) *"And I was with thee whithersoever thou wentest, and have cut off all thine enemies out of thy sight, and have made thee a great name, like unto the name of the great men that are in the earth. Moreover, I will appoint a place for my people Israel, and will plant them, that they may dwell in a place of their own, and move no more; neither shall the children of wickedness afflict them any more, as beforetime, And as since the time that I commanded judges to be over my people Israel, and have caused thee to rest from all thine enemies. Also, the Lord telleth thee that he will make thee an house. And when thy days be fulfilled, and thou shalt sleep with thy fathers, I will set up thy seed after thee, which shall proceed out of thy bowels, and I will establish his kingdom."*

Notice that David desires to build him a house, but he says he is going "to make you a house."

(2 Samuel 7:12-13) *"And when thy days be fulfilled, and thou shalt sleep with thy fathers, I will set up thy seed after thee, which shall proceed out of thy bowels, and I will establish his kingdom."*

(Speaking of Solomon):

"He shall build an house for my name, and I will stablish the throne of his kingdom for ever."

Here we see a word play. In one sense he is talking about Solomon, but did you know that Solomon will not live forever? He is saying, "I will establish the throne of his kingdom forever." We know that Solomon is not going to live forever, so who is he speaking of?

(2 Samuel 7:14) *"I will be his father, and he shall be my son. If he commit iniquity, I will chasten him with the rod of men, and with the stripes of the children of men:"*

Now he is speaking of Solomon. What he is saying here is that the scepter — now we are looking at a kingdom. We see that Father is speaking here to his prophet. He is telling him that he is going to establish his throne forever. So, he is speaking of that which is futuristic while at the same time speaking concerning that which shall come out of David's bowel (meaning his son).

(2 Samuel 7:15-17) *"But my mercy shall not depart away from him, as I took it from Saul, whom I put away before thee. And thine house and thy kingdom shall be established for ever before thee: thy throne shall be established for ever. According to all these words, and according to all this vision, so did Nathan speak unto David."*

We see here that YeHoVaH is speaking to Nathan the prophet to tell David that he is going to establish this kingdom. He is going to start it by building a house through Solomon, but this house is going to have everlasting significance.

What is interesting is that many people think and believe that all of the *Psalms* were written by David, but they weren't. David wrote some *Psalms*, but David was not the only writer of *Psalms*.

(Psalm 89:1-3) *"I will sing of the mercies of the LORD for ever: with my mouth will I make known thy faithfulness to all generations. For I have said, ,,Mercy shall be built up for ever: thy faithfulness shalt thou establish in the very heavens. I have made a covenant with my chosen, I have sworn unto David my servant,""*

We see here that this is a prayer of Ethan. Ethan is an Ezrahite. Ethan is praying. In this prayer there is a prophecy coming forward through the prayer. In verse 3 we see that YeHoVaH chose David and made a covenant with him.

(Psalm 89:4-5) *"Thy seed will I establish for ever, and build up thy throne to all generations. Selah. And the heavens shall praise thy wonders, O LORD: thy faithfulness also in the congregation of the saints."*

He is now going to establish his throne forever. When we look at the words of the promises of the covenant that God made with David, it was an unconditional covenant. This was not based upon what David did or did not do. It was not based upon what Solomon did or did not do. Regardless of what Solomon did, regardless of what David did, Father had already spoken all the way back in *Genesis* when he established the first Messianic prophecy. He said that Yeshua was going to crush the head of the serpent. The serpent's seed would bruise his heel, but the woman's seed would crush his head.

So that prophecy has already gone forward. It is also continued through Abraham and through David. Now we see that this is an unconditional covenant.

In *Matthew 1:1* we see the words of the covenant. It was by implication, an integral part of the Abrahamic Covenant. The major promise of the Davidic Covenant was that which involved the coming of Yeshua Messiah, who was the seed of David as well as the seed of Abraham.

(Matthew 1:1) *"The book of the generation of Yeshua Messiah, the son of David, the son of Abraham."*

In several instances in the gospel narratives, we see that there are those who call Yeshua the son of David. Did you know that Yeshua's biological dad was not David? There are many, many generations after David, and yet prophetically Yeshua is the offspring of David. Oftentimes in Hebrew idioms, the offspring of an individual is also in certain cases, considered to be a son.

This is a good case (if you would) or a great example. If you remember, there was this fellow named Jacob. Jacob had twelve sons. One of the sons Jacob had been named Joseph. Joseph had two sons, Ephraim and Manasseh. Jacob elevated Ephraim and Manasseh (his grandsons) to sonship status with equal inheritance with the sons. He went so far as to name a plot of land, a tribal land, the land of Ephraim and the land of Manasseh.

Later on, Ephraim became the representative (again if you would) of Israel. Ephraim and Israel were used interchangeably in certain places. Ephraim was considered to be the ten lost tribes.

As a matter of fact, there is a prayer or a prophecy that was spoken back in the Torah that the children of Israel would pray over their sons. "May YeHoVaH make you like Ephraim and Manasseh." Now, that is a prophecy. If we take time to really look at that, we can see that Father is speaking something prophetically. By the time that we get into New Testament writings, the Ephraimites and Manassites — their land was the land of Samaria. Samaria was the land of Ephraim and Manasseh.

This is one of the reasons why the Samaritan woman could claim Jacob as her Father. As a descendent of Ephraim, they could claim Jacob as their Father — at least that is what the Samaritan woman did.

He would take the throne of David and rule and reign upon it as a righteous king forever. There are many passages that address this:

Genesis 49:8-12   *1 Kings 8:20-25*   *2 Samuel 7:1-17*
Jeremiah 33:20-21   *Psalm 89:3-4, 34-35*   *Isaiah 9:6-9*
Psalms 132:11-12   *Luke 1:30-33*

Who is going to take the throne of David? We saw in *Matthew*. Yeshua Messiah is the son of David, who was the son of Abraham. We know that David was not the biological Father of David. Abraham had how many sons? **Eight sons**. None of them were named David.

It is interesting that many people think that Abraham only had two sons. Some would say that Abraham only had one real son. The covenant, the promise, was the lineage of Abraham through David and in which the Messiah came through what tribe? The tribe of Judah.

(Genesis 49:8-9) *"Judah, thou art he whom thy brethren shall praise: thy hand shall be in the neck of thine enemies; thy father's children shall bow down before thee. Judah is a lion's whelp: from the prey, my son, thou art gone up: he stooped down, he couched as a lion, and as an old lion; who shall rouse him up?"*

Oftentimes when you see the imagery of Judah, it is referred to as the lion of Judah.

(Genesis 49:10) *"The scepter shall not depart from Judah, nor a lawgiver from between his feet, until Shiloh come; and unto him shall the gathering of the people be."*

Father is speaking prophetically way back here in the book of *Genesis*. The question is, was Judah ever a king? And yet kings have scepters. The scepter is a sign of rulership, of kingship.

(Genesis 49:11-12) *"Binding his foal unto the vine, and his asks colt unto the choice vine; he washed his garments in wine, and his clothes in the blood of grapes: His eyes shall be red with wine, and his teeth white with milk."*

This is a prophecy that Jacob is pronouncing over his children. He is actually blessing them, but he is prophesying. He is speaking into their future. This is so important for us because when you speak words over your wife, when you speak words over your husband, when you speak over your children, your nieces and your nephews; understand that your words have power whether you intend them to have power or not. They just do.

I received an email from someone. I really don't think people understand the power of words. When I speak to my wife, I am very, very careful. When I did not know any better, I would say dumb things. A Father should never say to a son, "You will never amount to anything." A Mother should never speak those words over her children. A Father should never speak those words. A man should never call his wife out of her name or call her something derogatory.

You have heard people say (and this is a lie straight from the pit): "Sticks and stones will break my bones, but words will never hurt me." Let me tell you something. People have been healed from sticks and stones, but words are still like daggers in the hearts and minds of individuals. It puts up roadblocks, hurdles, stumbling blocks and even great gulfs between an individual and their destiny.

This is why when Fathers and Mothers would pronounce a name upon their child, that name typically would have prophetic significance. When you name a child something, you are literally speaking into that child's future by giving them that name. I think this is one of the reasons why many in the Hebrew Roots movement want to go around and change their name to something that sounds Hebrew.

If you really want to change your name, change it. Get it on your birth certificate or on your driver's license. That is really changing it. When you speak a word whether it be a name and the same with name calling, the enemy is taking your words and working them to his will. Your words have power. Death and life are in the power of the tongue. *(Proverbs 18:21)* With your words you will speak life or you will speak death.

I hear people say stuff and I am constantly correcting people. When people speak words, don't allow someone to speak words over you that you do not agree with for the sake of being cordial. My family used to say things like "That is an ugly child," or "That is a cute little devil." No, no, no. You don't speak those words over my children. You don't speak those words over anybody's children.

Some people might say, "Well, that is just trivial." Well, you can take it however you want, but **your words have power. Everything in the universe was created by words. Our words have power. Yeshua said that we will be held accountable for every idle word we speak.** We will be held accountable for every word we speak. When you understand that, there is no such thing as just having a casual conversation.

This is why I believe that *Proverbs* says that "many words cause sin." When people just want to talk, talk, talk, talk and talk, they run out of words. They just start making up stuff. They start adding fillers and words to the dictionary. "Uh, you know, um, uh and yeah." It is like, okay, spit it out. Typically, a person has either lost their train of thought; they have run out of words or they just like hearing themselves talk.

I am not trying to be mean, but if you spend your words like you spend your money, then you would spend your words a little differently. Your words are like money. You speak to them and what you say, you shall have. **What you say, you will have.** People will say, "I don't believe I can do that." No, you can't, if you believe that. If you don't believe, you are not going to make it happen.

(Matthew 12:36) "but I say unto you that every idle word that men shall speak they shall give account thereof in the day of judgment."

That is every word that you speak, every idle word. That word there says that every word that is idle or every word that is inoperable or every word that is not purposeful. We have to understand that our words have power.

When you speak words:

(Matthew 12:37) "for by thy words you shall be justified and by your words you shall be condemned."

Your words are going to justify you or your words are going to condemn you.

(2 Samuel 7:1-4) "And it came to pass, when the king sat in his house, and the LORD had given him rest round about from all his enemies; That the king said unto Nathan the prophet, „See now, I dwell in an house of cedar, but the ark of God dwelleth within curtains." And Nathan said to the king, „Go, do all that is in thine heart; for the LORD is with thee.""

As we read earlier, at that particular point David is saying, "I'm living in luxury, but the House of YeHoVaH is in a tent. I am living in my beautiful mansion, my palace, but the House of YeHoVaH is in a tent. Really those words have always been a challenge for me. They have always been a challenge, which is one of the reasons why when it comes down to trying to create an environment; when the people of YeHoVaH come and gather, that environment in my mind — we don't have to have gold trimmings and we don't have that kind of resource. But we can have a nice, beautiful, warm, welcoming Spirit-filled holy place. We should have that. We should not be in someplace that smells and bugs are running all over the place. That is just nasty. This place should be the most welcoming.

Every place that I have been, I have had people get to a place where they say, "You put more emphasis on the building than you do on the people." That is not true, not true at all, but I know this. The house or the place where people come to gather to worship and to fellowship should be a place where you should be comfortable inviting anybody. I don't care if it is the pope. If the pope walked in here, the pope should look around and say, "Nice." That is what he should do. If the king of Jordan walked in here, he should say, "Not bad." Anybody who walks in here should (I believe) feel the peace of YeHoVaH. They should feel welcomed and they should feel comfortable.

Have you ever been in a place where you are kind of nervous about sitting down? I have been in places where the seats are all dingy and it doesn't have to be that way. The house, the place where people gather and worship should be a nice place. It should be a place where people can come and fellowship and not be afraid or fearful that they are going to catch something by sitting on the seat or even if they lay upon the floor.

(Jeremiah 33:20-22) *"Thus saith the LORD; „If ye can break my covenant of the day, and my covenant of the night, and that there should not be day and night in their season; Then may also my covenant be broken with David my servant, that he should not have a son to reign upon his throne; and with the Levites the priests, my ministers. As the host of heaven cannot be numbered, neither the sand of the sea measured: so, will I multiply the seed of David my servant, and the Levites that minister unto me.""*

What you see here is as long as the night and day exist in their season, so shall my covenant be with David. The book of *Matthew* says that heaven and earth shall pass away before one jot or tittle of this word passes. Everything in this Bible will be fulfilled — everything. Heaven and earth will not pass away until every word be fulfilled. That is a promise.

(Luke 1:30-33) *"And the angel said unto her, „Fear not, Miriam: for thou hast found favour with Elohim. And, behold, thou shalt conceive in thy womb, and bring forth a son, and shalt call his name YESHUA. He shall be great, and shall be called the Son of the Highest: and YeHoVaH Elohim shall give unto him the throne of his father David: And he shall reign over the house of Jacob (Israel) for ever; and of his kingdom there shall be no end.""*

One of the problems you will find in the King James translation is that the translators have put "Jesus." Miriam (Mary) never called her son "Jesus" — never. None of his disciples ever called him "Jesus." No one in the first, second, third, fourth and on up to the sixteenth century ever called him "Jesus." The 1611 King James Bible clearly shows us the word "Jesus" is nowhere to be found in the Bible. And yet people are calling upon the name of "Jesus." Every knee is going to bow and every tongue is going to confess the name of "Jesus." "No other name I know whereby a man may be saved." You mean to say no other **transliterated** name. **It is not even a translation.**

It is unique because Yeshua was from the tribe of Yehudah or Judah — a Judean reigning over the House of Israel. When we look at the Renewed Covenant, we are going to see that YeHoVaH is going to bring Judah back into Israel. He is not going to take Israel and make Israel to be Jews, not the House of the Jews. Judah will be brought back into the commonwealth of Israel.

They will be called "Israel" (not Jews).

What do I mean "they'll be brought back into?" Well, right now you still have a divided kingdom. It is what we have. We will have a divided kingdom until the New or Renewed Covenant is established. What do I mean? Isn't the New Covenant established? The Renewed Covenant is only established with those who call upon the name of YeHoVaH.

Whosoever shall call upon the name of YeHoVaH shall be saved. Look at what Paul actually wrote. We will jump off here, but it is all within the covenant.

(Romans 10:9) *"For whosoever shall call upon the name of the Lord shall be saved."*

Oftentimes New Testament people look at that and they say it, translating it to, **"Whosoever shall call on the name of Jesus."** **That is not what it says.** That is not what Paul is writing. If you do your word study on that, you will see that he is saying, **"Whosoever shall call on the name of YeHoVaH shall be saved."** Look it up.

Notice that Paul is quoting from:

(Joel 2:32) *"And it shall come to pass, that whosoever shall call on the name of the LORD shall be delivered: for in mount Zion and in Jerusalem shall be deliverance, as the LORD hath said, and in the remnant whom the LORD shall call."*

The translation is "whosoever shall call on the name of YeHoVaH."

As we go back here, we see in *Luke 1* that this whole idea of the covenant of David is actually fulfilled or established, if you would. It is really not fulfilled yet. The scepter shall not leave his house. Right now, the scepter shall not leave the household of David.

There will always be one on the throne of the household of David. The question is this. Is Yeshua King of Kings yet? No, he is not. Is he Lord of Lords yet? No, he is not.

The blood of the Davidic Covenant is found in *2 Samuel 6* (before it was pronounced!).

(2 Samuel 6:15-18) *"So David and all the house of Israel brought up the ark of the LORD with shouting, and with the sound of the trumpet. And as the ark of the LORD came into the city of David, Michal Saul's daughter looked through a window, and saw king David leaping and dancing before the LORD; and she despised him in her heart. And they brought in the ark of the LORD, and set it in his place, in the midst of the tabernacle that David had pitched for it: and David offered burnt offerings and peace offerings before the LORD. And as soon as David had made an end of offering burnt offerings and peace offerings, he blessed the people in the name of the LORD of hosts."*

He pronounced the blessing on the people. As in all previous covenants, sacrificial blood was shed and so it was for the Davidic Covenant. David offered burnt offerings and peace offerings at the return of the Ark of the Covenant. It was at this time that the Everlasting Covenant was made with David concerning his seed, Yeshua Messiah.

The seal of the covenant is back over in *Psalms*. The *89th Psalm* is a prayer of Ethan, the Ezrahite.

(Psalm 89:27-34) *"Also I will make him my firstborn, higher than the kings of the earth. My mercy will I keep for him for evermore, and my covenant shall stand fast with him. His seed also will I make to endure for ever, and his throne as the days of heaven. If his children forsake my law, and walk not in my judgments; If they break my statutes, and keep not my commandments; Then will I visit their transgression with the rod, and their iniquity with stripes. Nevertheless, my lovingkindness will I not utterly take from him, nor suffer my faithfulness to fail.* ***My covenant will I not break, nor alter the thing that is gone out of my lips.****"*

Notice that unlike the Mosaic Covenant and unlike the Land Covenant (Palestinian), Father said that if they broke the law, if they broke the commandments, he would spew them out of the land. That was conditional. Here he is saying no matter what. In other words, the covenant that I have made with David is an Everlasting Covenant. It is forever. If his children break my laws, I will deal with them personally. Every person will have to give an account for their own life. Every person will have to give an account for what they do.

(Psalm 89:35-37) *"Once have I sworn by my holiness that I will not lie unto David. His seed shall endure for ever, and his throne as the sun before me. It shall be established for ever as the moon, and as a faithful witness in heaven. Selah."*

As long as there is a sun, the throne of David will be established. As you can see, this is a very powerful covenant that cannot be broken because YeHoVaH made this covenant an unconditional covenant. It is not based upon what someone does or does not do. YeHoVaH has promised.

Just as he made the rainbow the token of the Noahic Covenant, God here used the sun and the moon to be the token or seal of the Davidic Covenant. As long as we see the sun, as long as the sun rises and sets and as long as the moon waxes and wanes; if you can see the moon, if you can see the sun, then the throne of David is still established.

YeHoVaH promised David that as long as the sun and the moon existed, the seed of David would sit upon his throne. This seal finds its ultimate fulfillment in Yeshua Messiah, the King of Kings, Lord of Lords and ruler of this world.

The New Covenant

You are going to see some things here that you need to pay some very close attention to. It is through this that you will begin to see how individuals have a tendency to pervert the scriptures. As I put this together, I remember and reflect upon how I was indoctrinated as a believer and then indoctrinated as a minister into various denominations. Then I was indoctrinated to indoctrinate people into those denominations.

What is really interesting is that if you preach something with fire and passion, people believe it. People will believe it. Think about how long we spent in those places called churches. We believed things that we were taught, but never ever searched them out for ourselves. When we did read them, we read them within the context of the sermon.

You took notes. You took notes in the context of the sermon that was preached, so you have a verse here and a verse there. There is a heading. And you have this verse, this verse and this verse to back up the heading, which is actually what you would call one of those cut-and-paste sermons where they are just pulling verses. It is an eisegetic message where you take the verse out of the context and paste it into a context along with other verses. Now you have developed a principle based upon scriptures taken out of context.

This happens all the time. It even happens in Messianic circles. People make statements to me about certain individuals, certain teachers that are into Kabbalah-type teachings. They are taking Jewish sages' teachings and books they have read. Then they are preaching these messages. Here is the thing that I say to people and I will say it to you. If you receive a message that you can't apply; if you can't apply it, it is just information. It is knowledge. What does knowledge do? Knowledge puffs up.

You see, the word is something that we are to be living. This is a living word. It is not a dead word. Those things that are put into this book are for our admonition, for our learning, for us to walk out. These things were written as an example. Yeshua came not to give us a lot of knowledge and information, because we already had that.

There were people who were preaching. There were thousands and thousands of denominations when Yeshua came. There were several Jewish orders when Yeshua came. Yeshua just called them what they were: children of the devil, preaching traditions.

He did not come to establish a new denomination. He came to show the children of Israel how to live out this word in everyday life. So, if you receive information that you can't apply, then what good is the information?

The things that we are trying to share with you are how to search the scriptures for yourself so you are not dependent and so people can't pull the wool over your eyes. Let me tell you something. There are people out there preaching stuff that if you really sat down and thought about it, it really doesn't make sense.

But many people are out there in television land and in the Internet world. They don't have the time to research and study, so they go from this teacher to that teacher to that teacher. They are constantly on the Internet searching and searching. *Facebook* is giving them a platform to paste all of this stuff. They post this. They post that. They go to this place and go to that place. Pretty soon what you will find is that this is where people will say, "You shouldn't depend on one teacher."

Have you heard that before?

Can I give you some scripture? Because if that is the case, people shouldn't listen to Yeshua. They should have listened to all of the other Rabbis in Yeshua's day, but Yeshua is one who preached as having authority. They had all these other teachers. You have many teachers, but you don't have many Fathers. *(1 Corinthians 4:15)*

You see, the thing about a Father is that a Father loves his children. Most of these guys out here like the idea that you like them. They do and their identity is based upon how many people come to their services or to their conferences. It is amazing. I hear people out there boasting, "Well, we had the highest ratings," or "We had the most viewers." So what?

If that be the case, by John the Baptist's standards, he was a complete failure. By Yeshua's standards, when you think about it, he was a master teacher who had thousands and thousands of followers. Can you imagine the funeral procession? You have cars and mules and buggies for miles. That wasn't so at Yeshua's funeral. There were a handful of people. When you look at these individuals, you will find that there were not a whole lot of folks hanging around in mourning.

People today are getting their identity from how many people are watching their programs or showing up in their buildings. One of the things that *Livestream* has taken away from us is this.

We stopped putting the viewer count on our *Livestream* broadcasts.[5] Part of it is because I was on another broadcast and they were saying, "Oh man! Look at how many people have joined us today!" It seems like there are one or two or three individuals whose job online is to point out, "Wow! All these people! It is really growing! Wow!" Is that what it is all about?

Somewhere in the conversation when I get into conversation with people, they want to know how many you are running. How many people show up at the service? How many people are coming into your broadcast? What business is it? If you come and you are being ministered to and the Father is speaking to you, then you are the one that matters. You really are.

But some people feel that if they go into a building and there are not a whole lot of people, then maybe the Father is not in that.

I don't get my identity from how many people show up in this building. I am going to preach the same whether there are 5 or 5,000. Now the energy of 5,000 is a lot stronger than 5, so there is more energy that is there, but the message doesn't change. It really doesn't.

---

[5] We are keeping it off because we don't want count checkers. It doesn't matter.

Whether Yeshua was in a house or whether he was in a multitude — as a matter of fact if you look at it, he tried to get away from the multitude and speak to those people who really wanted to hear what he had to say. There were a whole lot of folks who were gawkers. Here in Charlotte, there are a lot of gawkers. You drive down the highway and there is something going on at the side of the road. The traffic is backed up because folks are driving by gawking and rubber-necking.

I was going to show you something. I hope you are ready. I really do. I want you to see this.

(Ecclesiastes 12:10-11) *"The preacher sought to find out acceptable words: and that which was written was upright, even words of truth. The words of the wise are as goads, and as nails fastened by the masters of assemblies, which are given from one shepherd."*

You see, you can't have two shepherds. You can't. You can't have two shepherds because two shepherds will lead the flock in different directions. They don't know who to follow. "My sheep know my voice." That is what Yeshua said. They hear my voice. Man should not live by bread alone, but by the word that proceeds out of the mouth of YeHoVaH.

One of the reasons why many of you are confused is because you are going all over the place. I remember when I was in the Baptist Church and they were preaching against the Holy Spirit and speaking in tongues and the gifts of the Spirit. Here it is that I am reading in the Bible about the gifts of the Spirit and the tongues and interpretations of tongues and all of this. These people are preaching against it. Then people who have been sitting under that for some time, the moment you hear somebody talk about the gifts, these people say that it is of the devil.

If somebody is in the congregation seeking to be filled with the Holy Spirit, these people are adamantly opposed to that. Now, if you are in a place that is preaching the prosperity of the gospel, the prosperity of the scriptures and not a prosperity gospel, I am talking about biblical prosperity. You are preaching healing. You are preaching faith. Then over here somebody is preaching a watered-down faith. "If God wants you to be healed, he'll heal you."

Let me tell you something. By his stripes you are *already* healed. You are already healed right now. He doesn't need to heal you. He has healed you already. You just have to come into agreement with that.

But people are coming into agreement with other stuff other than what the word says. You can hear what they are agreeing to. By the abundance of their heart, their mouth speaks. They are speaking what they believe and what they are saying is contradicting what he has said.

You are over here and you are over there and back over here, running all over the place and mixing up all of these teachings. One teacher is contradicting another teacher and another teacher is contradicting another one. You have all of this knowledge, but you are never coming to the knowledge of truth or the understanding of the truth so you can apply it. The truth is not what sets you free. You shall KNOW the truth. You shall become involved intimately; one with the word. *That* truth is what sets you free.

It is when you take that word, that truth and you do what it says. If all you are is a hearer, you are so deceived. Be a doer of the word, not just a hearer only. You have all of these folks who have ears. They are running here and there. And you are here at this time, there at that time. You are hearing all of these messages that don't jive. What it does is put all of these different signals into your spirit. It is just confusion.

You can just stop it. Don't spew your unbelief on me. Then you want me to pray for you. I am not trying to be mean. I just want to help people. You can't have many shepherds. You can have only one shepherd — one, just one. It is not biblical to have more than one shepherd. You can't. A shepherd cannot shepherd two flocks. What you have is a hireling.

The reason why I teach the way that I do is because I am not trying to get followers. I am trying to make disciples of Messiah. Messiah would tell you, "I am not nursing you up the hill. I am not nursing you through Samaria. I am not your nursemaid. Babes need nursemaids." I am making disciples of Messiah. Sometimes I try to be nice and have nice words. But if they are rough, it is because the words of YeHoVaH are rough and they are tough. But people want nice.

(Jeremiah 31:31) *""Behold, the days come," saith the* LORD, *"that I will make a new covenant with the house of Israel, and with the house of Judah:""*

With whom? With the Christian Church? No. With the Gentiles? No. Read it. It is with the House of Israel and the House of Judah. Where does the Gentile fit in? Paul made it clear that you are grafted into the commonwealth of Israel, not the commonwealth of Judah — but the commonwealth of Israel. They are the only two houses in this covenant.

So, for a Gentile who is not of the House of Judah or of the House of Israel, you only come into the covenant through being grafted in by accepting the King of Judah, Yeshua. That is the only way in. You can't join it, can't buy your way in and can't serve your way in.

(Jeremiah 31:32-33) *""Not according to the covenant that I made with their fathers in the day that I took them by the hand to bring them out of the land of Egypt; which my covenant they brake, although I was an husband unto them," saith the* LORD: *"But this shall be the covenant that I will make with the house of Israel; After those days," saith the* LORD, *"I will put my law in their inward parts, and write it in their hearts; and will be their God, and they shall be my people.""*

Notice here. Who is the New Covenant with? The House of Israel. Why? Because he brought Judah back into the House of Israel. It is one now. Yeshua is the King, the prophetic fulfillment of the Everlasting Covenant, the Davidic Covenant, the Abrahamic Covenant, the Noahic Covenant and the Everlasting Covenant. Through Yeshua, Judah and Israel (the House of Judah and the House of Israel) will become one again just as it was under King David. It was not a divided kingdom. It was one kingdom, the kingdom of Israel.

This is why at the last meeting, Yeshua's disciples had with him in the book of *Acts*, they said, "Are you at this time going to restore the kingdom to Israel?" Not the kingdom to the Jewish people. Not the kingdom of Judah, but the kingdom of Israel.

(Acts 1:6) *"When they therefore were come together, they asked of him, saying, "Lord, wilt thou at this time restore again the kingdom to Israel?""*

You have people out there that talk about how Israel is the homeland for the Jewish people. Yes, it is the homeland for Jews, but it is also the homeland for Benjamin, for Naphtali, for Manasseh, for Ephraim and for all the tribes. This is where this whole idea of Judaism comes in. Notice that when people come into Messianic Judaism, they think they have to look Jewish. They have to sound Jewish. They have to act Jewish.

Now to make aliyah into the land you have to convert to Judaism. There are people who have stolen, who have taken the identity of YeHoVaH's people. They have established a man-made religious system where even Yeshua Messiah is not welcome in the land. And no one who confesses Yeshua can make aliyah to the land.

That is an abomination!

You have all these people saying, "I love Israel." Let me tell you something. The state of Israel rejects Yeshua, but they take silly Christians' money. "Send us your money but keep your Jesus." And yes, you can come and visit and you can come and pray. You can come and stay for a few days, but you can't come live here because you are not welcome. The only way you can come and live in this land is if you reject that Jesus, you denounce that Yeshua and you become a Jew through Judaism conversion.

Any of you who have ears to hear, you know that I am telling the truth.

This is why it has to come down. Yeshua is going to send the enemies to surround it. That system has to come down. It will not stand. You might say, "God honors it." Does he really? He honors that just as much as he honors the United States or Russia.

This book is what he honors. This word will have the last word.

(Jeremiah 31:33-34) *",,But this shall be the covenant that I will make with the house of Israel; After those days," saith the LORD, ,,I will put my law in their inward parts, and write it in their hearts; and will be their God, and they shall be my people. And they shall teach no more every man his neighbour, and every man his brother, saying, Know the LORD:* **for they shall all know me, from the least of them unto the greatest of them,** *" saith the LORD: ,,for I will forgive their iniquity, and I will remember their sin no more.""*

This is how we know that the New Covenant is not fulfilled. It was ratified through Yeshua, but it is not fulfilled. Why? Because Yeshua says this gospel must be preached to the ends of the earth, THEN the end will come. Why? For a witness against the nations. The gospel has to go forth so people will have heard the truth. So, when they stand in judgment, they cannot say "I didn't know." Until the gospel goes out, the blood of the nations is upon our hands.

Verse 34 shows us:

"And they shall teach no more…"

There will be no more teaching. There will be no more gospels going to the nations of the world because it would have gone.

We are going to stop there. The next lesson is where we are going to dig deep into the Renewed Covenant. We are going to look at some scripture and we are going to go forward.

Class 57 Study Summary
Key Points

1. The Davidic Covenant is one by which we have our salvation and faith in the Messiah.
2. In the Bible Father makes it very clear who his people (Israel) are.
3. David did not write all of the *Psalms*. There were other writers.
4. The Davidic Covenant is an unconditional covenant. It was not based on what David did or did not do.
5. Some people think that Abraham had only two sons (Ishmael and Isaac) and one wife (Sarah). But he later remarried a woman named Keturah after Sarah passed and had at least six more children that were male. See **Genesis 25:1-2**.
6. The popular phrase "stick and stones" says that words "will never hurt me", but that is not true. Words can be like daggers in the hearts and minds of individuals. Our words are powerful. Everything in the universe was created by words. *Proverbs* says that "many words cause sin." We will have whatsoever we say.
7. Miriam (Mary) the Mother of our Savior never called her son "Jesus." His name is Yeshua.
8. YeHoVaH is not going to bring the tribe of Judah back into Israel. He is going to take Israel (people) and make Israel to be "Jews" (not the House of the Jews). He is going to bring Judah back into the commonwealth of Israel. They will be called "Israel" and not "Jews."
9. Whosoever shall call upon the name of YeHoVaH shall be saved (not "Jesus" or "Lord").
10. The Palestinian or Land Covenant is a conditional covenant. The people had to obey the commandments or YeHoVaH would spew them out of the land.
11. YeHoVaH has promised that as long as there is a sun, the throne of David will be established. This is an unconditional covenant that is not dependent upon what men do.
12. If you preach something with fire and with passion, most people will believe it and won't search it out for themselves.
13. Yeshua did not come to establish a new denomination. He came to show the children of Israel how to live out his word in their everyday life.
14. By the abundance of the heart, the mouth speaks. Most people are speaking what they believe and what they believe contradicts the word of YeHoVaH.
15. People have made laws in Israel that people cannot make aliyah to the land unless they convert to Judaism and denounce the Messiah Yeshua. Such things are anti-Messiah.
16. The book, the word that is in the book (Bible) is what YeHoVaH honors. His word will have the last word.
17. Until the gospel of the Kingdom goes out, the blood of the nations is upon our hands.
18. We will know that the New Covenant is fulfilled when the true gospel of the Kingdom has been preached to the whole word. There will be no more gospels. There will be no more teaching.

Review Exercise

1. Can you list all nine of the covenants we have been learning about?

   1. _____   6. _____

   2. _____   7. _____

   3. _____   8. _____

   4. _____   9. _____

   5. _____

2. What was promised in the Davidic Covenant (which was an unconditional covenant)?

   _____
   _____
   _____
   _____
   _____
   _____
   _____

3. David did not get to build the temple. Moses did not enter into the Promised Land (after putting up with those people all of those years!). Abraham died knowing that his progeny would spend 400 years in foreign captivity. Noah watched as all, but seven other people were destroyed while he and his sons fed, tended and cleaned up after a "boat load" of creatures for a year. The Messiah they all waited for came, died, resurrected and left a pitiful group of disciples with the charge of his entire message to the world. How then are we to think about these covenants?

   _____
   _____
   _____
   _____
   _____
   _____
   _____

4. If you have not read the scripture references in this lesson, please do so now.

   _____
   _____
   _____
   _____
   _____
   _____
   _____

Rate the following statements
by filling in the most appropriate number.

(1 = I do not agree 10 = I agree completely)

Objectives:

1. I can define the Davidic Covenant and its significance toward faith and salvation.

    1. ○   2. ○   3. ○   4. ○   5. ○   6. ○   7. ○   8. ○   9. ○   10. ○

2. I can compose an overview the New/Renewed Covenant.

    1. ○   2. ○   3. ○   4. ○   5. ○   6. ○   7. ○   8. ○   9. ○   10. ○

My Journal

What I learned from this class:

Discipleship Training Class 58

Principles of Interpretation — Covenantal Principle (part 7)

Objectives:

As a Discipleship student, at the end of this class you will be able to:

- Clarify what the New Covenant is and is not
- Define the interlocking and at times overlapping nature of the covenants

We have been looking at the various covenants and this lesson covers the Renewed Covenant, or what is commonly referred to as the New Covenant. It is vitally important for every believer to understand what the New Covenant is and what it is not. I know that it has been declared a lot of things, especially within the different denominational circles that I have been in. So, we are going to take a close look at the New or Renewed Covenant.

The Renewed Covenant

In the last lesson we looked at these particular verses relative to the Renewed/New Covenant.

Jeremiah 31:31-34   Matthew 26:26-29   Hebrews 8-10

What I want us to do is to start out looking at the prophet Jeremiah. In chapter 31 we see the first mention principle (if you would) of the Renewed Covenant.

(Jeremiah 31:31) *"„Behold, the days come," saith YeHoVaH, „that I will make a new covenant with the house of Israel, and with the house of Judah:""*

Notice with whom he is making a covenant: the House of Israel and the House of Judah. What Christianity has done is try to hijack the New Covenant. Translators have turned the New Testament into the New Covenant. If you look at the actual writings of the New Testament, the word "testament" is not found in the New Testament. It is the word "covenant." Father did not make testaments in the Old Testament. He made covenants.

We need to understand this because when we begin to look at the New Testament, we don't get the full impact of the covenant that the New Testament actually talks about.

He is going to make a New Covenant with the House of Israel and with the House of Judah. You will notice that some other Hebrew teachers and I will call it the Renewed Covenant. There is a reason why it is called the Renewed Covenant. We will see that as we read.

(Jeremiah 31:32) *"„Not according to the covenant that I made with their fathers in the day that I took them by the hand to bring them out of the land of Egypt, which my covenant they brake, although I was an husband unto them," saith YeHoVaH:"*

The Renewed Covenant is connected with the covenant that Jeremiah talks about concerning the

Fathers. Jeremiah is speaking and saying that this New Covenant is not going to be like the covenant that was made with the Fathers. We will see what the difference is.

(Jeremiah 31:33-34) "„But this shall be the covenant that I will make with the house of Israel; After those days," saith YeHoVaH, „I will put my law in their inward parts, and write it in their hearts; and will be their God, and they shall be my people. And they shall teach no more every man his neighbour, and every man his brother, saying, Know YeHoVaH: for they shall all know me, from the least of them unto the greatest of them," saith YeHoVaH: „for I will forgive their iniquity, and I will remember their sin no more.""

There will be no more teaching once this has happened. It is so important that you understand this because it is going to help us to understand the New Covenant when we get into the New Testament. He says when this happens there will be no more need to teach. What we are doing today is teaching. We are teaching and we are commissioned to take the true gospel of the kingdom to the ends of the earth. Then the Messiah shall come.

It is important that you understand this and not look at this through religious eyes. Verse 33 is an indication that the New Covenant has not been completed.

When we look at the difference between the Old Covenant and the New or Renewed Covenant, the difference is in where it is written. The Old Covenant was written upon tables of stone. The New Covenant will be written in our inward parts. It is the same covenant, the same law and the same writings, but they will be placed within us. The moral compass of the commands will now be seared within our conscious.

It would be a part of us, like breathing. There will no longer be a need to tell somebody they need to be saved, you need to ask Yeshua into your life or you need to give your heart to God. There will no longer be a need for that because everybody will have come to that place, so there will be no more need.

Yeshua Messiah is actually the New Covenant personified. He is the mediator of the New Covenant. Some would say that Yeshua ushered it in, and that is partially true. The New Covenant is also everlasting. This covenant is the consummation of all previous covenants which brings redeemed mankind into the Everlasting Covenant. It will never be superseded by another covenant because when completed, it fulfills all other covenants in itself.

Notice that I said, "when completed." There are those who would want us to think that the New Covenant has been completed because the Bible, the Old Covenant and the old New Covenant is complete. Because the Bible is complete and the second part of the Bible is called the New Testament; it says that by default, the New Testament is complete.

We see that is not true if we look at what the Bible teaches. When we think about this, we have to ask ourselves, "Well, if it is not completed now, when will it be completed and will it continue?"

The blood of the Renewed Covenant is revealed in *Matthew*.

(Matthew 26:26-28) "And as they were eating, Jesus took bread, and blessed it, and brake it, and gave it to the disciples, and said, „Take, eat; this is my body." And he took the cup, and gave thanks, and gave it to them, saying, „Drink ye all of it; For this is my blood of the new testament,"" [It is actually "of the New Covenant."] *"„which is shed for many for the remission of sins.""*

It is talking about Yeshua's blood, the blood of the Lamb, the actual human lamb slain before the foundation of the world. His blood is the blood of the covenant. This blood was shed on Calvary as we have been taught. It was shed when he gave his life upon the stake, upon the tree, upon the cross or whatever you want to call it. When they pierced that spear into his side, it actually went into the sac around his heart and blood and water came out of his body. Then he ascended. We are going to see in *Hebrews* that he shed his own blood upon the heavenly Ark for the remission of the sins of the world. No longer will there be a need for animal sacrifices.

(John 19:34-35) *"But one of the soldiers with a spear pierced his side, and forthwith came there out blood and water. And he that saw it bare record, and his record is true: and he knoweth that he saith true, that ye might believe."*

What he is saying here is that the person who is writing this was an actual eyewitness of what happened. Now the record is being shared with you and me.

(1 John 1:7) *"But if we walk in the light, as he is in the light, we have fellowship one with another, and the blood of Yeshua Messiah his Son cleanseth us from all sin."*

The blood of Yeshua Messiah (his Son) cleanses us from all sin. It is the blood of Yeshua which dealt with our sin. Yeshua paid that price once and for all. The precious and incorruptible blood of Yeshua is the blood of the New Covenant. As we have looked at all of the covenants, the New Covenant also has blood that was shed in order for the New Covenant to be ratified.

(Revelation 12:11) *"And they overcame him by the blood of the Lamb, and by the word of their testimony; and they loved not their lives unto the death."*

Because of what Yeshua has done, we have been given the power to overcome any situation, any obstacle. Let me tell you something. Your greatest adversary is not the devil. The devil has been defeated. The greatest adversary in your life is you. You are your biggest problem, not your husband, not your wife, not your Mom or Dad, not your sister or brother, not your son or daughter. It is YOU.

The sooner you deal with you, the better. But our focus, our problem, is always on someone else. We have this idea I think, that if we can fix the world around us, we will be okay. If we can just get the world to see things our way, then the world would be a much better place to live.

So, they believed. They understood. Speaking of those in the book of *Revelation*, these individuals endured hardship and difficulty. But they knew that what they were standing upon was not mere words. It was not sermons. It was not denominational doctrine. It was what the Lamb of YeHoVaH had done. By overcoming all that was in the world, he gave us power and authority to overcome.

When people say, "Yeshua has done it all," yes he did. Now you have to walk it out. You have to walk it out. For those who endure to the end, those who overcome until the end are the ones who have access to the Tree of Life. What if you don't? Well, you won't.

We are going to take a good look in the book of *Hebrews*.

(Hebrews 9:1-7) *"Then verily the first covenant had also ordinances of divine service, and a worldly sanctuary. For there was a tabernacle made; the first, wherein was the candlestick, and the table, and the shewbread; which is called the sanctuary. And after the second veil, the tabernacle which is called the holiest of all; Which had the golden censer, and the ark of the covenant overlaid round* *about with gold, wherein was the golden pot that had manna, and Aaron's rod that budded, and the tables of the covenant; And over it the cherubims of glory shadowing the mercyseat; of which we cannot now speak particularly. Now when these things were thus ordained, the priests went always into the first tabernacle, accomplishing the service of God. But into the second went the high priest alone once every year, not without blood, which he offered for himself, and for the errors of the people:"*

As we look at that and Yom Kippur, we see what the high priest actually had to go through.

(Hebrews 9:8) *"The Holy Ghost this signifying, that the way into the holiest of all was not yet made manifest, while as the first tabernacle was yet standing:"*

The first tabernacle was a shadow of things to come. Notice that he is dealing with the tabernacle service because this is where it was instituted.

(Hebrews 9:9) *"Which was a figure for the time then present, in which were offered both gifts and sacrifices, that could not make him that did the service perfect, as pertaining to the conscience;"*

What it did is that the blood actually atoned for the sins of the people. And yet people still had to deal with their thoughts, their issues and their attitudes. They were atoned for in the sight of YeHoVaH. But now they had the whole process of getting right, repenting and allowing the Father to govern their way of life through the instructions that he gave.

(Hebrews 9:10) *"Which stood only in meats and drinks, and divers washings, and carnal ordinances, imposed on them until the time of reformation."*

This time of Reformation is not speaking of the Reformation of Martin Luther. He is actually dealing with the coming of Messiah.

(Hebrews 9:11) *"But Messiah being come an high priest of good things to come, by a greater and more perfect tabernacle, not made with hands, that is to say, not of this building;"*

When we begin to talk about Messiah as a high priest, we know that people want to get into the idea that you are not a Levite. You are not a priest. Neither was Yeshua. Yeshua was not a Levite. Yeshua was of the tribe of Judah. Do you understand that? And yet he was a high priest. He was a high priest not after the priesthood of Aaron, but after the priesthood of the Melech Tzedek or Melchizedek, as it is known in the English Bible.

(Hebrews 9:12) *"Neither by the blood of goats and calves, but by his own blood he entered in once into the holy place, having obtained eternal redemption for us."*

Messiah Yeshua became the perfect sacrifice. Once he obtained this eternal redemption for us. How? By not submitting or succumbing to his flesh; to the temptations of HaSatan (Satan, the devil). He became the perfect human sacrifice that could once and for all take away the sins of human beings (you and I).

(Hebrews 9:13-14) *"For if the blood of bulls and of goats, and the ashes of an heifer sprinkling the unclean, sanctifieth to the purifying of the flesh: How much more shall the blood of Messiah, who through the eternal Spirit offered himself without spot to God, purge your conscience from dead works to serve the living Elohim?"*

Now what Yeshua did by what he did is this. It purged our conscience and here is how. (If you don't grasp this, you won't walk in it.) The way he purged our conscience is that he showed us that a human being just like us — for we have not a high priest that is not touched by the infirmities that we have. In the same way he was tempted like all of us, yet he did not sin. What he did is show us that human beings (we has human beings); by him as a human being living on planet earth, around and surrounded by wicked, evil people, could keep the Laws of YeHoVaH.

Now you have these crazy people running around here saying, "Well, if you could keep the whole law — nobody can keep the whole law." That is a lie. Yeshua did it. If people say such things, their conscience has not been purged. They are still under the same old fallen man conscience who does not believe. They say with their mouth, but do not believe in their heart that they can do all things in Messiah who gives them strength.

That means that you can walk in the authority of the law by the power of his Spirit just like Yeshua, a human being did. Yeshua was a man. He left his Godlikeness. He ate. He slept. He bled and he died just like a human being.

Therefore, he came as an example. He says, "Hold it! Up until this point no one has been able to walk out this command that the Almighty gave." There are few people in the history of the world (we read about them in *Hebrews 11*) <u>who lived a holy life</u>. They are in what we call the Hall of Faith. Every last one of those individuals were Old Testament, Old Covenant characters.

Why? Because there were no New Covenant characters or Renewed Covenant characters to use as an example when the book of *Hebrews* was written.

Since then, there are those who we probably won't know of. The Church Fathers. These guys made statements like "We are all sinners, saved by grace." "No, we can't keep the law." "No, the law is not…" They made all kinds of statements that disqualified them. They even came to the conclusion that the law was "done away with."

See, that is the doctrine of demons. This is the very thing that Paul said. He said that in the last days many will turn from the faith, giving heed to seducing spirits and doctrines of demons. It is a demon that tells you that you can't keep the law. Yeshua did it, but Yeshua was God. No, Yeshua was man. He was born of a woman and filled with the Holy Spirit. When the enemy tried to get him to exercise the authority that he obviously had, he refused. He could have come down off of that tree, that stake, that cross.

But he had to show us to the very end. And in all of that, only a couple of people got it, including a thief on a cross. "Yeshua, receive me when you come into your Kingdom."

As our example, Yeshua showed us that it is possible to live a human life here on planet Earth without succumbing to the sins of the world and the false authority that the devil claims; understanding that your biggest problem is you. The sooner you get that — this is what makes the garden of Gethsemane scene so powerful. The Bible lets us know that Yeshua agonized in that garden to bypass the cross. He cried three solid hours of crying out to YeHoVaH: "Let this cup be passed from me."

And yet he went to the cross and paid the ultimate price.

Our hope is not so much in his death. The forgiveness of our sin is in his death and the blood. Our hope is in the fact that he resurrected from the dead. What does that say to us? Here it is in a nutshell. You can either live your life on this side succumbing to your flesh, or you can deny your flesh and live eternally. Those who believe in him shall never die, but let me tell you something. You will have to make choices. You will have to make decisions. And the first decision you will make is whether or not you are going to get onto the broad way of religion or the narrow path that leads to life. And it is now.

It is not about judging other people. That is all part of trying to make the world around you conform to your belief system so you can live your little Torah-centered life as you see it. People are always trying to control other people.

The only person you have authority over to control is yourself. That's it.

(Hebrews 9:15) *"And for this cause he is the mediator of the new testament/covenant, that by means of death, for the redemption of the transgressions that were under the first testament/covenant, they which are called might receive the promise of eternal inheritance."*

Actually, it is the New Covenant, as we have said. If you look at the conversation, the conversation surrounds the tabernacle, the sacrifices, the blood of lambs, rams, bulls and goats. **Yeshua is the Lamb of YeHoVaH who takes away the sins of the world by his blood.**

"They which are called" means those who are called out. These are the set apart ones. To be called out of the world is to not conform to this world.

(Hebrews 9:16) *"For where a testament is, there must also of necessity be the death of the testator."*

It is interesting how this language now gets from a testament to a testator. Read and look that up. You will be surprised.

(Hebrews 9:17) *"For a testament is of force after men are dead: otherwise, it is of no strength at all while the testator liveth."*

When you look at this language, what you will see is that the testament goes into force once the testator is dead. People will look at this in natural human language and a natural realm. The fact is that no one who has left a will and testament has come back from the dead — none.

(Hebrews 9:18-20) *"Whereupon neither the first testament was dedicated without blood. For when Moses had spoken every precept to all the people according to the law, he took the blood of calves and of goats, with water, and scarlet wool, and hyssop, and sprinkled both the book, and all the people, Saying, „This is the blood of the testament which God hath enjoined unto you.""*

Not the testament! The word "testament" is not found in the Old Testament. But religion pulls people into the "New Testament" and drills a hatred in their heart toward the Old Testament. My son had a friend who came and my wife had some conversation with him. He said that he doesn't read the Old Testament because he likes the New Testament. For her, that was a revelation that people read what they like.

Here you have a 17- or 18-year-old boy who is actually telling you what 30, 40, 50-, 60-, 70-, and 80-year-old people do. Very few "New Testament believers" — when somebody says "I am a New Testament believer" what they are saying is that they don't believe the Old Testament. That is what they are saying, but they are not speaking that.

What they have done is taken YeHoVaH's word and reduced it to historical documents. Now when something comes on the *History Channel*, it becomes believable. They can read. They can listen to the *History Channel* and PBS and some of these other channels that show some of the foolishness that is there. They will believe it because they have already discounted the Old Testament. They have no knowledge or desire to learn the Old Testament After all, they like the New Testament primarily because the New Testament does not require anything except for faith in Jesus Christ.

It is interesting that the book of *Hebrews* is in the "Greek" writings. I find this to be interesting in and of itself.

(Hebrews 9:19-22) "For when Moses had spoken every precept to all the people according to the law, he took the blood of calves and of goats, with water, and scarlet wool, and hyssop, and sprinkled both the book, and all the people, Saying, „This is the blood of the testament which God hath enjoined unto you." Moreover he sprinkled with blood both the tabernacle, and all the vessels of the ministry. And almost all things are by the law purged with blood; and without shedding of blood is no remission."

The law was purged with blood; for without blood there is no remission of sin. Yom Kippur and the shedding of the blood of the sacrifice (the Yom Kippur sacrifice) remitted the sin for a year.

(Hebrews 9:23) "It was therefore necessary that the patterns of things in the heavens should be purified with these; but the heavenly things themselves with better sacrifices than these."

Now you have the things in heaven being purified just as the things in the earthly tabernacle were purified; except it was not purified with the blood of bulls, rams and goats, but with the blood of Messiah.

(Hebrews 9:24-26) "For Christ is not entered into the holy places made with hands, which are the figures of the true; but into heaven itself, now to appear in the presence of God for us: Nor yet that he should offer himself often, as the high priest entereth into the holy place every year with blood of others; For then must he often have suffered since the foundation of the world: but now once in the end of the world hath he appeared to put away sin by the sacrifice of himself."

In other words, this is a one-time thing.

*(Hebrews 9:27-28) "And as it is appointed unto men once to die, but after this the judgment: So, the Messiah was once offered to bear the sins of many; and **unto them that look for him shall he appear the second time without sin unto salvation.**"*

What is this saying? It is saying that when he comes a second time, he is going to bring salvation *to those who are looking for him*. Get this. For those who are looking for him, when he returns he is going to bring salvation. So, when does salvation occur?

All previous covenantal sacrificial blood pointed to his blood. The blood of Yeshua fulfills and abolishes all typical animal blood. It is the blood of the Everlasting Covenant.

(Hebrews 13:20) "Now the God of peace, that brought again from the dead our Lord Jesus, that great shepherd of the sheep, through the blood of the everlasting covenant,"

It was Yeshua's blood that brought in this Renewed Covenant, which is actually an Everlasting Covenant — the blood of the Lamb slain from the foundation of the world. This is a very interesting passage because what it shows us is that long before Yeshua manifested, this act had already taken place.

(1 Peter 1:19-20) "But with the precious blood of Christ, as of a lamb without blemish and without spot: Who verily was foreordained before the foundation of the world, but was manifest in these last times for you,"

I want to stop here. You need to understand something. I want you to focus in on this verse. Here is the thing about you and me, because just as Yeshua was, so are we. Now, this is not Mormonism. This has nothing to do with that. But here is the bottom line. **Father knows the end from the beginning.**

> **Right now, you and I are simply walking through the process of life in which we were foreordained to walk.**

The challenge is that Father has a plan and a path for you, but you will choose your own path. The key for you and I is to seek the Father for the path that he has laid out for us and to allow him to order our steps.

This is what the Psalmist was trying to convey to us in *Psalm 23*. Here is what he said:

(Psalm 23:1-4) "The LORD is my shepherd; I shall not want. He maketh me to lie down in green pastures: he leadeth me beside the still waters. He restoreth my soul: he leadeth me in the paths of righteousness for his name's sake. Yea, though I walk through the valley of the shadow of death, I will fear no evil: for thou art with me; thy rod and thy staff they comfort me."

He is leading me. I don't fear evil. If he is leading me, he is with me. And if he is with me, what do I have to fear? When he leads me and I am not reveling in my own way or doing my own thing:

(Psalm 23:5) "Thou preparest a table before me in the presence of mine enemies: thou anointest my head with oil; my cup runneth over."

Your way, your walk, your life has already been preordained just as Yeshua was preordained before the foundation of the earth, but manifested at a certain time. I tell people that my Mom and Dad got together so I could get here. If they had not gotten together, I would not be here. I would have to come another way. Father ordained that. This is why no matter what your parents have done, no matter what your Mom or your Dad has done or said, no matter what happened to you, the bottom line is that the Father used them to get you here for the purpose that he has ordained you to fulfill.

The enemy wants to put these burdens upon you. He wants to weigh you down with hurt, unforgiveness, failures, falls, mishaps and abuses and get you to focus upon yourself. That is because as long as you are focusing on yourself, you will never die. You will always look for ways to please yourself to make yourself feel better. In order to do that, you now have to manipulate and control everything around you and everybody so that you will be happy and you are still not happy.

Your identity is hidden in Messiah. The sooner you die, the better. I am not talking about physical suicide. I am talking about death to self, leaning not to your own understanding and letting YeHoVaH be your shepherd. Trust in him with all of your heart. In all ways acknowledge him that he might do what? That he might direct your path.

(Proverbs 3:5-6) "Trust in the LORD with all thine heart; and lean not unto thine own understanding. In all thy ways acknowledge him, and he shall direct thy paths."

Either he is directing your path, or you are directing your path. If you are directing your path, I will guarantee you that you are not on the path he has ordained. If you are not on the path that he has ordained, you are going through stuff you were not designed to go through. And these things add baggage to your journey. They weigh you down and slow you down. In some cases, they cause people to give up and to stop.

Even though some people keep going and going and going and going, they are stuck in their minds. I know people who are still stuck in the '60s or stuck in the '70s. Every conversation is "Do you remember how things used to be?" That was 25-30 years ago. Folks always want to remind you of your childhood; remind you of when you were way back yonder because that is where they are. Father has a plan and the plan was ordained for you before you got here.

This whole New Covenant is really to usher you into the perfect will of the Almighty. That is why he freed you, so that you can willingly submit your will to him without being hindered by the enemy. Father did not set you free so you can live your life. He set you free so that you can give your life to him and so that he can perfect you and cause you to reach your full destination.

This is what he is talking about: abundant life. Your abundant life is not in stuff and things. Your abundant life is walking in his perfect will. It is not being hindered or burdened down by stuff, by the weight of the world.

(Ephesians 2:8-10) *"For by grace are ye saved through faith; and that not of yourselves: it is the gift of God: Not of works, lest any man should boast. For we are his workmanship, created in Christ Jesus unto good works, which God hath before ordained that we should walk in them."*

Father has ordained a path for you. But if you don't get into his face, into his presence and learn his will for your life, you will wander in the wilderness of life trying to figure this thing out. That is why Rick Warren's book, *The Purpose Driven Life* was a number one bestseller for so long; because people wanted to know what their purpose was (like Rick Warren was going to tell them).

He made a lot of money telling people about it. But the bottom line is that the only way you are going to know your purpose is not going to come from your apostle, your prophet, your evangelist, pastor, teacher, elder, reverend, bishop, deacon, your husband or your wife. It is going to come from YeHoVaH himself.

(1 Peter 1:20-21) *"Who verily was foreordained before the foundation of the world, but was manifest in these last times for you, Who by him do believe in God, that raised him up from the dead, and gave him glory; that your faith and hope might be in God."*

It does not say "in Yeshua," does it? That your faith might be in YeHoVaH. It is the blood of God.

(Acts 20:28) *"Take heed therefore unto yourselves, and to all the flock, over the which the Holy Ghost hath made you overseers, to feed the church of God, which he hath purchased with his own blood."*

Who purchased the church? YeHoVaH, with his own blood. God will never return to animal blood for the remission of sin now that he has the blood of Yeshua.

(Hebrews 10:26-27) *"For if we sin willfully after that we have received the knowledge of the truth, there remaineth no more sacrifice for sins, But a certain fearful looking for of judgment and fiery indignation, which shall devour the adversaries."*

There are people out there right now who are willfully sinning, thinking that the blood of Jesus covers them. They make dumb statements like, "I am saved. I am always going to be saved. No matter what I do, I am covered by the blood." This is what they say, but notice what the scripture says:

(Hebrews 10:28-29) *"He that despised Moses" law died without mercy under two or three witnesses: Of how much sorer punishment, suppose ye, shall he be thought worthy, who hath trodden under foot the Son of God, and hath counted the blood of the covenant, wherewith he was sanctified, an unholy thing, and hath done despite unto the Spirit of grace?"*

Now when people sin, they literally trod underfoot what Yeshua has done. This includes when people fall into sin (i.e. when people fornicate, commit adultery, lie, steal or get drunk on a regular basis).

The sign and seal of the New/Renewed Covenant is the infilling or baptism of the Holy Spirit. This is the seal. **The Holy Spirit is the seal of the New Covenant.**

(2 Corinthians 1:21-22) *"Now he which stablisheth us with you in Christ, and hath anointed us, is YeHoVaH, Who hath also sealed us, and given the earnest of the Spirit in our hearts."*

(Ephesians 1:13) *"In whom ye also trusted, after that ye heard the word of truth, the gospel of your salvation: in whom also after that ye believed, ye were sealed with that holy Spirit of promise,"*

The Holy Spirit of promise is what Yeshua told the disciples to wait for in Jerusalem; for the promise of the Father which Joel spoke about. The Holy Spirit was going to be poured out on all flesh. Sons and daughters will prophesy.

The Master Yeshua had the seal of YeHoVaH upon him.

(John 3:32-34) *"And what he hath seen and heard, that he testifieth; and no man receiveth his testimony. He that hath received his testimony hath set to his seal that God is true. For he whom God hath sent speaketh the words of God: for God giveth not the Spirit by measure unto him."*

Yeshua was filled with the Holy Spirit in the Jordan. Now, why would God need to be filled with God's Spirit? Because he was a man. He was a human being. He said, "Listen, if I am God, so are you." "Have not I said in my word you are gods? …<u>and the scripture cannot be broken</u>." *(John 10:34-35)*

He went a step further. If you think I am God, then you need to understand that the works I (God) do, you (god) shall do and greater works than I (God) do. *(John 14:12)*

This is good stuff. I pray you get this. Just swim in it, because this is powerful stuff. It is not just words.

The believer in Messiah is also to receive the seal of YeHoVaH.

(Ephesians 1:13-14) *"In whom ye also trusted, after that ye heard the word of truth, the gospel of your salvation: in whom also after that ye believed, ye were sealed with that holy Spirit of promise, Which is the earnest of our inheritance **until** the redemption of the purchased possession, unto the praise of his glory."*

So, now what? **The Holy Spirit has been given to us; sealing us** until the Messiah our Redeemer comes and fully purchases us. If you look at it, the Holy Spirit is like a down payment. That is what the Holy Spirit is. It is a down payment. So now you have to allow the Holy Spirit to lead you into overcoming all things. Because to him that overcomes — and it is the Holy Spirit that enables us and gives us power and strength to overcome so that we are ready. Not only are we ready, but we are looking to his coming. Those who are looking for the return of Messiah are the ones who are going to enter into the salvation.

This is why we have to watch and pray. We don't want to be like those who fall asleep. For Yeshua is coming. No man knows the hour. They don't know the day. We just have to be ready. The way we are ready is that we are conscientiously and constantly focused upon the fact that he is coming.

He is coming — So today is the day of preparation. Yesterday was the day of preparation. Tomorrow is the day of preparation. Next week is the day of preparation.

Every day is the day of preparation.

I am not talking about the Sabbath. I am talking about the return. Father through Yeshua (by his Spirit, his word) is enabling us to overcome every obstacle, every issue, every problem. And most of all, to put to death the deeds of the flesh.

That is what people have struggles with. They want to blame somebody else for their problems. Those days are done. They have been done — you just didn't know it. I am sorry I have to tell you, but those days are done. It is time for you to take responsibility for your own actions, because you will be held accountable for every last one of them.

That is not a bad thing. Knowing this, you are mindful of your actions before you act. You think. You are quick to hear, slow to speak and slow to anger. You think before you speak. You meditate, day and night, upon his word. He guides and leads you.

(Ephesians 4:22-24) "That ye put off concerning the former conversation the old man, which is corrupt according to the deceitful lusts; And be renewed in the spirit of your mind; And that ye put on the new man, which after God is created in righteousness and true holiness."

There are many people who claim to be filled with the Spirit who are living and dwelling with the old man, 24/maybe 6. There are folks who on Sunday, try to act holy. There are folks on the Sabbath who try to live a Sabbath life. But he says that you have to put off the former conversation (all the foolishness, the jesting, the joking) which is corrupt, according to the deceitful lusts.

You know, here is one of the things that I have to say about that saying of "What Would Jesus Do?" that came out. Some folks wanted the "What Would Yeshua Do?" bracelets. The bottom line is that we really need to be thinking okay, would Yeshua be doing this? I am mindful of areas in my life where I need to come up. We have to be mindful of those areas.

*(Ephesians 4:25-30) "Wherefore putting away lying, speak every man truth with his neighbour: for we are members one of another. Be ye angry, and sin not: let not the sun go down upon your wrath: Neither give place to the devil. Let him that stole steal no more: but rather let him labour, working with his hands the thing, which is good, that he may have to give to him that needeth. Let no corrupt communication proceed out of your mouth, but that which is good to the use of edifying, that it may minister grace unto the hearers. And grieve not the holy Spirit of God, **whereby ye are sealed unto the day of redemption.**"*

(Ephesians 4:31-32) *"Let all bitterness, and wrath, and anger, and clamour, and evil speaking, be put away from you, with all malice: And be ye kind one to another, tenderhearted, forgiving one another, even as God for Christ's sake hath forgiven you."*

In light of the all-embracing revelation of God's covenants, the Bible is not to be viewed merely as a compilation of sixty-six books. Rather it is to be seen as ONE BOOK having ONE AUTHOR, with a progression of thought throughout.

When we think about the New Covenant, the Renewed Covenant, what we are literally dealing with is what Yeshua has done and is in the process of writing the Torah on our inward man. Why does he want us to write the Torah on our inward man? Because the Torah is YeHoVaH's instructions on how we are to live every single day — every day.

I will tell you. Because of life, busy-ness — I am really amazed at how few people know what the Bible says about certain situations which pertain to life and Godliness such as how you are to live your life or how you are to love your neighbor. It is amazing that people don't seek first the Kingdom of YeHoVaH and his righteousness the way the Bible tells us. We have to get away from seeking his face only when things are wrong and when things are not going the way we want them to go, or when we think our lives are in trouble.

The way you deal with disaster is preparing for it before it happens. You have to prepare for it. This is why preparation for marriage, preparation for children, preparation for everything that you do — you have to put some thought into it. Think about it. What does the Father say about that? How am I supposed to handle this? What are the instructions from the Torah concerning that? That requires that we search the word. We search it and let the Spirit lead us through the word.

This New Covenant is not the New Testament. This New Covenant is a covenant that YeHoVaH says is not going to be like the covenant he made with the children of Israel in the wilderness. There he wrote down the commands and gave them to Moses and they then broke them. Before the people of Israel broke the commands, Moses broke the physical commands. YeHoVaH gave him another set of commands. These commands are hidden in the Ark of the Covenant. These commands were to be pronounced over the people. The beauty of these commands is that they contain both blessings and curses.

People want to talk about blessings, but you don't know what the blessings are without the Torah. You don't know what the curses are without the Torah. Many people in the world around us are living in a cursed realm all because it has walked away from the Torah.

Let me tell you something. Our land, the United States of America, the land wherever we have a society of people that rejects the Torah of YeHoVaH — when we reject the Torah of YeHoVaH, we defile the land. The land becomes defiled. When the land becomes defiled, he spews people out of the land. We have laws that are being made every day that are a direct violation of the commands of the Almighty. I say to you that I am amazed at how many so-called believers are watching perverted programs. It is scandalous.

I love people, but I am not going to watch something that has people living and acting gay, living in fornication and corruption. Every time that I sit and watch that stuff, what it does is that it desensitizes my spirit. Pretty soon I am endorsing it by watching it because I am a "rate." All you believers who are watching these things, you increase the ratings. What that says is that it is the best new series. Many of those new series are being gazed upon by people who claim to be of the covenant.

Men are marrying men. Women are marrying women. Folks are divorcing and fornicating and committing adultery and living lies and reveling in lies. This is corruption and it brings a curse not only upon the people who do these things, but in some states they are electing individuals to represent that state. You have people who are electing openly homosexuals to represent an entire state. Can you imagine how that state is being viewed from heaven from a Kingdom perspective?

When the highest authority or the representation of that authority is representing that state among states, it is almost like in a natural sense, the elders at the city gate in the secular community are sleeping with same sexes.

When we begin to talk about the New Covenant, it would be wonderful for many people to say, "We don't have to deal with this new Old Covenant because now we get to make up our own laws." And you can make up your own laws. You can. You can live your life the way you want to live your life. That is your right.

But the day will come. The day of reckoning will come when you have to stand before the Almighty and give an account. If we are looking to the coming of the Messiah, then it causes us to constantly evaluate and search our own hearts so that when he comes, we hear, "Well done, good and faithful servant."

We are not out here condemning people. We are not out here judging people. We are not out here bashing people. We are not out here trying to send people to hell. Our job is to bring the true gospel of the Kingdom so people will grab hold of that gospel and come out of the world. They will commit their lives to the Kingdom and proclaim the good news just as it has been proclaimed to them.

The New Covenant was given to us for the purpose of freeing us from the bondage of sin, the bondage of the world. It was given to us so that we might be free from all of the control of the devil. Then we can freely commit our lives to the King of Glory and live for him until he comes.

Class 58 Study Summary
Key Points

1. Christianity has tried to hijack the New Covenant. It has turned it into the New Testament. The word "testament" is not found in the Old or the New Testaments. Father did not make testaments in the Old Testament. He made covenants.
2. The difference between the Old and the New Covenant is where it is written.
3. Yeshua is the New Covenant personified.
4. The blood of the New or Renewed Covenant is the blood of the Lamb. Yeshua is the Lamb of YeHoVaH who takes away the sins of the world by his blood. Without blood there is no remission for sins.
5. Yeshua was not a Levite. He was of the tribe of Judah. He was not a high priest after the priesthood of Aaron. He is our high priest after the order of Melchizedek.
6. Yeshua showed us that it is possible to live a human life without succumbing to the sins of the world.
7. Your biggest problem is you.
8. Our hope is not so much in Yeshua's death as it is in his resurrection.
9. People are always trying to control other people. The only one you have authority over is you.
10. Some people have taken the word of YeHoVaH and reduced it to historical documents.
11. When Yeshua returns, he is going to bring salvation to those who are looking for him.
12. YeHoVaH knows the end from the beginning. If we don't seek the Father, we will seek our own path and will not be on the path that the Father has for us. Either he is directing your path or you are.
13. Like Yeshua, our way has already been preordained. We are just manifesting it at a certain time.
14. The enemy wants to burden you with hurt, unforgiveness, failures, falls, mishaps and abuses.
15. As long as you focus on yourself, you will never "die" (to self). Your identity is hidden in the Messiah. The sooner you "die," the better.
16. YeHoVaH will never return to animal blood for the remission of sin now that he has the blood of Yeshua.
17. The sign and seal of the New or Renewed Covenant is the infilling or baptism of the Holy Spirit.
18. The Master Yeshua had the seal of YeHoVaH upon him. The believer also receives the Holy Spirit to seal them until the Messiah our Redeemer comes and fully purchases us.
19. Every day is a day of preparation for his return.
20. The day of reckoning is coming. We will have to stand before the Almighty and give an account. If we are looking to the coming of the Messiah, we will constantly evaluate ourselves so that we may hear "Well done, good and faithful servant."

Review Exercise

1. What are the signs that tell us that the New Covenant has yet to be fulfilled?

2. Looking back to lesson 52, The Everlasting Covenant and now looking at the New/Renewed Covenant, what are the commonalities? What would you say are the points of contrast? Use this diagram to convey what you find.

[Venn diagram with two overlapping circles labeled "Everlasting" and "New/Renewed"]

3. If there is anything that you should take away from this seven-lesson study about the covenant principle, it is that the Bible is ONE book with ONE author. How can we say that after we have just divided it up into at least nine covenants?

4. How will you explain the New Covenant as a Renewed Covenant to someone who most likely believes there is one situation for "the Jews" and another for "the church?"

Rate the following statements by filling in the most appropriate number.

(1 = I do not agree 10 = I agree completely)

Objectives:

1. I can clarify what the New Covenant is and is not.

    1. ○ 2. ○ 3. ○ 4. ○ 5. ○ 6. ○ 7. ○ 8. ○ 9. ○ 10. ○

2. I can define the interlocking and at times overlapping nature of the covenants.

    1. ○ 2. ○ 3. ○ 4. ○ 5. ○ 6. ○ 7. ○ 8. ○ 9. ○ 10. ○

My Journal

What I learned from this class:

_____
_____
_____
_____
_____
_____
_____
_____
_____
_____
_____
_____
_____
_____
_____
_____
_____
_____

Discipleship Training Class 59

Ethnic Division Principle (part 1)

Objectives:

As a Discipleship student, at the end of this class you will be able to:

- Define the Ethnic Division principle in scripture, and discover its importance
- Distinguish our perceptions and impressions of ethnicity

Our Discipleship Training is where we get into areas that you will probably never get into in a Shabbat message or at a church on Sunday. The kinds of things we are teaching here are what individuals would pay for in Bible College or Seminary classes. Hopefully you are honing your ability to go to the Bible for yourself utilizing the different principles that are there and are now able to search and study the word of YeHoVaH.

The Ethnic Division Principle

You can be in church and synagogue worship and Messianic Shuls and home groups and you will be exposed to the ethnic division principle, but you probably won't hear someone mention "ethnic division principle." But it is so deeply woven into the fabric of theology, so we might as well expose it and call it what it is. Let's see how we even got such a radical term as a principle in biblical hermeneutics.

The ethnic division principle is that principle by which the interpretation of any verse or passage of scripture is determined upon a consideration of YeHoVaH's appointed ethnic divisions. What I hope to do here is expose some of the racist ethnic division that exists and that allows people to derive their positions from the Bible. We are going to expose some things here that I am hoping you just hear it out and bear with it (before you get upset).

I have been given the tremendous task of saying things and teaching things that I understand why many people would shy away from. Some of the things that I say and some of the things that I teach do not fall in line with where a lot of Messianics and even Christians want to be. So, it challenges people. It challenges people to rethink and reexamine the things that they have been taught; and even to reevaluate what they believe and why they believe it. It is no mind to cause confusion or to introduce controversy, because all of that stuff already exists.

The purpose of what I am doing is to bring clarity. It is to bring clarity so that people can see clearly beyond all of the denominational spins that individuals have put upon the scriptures. I say this to you. Don't trust any man. Don't trust any woman. Don't trust anybody with your spiritual growth.

That is your responsibility. You are going to know that it is your responsibility because when you stand before YeHoVaH, all of those preachers and pastors and apostles, prophets, evangelists and teachers will be nowhere in sight. It will be you and the Almighty. You will give an account for your life and what you believe.

Too many people that I talk to are upset. Once they come into the knowledge of the truth, they are upset at the people who taught them. Listen. You did not have to believe anything anybody taught you. Just because you bought it hook, line and sinker does not give you the freedom or the right to blame someone else for your spiritual walk. That has always been your responsibility — always.

You can get upset, but you can get over it. No one (I think) is intentionally trying to mislead you. Those who have misled people are misled themselves (most of them).

As we look at these principles, I encourage you to just allow the Holy Spirit to show you what I am trying to share with you. The days of having the wool pulled over your eyes in certain areas will be over.

The definition of the word "ethnic" has to do with the basic divisions of mankind distinguished by culture. It is not based upon color. Oftentimes people want to associate ethnicity with color. But from a biblical perspective, it is dealing with culture.

I was speaking to a precious sister (actually via email). The idea was that individuals don't know the distinction. How did we get to a place where there are now Jews and Gentiles? As we look at some things, I want to challenge you because I have gone through and searched terms that are not even used in the first five or six books of the Bible. Interestingly enough, in every place with the exception of about five places, the term "Jew" is actually spoken by someone's mouth versus being spoken in the commentary of the Bible. You need to understand that. In *Matthew, Mark* and *Luke,* Yeshua never used the term. He uses it in the book of *John*.

I also find it interesting of Peter, James and Jude that none of Yeshua's disciples (the ones who actually followed him) used the term "Jew." And yet we have been divided and distinguished ethnically by the terms "Jew" and "Gentile." That is an ethnic division. The question is, who did it?

Four Hebraic Terms Surround Ethnicity

Oftentimes people put a title or a term upon us and put us into a box. We accept the box and then begin to regurgitate what others are calling us. We take on that identity. We are going to look at this.

The following four words that we are going to look at in the Hebrew are the main words used in scripture relative to distinguishing the culture of the ethnic divisions of mankind. These Hebrew words distinguish the ethnic divisions that man has been placed within. They are: *goy, am, lom* and *ummah*.

Goy

Some of us are possibly familiar with the term "goy," which is where the term "Gentile" derives. Individuals identify Gentiles using the term *goy,* which actually has four main words associated with it: *nation, people, Gentile,* and *heathen*.

Goy or *gowy* (go-ee); a foreign nation; hence a Gentile; also (figuratively) a troop of animals, or a flight of locusts, Gentile, heathen, nation, people.

What is interesting here is the phrase "foreign nation." That is from the Strong's Concordance. Every nation is foreign to another nation. Every people are foreign to another people. But even in the biblical material, dictionaries, concordances and lexicons, it makes the distinction in hindsight.

People today make distinctions based upon material that was presented hundreds of years ago. We have to ask ourselves, where did that come from? I want you to pay close attention. When we talk about Gentile minds and Gentile mindsets and Western mindsets and Jewish mindsets and all of those kinds of things, we have to ask ourselves, where did that come from? How did it become such a major part of our language today, especially in the Messianic community?

In the Christian community, it is "Christians" and "Jews." Christians don't necessarily identify themselves as Gentiles as much as Messianics do. When it comes down to Jew and Gentile, it becomes more prominent in the Messianic community than it is elsewhere. As a former Christian, I never identified myself as a Gentile. I was American, African American, Christian, Baptist, Pentecostal, Charismatic or Apostolic — but never Gentile.

The word appears in **Genesis 10:5:**

"By these were the isles of the Gentiles [H1471] *divided in their land; every one after his tongue, after their families, in their nations."* [H1471]

It associates itself with the tribe of Japheth. Let's look at this in context:

(Genesis 10:1) *"Now these are the generations of the sons of Noah, Shem, Ham, and Japheth: and unto them were sons born after the flood."*

Understand that after the flood this is what they argue. There are some today who want to argue that there were people still alive after the flood. Individuals who make that argument have to disregard the scriptures in order to do it, because according to the scriptures, all mankind was destroyed. YeHoVaH starts all over with Noah. We have no account of Noah having any more children after the flood, but he has three sons who each have a wife.[6]

As we continue on, the entire world, the entire earth was of one tongue. What the writer here is talking about is actually projecting "After his tongue," but there was only one tongue when this account occurs.

What you need to see here is the word "Gentile" and the word "nation" in the King James that is present in this one verse. They are both the same number, the same word *gowy* (Gentile and nation). So, you have:

(Genesis 10:5) *"By these were the isles of the **gowy** divided in their lands; every one after his tongue, after their families, in their **gowy**."*

Let's go back. I want you to look at it:

(Genesis 10:1-4) *"Now these are the generations of the sons of Noah, Shem, Ham, and Japheth: and unto them were sons born after the flood. **The sons of Japheth; Gomer, and Magog, and Madai, and Javan, and Tubal, and Meshech, and Tiras**. And the sons of Gomer; Ashkenaz, and Riphath, and Togarmah. And the sons of Javan; Elishah, and Tarshish, Kittim, and Dodanim."*

---

[6] I should not have to make a point of that, but there are those who would say that *Genesis 7:13* means that each son has three wives. In the Messianic community there are those who want to look at what YeHoVaH allowed back then and try to fast-forward that to today. In order to do that you have to disregard a ton of scripture in the process. When we talk about progressive revelation, we go back to YeHoVaH's intent. Everything we need to know about YeHoVaH and our purpose and plan is found in *Genesis 1-3*. We can get the entire counsel of YeHoVaH. Everything after *Genesis 3* is given to a fallen people. Adam was made and given a wife (not two wives and not a man).

*(**Genesis 10:6**) "And the sons of Ham; Cush, and Mizraim, and Phut, and Canaan."*

Connect verse 5 to verse 2. The isles of the Gentiles we connect with Japheth. Then in verse 6 we see "the sons of Ham." Now there is a transition from the sons of Japheth to the sons of Ham. If you go all the way down to verse 20 and then to verse 21 you see:

*(**Genesis 10:20-21**) "These are the sons of Ham, after their families, after their tongues, in their countries, and in their nations. ²¹Unto Shem also, the father of all the children of Eber, the brother of Japheth the elder, even to him were children born."*

It transitions away from Ham now to Shem. YeHoVaH in *Genesis 10* identifies the nation of Japheth, the nation of Ham and the nation of Shem. They are all considered *gowy* or Gentiles.

*(**Genesis 10:32**) "These are the families of the sons of Noah, after their generations, in their **nations/gowy**: and by these were the **nations/gowy** divided in the earth after the flood."*

So, they were all **gowy**. This is how we start. Before there is "Israel," everybody is a **gowy**/*goy*. Before YeHoVaH changes Jacob's name to Israel, everyone is a goy including Abraham. YeHoVaH never refers to Abraham as a Jew. He never referred to Shem as a Jew.

I am not picking on anybody. What I am trying to do is help you understand that the terms "Jew" and "Gentile" created division among YeHoVaH's people. And in today's society in some Messianic communities this has created first-class and second-class citizens in the household of faith. This is the hand of man. This is the work of manmade religion.

By addressing these things, it does not make me anti- anything other than anti-lie. I am against lies. I am against the lies that we have inherited that Jeremiah speaks about (*Jeremiah 16:19*). The only way to confront lies is to bring forth truth. Then people have to make the distinction.

I think the problem sometimes is that people are so saturated and inured to their doctrine and what they believe that they are not willing to reevaluate it even in light of what these scriptures actually teach.

Noah's sons' descendants were call **Gentiles**/*goy* or heathen or nation or people. So, you have these four terms: **Gentile, heathen, nation** and **people**. Now in a sense it is left up to the interpreter or the translator to decide which word is going to be used in the context of the entire passage. But if people are simply doing a word study and not a passage study, they will come away with the word of their own choosing.

We see in *Genesis 10:2-4*, the list of the sons of Noah's sons. Now we show *Genesis 10:5* as:

*(**Genesis 10:5**) "By these were the isles of the Gentiles divided in their lands; every one after his tongue, after their families, in their nations."*

You see "Gentiles" and "nations" where the translator here makes a distinction of the word *gowy*. In one place it is "Gentile" and in the other place it is "nation," but it is the same word.

Skip to verse 20 and compare:

*(**Genesis 10:20**) "These are the sons of Ham, after their families, after their tongues, in their countries, and in their **nations**."*

It is the same word, number [H1471] *goy*.

(Genesis 10:31) *"These are the sons of Shem, after their families, after their tongues, in their lands, after their **nations**."*

Same word, number [H1471].

Abraham was referred to by YeHoVaH as the "great and mighty goy" and all the goys of the Earth shall be blessed in him. He is not a great and mighty Jew and he is not the Father of the Jewish people.

(Genesis 18:18) *"Seeing that Abraham shall surely become a great and mighty nation/goy,* [H1471] *and all the nations/goy* [H1471] *of the earth shall be blessed in him?"*

Israel was a goy by YeHoVaH.

(Exodus 19:6) *"And ye shall be unto me a kingdom of priests, and an holy **nation/goy**.* [H1471] *These are the words which thou shalt speak unto the children of Israel."*

These are the words of YeHoVaH that they should speak.

(Exodus 32:10) *"Now therefore let me alone, that my wrath may wax hot against them, and that I may consume them: and I will make of thee a great **nation/goy**."*

This is what YeHoVaH is saying to Moses. He says, "Moses, I will make you a great **goy**."

Now we know that the word is either Gentile, heathen, nation, or people. But every time the word "Gentile" is referred to in the scripture, it deals with the word "**goy**." Rarely do people who use the word "Gentile" ever associate it with Israel, except for YeHoVaH.

(Exodus 33:13) *"Now therefore, I pray thee, if I have found grace in thy sight, shew me now thy way, that I may know thee, that I may find grace in thy sight: and consider that this **nation/goy** is thy **people**."*

Look up these scriptures and see the contexts in which they are written. There are a lot more scriptures. These are just a few to get you started:

Scripture References

Gentiles	*Genesis 10:5*	*Isaiah 11:10; 42:1, 6; 49:22; 54:3; 60:3, 5, 11, 16*
Nation(s)	*Genesis 10:31, 32*	*Deuteronomy 9:1, 4, 5*
	1 Chronicles 16:20	*Psalm 22:27, 28*
	Isaiah 2:2, 4; 52:15	*Malachi 3:12*
Heathen	*Psalms 2:1, 8; 102:15*	*Jeremiah 10:2*
	Ezekiel 11:12, 16, 29:21	*Malachi 1:11*
People	*Joshua 10:13*	*2 Kings 6:18*
	Daniel 11:23	

We see this word "goy" being referred to as Gentile, nation, heathen and people; but it is always the same word.

Today a popular word among practicing Jews in Judaism refers to the goy as Gentiles. Rarely would people associate goy with Israel or goy with a Jewish person.

Am

The second ethnic word in scripture is the word "Am." Some people would correlate that to our English word "am." It is the word:

H5971 *am* (am); from H5971 a people; specifically, a tribe (as those of Israel; hence (collectively) troops or attendants; figuratively, a flock: — folk men, nation, people.

You have to understand that Israel was not the only tribes that we know of, because Israel's twelve sons (each male) represented a tribe or a nation or a people. We saw the tribes of Shem, the tribes of Ham and the tribes of Japheth. These were all tribal people.

When it talked about their tongue, it talked about their tribal language. Today here in the United States, whenever people talk about "tribe," they think of Indian reservations. They never refer to tribes as non-Indian or non-Native Americans.

It is interesting how in the United States Indians are called "Indians" when Indians are from India; except the Indians that are called "Indians" in the United States are not from India.

We give people terms and then we put them in those boxes, even sometimes when it just doesn't make sense. In India you have tribal people. You have tribal people in Pakistan and tribal people in Africa. You have tribal people as an ethnic division.

(Genesis 11:6) "*And the Lord said, ,,Behold, the people/am* H5971 *is one, and they have all one language; and this they begin to do: and now nothing will be restrained from them, which they have imagined to do."*"

This is *Genesis 11*. But in *Genesis 10* we saw that these were according to their tongues. At some point as people began to scatter all over the earth and YeHoVaH confused or confounded the language, you now have tribal language associated with ethnic groups, therefore cultures are developed. Within the cultures are hairstyles, colors, growing of beards, holes in their ears and the kinds of clothes they wear. All of these things become associated with a culture.

We see even in today's cultures that you have the hip-hop culture, the classic culture. You have people who are divided and separated by their cultural likes and dislikes. You have cultural, ethnic food. We use terms like this, but we don't often pay much attention to it. But this is biblical language.

Here are some scripture references for you to look up with regard to "*am*." You will find the same word. This points to the importance of looking up words. Every time you see the word "nation," it does not mean that it is the word "goy." It could be "am." There are a couple of other English words translated from other words besides goy and am.

Scripture References

| Folk | *Genesis 33:15* | *Proverbs 30:26* |

| Nation(s) | *Exodus 21:81* | *Deuteronomy 30:3* |
| | *1Chronicles 16:24* | *Psalm 108:3* |

| People | *Psalms 29:11; 102:18, 22* | *Habakkuk 3:13* |
| | *Zechariah 8:22* | *Malachi 1:4* |

Lom

The third ethnic word mentioned in scripture is the word *lom*.

[H3816] *lom* (leh-ome), from an unused root meaning to gather; a community: — nation, people.

(Genesis 27:29) *"Let people serve thee, and nations/leom [H3816] bow down to thee: be lord over thy brethren, and let thy mother's sons bow down to thee: cursed be every one that curseth thee, and blessed be he that blesseth thee."*

When we look at this and identify the context, we see that it is dealing with Isaac.

(Genesis 27:26-28) *"And his father Isaac said unto him, ,,Come near now, and kiss me, my son." And he came near, and kissed him: and he smelled the smell of his raiment, and blessed him, and said, ,,See, the smell of my son is as the smell of a field which the LORD hath blessed: Therefore God give thee of the dew of heaven, and the fatness of the earth, and plenty of corn and wine:""*

We see that Isaac is about to pronounce a blessing over Jacob. What he does is say to "let the lom bow down to you, let the nations bow down to you." So, you have the word "nation," but it is not the word "goy." It is the word "lom." It is not even the word "am."

The bottom line is you need tools to research with. If you don't have research tools, you will always be at the mercy of individuals who tell you what the Bible says. You don't want to be at the mercy of people because as we all know, men have desecrated the scripture. They have "ethnicized" the scripture. They have culturalized the scripture, westernized the scripture and made it say a whole lot of things it really doesn't say.

We have all been at the mercy of these individuals, but not anymore. We are learning the tools and we are taking the time to do the study ourselves. If people are coming up with all kinds of stuff that is so far away from what we are coming up with — the mistake that I made is that I trusted individuals who had more experience, more seniority and more education. I trusted them more than I trusted the leading of the Holy Spirit, because to me, they knew more than I did.

The Father brought me full circle back to the place where he said, "You cannot put your trust in men to teach you what I said. Have a relationship with me and not them; and a greater relationship because you are willing to pay the price of walking with me." Not everybody is willing to pay that price.

I was watching a program. They were interviewing this Hasidic Jew who served in the Israeli Army. As you may know, the Hasidim don't have to serve, but this young man chose to serve. As he was talking,

I was just thinking. He said that he has a couple of brothers in his family. Their job from 7 o'clock in the morning until 12 o'clock at night is to study the Talmud, to study the holy books. That is what they do from 7 a.m. until 12 at night. And I thought, "Man, what a commitment."

That is a tremendous commitment to study the holy books. Unfortunately, a lot of what they study is the research of men. And they become very astute and very knowledgeable in the words of the sages and this Rabbi and that Rabbi and Hillel and Shammai and the history and all of these things. So, they have all of this information and all of this knowledge which comes from the commitment of studying the holy books from sun-up until midnight. Whoa.

My commitment is not that committed, but they have people who support them and care for them and look out for them and their role. That is more than a full-time job. In America, a full-time job is 40 hours a week. That is usually translated into 8½ to 9 hours a day. But from 7 o'clock in the morning until 12 o'clock at night; say what you want to, but that is a serious commitment. I applaud it. I really do. I just wish that the holy books contained the Torah and not just what the Rabbis said about the Torah.

But they have the opportunity to read the Torah and would even allow the Prophet to have some say. It is one thing to study about the Prophet and yet reject the Prophet. But it is not just Hasidics. It is not just religious Jewish people who will reject Yeshua. It is a lot of Christians and Messianics who claim to know him, but who deny his word from living within them. It is head knowledge.

We have to get beyond knowledge to the application of this knowledge. We have to get beyond just having the information, but get to the application of the information which brings about the manifestation of Father's plan.

This word "lom" means to "gather." It is a community. Again, we see "nation" and "people." Here are your scripture references for lom:

Scripture References

Nation *Genesis 27:29*   *Psalms 47:3, 57:9*

People *Genesis 25:23*   *Psalm 148:11*
        Isaiah 55:4

Folk   *Jeremiah 51:58*

Ummah

The fourth ethnic word mentioned in scripture is the word "*ummah*."

[H524] *ummah* (oom-maw); (Aramaic): — nation, people.

(Ezra 4:10) "*And the rest of the nations/ummah* [H524] *whom the great and noble Asnapper brought over, and set in the cities of Samaria, and the rest that are on this side the river, and at such a time.*"

Here the word "ummah" is the word "nation." Scripture references for your study are:

Scripture References

Nation(s)	*Ezra 4:10*	*Daniel 3:4, 7, 29*
People	*Numbers 25:15*	*Psalm 117:1*

Greek New Testament

We have seen how the words "ummah," "lom," "am" and "goy" are describing groups from the Hebrew standpoint. When we move over into the Greek New Testament, the Brit Chadasha, the Renewed Covenant, the word most prominently used is the word *ethnos* from which we get our word "ethnic."

Ethnos

(Matthew 10:5) "These twelve Jesus sent forth, and commanded them, saying, „Go not into the way of the Gentiles/goy, G1484 *and into any city of the Samaritans enter ye not:""*

Here Yeshua makes a distinction between Gentiles and Samaritans. I don't want to make an issue out of this, but I do want to make a point.

G1484 *ethnos* (e-thnos); probably from G1484 *etho*; a race (as of the same habit), i.e. a tribe; specially a foreign (non-Jewish) one (usually by implication pagan): — Gentile, heathen, nation, people.

The interesting thing is that what the Greek does, is that it says "probably." That is what we think it is. We get race, racism, racial. Then you begin to move into racial slurs. But it is people of the same habit. Now, people outside of the United States oftentimes don't have a clue. If you have not been introduced to tribal people, you will have no knowledge and no understanding of what tribalism is like.

When I went to Kenya, I believe there were 42 tribes of Kenyans all having a different dialect. You may recall when I was in a little place 30 miles from the Sudan border. It was in the bush (you would call it, even in Kenya). I literally had three people standing next to me translating from English to Swahili and from that to Kukuyu and from that to the native language of the Luo people. When I have gone into some communities even here in the United States, I have spoken and have had to have a translator because I was speaking to people who did not understand. There were some English speakers, but many people did not speak the language. Also, we had people in the audience correcting the translators who were translating for me.

At one point in my ministry, my thoughts were that all Hispanics were simply Hispanic. That is until I began to go into different communities and there were tribes or cultures or individuals who did not want to be confused with the people of another ethnic group. All Hispanics are not Mexicans. All Israelites are not Jews.

Today, even most Jews think that all of Israel is Jewish and that is not true.

All Africans are not South Africans. I know some White South Africans. In the 'hood they have actually had to change the language. That is because there was a time in American history that an African American was a Black person. That is not so today. You have to use the terms "Black African" and "White African" because I know some Africans who are not Black.

In places that I have been in the Philippines and as I have traveled here in the United States and in Canada, you are dealing with ethnicity where you have people who are very, very — I hate to use the term, but "proud" of their heritage. When people migrate to the United States, they want to preserve their culture. They want that culture to pass down to the next generation because it really doesn't take, but a generation to lose a culture.

You hear people talk about second generation Chinese or second-generation Vietnamese or second-generation German and third generation. It is difficult to find third generations of ethnicities who still speak the language. Many people want to blend in. They want to assimilate. They don't want to be distinguished, but YeHoVaH made distinctions in the scriptures.

Even as Jacob is pronouncing the blessings over his children, he is making distinctions between his sons and the tribes that would come after them. This is how you will know. This is this people. These people have a certain spirit. They have a certain culture and they try to preserve that culture.

People want to say, "Well, in Jesus it doesn't matter. In Yeshua it doesn't matter." Well, why are you waving your ethnic flag? Why are you getting license plates with the flag of your native home? Flags are a symbol of a culture. It is the symbol of a people, a race or an ethnic group.

The Bible is full of ethnicity that is to be shared and enjoyed. You are going to have people of every nation, of every tribe, of every tongue worshipping together. But today we want to separate and isolate and cause people to be separated by a style or a sound or a beat. I don't like that kind of music or I don't like that kind of dance. I don't like that kind of food. I don't like this. The beauty of nations is that you can identify the things about certain cultures that you like. You can identify the things that you don't like. Enjoy those things you like. Avoid the things you don't — without being racist.

Now we have so much racism that it is a work of the enemy. It plays a prominent part even among the people who confess Messiah. I am amazed at how much racism is in operation among the so-called "Messianic/Hebrew Roots" people because it has been part of this culture. This culture has been steeped in racism; even in the earliest of days when only the Whites could enjoy the language of scripture and the benefits of serving the Almighty; whereas Blacks were property and women were property. In some cases, in some people's minds, it is still that way.

That is because people don't understand this book. They justify ungodly behavior and belief systems and ways of seeing people that are different through those ethnic racist eyes. Those kinds of things are not to be named among YeHoVaH. It should not be named among his people.

These are the kinds of things when I was in the Christian Church that separated churches. You have the White Church and the Black Church. You have the Hispanic Church. You have the Asian Church. You have the Vietnamese Church. They all have their language and they speak in their native tongues during their services. So, if you don't know the language, they can say that you are welcome, but there is no translator. After a while you are not there anymore.

They are not trying to make you welcome because they are trying to preserve a culture. People are trying to preserve a culture. They are not trying to preserve the culture of the Kingdom because they don't understand the culture of the Kingdom. When we do come into the understanding of the culture of the Kingdom, our culture becomes secondary.

And so, this word *ethnos*:

G1484 *ethnos* (e-thnos); probably from G1484 *etho*; a race (as of the same habit), i.e. a tribe; specially a foreign (non-Jewish) one (usually by implication pagan): — Gentile, heathen, nation, people.

Who put "non-Jewish" in there? You will notice that when we looked at *gowy*, it also said a foreign nation. Now you have individuals who are associating the definition to words from a modern-day mindset. They are inserting those words into the Bible. How does that happen? Well, where did the definition of *ethnos* come from? It came from Strong's.

As we are trying to identify and define words, Webster and Strong and all of these guys are like, "Okay, let's try to give it a definition based upon what it means." So, the word "gowy" became a foreign nation. The bottom line is that all nations were foreign to one another.

Here are some New Testament scripture references:

Scripture References

Gentile	*Matthew 10:5, 28*	*Mark 10:45Romans 9:24, 30*
	Acts 4:27	*Romans 9:24, 30*
Heathen	*2 Corinthians 11:27*	*Galatians 1:15; 3:8*
Nation(s)	*Mark 11:17*	*John 11:50-52*
	Acts 14:16	*Romans 4:17, 18*
People	*Romans 10:19*	

So, you see people, nation, heathen and Gentile all come from the word *ethnos*.

Here in the New Testament, you have the word "Jew." Again, my whole purpose is to bring clarity. Understand this. *Matthew* does not. *Mark* does not and *Luke* does not use the word. Again, in the commentary you will find the word "Jew."

In the book of *John* chapter 4, we find this conversation taking place. What I am about to share with you is going to really bless you, so eliminate the distractions. You don't want to miss it. The enemy does not want you to hear, so I am warning you right now. Pay attention.

Yeshua is having this conversation with the woman at the well:

(John 4:16-18) "Jesus saith unto her, „Go, call thy husband, and come hither." The woman answered and said, „I have no husband." Jesus said unto her, „Thou hast well said, I have no husband: For thou hast had five husbands; and he whom thou now hast is not thy husband: in that saidst thou truly.""

Think about this. Why would Yeshua ask the woman to go get her husband if he knows that she does not have a husband? Throughout the Bible what you will find is that Father and Yeshua test people to know what is in their hearts. It is not for him to know what is in their hearts, but he tests them to prove them. He gives them the opportunity to tell the truth or to tell a lie. He is hoping that based upon their response, he will determine whether or not he can go further with them. He is testing this woman to see if he can drop this revelation upon her because he is only going to reveal the revelation of heaven to those who are sincere, honest, open, truthful, faithful and committed. Yeshua did not go around casting his pearls among swine.

Believe me, the Jews considered the Samaritans to be swine, but Yeshua did not. People will give us a belief system if we let them. And if they give us their belief system and teach us "this is what this means," then we will believe it regardless of what the Bible teaches. We don't want to discount the Bible because of some sermon.

*(**John 4:19-22**) "The woman saith unto him, „Sir, I perceive that thou art a prophet. Our fathers worshipped in this mountain; and ye say, that in Jerusalem is the place where men ought to worship." Jesus saith unto her, „Woman, believe me, the hour cometh, when ye shall neither in this mountain, nor yet at Jerusalem, worship the Father. Ye worship ye know not what: we know what we worship: for salvation is of the Jews.""*

Notice what the translator does here. If you were to get a Bible dictionary or a concordance, what you will find is that Yeshua says, "Salvation is of Judah," not the Jews. Salvation did not come through the Jewish people. Salvation came through the tribe of Judah. It came through Judah and Yeshua was of the lineage of Judah.

The Jews did not bring salvation. Yeshua did.

Get this. There are people who are looking to the Jewish people instead of looking to Yeshua. He is not the Lion of Jews. He is the Lion of Judah. He is the offspring of David of the tribe of Jesse. Do you see this?

The word there is "Yehudah." It is "Judah" in reference to how Father is going to bring the Messiah. Not through Levi, not through the Levitical priesthood. The Prophet is going to come through Judah, the tribe of Judah, the Lion of Judah.

The next lesson will address the ethnic division that has been wrongfully inserted into scripture. There is no way in the world that you will ever be able to enjoy the ethnics of scripture Yah's way until we address the ethnics that have been inserted into scripture by men in an attempt to divide.

That is exactly what it has done. YeHoVaH never referred to his people as Jews. When you look at the book of *Revelation*, there are only two places where the term is referred to. You don't find it in the books of *James*, *Peter* or *Jude*. Two places in *Revelation* are not nice places for it to be.

We have to reevaluate and look at it and understand the ethnic division principle. We have to address that principle according to scripture. This is so that we can begin to appreciate our brothers and sisters regardless of the color of their skin, their dialect or their language, because in essence we become one culture. It is the culture of the Kingdom in which we can celebrate all of the cultures.

Class 59 Study Summary
Key Points

1. The ethnic division principle is the principle by which the interpretation of any verse or passage of scripture is determined upon a consideration of YeHoVaH's appointed ethnic divisions.

2. The definition of the word "ethnic" has to do with the basic divisions of mankind distinguished by culture. It is not based upon color.

3. None of Yeshua's disciples used the term "Jew," yet people today have been divided and distinguished by the terms "Jew" and "Gentile." This is ethnic division. It creates first and second-class citizens.

4. Four Hebraic terms surround ethnicity. They are *Goy, Am, Lom* and *Ummah*.

5. People today who make the argument that there were still people around after the flood have to disregard the scriptures in order to make that argument.

6. The nations of Shem, Ham and Japheth are all considered to be *gowy*, or Gentiles.

7. Abraham was referred to by YeHoVaH as the "great and mighty goy."

8. Not everyone is willing to pay the price of walking with the Father, but he says that we cannot put our trust in men to teach us what he has said. We are to have a relationship with him.

9. Today most Jews think that all of Israel is Jewish, but that is not true. There is a difference between being of the tribe of Judah and being in the religion of Judaism.

10. The Bible is full of ethnicity that is to be shard and enjoyed. People of every nation, tribe and tongue are to be worshipping together, but there is so much racism in the world.

11. People can justify their ungodly behavior and belief systems because they don't know or understand the Bible.

12. Throughout the Bible we see that Yeshua and YeHoVaH test people to prove them and to show what is in their hearts.

13. In the Bible, the Jews considered the Samaritans to be swine, but Yeshua did not. People will give us a belief system if we let them, even if it is not biblical.

14. The Jews did not bring salvation. Yeshua did. There are people looking to the Jewish people for salvation instead of to Yeshua. He is not the Lion of the Jews. He is the Lion of Judah.

Review Exercise

1. What are the four Hebrew words indicative of ethnicity that we learned about?

    1._____ 3._____

    2._____ 4._____

2. For many people in the United States (especially), this lesson introduces a very different way of viewing "diversity." Discuss the biggest difference in the two perspectives; one being the way we have been accustomed to think about it and the other being the biblical way to think about it.

    _____
    _____
    _____
    _____
    _____
    _____
    _____

3. Among the many biblical precepts that runs 180 degrees counter to our culture and our society is this idea of ethnicity as considered in the "Kingdom culture." Do you think it is workable for *you today* to operate in this mindset? Why or why not?

    _____
    _____
    _____
    _____
    _____
    _____
    _____

4. The phrase "It is always 5 o'clock somewhere" is indicative of a sort of moveable frame of reference in that it all depends upon where you are. How can we use a moveable or flexible frame of reference in thinking about terms like "foreign?"

    _____
    _____
    _____
    _____
    _____
    _____
    _____

5. If you did not look up the many scripture references in this lesson, I strongly suggest that you do so now.

Rate the following statements
by filling in the most appropriate number.

(1 = I do not agree 10 = I agree completely)

1. I can define the ethnic division principle in scripture and discover its importance.

    1. ○ 2. ○ 3. ○ 4. ○ 5. ○ 6. ○ 7. ○ 8. ○ 9. ○ 10. ○

2. I can distinguish our perceptions and impressions of ethnicity.

    1. ○ 2. ○ 3. ○ 4. ○ 5. ○ 6. ○ 7. ○ 8. ○ 9. ○ 10. ○

My Journal

What I learned from this class:

Discipleship Training Class 60

Ethnic Division Principle (part 2)

Objectives:

As a Discipleship student, at the end of this class you will be able to:

- Define a deeper understanding of the ethnic division principle introduced in Lesson 59
- Explain the New Testament understanding of ethnicity
- Clarify why YeHoVaH chose Israel and for what

As I have been spending time with this particular principle, I see such an important need. I could dwell in this area for a while. Have you ever heard people say things like, ‑God doesn't care about color or race in Messiah, or ‑It doesn't matter, and all of that? I think there is some truth to that. However, as we look at these particular principles, you are going to see that Father celebrates the diversity of his people and we should celebrate the diversity of the people that Father is bringing into his Kingdom.

This ethnic division principle will help us to understand scripture from an ethnic perspective because there are certain scriptures that are written to ethnic groups. The more we understand the different principles that are here in the Bible, the better we can interpret the scriptures and the better we will understand the scriptures that are pertaining to the diversity of people.

Discipleship as you know is an ongoing process. We are learning how to search and study the word. This is a lifelong endeavor. It is not something that you are going to do for a year or two. It is not something where you read the Bible and you boast for the next twenty years how you have read the Bible all the way through twice or three times. **It is about searching the scriptures** because therein (as Yeshua told the Pharisees), the scriptures speak of him.

There are those who thought that they had eternal life, but they failed to realize that **the scriptures are not words for religious dogma or things that you practice as a people. The words of YeHoVaH are words of life.** They are life-giving words; Spirit-filled words, words that will sustain you through the darkest moments on earth and in your life.

It is important that we don't look at the Bible as simply a book with words in there that you can easily turn into legalistic dogma. We should look at the scripture and at the words of YeHoVaH as words of life. They are like food is to the physical body. His words are food for our spirit man.

Let's review from part 1 and then move on into part 2.

Part 1 Recap

In the last lesson we moved into the New Testament looking at *ethnos*. What we were looking at when we looked at the ethnic division principle is the ethnicity that is found in scripture. We looked at it from a

Tanakh/Old Testament perspective. The last lesson concluded just as we began to look at it from a New Testament Greek perspective.

> *(**Matthew 10:5**) "These twelve Jesus sent forth, and commanded them, saying, „Go not into the way of the Gentiles [goy^{G1484}] and into any city of the Samaritans enter ye not:""*

We noticed that here Yeshua makes a distinction between the Gentiles and the Samaritans. There are many who tell us that the Samaritans are Gentiles and there is some degree of truth to that. But here is the thing that we have learned as we have looked at *John 4*. Understand that **the Messianic community did not call themselves "Christians**. The Bible says that they were first called Christians at Antioch. People put the title upon them. People put titles upon you. If you are not careful, you will take on the title that a person puts on you.

This is what people have done in religion. They put everybody in a box. Pretty soon you will begin to call yourself what they who developed the boxes say that you are. –I am a Baptist or –I am a Methodist or –I am a Pentecostal. –I am a Christian. –I am a Jew. These boxes were generated. There were boxes generated for the Samaritans. As a matter of fact, you will notice that the Bible says what the woman at the well said to Yeshua, –I am a Samaritan. You Jews have nothing to do with us. We see that by the time of Yeshua they (the Jews of that day) had already put the Samaritans into a particular box.

But the woman knew who she was. She said, –Are you greater than our Father Jacob? She identified herself as the family of YeHoVaH. The Jews, the religious leaders identified her as a heathen and as someone who was lower than dirt. As a matter of fact, they did not want anything to do with them. Even today there are those who teach that the Samaritans were Gentiles and were people who were not part of the covenant. And yet this woman identified herself.

That is not what this teaching is about. What I am trying to show you is that people will put you into a box. They will give you a name. They will give you a title. They will define you. You either define yourself or you take on the definition by which they define you.

^{G1484} *ethnos* (e-thnos); probably from <1486> *etho*; a race (as of the same habit), i.e. a tribe; specially a foreign (non-Jewish) one (usually by implication pagan): — Gentile, heathen, nation, people.

Notice the parenthetical about it defining non-Jewish. This is added by Strong's. By this time in biblical history there were literally two distinct groups of people (namely Jews and Gentiles). This is the division that the Bible placed them in. YeHoVaH did not put that there. This is the work of men.

So Strong is trying to give a definition to the word *ethnos* — Gentile, heathen, nation, people. These are the words that are associated with Israel. Israel was called Gentile, heathen, a nation, a people. Israel was called *gowy*, which is what the word is in the Hebrew.

Again, here are the scripture references to that:

<u>Gentile</u>	*Matthew 10:5, 28*	*Mark 10:45*
	Acts 4:27	*Romans 9:24, 30*
<u>Heathen</u>	*2 Corinthians 11:27*	*Galatians 1:15; 3:8*
<u>Nation(s)</u>	*Mark 11:17*	*John 11:50-52*
	Acts 14:16	*Romans 4:17, 18*
<u>People</u>	*Romans 10:19*	

I reviewed that with you because I want to take you to a new Greek word relating to people. It is the word *genos*.

It means offspring, family, nation, the aggregate of many individuals of the same nature, kind, sort, species.

You won't hear much about this word from a biblical standpoint. You will read right over these words in the New Testament and not realize that it is a different word for people.

Israel had offspring. Israel was a family. Israel was a nation.

Basically, what you are looking at in this word *genos* is the word –community. We will see that the word is also dealing with the word –born *(Acts 18:2, 24; 4:36; 2 Corinthians 11:26)*. Let's take a look at a couple of these.

(Acts 18:1-2) *"After these things Paul departed from Athens, and came to Corinth; And found a certain Jew named Aquila, born/genos in Pontus, lately come from Italy, with his wife Priscilla; (because that Claudius had commanded all Jews to depart from Rome) and came unto them."*

Aquila was a Jew born in Pontus. I really want you to take off the glasses. Take off the shades. Open your mind and your spirit. We are not going to try to sneak anything foreign in here, but I want you to remove the prejudices. We look at the Bible with prejudice. It doesn't mean something racist, as much as it means –prejudge. We approach the scriptures with the idea that we already know what it says.

When you read the Bible with the idea that you already know what it says, you will simply read over words. You don't <u>read</u> it. YeHoVaH told Philip to pull himself up next to this man of Ethiopia. This man was an Ethiopian eunuch and he was reading the scriptures.

When Philip walked up to him, the guy was stuck. He was stuck in Isaiah. –Is the prophet speaking of himself or is he speaking of someone else? Those of us today read the Bible and say that the prophet was speaking of himself, based upon what Philip said. We don't have to ponder that like the Ethiopian because we believe that we know, but we need to be like the Ethiopian when we read the Bible.

Otherwise, you will read the Bible like you already know what it says and you will read right over stuff that is clearly right there before you. You won't see it.

So, we see Aquila was born. That word is –*genos*.

Another unique word is the word –diversity. We find that in *1 Corinthians 12:28*.

(1 Corinthians 12:28) *"And God hath set some in the church, first apostles, secondarily prophets, thirdly teachers, after that miracles, then gifts of healings, helps, governments, diversities [genos] of tongues."*

We also get the word –kindred. And if we go back to *Acts 7:*

(Acts 7:13) *"And at the second time Joseph was made known to his brethren; and Joseph's kindred [genos] was made known unto Pharaoh."*

We can see that this word *genos* deals with a group of people who have like culture, like minds and like practices.

Genos as nation:

(Mark 7:26) "The woman was a Greek, a Syrophenician by nation; and she besought him that he would cast forth the devil out of her daughter."

People were identified by the place they were born. This is going to be very important when we get into the latter part of this teaching. This is why I am laying this out for you right now. Again, we identify people today by two groups: Jews and Gentiles. You are either a Jew or you are not (and that is an insult to scripture).

It is also an insult (I believe) to the Almighty, because now you have taken his creation and put it into a box. I don't believe that he likes that because we are doing something he has not done and we are forcing the world to accept this, which is not right.

Genos as offspring: **Acts 17:28, 29; Revelation 22:16**

Genos as stock: **Acts 13:27; Philippians 3:5**

The above words indicate that an ethnic group is to be viewed as a community of persons sharing the same ancestry and participating in the culture. These words are applied to Israel/Judah, Gentile nations and the church/ekklesia. What you are going to find is that there are cultural similarities in people who are raised up in certain neighborhoods, certain communities and on certain sides of the tracks or the highway.

This is one of the things that I think David was alluding to when he said he was born in sin and shapen in iniquity. In other words, the culture in which he was born shaped him. You have heard the old saying that it takes a village to raise a child. The child gets its identity from the village in which it is raised. It understands its pecking order and where it fits into the whole scheme of things. For lack of a better term or phrase, it knows where its place is on the totem pole. I hate using that term, but I think some would identify with what I am trying to say. You know the order.

In every household, there is an order and you need to find out where you fit. Otherwise, you will find yourself stepping out of line.

This also goes on in business. There are levels of authority. You need to make sure that you follow the chain lest you find yourself offending someone by bypassing someone. When you bypass someone who is of authority, you have lost that person as an ally. You have alienated yourself. Within a community there is a culture. There is an understanding of that culture. People try very hard to preserve that culture.

It happens in denominations because denominations are a broad community. Then in the local assembly there is a more unique community of people within that local assembly.

We identify –church, which comes from American Bibles. The Greek word is *ekklesia* (eh- kleh-see-ah), which comes from a Hebrew ideology, meaning the –called out ones. Oftentimes you will hear Christians refer to the church as the –spiritual Israel.

POPPYCOCK!

That is malarkey. What you have is an identity that has given a name, a term, a definition. It has created a box. This box is called –the church. In many of the minds of those who established this box, this has replaced Israel. It is replacement theology at its worst.

Classification

The apostle Paul recognized that while YeHoVaH is no respecter of person, he has instituted certain ethnic distinctions. Paul noted the three basic ethnic divisions in the New Testament Bible in his letter to the Corinthians.

(1 Corinthians 10:32) "Give none offense, neither to the Jews, nor to the Gentiles, nor to the church (ekklesia) of YeHoVaH."

What I need for you to understand is that when Paul wrote this, Paul was not referring to them in these terms. He did not like –the church, so this word –church was inserted hundreds of years later. He talked about the –called out ones because the church was not born on Pentecost/Shavuot as Christians would put it. YeHoVaH is now calling people out of Judaism. He is calling people out of religion. He is calling his people out.

The first called out ones were all Hebrews. They were not Gentiles (if you would) as it relates to the New Testament Bible translation or Strong's Concordance. Strong's Concordance refers to Gentiles as non-Jews. This is the same word for the word *gowy*. When we find that in the Hebrew Scriptures, the word *gowy* was used to refer to people who are called Jews. It is a mangled mingling of words.

The interpreters of the Bible have used words in such a way as to lead people in their thinking. This causes one to read right over what is right there in front of them. This is how many people read the Bible. They read the Bible with blinders on because they assume they already know what it says.

The Jews had several ethnic distinctions in the New Testament Bible. We need to see this. I have tried to point this out in my teachings for many, many months — a couple of years now. Some people wrongly conclude that I have some kind of anti-Semitic belief or thought and it is so far from the truth. I won't let people try to put me into a box and back me up from what the Bible actually says, however it may seem.

What is really interesting is that the people who have the biggest issues with the things that I am saying are Gentiles — Jew-wannabe's. I have many Jewish people who compliment and tell me, –Keep it up! People need to know this stuff.

Notice that the Bible referred to the Syrophenician by nation. That word is *genos*.

(Acts 2:7) "And they were all amazed and marvelled, saying one to another, „Behold, are not all these which speak Galilaeans?""

Were they Jews? That is not what it says. It says –Galileans. They were identified by their region. Who are they referring to? It is referring to the 120 in the upper room. You have to know they were not Gentiles as the New Testament church defines Gentiles. These were Hebrews. These were Israelites, but they are not referred to as Jews.

What is interesting in the Bible is that there are times when Jewish people or Israelites or Hebrew people are referred to not as Jews or Hebrews or Israel. Then there are times that they are. You have to look at who is doing the referring. Is it the commentator? That is because we read the Bible as the commentator or as if the commentary from the commentator is actually the words of YeHoVaH.

–They are inspired. Who said they are inspired? They are commentary. We can go and get some of

Calvin's commentaries. He is commenting and making commentary on the Bible. Is that scripture? How can we take commentary that is clearly marked as commentary and say that they are not scripture, but apply commentary in the Bible as if it's scripture?

It is commentary.

I was having an interesting conversation with a pastor. Then I was talking to the pastor and his wife. I love when that happens.

When that conversation ensued on the phone, that is where the life of YeHoVaH just began to flow. I understand what Yeshua said after he sent his disciples into town to buy meat in *John 4*. They came back with food, saying, −Wait a minute. He won't eat. Has somebody given him something to eat? He says no that he had meat that they knew not of. His meat was to do the will of the Father.

There is something about doing Father's will. Before I get started preaching sometimes, I am dragging. I am ready to take a nap. But getting into that place where you are saying, −Okay, Father. Here I am. Use me. It is the life source that begins to flow. All of us need to learn how to flow in the life of YeHoVaH, because our physical body will not be able to sustain the calling that he has placed upon our lives.

If we are trying to do his will in our own strength, we will get burned out. I want you to look at verse 5 for a second. Notice what it starts out saying:

(Acts 2:5) "*And there were dwelling at Jerusalem Jews, devout men,* **out of every nation** *under heaven.*"

(Acts 2:8) "*And how hear we every man in* **our own tongue**, *wherein we were born?*"

What is the tongue of the Jews? It is Hebrew. That is what you would assume. That is the assumption. He says, −We are hearing these men in our own native languages, in our own tongue. But the assumption is that Jewish people speak Hebrew. Well, these Jews spoke another tongue. Maybe they spoke Hebrew as well. If that was the case, all of the hundred — the one hundred and twenty or those who were filled with the Holy Spirit began to speak in tongues. All they had to do was speak in Hebrew and everybody would have known what they were saying.

Instead, they were speaking to people who were:

(Acts 2:9-11) "*Parthians, and Medes, and Elamites, and the dwellers in Mesopotamia, and in Judaea, and Cappadocia, in Pontus, and Asia, Phrygia, and Pamphylia, in Egypt, and in the parts of Libya about Cyrene, and strangers of Rome, Jews and proselytes, Cretes and Arabians, we do hear them speak in our tongues the wonderful works of God.*"

These were their native languages. Just like today you have English speaking Jewish people who live here in the United States who don't speak Hebrew. If they would go to Israel, they would need an interpreter if they were speaking to someone who speaks Hebrew. (The majority, or a great deal of people in Israel speak English (both Jews and Arabs) because English is an international language and the language of currency.)

You have all of these languages. Whoever is speaking is making the distinction of the ethnicity of these individuals by the language and region from whence they have come. They said, −How is it that we hear these men in our own native tongue? But wait a minute. They are Jews. Shouldn't they be speaking Hebrew?

You see, they put the idea of –Jews in verse 5. That created the image in our minds and put blinders on our eyes. You see it, but you don't see it. –That is the Holy Spirit, brother.

Well, yeah it is, but these individuals specifically said that we are Parthinian Jews. We are Roman Jews. We are Mesopotamian Jews. We are Median Jews. We are Elamite Jews. Then there were Jew Jews, Jews from Judea. But the word here is Judeans. It really should be Israelites.

You have Israelites who come from all over in honor of the Feast of Shavuot which was a pilgrimage feast. Now the church has totally separated the pilgrimage feast from the rest of the Torah. –Well, the church was born on the day of Pentecost, they will say. Do you know what Pentecost was? And do you know that Gentiles were not in Jerusalem for Pentecost? The Gentiles here were proselytes from Rome. These Gentiles identified as proselytes from Rome says to the reader that you have some Gentiles who have converted to Judaism.

When you look at the ethnic culture here, you are going to also see that these Gentiles who have converted to Judaism have converted to a religion. This brings into question: Is being a Jew ethnic or is being Jewish one who practices Judaism?

When you think about conversion, a proselyte is a Gentile who converted to being a Jew (like you are going to convert to being an African or you are going to convert to being Chinese or you are going to convert to being Japanese). The only thing you can do is citizenship. You renounce one citizenship and you take on the citizenship of another nation, but that does not make you Japanese or Chinese. You are still an American with a Chinese or Japanese or African citizenship.

How can you convert to being a Jew? Do you follow what I am saying? (If it is an ethnicity.) What you can do is you can convert. You can become an Israelite by entering into covenant with YeHoVaH. It does not bring you into the commonwealth of the Jewish people. It brings you into the commonwealth of **ISRAEL.**

We have another issue.

(Acts 6:1) "And in those days, when the number of the disciples was multiplied, there arose a murmuring of the Grecians against the Hebrews, because their widows were neglected in the daily ministration."

The Greek speaking Jews were murmuring against the Ivri or Hebrew speaking Jews. This is what it says. Now you have some ethnic among the Jewish people. One is a Greek culture and the other is a Hebrew culture. Two different cultures are clashing in the Messianic community.

From *Genesis* to *Revelation*, Israel is divided into twelve tribes, not one. Let's look at some scriptures. Mark these in your own Bible so that you have a place of reference.

<u>Scripture References</u>

(Genesis 49:28) "All these are the twelve tribes of Israel: and this is it that their father spake unto them, and blessed them; every one according to his blessing he blessed them."

*(Exodus 24:4) "And Moses wrote all the words of the LORD, and rose up early in the morning, and builded an altar under the hill, and twelve pillars, **according to the twelve tribes of Israel**."*

*(Exodus 28:21) "And the stones shall be with the **names of the children of Israel, twelve**, according to their names, like the engravings of a signet; every one with his name shall they be according to the twelve tribes."*

The ephod that the high priest wears has twelve stones which represent twelve tribes. When the high priest went into the holy of holies during Yom Kippur, all twelve tribes were represented.

(Exodus 39:14) *"And the stones were according to the names of the children of Israel,* ***twelve, according to their names****, like the engravings of a signet, every one with his name, according to the twelve tribes."*

Each stone would have the name of a tribe. You did not have one giant stone representing all twelve tribes of Israel (now called Jews).

(Ezekiel 47:13) *" Thus saith the Lord GOD; „This shall be the border, whereby ye shall inherit the* ***land according to the twelve tribes of Israel****: Joseph shall have two portions.""*

I want you to see this because people are so concerned about the dividing of Jerusalem. They are totally unaware that a people called Jews have control of all of the land that was given to twelve tribes. There are individuals who have taken on the governance and the responsibility over the land. They are the ones who have (how would you put it?) taken that which belongs to YeHoVaH as their own. They have hijacked it.

Now the only way you can get in there is if you convert to Judaism.

I am going to say something and this is just for your own pleasure. The next time someone tells you that they are Jewish, ask them, –What tribe are you from? That is going to confound the majority of them. —Well, I am Jewish. What do you mean, what tribe am I from?

If I introduce myself as Jewish, I hear two questions: –Did you convert? or –Are you Ethiopian? Either I converted or I am an Ethiopian Jew. Why? It is because I am Black.

We have been taught to look at people by the tone of their skin. When we see dark brown people with a certain type of hair, they –must be Muslims. It has nothing to do with dressing. You can look at a person who is in a suit. Take a dark brown skinned guy (me) and a White guy and put them in a line-up. People are already going to stereotype. We have a Muslim, an African, and a Jew. I have friends that if I were to introduce them as African, you would say no, because they are White, but they are Africans. The idea is that all Africans are Black.

I was in the Philippines and I was amazed. I was so amazed. There was this community of Black Filipinos. They had hair like mine and dark skin. We are the ones here in the United States who have the biggest issue. Folks outside of the United States don't have nearly the kinds of issues of stereotyping people that we do here in the United States. When we translate this Bible into their languages, we translate the stereotypes, the prejudices and the racism. And we send them Jesus — a White, Western, blue-eyed, blonde-haired Jesus. We have that picture in many of the churches in the United States. That is what he looked like. That is amazing. That photograph has really stood the test of time. How in the world were you able to preserve such an immaculate photo for 2,000 years? Wow.

I am annihilating racism. People talk about how –we should be color-blind. Yeah, you say we should be color-blind, but you aren't. It sounds good, but you aren't and we should be working at it. Color should not matter in the body of Messiah, but it does. I have been in various denominations and in every denomination you have divisions. In the Baptists you have Black Baptists and White Baptists, Southern Baptists and Northern Baptists. In the Pentecostals you have White Pentecostals, Black Pentecostals and Hispanic Pentecostals. In the Reformed or the Lutheran, it doesn't matter. Ethnicity, race, is the dividing line.

In some multicultural churches, there are Whites on one side and Blacks on the other. It just happens. People come into House Of Israel and they just gravitate to their ethnicity. They don't even think about it. They talk about the cafeteria study where Blacks go and sit at the Black table and Asians go and sit at the Asian table and Hispanics sit at the Hispanic table because birds of a feather do flock together. There is a mentality that has been established in us from a culture. Absolutely this culture is what drives us. We don't understand Kingdom culture. We have taken on Western culture.

(Matthew 19:28) *"And* **Yeshua** *said unto them, ,, Verily I say unto you, That ye which have followed me, in the regeneration when the Son of man shall sit in the throne of his glory, ye also shall sit upon* **twelve thrones, judging the twelve tribes of Israel.** *""*

(Luke 22:30) *"That ye may eat and drink at my table in my kingdom, and sit on thrones* **judging the twelve tribes of Israel.***"*

(Acts 26:7) **"Unto which promise our twelve tribes,** *instantly serving God day and night, hope to come. For which hope's sake, king Agrippa, I am accused of the Jews."*

This is amazing right here. Understand that Paul understood that the Jews were Judeans. They knew who the Jews were. They were Judeans. Yeshua came to his own. People will say that Yeshua came to Israel. No. Yeshua came to Judea. He came to his own, the Judeans. Yeshua was Judean. The Judeans were the religious leaders. Those are the ones he came to who received him not.

Now they say –Israel rejected him. They put Israel into the boat of the Jewish people. They say, – The Jews rejected Jesus. The Jews killed Jesus. They fail to realize that all of Yeshua's disciples were Israelites. The 120 in the upper room were Israelites. The 3,000 added on the day of Shavuot were Israelites. The 5,000 were Israelites. The myriad were Israelites. The priests who accepted the Messiah were Israelites and were considered (in today's vernacular) Jews.

Ask yourself which of the 120 killed Jesus? It was the religious leaders, the Judeans who were in authority who were responsible for following the will of the Almighty unawares. They were working for their Daddy, the devil.

Yeshua says, –Your Daddy is the devil because you are trying to kill me. Murder is an action of the evil one. Hatred in one's heart is an action of the evil one. When you hate your brother without cause, that is an action of Satan. That is a violation of Torah. As Yeshua said, if you hate your brother, you are guilty of murder.

(James 1:1) *"James, a servant of God and of the Lord Jesus Christ, to the twelve tribes which are scattered abroad, greeting."*

James is not for everybody. James is only for the twelve tribes of Israel. You have to fit into the twelve tribes in order to partake of James. James makes it clear. This is who this is written to. This is not written to some –spiritual Israel.

(Revelation 21:12) *"And had a wall great and high, and had twelve gates, and at the gates twelve angels, and names written thereon,* **which are the names of the twelve tribes of the children of Israel:***"*

From *Genesis* to *Revelation,* they are never reduced by YeHoVaH or Yeshua or even the disciples. It is reduced by people, translators.

I need to drive this home. The more you use the terms –Jew and –Gentile, you are as much a part of the problem. This is why I purposely use the term –Hebrew, –Israelite. I continually and consistently knock out this idea that there are two groups of people, Jews and Gentiles. That is not YeHoVaH's plan from *Genesis* to *Revelation*.

I think that the more we expose it, the easier it would be for people to deal with it. My wife and I had the conversation years ago, –How would you feel if your daughter married a White guy? My only thing is that as long as he believed like we believe; I am good with that. The same goes with my sons. There are some people who have a real issue with it and you have to ask yourself, why?

For a long time, religious fanatics felt that you could not mingle the races. Only less than ten years ago has that changed in some Christian Colleges. They were not allowed to mix (earlier than ten years ago). That is the prejudices. That is the human religion. That is not biblical religion. That is not true religion. That is manmade religion based upon their skewed interpretations.

It was not the Jews who did this. The book where it is written and given is in the Gentile portion of the scriptures. The Judeans, those who practice Judaism, don't even read this part of the Bible, so they are not responsible for this. They did not translate this. They are saying, –That is your Bible.

Thus, the New Testament translators have condensed the human race into three main divisions: the Jews, the Gentiles and the church/ekklesia (which is supposed to be Jews and Gentiles). The called-out ones are of the twelve tribes of Israel and those who have joined themselves with Israel.

It is as if these people teach that YeHoVaH had plan A. Plan A failed, so he established plan B. He initiated plan B so that when plan B succeeds, he would go back to plan A. Plan A was to reach out to the Jews. They rejected Jesus, so he established plan B to reach out to the Gentiles.

The Gentiles all come in through the Jewish scriptures. Now he is going to go back and get the Jews.

We believed that stuff for a long time, but logically it doesn't even make sense. If he had plan A and it did not work, what makes you think plan B is going to work? Then plan B is going to go so well that plan A is now going to work (because plan B works so well). Those who were part of plan A have seen how well plan B worked, so now they are going to come on board.

The Origination of These Ethnic Groups

From the creation of Adam to the Tower of Babel *(Genesis 1:1-11:9)*, mankind is one race and speaking one language. The event recorded in *Genesis 11* gives us background of the reason for the division of mankind into diverse nations. The origin of the nations is described in this chapter. Out of these nations, YeHoVaH chose a nation for himself and for his own purposes.

In the Old Testament there are two major ethnic divisions: the chosen nation (Israel, twelve sons/tribes of Jacob/Israel) and the Gentile nations. The more you understand the Torah you will find that YeHoVaH changed Jacob's name to Israel so –Jacob and –Israel are used interchangeably. Sometimes it refers to Jacob and sometimes it refers to Israel. Israel was Jacob who had a name change by YeHoVaH. The twelve tribes of Israel are the twelve sons of Jacob.

We are not going to get into all of that, but there is so much there that it would really be worth getting into at some point.

The New Testament introduces a third major ethnic division, which is the church/ekklesia. It is composed of both Israel/Jew and Gentile (Israel and Non-Israel). When you look at the scriptures without the glasses, when you look at the scriptures without thinking you already know what the scriptures say, you will see what I am saying here. As we think about the chosen, scripture reveals that Israel was the nation which YeHoVaH chose to fulfill his own purposes. YeHoVaH took Israel as a nation from the midst of the nations and made a great nation out of them by his statutes, laws and judgments. *(Deuteronomy 4:6-8, 34)*

In the covenant with Abraham, YeHoVaH said that he would make of him a great nation *(Genesis 12:2-3)*. YeHoVaH also promised Abraham that he would make him the Father of many nations *(Genesis 17:1-7)*. We saw that as we talked about covenants (and specifically the Abrahamic covenant).

The Reason

YeHoVaH chose Israel to be a special people to himself above all of the people on the earth because of his love and the covenant he made with Israel's Father Abraham (Isaac and Jacob/Israel). *(Deuteronomy 7:6-9; 9:1-6)* There were a number of things involved in the purpose of this divine choice.

The people were chosen to bless all nations. *(Genesis 9:27; 12:2-3; 17:4-7; 18:18; 22:16-18)*

The people are scattered. They are all YeHoVaH's people because they came from Adam. There is one nation and one group of people. There was Adam. Father destroyed the people of the earth through the flood. Then we had Noah, his three sons and their wives, who repopulated the earth. In essence, the three sons came out of Noah. Noah traces his lineage back to Adam. We all came from Adam. That is every person on the planet.

You can call yourself whatever you want. You can identify yourself by your culture. You can identify yourself by your ethnicity. You can identify yourself by the ancestry or by the places of your ancestors. You can hear it as people talk. You can feel the pride coming out of people when they begin to talk about their ancestry.

There are certain groups of people that this is strong among. One group is the Jews. Another group is the Dutch. Another is the Irish. Another is the Germans and then the Greeks. Have you seen the movie *My Big Fat Greek Wedding*? They believe that every word on the planet came from the Greek language and is based on the New Testament. They could say, yeah, that is true.

When you look at it, there is this pride that is associated with one's ethnicity that overshadows the Kingdom. The culture of the Kingdom supersedes all culture. It is a new culture that we come into where we now have to learn the culture of the Kingdom. We have to begin to treat one another according to the statutes of the Kingdom. This is the whole purpose of the commandments: how to love the Father, the King of the Kingdom and how to love the people of the Kingdom.

We live in two kingdoms: the kingdom of this world controlled and owned by Satan and the Kingdom of YeHoVaH. Those who live in the kingdom and who identify with their ethnic culture are relegated and confined to worldly kingdom relationships. But when we come into the Kingdom of YeHoVaH, our relationships change.

Because people don't understand the body of Messiah, many of them are dying. Many of them are sleeping. Many of them are sick. Many of them are weak. You can take communion all you want, but if you don't discern the body of Mashiach (the body of Mashiach are those who are blood-bought) – those who have been brought out of darkness into light, those who have come into the Kingdom of YeHoVaH, the body of Messiah, that is the true family of YeHoVaH.

Those who don't understand it don't discern it properly. Therefore, they don't treat the Kingdom of YeHoVaH and his people properly. **When we come into the Kingdom, that means that the King lives in us. Therefore, how you treat the King in me is going to have an effect upon your life because you don't discern who I represent.** This is why I warn you about all of that murmuring, complaining, backbiting, unforgiveness, bitterness, hatred, tongue-lashing and all of that mess that people think they can do on *Facebook* and in private chats and private messaging and all of that stuff. Father knows who you are. He knows who I am.

I have to love people who don't even like me. People that I just want to take a bat and knock their head from here to New York Father says, —No, that is the wrong spirit. Now I am convicted. I am not the only one. The Father says that if your enemy is hungry, you have to feed him. You have to pray for them that use you. You don't rejoice when he takes vengeance upon those who have wronged you, otherwise it will be turned on you. If you are going to take on Father's Spirit, you are going to have to walk in the love. That is because by the love you have for one another is how the world is going to know you are truly mine.

You can't fake this. You just can't fake it. There are too many people trying to fake it till they make it. You can't fake this. It is either in you or it is not. Those who have discernment will discern what Spirit you are. It may take them a little while, just as you discern people's spirits.

YeHoVaH chose this group of people to bless the world. He says, –Don't get all prideful and lifted up because I chose you, because I could have chosen anybody. I just chose you. I am going to take you and set you up as an example that all of the nations of the world will have as an example.

Whether you know this or not or believe this or not (and those of you who have come to maturity realize this), that for any area you want to excel in, you need a mentor. The Bible calls them a disciple. It is one who disciples. This is what we are supposed to be. We are supposed to be discipled. Then we are supposed to make disciples. If you are going to walk this journey, you have to be discipled. –I don't need nobody to tell me nothing. I have the Holy Ghost. I can tell by your spirit. You have something. It is a ghost, but I don't know how holy it is.

The people were chosen to receive the oracles of YeHoVaH. *(Romans 3:2)*

This is why he chose Israel. Father says, –I want to give my commands to a people. When the children of the earth built that tower at Babel, basically they were saying, –We want to be self-ruled. That is what a democracy is. It is a government by the people, for the people. It is self-ruled.

According to the Kingdom, we are supposed to be self-ruled, but it is the Holy Spirit that is doing the ruling in ourselves. We are supposed to be self-governed by the Spirit that is within us. This is why it is important for us to be filled with the Spirit so that the Spirit within us can govern us. This is how the governance of the Kingdom is going to operate. Self-control, self- government — you don't need somebody to tell you what to do if you are yielded to the Holy Spirit because the Holy Spirit is going to lead you into all truth. But most people would not know the Holy Spirit if he slapped them. It is unfortunate. I did a series on *How to Hear the Voice of God,*[7] *The Power of the Spirit* and *Understanding Things of the Spirit.* All of these things that I am trying to teach are so that people won't be dependent upon me.

---

[7] See our web site at *www.ArthurBaileyMinistries.com*.

I don't want you dependent upon me. My job is to try to get you connected to him. If I do that right, you will not become dependent upon me. And if you choose to become dependent upon me, then guess what? I am going to get away from you. I am not going to let you become dependent upon me. That is a dangerous place. YeHoVaH is jealous. He is not going to allow anyone to stand as –God in your life, but him. He will kill you first and he will kill anybody who tries to do it. He is jealous and vengeance is his. He says for you to put no other gods before him, no man, woman or child. That is nothing in the heavens, on the earth or in the water. You don't put anybody or anything before him. Anybody who allows themself to be put between that person and the Almighty, let me tell you something. That is a dangerous place to be.

The people were chosen to receive the blessing of YeHoVaH. *(Romans 9:4-5)*

I want you to see this:

(Romans 3:1-4) *"What advantage then hath the Jew? or what profit is there of circumcision? Much every way: chiefly, because that unto them were committed the oracles of God. For what if some did not believe? shall their unbelief make the faith of God without effect? God forbid: yea, let God be true, but every man a liar; as it is written, That thou mightest be justified in thy sayings, and mightest overcome when thou art judged."*

(Roman 9:4) *"Who are Israelites; to whom pertaineth the adoption, and the glory, and the covenants, and the giving of the law, and the service of God, and the promises;"*

Notice here what he says. The Israelites were adopted. YeHoVaH adopted Israel just like he adopts you. He chose them. You are chosen. The Israelites are no different than you. YeHoVaH chose a people unto himself. We are fortunate if he chooses to reveal himself to us. That is not to get big-headed and puffed up and prideful. It should humble you.

All the covenants were given. Every covenant in the Bible given by YeHoVaH were given to Israel. When you think about Adam, Noah and all the way down to the New Covenant/Renewed Covenant, it all had to do with the people that he had chosen out of the world for himself. Everybody else is going to hell. Everybody else is going into the Lake. Those who do not enter into covenant with YeHoVaH and who become the household of YeHoVaH (that is the Israelites and all who join themselves with them through faith in Yeshua), will not inherit the Kingdom. It is that simple.

(Romans 9:5) *"Whose are the fathers, and of whom as concerning the flesh Christ came, who is over all, God blessed for ever. Amen."*

Class 60 Study Summary
Key Points

1. YeHoVaH celebrates the diversity of his people.
2. The ethnic division principle helps us to understand scripture from an ethnic perspective because certain scriptures are written to ethnic groups.
3. Discipleship is an ongoing, lifelong process. We are learning to search and to study the word.
4. The scriptures are not words for religious dogma or things that you practice as a people. They are words of life. They are YeHoVaH's life-giving words. They are Spirit.
5. The earliest Messianic community did not call themselves –Christians.
6. The work of men was to divide the people into two groups, the Jews and the Gentiles. YeHoVaH and his word did not do this. Such simplification is an insult to scripture.
7. If you do not take the time to look up the meaning of words, you will read right over them and think they mean one definition when they mean something entirely different.
8. What David was alluding to when he said that he was –born in sin and shapen in iniquity was that the culture that he was born into shaped him.
9. The word –church comes from American Bibles. In the Greek the word is –*ekklesia* or called out ones.
10. There is no –spiritual Israel. It is a made-up term.
11. YeHoVaH is calling people out of Judaism. He is calling people out of religions.
12. The first called out ones were all Hebrews. They were not Gentiles as it relates to the New Testament translations or even Strong's Concordance.
13. Gentiles are not non-Jews. They are non-believers (and can include Jews).
14. The interpreters of the Bible have used words in a way that leads people in their thinking.
15. The Jews had several ethnic distinctions in the New Testament Bible. This is not anti- Semitic.
16. When we study the Bible we must look at who is speaking. At times we are reading commentary. It is not the word of YeHoVaH. It is commentary.
17. If we are trying to do YeHoVaH's will within our own strength, we will become burned out.
18. The one hundred and twenty that were filled with the Holy Spirit on Shavuot and who began to speak in tongues were speaking to people who were hearing them in their native tongues. They were not all speaking Hebrew. Those listening were from different countries.
19. The modern church has separated the pilgrimage feast from the rest of the Torah. They say that the –church was born on the day of Pentecost.
20. Gentiles were not in Jerusalem for the Feast Pentecost. The Gentiles that were there were proselytes from Rome who had converted to the religion of Judaism.
21. From *Genesis* to *Revelation*, Israel is divided into twelve tribes, not one.
22. The ephod that the high priest wears have twelve stones which represent twelve tribes.
23. The people who control the land of Israel today are those who are in Judaism and who call themselves Jews. They control all the land given to the twelve tribes (not just Judah). They have effectively hijacked the land and taken what belongs to YeHoVaH as their own.
24. YeHoVaH chose Israel to be a special people to himself above all of the people of the earth.
25. We who are believers live in two kingdoms: the kingdom of this world and the Kingdom of YeHoVaH.

Review Exercise

1. Most people in Latin countries self-identify by nationality. It is primarily in the United States that we are asked our –race as an ethnic identification. Oddly enough, we are the nation with probably the most urgent problems in the area of ethnicity and diversity. Why do you think that is and how exactly does that mesh with the perception of the U.S. as a –melting pot (or maybe –salad bowl)? How might –the church has influenced the perception and the reality?

   _____
   _____
   _____
   _____
   _____
   _____
   _____
   _____

2. Again, we see the interplay of biblical interpretation and replacement theology. We all need to be confident in our capacity to walk the fine line of correct interpretation without being accused of anti-Semitism. Can you explain in 100 words or fewer, how it is that Israel was chosen by YeHoVaH and how that doesn't necessarily mean –the Jews only?

   _____
   _____
   _____
   _____
   _____
   _____

3. Israel was chosen for three purposes. They are:

   a Chosen to _____

   b Chosen to _____

   c Chosen to _____

4. The Hebrew word *bachar* (ba-khar) is the word for –chosen. According to Gesenius' Lexicon, it means –to prove, to try, to examine, to approve, to appoint. How does this view of the word –chosen compare with your perceptions around the word –chosen? How does this change the whole –chosen people idea for you, if at all?

   _____
   _____
   _____
   _____
   _____
   _____

Rate the following statements
by filling in the most appropriate number.

(1 = I do not agree   10 = I agree completely)

Objectives:

1. I can define a deeper understanding of the ethnic division principle introduced in Lesson 59.

   1. ◯   2. ◯   3. ◯   4. ◯   5. ◯   6. ◯   7. ◯   8. ◯   9. ◯   10. ◯

2. I can explain the New Testament understanding of ethnicity.

   1. ◯   2. ◯   3. ◯   4. ◯   5. ◯   6. ◯   7. ◯   8. ◯   9. ◯   10. ◯

3. I can clarify why YeHoVaH chose Israel and for what.

   1. ◯   2. ◯   3. ◯   4. ◯   5. ◯   6. ◯   7. ◯   8. ◯   9. ◯   10. ◯

My Journal
What I learned from this class:

_____
_____
_____
_____
_____
_____
_____
_____
_____
_____
_____
_____
_____
_____
_____
_____
_____

Discipleship Training Class 61

Ethnic Division Principle (part 3)

Objectives:

As a Discipleship student, at the end of this class you will be able to:

- Distinguish the called-out ones as an ethnic division
- Interpret the scope of being "called" as a work of responsibility; an appointment
- Define the dangers of cultural mysticism as being applied to scripture

One of the biggest challenges we have today in searching and studying the scriptures are the letters that Paul wrote and how these letters are interpreted. These letters are interpreted by different people. Often it is from a Western perspective without understanding the Hebrew culture and the culture in which Paul was writing. They are also typically interpreted without understanding Paul's knowledge of the Torah. We have to have some knowledge and understanding of the mindset of Paul and know where Paul was coming from in order to understand his writings today.

Those who have divorced themselves from the Torah and from the Old Testament and those who are focused solely upon the New Testament are not going to glean. They will not grasp a lot of what Paul was talking about. Even in Paul's day, Peter wrote that many people misunderstand the letters of Paul and his writings. Therefore, they have a tendency to misinterpret the scriptures. They malign them. They do not come away with the right understanding. If you do not have the right understanding, you certainly can't apply the truth that sets you free. Therefore, you will be in bondage.

Paul's letters were actually able to summarize the spiritual condition of the Gentile population (the *gowy*, of his day). He wrote that:

(Ephesians 4:18) *"...having their understanding darkened, being alienated from the life of YeHoVaH through the ignorance that is in them, because of the blindness of their heart."*

Why? Only the Hebrew people had access to the Torah. The life of YeHoVaH was from the Torah and the prophets and the *Psalms*. Those who were not reading the Torah, those who were not reading the prophets and those who were not reading the *Psalms* didn't understand the life of YeHoVaH.

It is the same today. Yeshua didn't come with something new. Yeshua came to show us how to apply the words of YeHoVaH. He was the word. The living word took on human flesh. Those who were without the Torah, without the prophets and without the *Psalms* were alienated from the life of YeHoVaH. Their understanding was darkened through their ignorance.

It is the same with the Gentile Church. Those who reject the Torah are still darkened in their understanding.

Read *Romans 1:18-32*. I want you to actually read it. You need to go back to verse 16 because the words "the Jew" here are talking about the Judean. Why? Because Yeshua was a Judean. Yeshua was of the tribe of Judah. Yeshua came to his own. Who? It was not the Israelites. He came to seek and to save the lost sheep of Israel, but that included them all. His own were Judea, Judah, the tribe of Judah.

Judah and those who were of Judah is where the term "Jew" came from (Yehudah). Those were the ones who were literally running things in the temple in the days of Yeshua. The Pharisees, the Sadducees in Judah were there in Jerusalem, in the land of Judah. (That is where Jerusalem was, where the temple was, where the religious center of Hebraic life was.) Yeshua was from the tribe of Judah.

(Romans 1:17) "For therein is the righteousness of YeHoVaH revealed from faith to faith: as it is written, The just shall live by faith."

Now, "the just shall live by faith." We see this in the prophets. Paul here is quoting the prophet, "as it is written." He is not quoting his writing. He is quoting what has been written.

Read *Romans 1:18-23*. This is what was happening to the nations around Israel. YeHoVaH had clearly told the children of Israel that they were not to make graven images. They were not to make images, call those images "God" and then bow down to those images.

All mankind has this innate desire to worship, to look to something. The world may call it a higher power. Some call it our better angels. There is terminology that people in the world use today. They talk about "spirituality" because people want to be connected to the realm of the Spirit, whether they know that realm or not.

I was listening to politicians. There are those out there who consider the Holy Spirit a "she." They consider God a "she." They want to put gender to it. They want equality. They want all of the things that are associated with male/female gender incorporated into the "Creator of the universe." So, you have this ideology that there is the desire to worship something greater than ourselves. This is part of mankind.

YeHoVaH says, "Listen, that desire is in you. Therefore, you need to know who you are supposed to worship and not worship that which you are not supposed to worship." This is what the world around was doing. YeHoVaH says, "You are not to worship me as the nations around you worship their gods." The nations that surrounded Israel were all engaged in worship; every one of them and they had images that they called their gods.

(Romans 1:24) "Wherefore God also gave them up to uncleanness through the lusts of their own hearts, to dishonour their own bodies between themselves:"

This is still going on today. You have people today who are in churches and who believe that YeHoVaH does not have an issue with men marrying men and women marrying women. Because YeHoVaH does not strike them down dead, they think that it is okay.

The whole movement is this. If the Church of God is the image and the presence of God on the earth and those who are the representatives of God are the clergy; if we want God to accept our way of life, then we have to force this way of life upon the church and upon God's representation on the earth. We have to force them to accept it. Therefore, we need to make sure that the clergy (God's representatives, spokesman, mouthpieces) sanction what we do. And if the church and the clergy sanctions what we do, then it "has" to be acceptable by God.

They are forcing this lifestyle. So, when the church and the President of the United States sanctions this and when the states sanction this and the churches begin to sanction homosexuality and lesbianism and transgender lifestyles and accept these clergy, pastors, elders and bishops; then this is "God's house" and "God's spokesmen." So, if they accept it, "God" accepts it.

God says, "Well, you know, NOT TRUE! These people who call themselves my representatives are hirelings. They do not represent me. They are telling you what you want to hear. They are going to have to pay the same price that you all pay for your unrighteousness."

Elohim gave them up to uncleanness through the lusts of their own hearts.

(Romans 1:25) *"Who changed the truth of God into a lie, and worshipped and served the creature more than the Creator, who is blessed for ever. Amen."*

They have taken the truth. They have turned it into a lie and they are saying, "That is not what God really meant when he said that."

(Romans 1:26-27) *"For this cause God gave them up unto vile affections: for even their women did change the natural use into that which is against nature: And likewise, also the men, leaving the natural use of the woman, burned in their lust one toward another; men with men working that which is unseemly, and receiving in themselves that recompense of their error which was meet (fit)."*

You have men sleeping with men. There is no way that is productive. You have women sleeping with women and there is not a way they can be productive. Now they have to change the whole adoption process and therefore develop what we know today by television vernacular as a "modern family."

Now you have moms dressing up their boys as "princess boys." They are dressing up their girls as little boys. You have all kinds of pedophilia going on. You have all manner of corruption taking place. There are just abominations on top of abominations in these whorehouses called "churches" and in some of these Messianic communities as well.

(Romans 1:28) *"And even as they did not like to retain God in their knowledge, God gave them over to a reprobate mind, to do those things which are not convenient (fit)."*

When a person's mind is reprobate, they actually are given the ability to enjoy their ungodly lifestyle while they are living because they are going to pay the price when they die or when they face the judgment.

(Romans 1:29-32) *"Being filled with all unrighteousness, fornication, wickedness, covetousness, maliciousness; full of envy, murder, debate, deceit, malignity; whisperers, backbiters, haters of God, despiteful, proud, boasters, inventors of evil things, disobedient to parents, Without understanding, covenant breakers, without natural affection, implacable, unmerciful: Who knowing the judgment of God, that they which commit such things are worthy of death, not only do the same, but have pleasure in them that do them."*

In the churches you have a Christian culture that is so similar to the world's culture. Christianity is a state religion. It really is. It doesn't mean that it is sanctioned by YeHoVaH, but it is certainly sanctioned by the state. It is sanctioned by the federal government. Those on Capitol Hill — they go to church. These ministers and these people are living these lifestyles. They know that YeHoVaH is going to deal with them, but if they can get the church to accept this behavior, then obviously it is "okay" with the Almighty.

Now folks want to be "tolerant." They have to be tolerant to the lifestyles of people. So, as you can see, that is that culture.

When it comes down to the salvation of Gentiles, the writers of the Old Testament scriptures were concerned primarily with the chosen nation. They only dealt with the Gentile nations as they related to it. Keep your Bible close now and put it into fifth gear. We are getting into high speed.

*(**Deuteronomy 32:8**) "When the Most High divided to the nations their inheritance, when he separated the sons of Adam, he set the bounds of the people according to the number of the children of Israel."*

From the very beginning you have to remember that YeHoVaH chose the Hebrew nation, Israel, to give the oracles to. Israel's responsibility was to share them with all of the nations. Why? <u>Because all of the nations belong to YeHoVaH</u>. The earth is his, the fullness thereof, they and all that dwell therein.

*(**Acts 17:18-26**) "Then certain philosophers of the Epicureans, and of the Stoicks, encountered him (Paul). And some said, ,,What will this babbler say?" other some, He seemeth to be a setter forth of strange gods: because he preached unto them Jesus, and the resurrection. And they took him, and brought him unto Areopagus, saying, ,,May we know what this new doctrine, whereof thou speakest, is? For thou bringest certain strange things to our ears: we would know therefore what these things mean." (For all the Athenians and strangers which were there spent their time in nothing else, but either to tell, or to hear some new thing.) Then Paul stood in the midst of Mars" Hill, and said, ,,Ye men of Athens, I perceive that in all things ye are too superstitious. For as I passed by, and beheld your devotions, I found an altar with this inscription, TO THE UNKNOWN GOD. Whom therefore ye ignorantly worship, him declare I unto you. God that made the world and all things therein, seeing that he is Lord of heaven and earth, dwelleth not in temples made with hands; Neither is worshipped with men's hands, as though he needed any thing, seeing he giveth to all life, and breath, and all things; And hath made of one blood all nations of men for to dwell on all the face of the earth, and hath determined the times before appointed, and the bounds of their habitation;""*

Some Bibles say "demons" in verse 18 for the "gods." If you were to do a word study there, the word is "strange demons." It is not the word "Elohim," but instead *daimonion* or demons. These individuals knew that they were worshipping demons. And now here comes somebody who is a setter forth of a "strange demon" we haven't heard of.

There are people out there who worship spirits. There are spiritists, devil worshippers and individuals who do séances. They know that they are communing with demons and they have no issue with it.

*(**Acts 17:19-20**) "And they took him, and brought him unto Areopagus, saying, ,,May we know what this new doctrine, whereof thou speakest, is? For thou bringest certain strange things to our ears: we would know therefore what these things mean.""*

In other words, "We want to know what you are talking about."

*(**Acts 17:21**) "(For all the Athenians and strangers which were there spent their time in nothing else, but either to tell, or to hear some new thing.)"*

This is the way that the Western society, the European society, is more of a Greek mindset. A Western Gentile mentality is more of a Greek mindset and a famous newspaper, a tabloid, is as well because "inquiring minds want to know." You have people who want to know. They just want to know.

These individuals had this inquisitive mindset just like people today are very inquisitive.

(Acts 17:22-23) "Then Paul stood in the midst of Mars" hill, and said, ,, Ye men of Athens, I perceive that in all things ye are too superstitious. For as I passed by, and beheld your devotions, I found an altar with this inscription, TO THE UNKNOWN GOD. Whom therefore ye ignorantly worship, him declare I unto you.""

What we see here is that in this environment you have people who were worshipping but they just did not know who they worshipped. The Samaritans worshipped, but as Yeshua said, they did not know who they worshipped. The churches worship, but in many senses they do not know who they worship and that is unfortunate.

*(Acts 1:24-26) "God that made the world and all things therein, seeing that he is Lord of heaven and earth, dwelleth not in temples made with hands; Neither is worshipped with men's hands, as though he needed any thing, seeing he giveth to all life, and breath, and all things; And **hath made of one blood all nations of men** for to dwell on all the face of the earth, and hath determined the times before appointed, and the bounds of their habitation;"*

Notice that he has made them <u>of one blood</u>. Your blood and my blood are no different. You may have a different type because of your parents, but it is all blood that flowed through Adam. Every person born — your blood is the same blood, just a different type because of the differences of the ethnicities that have intermarried over the centuries of man's existence on the planet.

But all of us come from Noah by way of Adam. All of us, the human family are all brothers and sisters in the human realm. That is tough. I know that there is dark skin, light skin, Whites and Blacks. There is coarse hair, fine hair and all types of different pigmentations, but the bottom line is this about every last one of them. You can get on *ancestry.com*, but if you go back far enough, we all go back to Adam. You can be proud of whatever culture or whatever ethnicity you want, but we all go back to one man — Adam.

YeHoVaH determined (according to verse 26) where people would stay and where they would live. He knew the end from the beginning. The whole purpose of this whole ethnic division principle is first to help us to understand that YeHoVaH separated mankind. He confounded the language, but men began to give themselves titles and names. They began to determine, based on the region in which they lived, what they called themselves or what others called them.

The scriptures also plainly declare that YeHoVaH is no respecter of persons. *(Acts 10:34-35)* As already noted, Israel was chosen as a nation to eventually bless all other nations. The following scriptures attest to this:

- *All nations were to be blessed through the seed of Abraham.* **(Genesis 22:18)**

- *All families of the earth to be blessed* **(Genesis 26:4)**

- *All kindred of the nations to worship God* **(Psalm 22:27-28)**

*(Psalm 22:27-28) "All the ends of the world shall remember and turn unto YeHoVaH: and all the kindreds of the nations shall worship before thee. For the kingdom is the LORD"s: and he is **the governor among the nations**."*

He is the Governor among Iraq, Iran, North Korea, South Korea, Russia, Germany, Israel, America, and Australia. It doesn't matter where you come from. You belong to YeHoVaH whether you admit it, acknowledge it or not.

You are his property although you may not have come into covenant with him through the blood of Yeshua. Those who do not come into covenant with him are going to have hell to pay.

- *All nations to flow to the House of YeHoVaH (**Isaiah 2:2-3**)*

I am really setting you up because the scripture sets us up. When we look at it, we see:

*(**Isaiah 2:2-3**) "And it shall come to pass in the last days, that the mountain of YeHoVaH's house shall be established in the top of the mountains, and shall be exalted above the hills; and **all nations shall flow unto it**. And many people shall go and say, „Come ye, and let us go up to the mountain of YeHoVaH, to the house of the God of Jacob; and he will teach us of his ways, and we will walk in his paths: for out of Zion shall go forth the law, and the word of YeHoVaH from Jerusalem.""*

We see this taking place in the book of *Revelation*. We see the end of *Isaiah* and *Zechariah*. Every nation on the planet is going to have to go up to Jerusalem. It doesn't matter whether you are a Jew, Gentile, Israelite, Hebrew, alien, stranger or foreigner. It doesn't matter what your religion is today. In the end there is only going to be one — as it was in the beginning.

Gentiles will seek the root of Jesse.

*(**Isaiah 11:10**) "And in that day there shall be a root of Jesse, which shall stand for an ensign of the people; **to it shall the Gentiles seek**: and his rest shall be glorious."*

This is YeHoVaH's doing. All of this was prophesied.

Messiah will sprinkle many nations with blood.

*(**Isaiah 52:15**) "So shall he sprinkle many nations; the kings shall shut their mouths at him: for that which had not been told them shall they see; and that which they had not heard shall they consider."*

What we see is that we can exalt a nation and try to be like a people. It is amazing that in the Messianic community you have followers of Yeshua who are trying to imitate individuals who do not follow Yeshua.

I want to share an email with you that I got out of nowhere. It was entitled "Discipleship classes and mysticism."

"I want to thank you Arthur, for making your Discipleship teachings available online. I discovered your teachings just a couple of weeks ago and I've gone through the first seven so far. I am hooked. In part 7 you mention about the Talmud and mysticism. I agree with you 100%. Then just now I was looking at a web site that has Jewish vocabulary software, etc."

This is one of the traps. When I talk about religious traps, I get some scathing emails. Some people are totally upset with me because I put that. They call it "garbage." They talk about my $10 tallit that I got from China (it came from Israel). They are just angry and that is okay. I understand. But oftentimes when people begin to learn Hebrew, they find themselves in places learning Hebrew. As the saying goes, "You can't go into a smoky room and not come out smelling like smoke." When you go into certain places, you pick up stuff that you are not even trying to pick up.

You have people who are learning Hebrew in places. They are learning words and do not even know that by the very environment that this learning is taking place in, that they are picking up spirits.

The email continues:

*"I was on a site looking and came across the following e-book, „The Mystic Jewish Secrets of the Occult."" *

The writer quotes from the book blurb:

"„This is a most fascinating book – it is based on the Talmud and introduces you to many secrets of the occult. Rabbi Bisker guides us through a world that we can't see, yet we know it is there. The Rabbi peels back layers [of] darkness and gives us a glimpse of these powerful forces. The reader will be mesmerized by the mystical insight from a Talmudic perspective. This book could be a life changer!""

There are those four layers of Torah again.

So now the person is looking for Hebrew and finding themselves in the occult. There is that inquisitive mindset.

I did something and I know how this works, because I am just as guilty of it. When I first came into this movement, I bought books on Kabbalah. I bought books on mysticism. I bought books on the Jewish perspective of the Garden of Eden. I've got two boxes of Jewish books at home. I think when people come into the Hebrew Roots and the Messianic community, by default they sometimes kind of go over into Judaism.

This is one of the reasons why I made *The Religious Traps* teaching. This is one of the reasons why I teach the way I do. I avoid the Rabbis. These individuals out there who want to quote the Rabbis. They have inquisitive minds. If a Messianic Hebrew teacher is teaching out of the Talmud, his listeners are going to want to know. "Okay, where is that at?" It is in the Talmud. Well, how are you going to find that? You are going to end up in the Talmud.

If you are quoting from mysticism, you are quoting from some author. The moment you mention the name of that author, you have people "Googling." We have to avoid that. This is one of those times where just by reading and sharing that email, I would not be surprised if there are people "Googling" the name that I just mentioned.

You have to be careful. You are free to go wherever you go, but just know something. You can't go into a smoky room and come out not smelling like smoke. You can't go into a place and not be infected or affected or influenced by the place that you have gone. I know you are smart. I know you are not easily influenced, but you are either being influenced or you are influencing. There is no in between.

The same way that Moses put the blood of the covenant on the people, Yeshua's blood is going to be the blood that gives access to every nation who seeks YeHoVaH.

- *Many nations will be joined to YeHoVaH in that day* (**Zechariah 2:11**)

- *The name of YeHoVaH to be great among the Gentiles.* (**Malachi 1:11**)

The reason why the church today is in the condition that it is in is because it has been given a skewed, Western gospel. Now, I believe that there are those in the churches, in the congregations and in the denominations that are going to hear the truth. But there are thousands, hundreds of thousands or millions of people who are not satisfied with the stuff they are hearing. They know that something is wrong with it. They just don't know what.

When the true gospel of the Kingdom hits their ears, they are going to perk up. They are going to know that there is something different. Just like when Yeshua came, the people were very familiar with the Rabbis, with the Sadducees and the Pharisees of their day (the religious leaders). But when Yeshua came with the true gospel, they knew there was something different. There is an authority that He spoke with. The words that He spoke are resonating with the Spirit.

You see, the words that Yeshua spoke were Spirit. These words are Spirit. The Spirit and the life of YeHoVaH is in the Torah. It is in the prophets. And if we do not have that access, if you are a New Testament believer and have rejected the law, the life of YeHoVaH can't flow. It won't flow. Blinders will be on. Just as the religious leaders in the days of Yeshua put the blinders on the people of their day, the religious leaders of our day are putting blinders on people today. People are trusting the religious leaders more than they trust what they read with their own eyes.

But they know that something is wrong, just like how we knew something was wrong but we didn't know what was wrong until we heard the truth. As long as you have hundreds of thousands of ministers out there preaching about Jesus Christ (the death, burial and resurrection of Jesus Christ) and "give your life to Jesus and send us your money"; as long as that is out there and no other voice, we literally are like the voice crying out in the wilderness. That is what we are. We are John the Immerser, Yohanan the Immerser of our day saying, "Prepare the way for YeHoVaH!"

We have to get out there. The people have to hear us. It is not enough for us alone.

(Malachi 1:11) "For from the rising of the sun even unto the going down of the same my name shall be great among the Gentiles; and in every place incense shall be offered unto my name, and a pure offering: for my name shall be great among the heathen, saith the LORD of hosts."

(You probably do not get to *Malachi* much unless it is offering time, but this is not an offering.)

Gentiles will trust in YeHoVaH's name.

(Matthew 12:21) "And in his name shall the Gentiles trust."

The great commission involves taking the gospel of Messiah to every creature, making disciples of all nations. *(Matthew 18:19; Mark 16:17; Luke 24:47; Acts 1:8)* These are the commissions. When we talk about the Ethnic Division principle, we look at two different classes of people so far.

The books of *Acts* shows that YeHoVaH is opening the door to the Gentile nations in order to take out of them, a people for his name. *(Acts 9:15; 13:44-49; 14:1-2; 15:14-18; 28:23-31)*

YeHoVaH did this to provoke Israel to jealousy. *(Romans 10:19, 11:11, 14)* Let's look at these:

(Romans 10:19) "But I say, Did not Israel know? First Moses saith, „I will provoke you to jealousy by them that are no people, and by a foolish nation I will anger you.""

(Romans 11:11, 14) *"I say then, Have they stumbled that they should fall? God forbid: but rather through their fall salvation is come unto the Gentiles, for to provoke them to jealousy…If by any means I may provoke to emulation them which are my flesh, and might save some of them."*

I do not understand this idea. When I first came into the Messianic community, it was like, okay, we want to look Jewish. Wait a minute, why do you want to look Jewish? Why are Gentiles trying to look Jewish, to provoke the Jewish people to jealousy?

No. You are looking more Jewish than they do.

The Jewish people are saying, "These people are trying to be Jews? They are trying to be like us? How is that going to provoke us?" It doesn't work that way. Be YOU. I remember when folks found out. Folks think that if I say that I am Jewish, I must be from Ethiopia. Why? Because I am Black.

The idea that I am trying to be anything but me — I am not from Ethiopia. I am not a Jew. "Then why are you keeping the commands?" "I am keeping the commands." "But aren't you a Christian? Don't you celebrate Easter?"

That always gets them. This Hasidic Jew asked me, "Don't you celebrate Easter?" He was hoping I'd say yes. "What about Christmas?" Now he is scratching his head. You are not Ethiopian. You are wearing tzitzits. You do not celebrate Easter or Christmas.

I can imagine that became conversation back in his group. "I met this Black guy and…" Yeah.

We looked at the Hebrew nation and the Gentile nations. There is a third group.

The Called-Out Ones

This third group consists of both Hebrews and non-Hebrews. The third group mentioned by Paul in *1 Corinthians 10:32* is *"the church/ekklesia/the ekklesia of God"* — the "called out ones." The word "church/ekklesia" is a translation of the Greek word *ekklesia*, which is made up of two other words:

"ek" meaning "out of"

"kaleo" which means "to call."

Thus, the word *ekklesia* literally means "the called-out ones." It is used in scripture to refer to the nation of Israel and to the Messianic community of believers (whether in heaven or on earth).

Israel — the church/ekklesia in the wilderness:

(Acts 7:38) *"This is he, that was in the church (ekklesia) in the wilderness with the angel which spake to him in the mount Sinai, and with our fathers: who received the lively oracles to give unto us:"*

When I point this out to my Christian friends, they think that the church, the called-out ones, started in *Acts 2* on the day of Pentecost. Israel was considered, according to the same writing of the book of *Acts*, as the called-out ones. We see that it is the called-out ones in the wilderness, the church in the wilderness with the angel who received the "lively oracles to give unto us." Compare:

(Hebrews 12:22-23) *"But ye are come unto mount Sion, and unto the city of the living God, the heavenly Jerusalem, and to an innumerable company of angels, To the general assembly and church of the firstborn, which are written in heaven, and to God the Judge of all, and to the spirits of just men made perfect,"*

There are no saints in heaven. I know people want to think their Mom and their Dad and everybody passed is there, but they are not there yet. They are written. How are they written? In the Lamb's Book of Life. They are written in the Book. The day will come when the dead in Messiah will rise first. Those who are dead in Messiah are still in hell (the grave). **There are saints in hell? Absolutely. It is the grave. Hell is the grave.**

(Hebrews 12:24) *"And to Jesus the mediator of the new covenant, and to the blood of sprinkling, that speaketh better things than that of Abel."*

Saints on Earth

(Revelation 1:11) *"Saying, I am Alpha and Omega, the first and the last: and, What thou seest, write in a book, and send it unto the seven churches/ekklesia, (pl.) ekklesiaes which are in Asia; unto Ephesus, and unto Smyrna, and unto Pergamos, and unto Thyatira, and unto Sardis, and unto Philadelphia, and unto Laodicea."*

In these three, the word "church" or *ekklesia* is used in its two basic senses: universal and local. We understand the universal church/ekklesia to include the redeemed of all ages — both which are written in heaven and the local church/ekklesia to be a visible expression of it.

I want to drill in your mind to stop using the word "church." The word "church" is a translation. It takes away from the idea of the called-out ones. It is not a building. People call the building "the church," not the people. The literal word refers to the people, not brick and mortar or wood.

I remember when I was in the church the people said,

"Well, where's your church at?"

I would say,

"You are looking at it. I am the church. I am not the whole body of Messiah, but I am a member and wherever I am, church is."

Why? It is because I am a called out one. That is who you are.

I had to reeducate my children. We are not a church. We are called out ones. When we understand that, now we can apply the right definition of who we are. They were first called "Christians" at Antioch. Who called them Christians? They weren't called "Christians." They were called "Messianics" or "Messiahans" at Antioch.

Who called them that? The Antiochans (an-TIE-uh-kinz). This is the thing. People will give you a title. They will put you in a box if you let them.

"What denomination are you?"

"What church do you attend?"

They are asking these questions and we play right into it.

"I am (this)" or "I am (that)."

Isn't being called "Messianic" putting yourself in a box too? Most people say, "What's that?"

The average person in the church today doesn't even know what a Messianic is. The thing most church people know is the Messianic prophecy found in *Genesis*: *"the serpent will bruise his heel and he will crush his head."* That's the first Messianic prophecy. That is as far and as much about "Messianic" as most people in church know.

We talk about assembly, *kehilah*, gathering, congregation, called out ones. The place where the called-out ones assemble is an assembly. We assemble together. That is what we do. We come together as a body of Mashiach in a local setting, but we have brothers and sisters all around the globe.

Calling of the Church/Ekklesia

YeHoVaH has always had a people for himself; a company of called out ones. Being a "called out one" involves:

• *Being called out of darkness into light (**1 Peter 2:9**)*

When you look at the Hebrew culture, the Israeli culture today is as close as people can get to a Hebrew culture, but that is really not so. The Bible is the closest you can get. You can begin to imagine. In Israel, unless you get out of the cities and the towns; Israel is a tourist trap (for the most part). You have to get out where the nomadic people are. You get outside of the places where cars and buses and hotels are. You get out to where people are riding on donkeys and herding sheep and goats and searching for water and living in tents. That is the nomadic culture.

What is interesting is that when I went to Kenya several years ago, I experienced the presence of YeHoVaH like I had never experienced it in my life. I have been to Israel. I have experienced a greater presence of YeHoVaH on the Nile River in Egypt than I did in the land of Israel.

What I experienced in the land of Israel was from a religious perspective. I experienced the awe of church people being in what is called "The Holy Land" and being able to get baptized in the Jordan River. There is this awe of being in the places where Jesus walked. Of course, we know of the road that Constantine's Mama laid out, the Via Dolorosa as it is called by many. These sites that they say where all of these places are, are for tourists. The church (the Greek Orthodox, Catholics) has put its mark upon a lot of these things. The mark of religion is all over the place.

Here I am angry because I am experiencing God's presence in Egypt and I do not experience his presence in Israel. I go to Kenya out in the bush, for real. We are about 25-30 miles from any running water. I am talking about where people search for days looking for water. There are poisonous snakes and frogs. The moon at night you could see just as clearly as if it were in the daytime. The worship of these people was so awesome that it put my little Western worship mindset to shame.

Here we are going out to preach to them, but these nomadic people had such a connection with heaven that I literally got jealous out there. I wanted to bottle that up and take it home. I went to take pictures and my camera stopped. I distinctly heard the voice of YeHoVaH saying, "This is mine. No, you are not going to market this. You are not going to take these pictures home and put them in your newsletter." He allowed me to see it, but he would not allow me to take it with me. The only images that I have are the ones that are in my head.

But it is the most awesome experience and encounter with the Almighty I have ever had in my life, there in the deserts of Kenya. I have come to find that those nomadic people believed that they were direct descendants of Israel. That is what they told me.

Interestingly enough, the people in Kenya, the Kukuyu (one of the tribes) have had three presidents in Kenya. Two of them are Kukuyu. The Kukuyu people believe that they are Israel. They are Israelites. And again, those nomadic people out there are awesome.

Peter tells us that the more we lose and get away from the land and working with our hands, the farther we get from the Almighty. Now, I am not one who is going to run to the mountains or to the hills to build myself a bunker, but I do believe that YeHoVaH's people should have some land, that we should raise animals and that we should raise our own food.

I believe that that is something that every last one of us needs to think about because the closer we are to the land it seems, the closer we are to the Almighty and the more we begin to understand the Almighty. I am not talking about buying flowers that have been raised on some farm for the purpose of cutting and selling in a florist shop. I am talking about the beauty of seeing nature and walking in it and living in it and working the land. I am talking about seeing the beauty of his creation without the hustle and bustle of airplanes and jets and the buzz going through electric cables over and under us. There is television and cell phones and all of the stuff that has caused us to be so disconnected from the Spirit realm.

We are called out of darkness into light.

*(**1 Peter 2:9**) "But ye are a chosen generation, a royal priesthood, an holy nation, a peculiar people; that ye should shew forth the praises of him who hath called you out of darkness into his marvelous light;"*

This is one of those verses of scripture that the believers should know. You should know who you are. **Every believer in Messiah, you are a chosen generation. You are royalty. You are a royal priesthood. You are a holy nation, a holy people, a *segulah*, a peculiar, special people.**

It doesn't mean "short bus" special. That is not what I am saying. I am talking about special as in the apple of YeHoVaH's eye. Isn't Israel the apple of his eye? Absolutely. Those who come into Messiah come into Israel.

Now, we are going to look at some scriptures, like Paul said. All who call themselves Israel aren't Israel.[8] There are people who call themselves Israel, but they are not. There are people who call themselves Jews, but they are not.

As people of Israel (whether born into or grafted in) — and when I say, "born into," I am really talking about born again into. That is really the only way you get into this Israel. I am not talking about some spiritual Israel, although we come in by the Spirit.

---

[8] *(**Romans 9:6**) "Not as though the word of God hath taken none effect. For they are not all Israel, which are of Israel:"*

This light is the light of the word. We do not hide. We are the light of the world. Why? It is because we have the light of the word. We have the true gospel. This is the gospel that lightens the mind and the heart of man. He has called us out of darkness. He has removed the veil of darkness from us. Now we have the mind of Messiah and we should operate in that.

Again, what does it mean to be a called out one? It means being called to a calling. In the King James it uses the word "vocation," but you will see:

*(**Ephesians 4:1**)* *"I therefore, the prisoner of the Lord, beseech you that ye walk worthy of the vocation wherewith ye are called,"*

You arc to walk worthy of the calling to which you are called. Every person has been called and given a calling. Now it is a matter of identifying what that calling is.

*(**Ephesians 4:4**)* *"There is one body, and one Spirit, even as ye are called in one hope of your calling;"*

Every one of you has a calling. This calling is a calling of hope. We bring hope to a hopeless generation. In Michigan, our mission for *Abundant Life Ministries* and *Abundant Life International Ministry* was bringing hope to our community and its families, one person at a time. We are the proclaimers of hope. We declare hope and we live among a people who seem and who feel hopeless.

- *This calling we have is holy. (**2 Timothy 1:9**)*

We have been called with a holy calling.

*(**2 Timothy 1:9**)* *"Who hath saved us, and called us with an holy calling, not according to our works, but according to his own purpose and grace, which was given us in Christ Jesus before the world began,"*

This is the called-out ones. This is a people. We are the called-out ones of Jews, Gentiles, Hebrews, Israel — *gowy*. We are a mixed breed, but we are all family.

Notice: *"...before the world began."* Your calling was given before you were even born. Unfortunately, we are closer to our calling as children. The longer we live, the farther it seems we get away from that calling and from hearing his voice. Yeshua says that in some situations, *"except you be like little children."* I remember when I was around ten or eleven years old. My calling was much clearer to me than it was when I was twenty-five. I've now had to go backwards, if you would, back to when I was a child. I remember that calling. Now Father is saying, "Yeah, I called you way back then."

Many of us have been called "way back then," but life and circumstances and all kinds of other things have a tendency to choke the calling out of us.

Being called to a high calling:

*(**Philippians 3:14**)* *"I press toward the mark for the prize of the high calling of God in Christ Jesus."*

This is a high calling.

Being called to a heavenly calling:

(Hebrews 3:1-2) *"Wherefore, holy brethren, partakers of the heavenly calling, consider the Apostle and High Priest of our profession, Christ Jesus, Who was faithful to him that appointed him, as also Moses was faithful in all his house."*

We have been called to a heavenly calling.

Being called unto eternal glory by Messiah Yeshua:

(1 Peter 5:10) *"But the God of all grace, who hath called us unto his eternal glory by Christ Jesus, after that ye have suffered a while, make you perfect, stablish, strengthen, settle you."*

Your perfection is going to come through your suffering. He is going to establish you and strengthen you by the things you suffer.

(Hebrews 5:7-8) *"Who in the days of his flesh, when he had offered up prayers and supplications with strong crying and tears unto him that was able to save him from death, and was heard in that he feared; Though he were a Son, yet learned he obedience by the things which he suffered;"*

Being called to his Kingdom and glory:

(1 Thessalonians 2:12) *"That ye would walk worthy of God, who hath called you unto his kingdom and glory."*

He has called us into his Kingdom and glory (or rather) he shared his glory with us. Yeshua said the glory that the Father gave him; he has now given to us.

Composition of the Ekklesia

The composition of the church/*ekklesia* as it is revealed in the New Testament is composed of both Israel and Gentiles. As God called Israel as a nation from the midst of the nations and constituted them as his ekklesia in the Old Testament, so God now calls people unto himself out of every nation, whether Israel or Gentile and constitutes them as his church/ekklesia in the New Testament.

The New Testament/Covenant church/ekklesia is revealed in the body of Messiah. It is composed of Hebrew and Gentiles. Messiah as the builder of his church/ekklesia:

(Matthew 16:18) *"And I say also unto thee, That thou art Peter, and upon this rock I will build my church; and the gates of hell shall not prevail against it."*

He adds to his church/ekklesia:

(Acts 2:47) *"Praising God, and having favour with all the people. And the Lord added to the church daily such as should be saved."*

Messiah is the head of the body — the church/ekklesia.

(Colossians 2:19) *"And not holding the head, from which all the body by joints and bands having nourishment ministered, and knit together, increaseth with the increase of God."*

The church/ekklesia is Messiah's body.

(Ephesians 1:22-23) *"And hath put all things under his feet, and gave him to be the head over all things to the church, Which is his body, the fulness of him that filleth all in all."*

Jew/Israel and Gentile are all baptized into one body.

(1 Corinthians 12:13-14) *"For by one Spirit are we all baptized into one body, whether we be Jews or Gentiles, whether we be bond or free; and have been all made to drink into one Spirit. For the body is not one member, but many."*

Jew/Israel and Gentile are one new man in Messiah.

(Ephesians 2:15-16) *"Having abolished in his flesh the enmity, even the law of commandments contained in ordinances; for to make in himself of twain one new man, so making peace; And that he might reconcile both unto God in one body by the cross, having slain the enmity thereby:"*

There is no distinction.

Jew/Israel and Gentile are fellow heirs in the same body.

(Ephesians 3:6) *"That the Gentiles should be fellow-heirs, and of the same body, and partakers of his promise in Christ by the gospel:"*

There is no first class and second class. There are no Jews and "others." We are not proselytes. We are not converts. We are part of his family.

Thus, the church/ekklesia, being the third major ethnic division, is a called-out company. It consists of Jew/Israel and Gentile, circumcision and uncircumcision, chosen nation and Gentile nation in one body of Messiah.

National divisions are determined by natural birth, but by spiritual birth all national distinctions cease to exist. For:

- *"There is neither Jew nor Greek, there is neither bond nor free, there is neither male or female: for ye are all one in Messiah Yeshua." (Galatians 3:28)*

- *"For in Messiah Yeshua neither circumcision avails anything, nor uncircumcision, but a new creature." (Galatians 6:15)*

Significance of the Church/Ekklesia

This church/ekklesia is taken out of every kindred, tongue, people and nation and now constitutes God's nation.

(Revelation 5:9) *"And they sung a new song, saying, „Thou art worthy to take the book, and to open the seals thereof: for thou wast slain, and hast redeemed us to God by thy blood out of every kindred, and tongue, and people, and nation;""*

Now we are one nation under YeHoVaH.[9]

---

[9] I am not talking about the United States. I know it is in the Constitution, but that is about as far as it goes.

Class 61 Study Summary
Key Points

1. One of the biggest challenges we have today in searching and studying the scriptures are the letters that Paul wrote and how those letters have been interpreted.
2. Paul's letters were able to summarize the spiritual condition of the Gentile population (gowy) of his day.
3. Only the Hebrew people had access to the Torah. The life of YeHoVaH was from the Torah and the prophets and *Psalms*. He is the living word. The living word took on human flesh. Yeshua didn't come with something new. He brought his Father's word and laws.
4. Those who reject the Torah today are still darkened in their understanding.
5. Judah and those who were of Judah is where the term "Jew" came from (Yehudah). They were the ones who were literally running the things in the temple in the days of Yeshua.
6. The just shall live by faith.
7. The people of the world use the term "spirituality." They want to be connected to the realm of the Spirit whether they know that realm or not.
8. YeHoVaH says that the desire to worship is within us. We need to know that which we are supposed to worship and not worship what we are not supposed to worship.
9. There are people in the world today who believe that YeHoVaH does not have an issue with men marrying men or women marrying women. They think that because a "church" allows this, that God allows it. But God says "NOT SO."
10. YeHoVaH calls those who say they represent him but who are teaching contrary to scripture "hirelings." He says they do not represent him and they tell people what they want to hear.
11. When a person's mind is reprobate, they are given the ability to enjoy their ungodly lifestyle.
12. The Christian culture in the church is similar to the world's culture. Christianity is a state religion. It is sanctioned not by YeHoVaH, but by the state.
13. From the very beginning YeHoVaH chose to give the oracles (commandments) to the Hebrew nation.
14. YeHoVaH has made all nations of men of one blood. We are all from the blood of Adam. We are all the same.
15. The book of *Revelation* reveals that every nation on the planet is going to have to go up to Jerusalem for the feast days.
16. Mysticism and the four levels of Torah are some of the traps that people can fall into when trying to walk as a Messianic. They are among many religious traps.
17. The words Yeshua spoke are Spirit. The Spirit and the life of YeHoVaH are in the Torah.
18. The called-out ones consist of both Hebrews and non-Hebrews. It is the *ekklesia*, which literally means "called out ones." This did not begin on the day of Pentecost. The word "church" is a translation. The *ekklesia* is not a building. It is a group of called out ones.
19. There are saints in hell. Hell is the grave. It is not the Lake of Fire.
20. We are called out of the darkness into the light. The word is the light of the world. We are to be that light.
21. We are to be worthy of the calling to which we are being called. Each person has a calling.
22. The ekklesia is taken from every kindred, tongue, people and nation to make God's nation.

Review Exercise

1. Summarize the ways in which Israel was to be a blessing to the nations (using the bullet points starting in this chapter).

2. Reconcile the "chosen" aspect of Israel with the "called out" nature of believers. You can use a Venn diagram below with overlapping circles to compare or contrast or simply a couple of paragraphs.

3. What potential for entrapment exists when the line between "Israel" and believers gets blurred by adopting "Jewish" culture?

4. What is your calling and how does it translate as an "appointment" (as in to an office or title) by YeHoVaH on your life? (If you are unsure of a specific calling of Yah upon you personally, think more broadly to your calling as a believer. What is every believer called to?)

Rate the following statements by filling in the most appropriate number.

(1 = I do not agree 10 = I agree completely)

Objectives:

1. I can distinguish the called-out ones as an ethnic division.

   1.○ 2.○ 3.○ 4.○ 5.○ 6.○ 7.○ 8.○ 9.○ 10.○

2. I can interpret the scope of being "called" as a work of responsibility, an appointment.

   1.○ 2.○ 3.○ 4.○ 5.○ 6.○ 7.○ 8.○ 9.○ 10.○

3. I can define the dangers of cultural mysticism as being applied to scripture.

   1.○ 2.○ 3.○ 4.○ 5.○ 6.○ 7.○ 8.○ 9.○ 10.○

My Journal

What I learned from this class:

_____
_____
_____
_____
_____
_____
_____
_____
_____
_____
_____
_____
_____
_____
_____
_____
_____

Discipleship Training Class 62

Ethnic Division Principle (part 4)

Objectives:

As a Discipleship student, at the end of this class you will be able to:

- Describe how to use the ethnic division principle in study
- Identify the various people referred to by the term "Israel"
- Explain how to determine to whom the pastoral and Pauline epistles were written

As we noted in the last lesson and really all the lessons dealing with the ethnic division principle, we see that there were three main divisions in reference to the ethnicity that the scriptures address. As we look at this principle, we have to understand. How do we use this principle when we are approaching the word? How do we apply the ethnic division principle when it comes down to interpreting what the Bible says and coming with an understanding from our study?

The ethnic principle is used to determine whether the verse or passage under consideration is relevant to any of the three main ethnic divisions. What are the three main ethnic divisions?

1. Israel
2. Gentiles
3. Ekklesia (called out ones, known as the church)

As noted in the first teaching on this principle (Lesson 59) and with the word *gowy*, there are certain places in the Tanakh where Israel is considered gowy as it relates to the word "nation." So as far as ethnicity, we have Israel, Gentiles and the called-out ones.

Using the Ethnic Division Principle

When using this principle, one may ask the following questions. It is so important when you approach the Bible that you ask questions. Who are you asking these questions to? You are approaching the Bible not from a position that you know everything.

If you go to the Bible and you do not ask questions — understand that when you get into this word, YeHoVaH and his word are one. "In the beginning was YeHoVaH." As we see in the book of *John* it says, "In the beginning was the word." It takes more of a reverse order. "In the beginning was the word and the word was with Elohim and the word was Elohim. And Elohim (the word) became flesh and dwelt among us and we beheld his glory as the glory of the only begotten full of grace and truth."

Yeshua is YeHoVaH/the word made flesh. When we look at this ethnic division principle, you are asking questions. The person you are directing these questions to is the Father. You are approaching his word, just like Yeshua's disciples approached Yeshua. They did not understand and you do not understand the Bible.

You may understand the traditional, religious denominational interpretation of the Bible, but Father has in this word, things that are hidden. The more your relationship goes deeper, the more he reveals himself through his word.

Here is where evolution makes any sense. It is the *only* place where evolution makes sense. We are constantly evolving. We are growing in spirit. Whether you started off last year, three years ago, five years ago or ten years ago; do you know that today, no matter what age you are in the natural, you are older than you were yesterday, last week, last month or last year? Now, I hope you know a little more today than you knew last week, last month, last year or ten years ago. So, we are constantly learning. The day we stop learning is the day it is time to leave. But we are constantly learning.

As we are walking with the Father, he is revealing himself to us more and more and more. Some of the things that we are discussing here today, last week, the week before last; some of you are hearing this stuff for the first time. With what we have been dealing with in these Discipleship classes, many of you have heard messages that were designed and developed from these principles. But you did not know it was those principles that were behind the messages. We are taking you behind the scenes and showing you how the messages are developed so that when you hear these messages, you will hear the principles.

When you go to the word, you will see the principles. You are learning how to apply the principles so that when you approach the word, you approach it as if you were sitting at the feet of Yeshua. You approach it as if you are sitting in the presence of the Almighty. And now you are talking to him. You are asking questions.

As you are looking at this Bible, the verse, the passage or the book, you have to ask yourself. Does this verse refer to the united nation of Israel? In other words, is this all Israel? **That is one question**.

In dealing with the ethnic division principle, you are looking at three main ethnic groups: Israel, the Gentile nations and the called-out ones. The called-out ones are a mixture of Israel and Gentiles.

The second question is, "Does this verse refer to the ten tribes of the House of Israel, the Northern Kingdom?

Third, does it refer to the two tribes of the House of Judah, the Southern Kingdom (Judah, Benjamin plus the Levites)? When you see Israel, you are going to see Israel in the Bible refer to multiple definitions. When you see "Israel," you have to know which Israel you are talking about. What Israel are you reading about?

Fourth, does it refer to the Gentile nations?

Fifth, does it refer to the ekklesia/called out ones chosen out of every nation (the church)?

In interpretation, extreme caution must be used in order to avoid confusing these ethnic divisions. That which is said of one division, must not be interpreted as referring to another.

CAUTION
Ethnic
Confusion
Area Ahead

It is important for you to understand this. The same is true of certain divisions within these main divisions. There is a lot of stuff behind this, but once you get the concepts, it becomes easy. It really does. And now when you are talking Bible, you are able to communicate Bible apart from traditional beliefs, knowledge and understanding. This is going to affect people who are on a traditional belief system. Their eyes will be rolling backward in their heads. You will now be able to articulate and show it to them right there in their Bible without having to argue with people.

I am going to lay some things out for you.

It becomes especially important when you are looking at the prophets. For those of you who have seen my books, you will note that anytime you are approaching the Bible, you have to have some rules. You have to understand the rules. Even in every Bible they give you some instructions on how to approach this book. Any Bible that has any value to it is going to give you instructions. But like most people, you skip the instructions and go straight to *Genesis* or straight to the back. **You have to read the instructions.**

When I put my book *Sunday is Not the Sabbath?* together I established six ground rules. These ground rules are what help people to understand (as you are looking at my book) what the rules are. They are right in chapter one. If you do not get the rules, you might look at a chapter to see what this babbler has to say about this particular subject and skip over the rules. You may skip the instructions and then enter into an argument. We do not want to do that.

A lot of the people you are dealing with have skipped the instructions. They have gone straight to an argument. They will challenge you and what you are trying to say. You have to take them back to the beginning. If you discern, you will see really quickly where they are coming from.

When you are looking at the prophets, you have to understand these ethnic divisions. Some of the prophets ministered distinctly to the House of Israel while others ministered to the House of Judah. However, even though the prophets were generally sent to one specific house, sometimes they prophesied concerning both houses.

Sometimes people look at the *Kings* and they think that the kings were over all of Israel. There were only three kings who were over the entire united nation of Israel: Saul, David and Solomon. Every king after Solomon that is mentioned in the Bible was either King of Judah or King of Israel. So, when a king pronounced something, they were speaking to a particular people because they had no jurisdiction over the other nations.

We are going to see some things as we look at Paul's writings about this.

Isaiah and Jeremiah were sent to the House of Judah. Hosea was sent to the House of Israel. Micah was sent to both houses. And yet all of these prophets at times gave utterances involving both houses. For instance:

(Isaiah 1:1-2) *"The vision of Isaiah the son of Amoz, which he saw concerning Judah and Jerusalem in the days of Uzziah, Jotham, Ahaz, and Hezekiah, kings of Judah. „Hear, O heavens, and give ear, O earth: for the LORD hath spoken, I have nourished and brought up children, and they have rebelled against me." "*

Here we see that Isaiah's vision pertains to Judah. Under Isaiah's prophetic ministry, there was Uzziah, Jothan, Ahaz, and Hezekiah — kings of Judah. Actually, it was in the year that King Uzziah died, so Isaiah was born during Uzziah's reign. His prophetic ministry began when Uzziah died. He was a prophet to Jothan, Ahaz and Hezekiah. This was the span of Isaiah's ministry.

Who is Isaiah speaking to in the verse above? This now becomes important because you might say that he is speaking to us. No, he is not! There are things that he spoke in the days of Isaiah that if he sent a prophet today, he would probably say some similar things.

(Jeremiah 1:1-3) *"The words of Jeremiah the son of Hilkiah, of the priests that were in Anathoth in the land of Benjamin: "To whom the word of the LORD came in the days of Josiah the son of Amon king of Judah, in the thirteenth year of his reign. It came also in the days of Jehoiakim the son of Josiah king of Judah, unto the end of the eleventh year of Zedekiah the son of Josiah king of Judah, unto the carrying away of Jerusalem captive in the fifth month.""*

We see that Jeremiah prophesied under Josiah, the son of Amon and also Josiah's son, Jehoiakim and then his son Zedekiah.

We can see from this, the introductions to these prophesies. This is why it is so important. Christians want to take you to the middle of the book. "What about *Galatians* 6?" "Well, do you understand *Galatians* 1?" You are building an argument on chapter 6 as if chapter 6 is the beginning of the book.

We have to make sure that people understand that we have arrived where we are somehow. You do not get to *Galatians* 6 by skipping over *Galatians* 1, 2, 3, 4 and 5.

(Micah 1:2) *"Hear, all ye people; hearken, O earth, and all that therein is: and let the Lord GOD be witness against you, the LORD from his holy temple."*

We see that Micah says "hearken, O <u>earth</u>."

(Hosea 1:1-3) *"The word of the Lord that came unto Hosea, the son of Beeri, in the days of Uzziah, Jotham, Ahaz, and Hezekiah, kings of Judah, and in the days of Jeroboam the son of Joash, king of Israel. The beginning of the word of the Lord by Hosea. And the Lord said to Hosea, „Go, take unto thee a wife of whoredoms and children of whoredoms: for the land hath committed great whoredom, departing from the Lord." So he went and took Gomer the daughter of Diblaim; which conceived, and bare him a son."*

Do you see any names that you have seen recently? Who else prophesied under these kings? Isaiah. So, Isaiah and Micah and Hosea were there under the same reigns. People say they are contemporaries. What does contemporary mean? It means that their ministries were kind of parallel to one another, even though they were in different kingdoms.

Hosea is ministering to both kingdoms.

(Jeremiah 31:31-34) *"„Behold, the days come," saith the LORD, „that I will make a new covenant with the house of Israel, and with the house of Judah: Not according to the covenant that I made with their fathers in the day that I took them by the hand to bring them out of the land of Egypt; which my covenant they brake, although I was an husband unto them," saith the LORD: „But this shall be the covenant that I will make with the house of Israel; **After those days**," saith the LORD, „I will put my law in their inward parts, and write it in their hearts; and will be their God, and they shall be my people. And they shall teach no more every man his neighbour, and every man his brother, saying, Know the LORD: for they shall all know me, from the least of them unto the greatest of them," saith the LORD: „for I will forgive their iniquity, and I will remember their sin no more.""*

Here is something that people can easily miss. If you notice, the prophecy starts out with the House of Israel and the House of Judah. But then in verse 33 the prophecy is House of Israel. Then there is "after those days." If you have questions when you approach the Bible, you would say, "**Well, after *what* days?**"

How do you get from making a covenant with the House of Israel and the House of Judah and now you are only making a covenant with the House of Israel? And there are some days after which this covenant is going to be made. YeHoVaH is not bringing Israel into Judah. He is not bringing Israel into Judaism. He is not bringing Gentiles into Judaism. He is not bringing Gentiles into the kingdom of Judah.

The covenant starts out with the House of Israel and the House of Judah. It ends up with the House of Israel because they are going to be one house. The two shall become one. They started off as one. YeHoVaH is going to bring the two houses back together. It will be one house and it will not be the House of the Jews.

It will be the House of Israel, consisting of all the twelve tribes including the Gentiles, the gowy who believed and confessed with Yeshua and keep the commandments of YeHoVaH and Yehudans (Jews) who believe in Yeshua and who keep the commandments of YeHoVaH.

Verse 34 is how you know the New Covenant has been established. There will be no more teaching. (**See also *Hebrews 8:11*.**) No more evangelizing. No more taking the gospel of the Kingdom to the whole world. That is how you will know the New Covenant has been established. It has been ratified. Yeshua established or ratified it at the last supper.

*"This is the new testament/new covenant in my blood." (**Matthew 26:28; Luke 22:20**)*

So, he ratified the New Covenant. But when the New Covenant is established, he is going to be the King of Kings reigning in the earth.

(Isaiah 8:14) *"And he shall be for a sanctuary; but for a stone of stumbling and for a rock of offence to **both the houses of Israel**, for a gin and for a snare to the inhabitants of Jerusalem."*

Notice here the words "houses of Israel." This is because within Israel are ten houses; the ten tribes plus Levites. Even in the House of Judah you still have two houses (Benjamin and Judah). We will see that a little bit later.

(Hosea 1:4-7) *"And the L*ORD* said unto him, „Call his name Jezreel; for yet a little while, and I will avenge the blood of Jezreel upon the house of Jehu, and will cause to cease **the kingdom of the house of Israel**. And it shall come to pass at that day, that I will break the bow of Israel, in the valley of Jezreel." And she conceived again, and bare a daughter. And God said unto him, „Call her name Loruhamah: for I will no more have mercy upon the house of Israel; but I will utterly take them away. But I will have mercy upon the house of Judah, and will save them by the L*ORD* their God, and will not save them by bow, nor by sword, nor by battle, by horses, nor by horsemen.""*

So, Father is going to remove Israel. They are not going to go to war. YeHoVaH is going to deliver them. We have seen how YeHoVaH has delivered his people without a bow or arrow. Remember Cyrus? Cyrus issued a decree and sent them all back. There was no war and no battle. He just released them.

YeHoVaH has a way of touching the heart of those who do not even call upon his name. The heart of men is in his hands. He puts up one and takes down another. So that is why we have to put our faith in him and not in men. No man can undo what Father does.

If Father opens a door, no man can shut it. And if he shuts a door, no man can open it.

He has the heart of men in his hands. And those who rebel against him, those who do not want to hear what he has to say, he just moves them out of the way. He takes them down and puts someone else up who will listen. Sometimes he will put somebody in the place who is designed to bring destruction and calamity upon his people. He raised up Pharaoh. He has raised up tyrants in the history of both Israel and Judah. He sent them into captivity. He brought an army in to destroy them and to take them into bondage. This is YeHoVaH's doing.

Unless this distinction is maintained, the prophets may seem to contradict each other.

The Pauline Epistles

The same holds true with writers of the New Testament. Are you ready for this? I need you to take off your religious glasses. Take off your denominational ears because I want to show you things that we looked over because of religion and tradition. I hope you are ready.

Paul wrote the book of *Romans,* but who did he write it to?

(Romans 1:7) *"To all that be in Rome, beloved of God, called to be saints: Grace to you and peace from God our Father, and the Lord Jesus Christ."*

It does not say it is "to all that be in Rome, beloved of God, called to be saints." When you say "believer," you have to clarify what you mean. There were those who believed in God, but they did not believe in Yeshua.

Here is the key. He wrote to Rome. There are specific things in Paul's letter that only pertain to the Romans. It is going to get a little tricky here, but stay with me.

(1 Corinthians 1:2) *"Unto the church* [ekklesia/called out ones] *of God, which is at Corinth, to them that are sanctified in Christ Jesus, called to be saints, with all that in every place call upon the name of Jesus Christ our Lord, both their's and our's:"*

He is writing a letter to the Corinthians. He is writing to the Corinthians who call upon the name of Yeshua, along with others everywhere in every place. So, they are our brothers and our sisters. But the letter that he is writing to them, he is writing **to them**. He tells us who he is writing it to.

(2 Corinthians 1:1) *"Paul, an apostle of Jesus Christ* [called out ones] *by the will of God, and Timothy our brother, unto the church of God, which is at Corinth, with all the saints which are in all Achaia:"*

He is writing to those who are at Corinth and those who are in Achaia, so how do we get to the church at Charlotte? To the called-out ones in Namibia? Well, let's keep looking.

(Galatians 1:1-2) *"Paul, an apostle, (not of men, neither by man, but by Jesus Christ, and God the Father, who raised him from the dead;) And all the brethren which are with me, unto the* **churches** [ekklesia, called out ones] ***of Galatia:"***

This is why his letters are different. He writes to Galatia. He is writing to Galatia. He gives instructions to those in Galatia, which happens to be a region and not a city. He writes a different letter to the Corinthians. Paul could have just written one letter and said, "To believers everywhere," but he did not.

(Ephesians 1:1) *"Paul, an apostle of Jesus Christ by the will of God, to the saints which are at Ephesus, and to the faithful in Christ Jesus:"*

This is one of those letters that you can say, okay. He is writing to the Ephesians and to the faithful.

(Philippians 1:1) *"Paul and Timotheus, the servants of Jesus Christ, to all the saints in Christ Jesus* **which are at Philippi**, *with the bishops and deacons:"*

He is writing to the bishops, deacons and saints at Philippi. There were different issues in Ephesus than there were in Philippi. Remember. Paul is responding to letters that were written to him.

(Colossians 1:2) *"To the saints and faithful brethren in Christ which are at Colosse: Grace be unto you, and peace, from God our Father and the Lord Jesus Christ."*

We can read over that and say, okay. He is writing to believers everywhere, but that is not what he is saying. He writes "at Colosse," not in Galatia, not in Corinth, not in Thessalonica. It was to those who are at Colosse. That is who got the letter. Paul's own letter tells us who he is writing to. We can't just cross that out and say that he is writing to us. He isn't. Are there things in those letters that we can apply? Absolutely, but he is very specific about who he is writing to, just as the prophets were very specific about who they were prophesying to.

Ask who is it addressed to?

Now, if you mingle it all together and mix it all up, you are going to come out with a smorgasbord of traditions (spirituality). The scriptures then are not distinct. They are unclear. They are vague. You can read into it and make them say whatever you want them to say, so you have to start out approaching the scriptures (especially the New Testament writings) with the understanding that every one of these writers wrote to a specific audience. Every one of them. Even when we get to *Revelation* we see that there were seven specific congregations that John addressed his letters to.

This messes with some people's minds. If you want to keep your traditional religious glasses on, then be my guest, but this in no wise minimizes Paul's writings. It does not deflect or take away from the Bible.

We are now drilling down. Father is showing us that if you read this book with these broad-spectrum lenses, you are going to come away with a broad view. That is because you are on a broad road. We all know where the broad way leads.

(1 Thessalonians 1:1) *"Paul, and Silvanus, and Timotheus, unto the church* [called out ones] *of the Thessalonians which is in God the Father and in the Lord Jesus Christ: Grace be unto you, and peace, from God our Father, and the Lord Jesus Christ."*

Who? To the ones where? Thessalonica. If I am going to read the letter of Paul to the Thessalonians, in order for me to understand Paul's letter to them, I have to now get some history of Thessalonica during Paul's day. I have to get some history of Ephesus during Paul's day. There are certain things that I am not going to be able to put into perspective without a historical view. Otherwise, I am going to apply a modern time and a modern view. Therefore, I do the scriptures a major disservice.

(2 Thessalonians 1:1) *"Paul, and Silvanus, and Timotheus, unto the church* [called out ones] *of the Thessalonians in God our Father and the Lord Jesus Christ:"*

Paul is very specific about who he is writing to and where he is writing to.

The Pastoral Epistles

Most people won't know or hear the term "Pastoral Epistles" unless you have had some kind of Bible study, Bible class, or Bible College. Let's look now at the pastoral epistles, because they are letters that Paul wrote that the church says are for pastors today. Every pastor needs to understand the pastoral letters.

Here is what you want to understand. Every apostle oversees the congregation they established. You need to really understand this because I want to show you something now that is going to put these letters into much more of a narrow focus. We are going to put them into focus and stop looking through bifocals and seeing things blurry, because the lines get blurry when you do not put things into focus.

(1 Timothy 1:2) *"Unto Timothy,* **my own son** *in the faith: Grace, mercy, and peace, from God our Father and Jesus Christ our Lord."*

Just in case you want to put your name in there, Paul is not my Father. Paul is not my spiritual Dad. He is speaking of his disciple — the one he trained, the one he raised, the one he discipled, the one he sent out to look over congregations he established. Can you handle this?

(2 Timothy 1:2) *"To Timothy,* **my dearly beloved son***: Grace, mercy, and peace, from God the Father and Christ Jesus our Lord."*

Both of these letters (make no mistake) are *not* written to Reverend Joe. They are *not* written to you. They are written to his beloved son, just as I would write to my own sons. If I planted a ministry or people wanted oversight, they would be looking for guidance, for instruction.

Benchmarks

Have you ever heard the term "benchmark?" Unless you are a trailblazer and doing something that has never been done, if it has been done before, there are examples out here. Some of them work and some do not. What corporations and companies do is look for the benchmarks that work. They are called benchmarks because hey, somebody set a mark. There is a standard and this is the highest standard that has been set so far.

Now, that is a benchmark. If somebody comes along and sets an even higher standard, then they have just raised the bar. We do this in business. We do this in education. Some people do not want to go to certain schools because that school is not a leader in the field that they want to study. Sha'ul/Paul can boast. He says, "I sat at the feet of Gamaliel." All of the Jews who studied the Talmud did not sit at Gamaliel's feet.

There is a difference between Community College and a University. There is a difference between a government institution and a private institution. There is a difference in a public school and a Christian school or a Hebrew school. There is a difference between the University of North Carolina and Harvard. There is a difference between Harvard, Yale and Oxford. They call some schools "Ivy League." There are certain schools you have to have a GPA of a certain level just to even be considered.

There are all these levels and marks and benchmarks. You might ask what does that have to do with this?

When you begin to look at a ministry that works — and this is what a lot of churches do today. They look at ministries that work and then they send their delegation. They send their music minister or their executive pastor or the pastor. He goes on a "retreat" and takes all of these notes and buys all of these binders and gets all of these videos. Then he comes home and tries to implement that in the church because they say that it worked for them. They have this phenomenal growth and if we apply the principles that they applied, then we should see the same growth. They have established a benchmark.

This is what happens whenever a church splits. The church that split from the main church establishes another church with the same kind of leadership structure. They just split hairs on an issue. So now they go and start a ministry over here with the same doctrine. A Baptist Church becomes another Baptist Church. It splits and becomes two Baptist Churches. A Pentecostal split and becomes two Pentecostal Churches. A Messianic congregation splits and becomes two Messianic congregations.

There is a righteous split or separation and an unrighteous one. The righteous one — when they separate, communication is in order. It is intact (the love, the fellowship). When there is an unrighteous split. Nobody is talking to one another. We have more of those than righteous ones. There isn't multiplication. There is separation. There is division.

And now with *Facebook*, you have prophets and pastors and elders. You have *Facebook* pastors and *Facebook* prophets. They are prophesying and sharing dreams. You have dream blogs. But let me tell you something. There is always somebody who is willing to follow anybody. There will be those who will depart from the faith, giving heed to seducing spirits and doctrines of demons.

(Titus 1:4) *"To Titus, mine own son after the common faith: Grace, mercy, and peace, from God the Father and the Lord Jesus Christ our Savior."*

People read over that. Timothy my beloved son, Timothy my own son, Titus my own son. Titus and Timothy probably took on Paul's spirit. They were discipled by Paul. What Paul believed, they believed. What Paul taught, they taught. Paul told them what to teach.

What is really interesting is that the Baptists over there are preaching Paul's letters. The Pentecostals over there are preaching Paul's letters and yet the Baptists disagree with Paul on these areas. They take some of Paul's stuff and leave the rest. These guys over here take some of Paul's stuff and leave the rest and they all want to argue Paul.

Let's talk about Paul. What of Paul do you believe and what don't you believe? Everybody who argues Paul does not believe all of Paul. (Like Paul died for them and shed his blood.)

Again, this does not diminish from Paul. It does not deflect from him. It is putting what Paul had to say into perspective. It is amazing how the world around us would elevate Paul to such a status when Peter, James, John, Matthew — these guys were discipled by the Master and people do not elevate them to that status. Paul had an encounter on the Damascus Road and spent three years in the desert. He had a vision where he was taken to the third heaven and all of a sudden that elevates Paul above Yeshua in the eyes of many of these people.

It is very scary. We have to put Paul into perspective if we are going to fully understand what Paul is saying, but people idolize Paul and make Paul a deity. They worship Paul, teach Paul and bow down to Paul.

Understand this. Paul wrote letters. He taught scripture.

In this particular letter, he did not write to Timothy. Timothy's name is not on this letter. Timothy's name was on the other two, but he is not confused about who he is writing to. I am not digging on Paul's writings. I just want you to see who he is writing to so that you make no mistake. If you do not look and see, if you do not read the Bible within the perspective that it is written in and understand the ethnic division principle, you will muddle it all up. Now he is talking to everybody everywhere because "it is all spirit."

Well, now there is a spirit Israel, the spiritual Israel. *That is replacement theology.*

(Philemon 1:1-2) *"Paul, a prisoner of Jesus Christ, and Timothy our brother, unto Philemon our dearly beloved, and fellow labourer, And to our beloved Apphia, and Archippus our fellow soldier, and to the church in thy house:"*

Now he is writing to Philemon.

(1 Peter 1:1) *"Peter, an apostle of Jesus Christ, to the strangers scattered throughout Pontus, Galatia, Cappadocia, Asia, and Bithynia"*

This is as far as the believers had gone at this particular point in time. Peter's letters are universal — to the strangers. They are not to Philemon, not to Titus, not to Timothy, not to the church at Corinth, or Philippi, or Ephesus but to the scattered strangers.

(2 Peter 1:1) *"Simon Peter, a servant and an apostle of Jesus Christ,* **to them that have obtained like precious faith with us** *through the righteousness of God and our Savior Jesus Christ:"*

So, if you believe like Peter believes, he makes it very clear. He is not sending his letter to a particular region or person. He says that every person who has the opportunity to see these writings — if you believe in Messiah like we believe in Messiah, then this is for you.

(2 John 1:1) *"The elder unto the elect lady and her children, whom I love in the truth; and not I only, but also all they that have known the truth;"*

John does a similar thing because John doesn't necessarily address a particular person.

(3 John 1:1) *"The elder unto the well beloved Gaius, whom I love in the truth."*

Now he is specifically writing to Gaius.

(Jude 1:1) *"Jude, the servant of Jesus Christ, and brother of James, to them that are sanctified by God the Father, and preserved in Jesus Christ, and called:"*

He doesn't limit his writings to a group of people, because his writings are universal. Paul's writings are to those whom he established. This is to those he planted, those to whom he taught and set elders and pastors over to oversee. When Paul did his missionary journeys, where did he go? He went to those places that he established.

Will the real Israel please stand up?

When you see "Israel" in the Bible, you have to know which Israel is being referred to. When interpreting the Bible, you must realize that the same "Israel" is used in scripture to refer to:

• The patriarch Jacob. *(Genesis 49:1-2)* The first Israel we see specifically talks about Jacob.

• The 12 tribes of Israel. *(Exodus 19:3)* What is the "House of Jacob?" Those who came through Jacob. You have the children of Jacob (which is Israel) and you have Jacob who is Israel.

• The ten tribe House of Israel,[10] the Northern Kingdom. *(1 Kings 12:21)* What House of Israel are you talking about?

• The two-tribe House of Judah *(Ezra 6:21)* spoken of as children of Israel. Although they were of the tribe of Judah, they were children of Jacob (Israel). The tribe of Benjamin were not Jews. They were Benjamites. The Bible makes distinctions.

• The church/ekklesia/called out ones, the Israel of YeHoVaH, of Elohim, of God. *(Galatians 6:15; Romans 9:6)* Not the "spiritual" Israel. God only has one Israel, not two or three. He has one. He always has, and always will.

This looks confusing, but it isn't. There are people who call themselves "saved" who are not saved. There are people who call themselves "children of God," but they are not children of God. The world will tell you we are all children of God. No, those who believe in Yeshua, those who received him and believe on his name — to them he gave power to become the children of God. You do not become something you already are. We are all God's creation. But to be a son or daughter of YeHoVaH, you have to be born of him.

Be sure to read these references in your Bible for yourself. This should be clarity for you. You can't just read this book. You have to know what you are reading. When Philip when up to the Ethiopian's chariot, he said, "Do you understand what you are reading?" At least he had enough sense to say, "Honestly I am glad you showed up, because I don't."

People assume they know because they have heard a few sermons.

If we do not see these distinctions that the Bible makes, we muddle it all up. We have to examine the context. Now, no matter how much the tribe of Judah wants to identify with Judah, they are Israel's sons. They are sons of the tribes of Israel; one tribe of the twelve tribes of Israel. They will always be "Israel."

It is important to decide if you are going to believe your Bible or believe your preacher.

Israel is used as a collective name and thus may involve both houses. <u>Judah</u> however **is never used** in a collective sense of the whole twelve-tribed nation. Nowhere in the Bible do you see this — only in America.

Some interpreters have haphazardly interpreted prophecies given concerning Israel and Judah to be relevant primarily to the church/ekklesia/called out ones. They take prophesies that were spoken either to Israel or to Judah. They just take them and rip them off and apply them arbitrarily to themselves. This is just like people who call themselves Jews but who are not. Yeshua says that and nobody gets upset. I say it and now I have a problem.

---

[10] Folks are used to two houses. Well, no, there are 12 houses. The two houses have been reduced to one house called Jews. No, there is one house called Judah within the 12 houses. Read *Revelation*: 144,000 from each of the 12 tribes.

I am not backing down. I am simply trying to give you what the word says whether you want to see it or not. That is my job. My hands are clean after that.

Some Bibles, with their marginal headings, have brought much confusion to Bible students by randomly assigning the blessings and promises in the prophets to the New Testament church/ekklesia/called out ones. They leave all of the curses and judgments to Israel and Judah. These are the Bibles with the commentary on the sides that people read as scripture because it is in the book. The church claims the blessings, but they leave the curses to the Jews. That is sad. That is sick. That is improper interpretation.

Great care should be taken in looking for the church/ekklesia/called out ones in the prophets. Other interpreters completely fail to see the church/ekklesia/called out ones at all in the Old Testament; thus, missing a vital link in the purposes of YeHoVaH. They say that the church was born on Pentecost.

There is an interpretive danger of exalting the chosen nation and the natural birth above the church/ekklesia/called out ones and spiritual birth. That is what a lot of Messianics do. They are looking to the Jews in Talmud who reject Yeshua Messiah. And if they reject Yeshua Messiah, then is it possible that their doctrine, their revelation, their interpretation are all drawn by man-made devices and spiritualism or mysticism and not by the Spirit of YeHoVaH.

You cannot be filled with the Holy Spirit and reject Yeshua. I do not care what you say. You can talk about people being led by the Spirit. The question is, what spirit are you being led by? Yeshua says very clearly.

If you do not have the Holy Spirit, you are not of him. **The only way you get the Holy Spirit is for you to believe in Yeshua and to keep the commands of YeHoVaH.**

I am not making this stuff up. You can believe what you want to believe, but I just tell you what is in the book.

Even in the Messianic community you have these two houses and these first- and second- class citizens. It is all because of this faulty understanding and exalting somebody who calls themselves a Jew. What tribe are they from? Just because you are from Israel does not mean you are Jewish. There are people who converted. Now, if you convert to being a Jew, then can you convert to being an African or an Asian? I would like to see people converting to being Chinese.

Generally, the key to finding the church/ekklesia/called out ones in the Old Testament prophets is found in the prophecies concerning the coming of the Gentiles into Messianic blessings through the New Covenant in Messiah.

In the next lesson we will pick this up with the significance of Gentiles in the Old Testament.

Class 62 Study Summary

Key Points

1. There are three main divisions in reference to ethnicity that the scriptures address. These are Israel, Gentiles and the Ekklesia.
2. It is important when you approach the Bible that you ask questions. The person you are directing your questions to is the Father. YeHoVaH and his word are one.
3. The only place where evolution makes sense is in understanding that we are constantly evolving and growing in the spirit. Where we began last year or last week is not where we are today.
4. We have to read the instructions at the front of every Bible or related book of study. If we do not do that, we will misinterpret and/or not understand what we are reading or studying.
5. We must read the entire book. We cannot take scriptures out of context and apply them to defend our position or doctrine. We must build our arguments in the context in which they are written and apply scriptures in context. Unless we do that, we can read into scriptures whatever we want and use them to build any doctrine we like.
6. The Pauline Epistles are simply letters that Paul wrote to specific people about specific topics meant to address issues those people were having in their congregations. Paul tells us who he is writing to. He is not writing these letters to the people of today.
7. When you see the word "Israel" in the Bible, you have to know which Israel is being referred to. Is it the patriarch Jacob? Is it the twelve tribes? Is it the ten tribes (Northern Kingdom)? Is it the two-tribed House of Judah? Is it the called-out ones, the ekklesia?
8. It is important to decide if you are going to believe your Bible or your preacher.
9. You cannot be filled with the Holy Spirit and reject Yeshua. The only way you get the Holy Spirit is that you believe in Yeshua and you keep the commandments of YeHoVaH.

Key Questions

When we approach the word, we will see principles. We should approach it as if we are sitting at the feet of Yeshua. We have to ask ourselves key questions.

1. Does the verse/passage refer to the nation of Israel?
2. Does it refer to the ten tribes of the House of Israel, the Northern Kingdom?
3. Does it refer to the two tribes of the House of Judah, the Southern Kingdom (Judah, Benjamin plus the Levites)?
4. Does it refer to the Gentile nations?
5. Does it refer to the ekklesia/called out ones chosen out of every nation (the church)?

Review Exercise

1. List the five distinctions applicable to the term "Israel."

    1. _____

    2. _____

    3. _____

    4. _____

    5. _____

2. Place an "x" in the row that applies to whom the prophet was ministering.

Prophet	To the House of Israel	To the House of Judah
Isaiah		
Jeremiah		
Hosea		
Micah		

3. Explain how the concept of "benchmarks" applies to churches/ministries today.

   _____
   _____
   _____
   _____
   _____
   _____

4. If the letters in the New Testament were written to specific persons and/or congregations, what value are they to the believer?

   _____
   _____
   _____
   _____
   _____
   _____
   _____

5. The ethnic division principle focuses on the three main ethnic designations of the Bible. Tell why it is important to understand these ethnicities as it relates to interpreting the Bible. Include in your answer the significance of asking questions in the interpretive process that center on ethnicity.

_____
_____
_____
_____
_____
_____

Rate the following statements by filling in the most appropriate number.

(1 = I do not agree 10 = I agree completely)

1. I can describe how to use the ethnic division principle in study.

   1. ○   2. ○   3. ○   4. ○   5. ○   6. ○   7. ○   8. ○   9. ○   10. ○

2. I can identify the various people referred to by the term "Israel."

   1. ○   2. ○   3. ○   4. ○   5. ○   6. ○   7. ○   8. ○   9. ○   10. ○

3. I can explain how to determine to whom the pastoral and Pauline epistles were written.

   1. ○   2. ○   3. ○   4. ○   5. ○   6. ○   7. ○   8. ○   9. ○   10. ○

My Journal

What I learned from this class:

Discipleship Training Class 63

Ethnic Division Principle (part 5)

Objectives:

As a Discipleship student, at the end of this class you will be able to:

- Describe more in-depth what the scriptural idea of "Gentles" is
- Compare the concepts of "covenant" and "election"
- Contrast a passage of the New Testament which is supposedly quoting from the Old

As we talked about the ethnic division principle, we began to look at the steps on how to use these principles. It is one thing to have tools, but you have to know how to use them.

You know, I am fascinated by electricity, by electricians. We have a few people here who do work on furnaces and air conditioners and lighting for which I have a very, very healthy respect (around electricity). And I see these tools that they just pull in and out of their tool belts. They put things together and make it work. If you do not have the right tools, the last thing you want to do is try to work on something. It is another thing to have all the tools you need and not know what you are doing.

The knowledge and the tools to apply, to work with the tools and the knowledge are what bring about the results. You have to know how to use these principles. It is one thing to have them. It is another thing to know how to apply them in studying and researching the word.

The first step in using the ethnic division principle is to determine whether the verse or passage under consideration is relevant to any of the three main ethnic divisions. To review, those three divisions are: 1) Israel, 2) Gentiles and 3) the church/ekklesia/called out ones.

We know that Israel had several meanings that we looked at in class 62. We looked at Israel as it relates to the two houses — the House of Israel and the House of Judah.[11]

We have looked at the Gentiles and the words that are associated with that.

Then we looked at the church/ekklesia/called out ones. Notice when I utilize the word "church" I also make sure I add "ekklesia" and "called out ones." This is because the word "church" is used by many in the Christian world. But to those who have come out of the Christian world who still use "Jesus" in the Messianic community and the word "church," I have to tell those people that this is not a church. We do not go to church. We are the community. Even when I was in "the church" I would tell people, "No, we do not go to church. We *are* the church." We are the called-out ones. We are the *ekklesia*. That is the third group and we are going to move into that a little bit more.

---

[11] Not the various two-house doctrines that are being perpetuated. This is the actual biblical House of Israel and House of Judah in *Jeremiah 31*.

Ethnicity in Prophecy

Some interpreters have haphazardly interpreted prophecies given concerning Israel and Judah to be relevant primarily to the church/ekklesia/called out ones. That is a manner that we know of as *replacement theology*. You take all of the prophecy that is prophesied to Israel or prophesied to Judah and you attach them to the church as the "spiritual Israel." **There is no such thing**. You are either Israel or you are not. We have to make sure that we are not doing that.

The marginal headings in some Bibles have brought much confusion to Bible students. They do this by randomly assigning the blessings and promises in the prophets to the New Testament church/ekklesia/called out ones. They leave all of the curses and judgments to Israel and to Judah. They take the blessings and leave the curses. Great care should be taken in looking for the church/ekklesia/called out ones in the prophets.

There are prophets who prophesied to Israel. There were prophets who prophesied strictly to Judah. There were prophets who prophesied both to Israel and to Judah. We are going to find that there are prophesies concerning the Gentiles. There are prophesies concerning curses and destruction as well as blessings. We need to be able to look at these prophecies through the ethnic division principle to understand who the prophets are prophesying to and how to apply it.

Other interpreters completely fail to see the church/ekklesia/called out ones at all in the Old Testament. Thus, they miss a vital link in the purposes of YeHoVaH. In other words, the assumption is that the church did not start until *Acts 2* during the day of Pentecost. You have to think that if that is when the church started, if that is when the New Testament church started, then it is reasonable that the gospels *Matthew, Mark, Luke* and *John* are <u>Old Testament</u>.

Even when we say that the body of Messiah did not come into existence until after the Messiah's death, understand that his death came at the end of the gospel records. And if the New Testament begins at his death, then *Matthew, Mark, Luke* and *John* would be in the Old Testament scriptures! But they are not.

There is an interpretive danger of exalting the chosen nation and natural birth above the church/ekklesia/called out ones and spiritual birth — which many in the Messianic communities do. There are now two classes: the Jews and the Gentiles. There are the first-class citizens and the second-class citizens. In Judaism, this mindset was established because you had what is called one who is a proselyte (who is not a native-born but one who converted).

There is no two-class citizenship. There are people in the Messianic community who believe (and they teach this) that there is the Torah for the Jews and the Noahide laws for the Gentiles. There are people who believe that there are the commands that only Israel can keep. The Jewish people have to keep them. But the church, the New Testament, the Messianic community who believe in Messiah, we "get" to keep them. They *have* to, but we *get* to.

People want to change "the law" to the Torah or the instructions, in order to minimize the impact of the word "law." We do not want to play those games, so we do not want to get into exalting those who are Israel by birth over those who are grafted in (those who are brought in).

This creates a problem in another way because when you think along those lines, then one assumes that if a person is born "Jewish," they call them a "fulfilled Jew" if they receive Yeshua. There are people who boast about the fact that they have Jews in their congregation. We need to get off of that. We really do. People are people. There is no distinction between Jew and Gentile in the Messianic community.

Generally, the key to finding the church/ekklesia/called out ones in the Old Testament prophets is found in the prophecies concerning the coming of the Gentiles into Messianic blessing through the New Covenant in Messiah.

The term "Gentile" has a two-fold significance in the Old Testament:

1. It is used as a collective term referring to the heathen nations surrounding Israel.

(Jeremiah 46:1) *"The word of the LORD which came to Jeremiah the prophet against the Gentiles;"*

There is another prophet that we will look at later, but the interesting thing here is that in *Jeremiah* and *Ezekiel* there were specific prophesies that were prophesied against the Gentiles who rejected YeHoVaH. These are the curses, the destruction that is going to come. What people need to understand is that just as there were Gentiles in Israel's day, there are Gentiles today. Just as there were Israelites in Israel's day, there are Israelites today and there are those who are true Israel.

2. It is used to designate those out of all nations who would come to Messiah.

(Romans 15:8-12) *"Now I say that Jesus Christ was a minister of the circumcision for the truth of God, to confirm the promises made unto the fathers: And that the Gentiles might glorify God for his mercy; as it is written, For this cause I will confess to thee among the Gentiles, and sing unto thy name. And again, he saith, Rejoice, ye Gentiles, with his people. And again, Praise the Lord, all ye Gentiles; and laud him, all ye people. And again, Esaias saith, There shall be a root of Jesse, and he that shall rise to reign over the Gentiles; in him shall the Gentiles trust."*

There are those who reject God the Father, but who believe in Jesus the Christ. The Son delivered us from the Father. This is a doctrine that they teach — that Jesus set us free. Anyone who keeps the law that the Father gave is "under a curse." The Son delivered us from the curse of the law that the Father put on us. That is the rationale behind this, but *it isn't even logical.*

When we look at *Romans 15,* we see that there are blessings that are associated with those who are not Hebrew (not Israelites who receive the Messiah).

Now, unfortunately the ideology and theology behind this receiving the Messiah is that we receive Jesus by faith. We are no longer under bondage or the "curse of the law" (like Yeshua came with another agenda). He said very clearly that he did not come to abolish the law or the prophets, but that is exactly what people teach. "He came to abolish, to do away with the law and the prophets. We do not have to <u>do</u> the law."

But the blessings are found in the law! How can you have the blessings that come from the law and reject the law? If you reject the law, you have to reject the blessings. You can't take a part of the law and not take all of the law. That is the main thing that the Gentiles teach. "If you keep one part of the law, you have to keep all of the law." Well, if you take a part of the law called the blessings, you have to take all of it.

Covenant and Election

The ethnic division principle should be used in connection with the covenantal and the election principles. We have looked at this before, but we are going to drill a little deeper.

The chosen nation:

(Jeremiah 31:31) "„Behold, the days come," saith the LORD, „that I will make a new covenant with the house of Israel, and with the house of Judah:""

The burden of this passage involves YeHoVaH making a New Covenant with the ethnic division of the human race known as Israel and Judah. You can't put the Gentiles in this. It is very clear what the passage is saying: the House of Israel and the House of Judah, period. The prophet speaks of a time when YeHoVaH took the nation of Israel out of Egypt and brought them to Mount Sinai, where he made a covenant with them. This was the Mosaic Covenant. It is referred to specifically in scripture as the Old Covenant. *(Hebrews 8:8-13)*

The Western/Eastern "Church" refers to the Old Covenant as "the law." When you think of the Western Church, we think of the Americas and specifically North America. When you think of the Eastern, you think of the Eastern Orthodox. Did you know that the faith once delivered to the saints came out of the "East?" It came to the West. It started in the East.

You have the Eastern Church referring to the Old Covenant as "the law." Here is where the play on words with the church is. You are going to see here in the Bible that there is a play on words when it comes down to translation (and therefore, interpretation). And if you do not see this and do not catch it, what is going to happen is that you will read right over and pass it. But I believe that there are translation errors. Some of them were by mistake and some intentionally. I am going to show you one critical one.

(Hebrews 8:8) "For finding fault with them, he saith, „Behold, the days come," saith the Lord, „when I will make a new covenant with the house of Israel and with the house of Judah:""

Notice *Hebrews 8* is quoting *Jeremiah 31*.

(Hebrews 8:9-10) "„Not according to the covenant that I made with their fathers in the day when I took them by the hand to lead them out of the land of Egypt; because they continued not in my covenant, and I regarded them not," saith the Lord. "For this is the covenant that I will make with the house of Israel after those days," saith the Lord; „I will put my laws into their mind, and write them in their hearts: and I will be to them a God, and they shall be tome a people:""

This is why the church will tell you that the church is the "spiritual Israel." This is because it has to become some kind of Israel in order to take this prophecy. They know that the covenant is made with Israel. Well, how do Gentiles become Israel? They become "spiritual Israel."

And once they become spiritual Israel, they can take the prophecies concerning Israel and attach them to themselves. We're just going to hijack the prophecies. Imagine that. It is like stealing your identity.

My son does business and much of what he does is dealing in cash. A couple of days ago he was doing some business and he was given some currency. He showed me a counterfeit $20 bill. When you hold it up next to a real $20 bill, it does not look different at all. When it comes to the feel, there is a slight difference in the feel. The texture is about the same. You look at them and they look very, very close. They look really close to the untrained eye.

He was given two of them and this is favor. According to the law, if you give a counterfeit bill to a merchant, they are supposed to take it and call the police. They marked it up, but those pens that they use do not change colors on the fakes. There is a new counterfeit these days where they are bleaching $5 bills, because the pen reacts to the paper. They take a $5 bill, bleach it out and print upon that $5 bill.

Now they are putting out $20s and $50s, but there is a mark. What is missing on the counterfeit is that there is a face that you can't see unless you hold it up to the light. You can't see the face over on the right-hand corner on the fakes, that is on the real money. Not only is there a face, but there is also a vertical line that says "TWENTY TWENTY TWENTY"

If you happen to get a $5 that has been "repurposed," the face will be there, but the face won't match the face that is in the center. It will just be a face and it will say "FIVE FIVE FIVE," but a pencil won't detect it.

What does this have to do with our study? You have the "spiritual Israel" that does not have the marks. It looks like the real Israel, but the mark that Father established with this people is the Sabbath. That is the key.

You have to have the mark. You can't just be a counterfeit. You can't look like Israel. You have to have the markings. The markings of the true Israel are those who keep the commands of YeHoVaH and who have faith in Yeshua. *(Revelation 14:12)*

(Hebrews 8:10) *"„For this is the covenant that I will make with the house of Israel after those days," saith the Lord; „I will put my laws into their mind, and write them in their hearts: and I will be to them a God, and they shall be to me a people:""*

There are people today who want to say, "Our heart is circumcised and he is putting his law into it." Well, what law is he putting into your heart? The true Israel is going to have the law of YeHoVaH in their mind and in their heart. That is the true Israel, whether you are claiming to be "spiritual" or natural. You are going to keep the commands of YeHoVaH as well as have faith in Messiah.

(Hebrews 8:11) *"And they shall not teach every man his neighbor, and every man his brother, saying, „Know the Lord: for all shall know me, from the least to the greatest.""*

This is how we know the New Covenant has not been fulfilled, because we are still teaching "every man his neighbor and every man his brother" and because all do not know him.

(Hebrews 8:12-13) *"„For I will be merciful to their unrighteousness, and their sins and their iniquities will I remember no more." In that he saith, „A new covenant, he hath made the first old. Now that which decayeth and waxeth old is ready to vanish away.""*

That means it is getting there. It is ready to vanish, but it hasn't because there has to be the law that he is writing upon our hearts. That is the law that he wrote upon stone tablets.

Jeremiah points out that they broke this covenant, divorcing themselves from YeHoVaH their husband.

(Jeremiah 3:6) *"The LORD said also unto me in the days of Josiah the king, „Hast thou seen that which backsliding Israel hath done? she is gone up upon every high mountain and under every green tree, and there hath played the harlot.""*

What Israel as a nation did in committing adultery is they started worshipping idols. YeHoVaH looked at the worship of idols as if a man goes out and cheats on his wife with another woman or a woman goes out and cheats on her husband with another man. Israel, his bride, is now with another "El," another god, an idol which is not god at all — worshipping. They are married to the true Elohim, but worshipping with an idol, another man. But it was not just Israel.

(Jeremiah 3:7) *"And I said after she had done all these things, „Turn thou unto me. But she returned not. And her treacherous sister Judah saw it.""*

This is why you have to deal with sin in the midst of you. You have to deal with sin in your home, sin in the camp (if you would). That is because if you do not deal with it, other people will see it and then they will think (just like your children will say), "Well, you let them do it. It is not fair. You are showing favor."

It works the same way in the opposite direction when you see somebody who is doing wrong. The parents do not correct that behavior and other children do it and then that person gets corrected when the other one did not get corrected.

(Jeremiah 3:8) *"And I saw, when for all the causes whereby backsliding Israel committed adultery I had put her away, and given her a bill of divorce; yet her treacherous sister Judah feared not, but went and played the harlot also."*

Now here is the thing that really gets to me.

(Jeremiah 3:9) *"And it came to pass through the lightness of her whoredom, that she defiled the land, and committed adultery with stones and with stocks."*

There is this relationship that takes place between people and idols and between a man and woman where there is a consummation. When you go after idols or when you have a relationship with someone that is not your spouse, it is almost like having a relationship with an animal. It is not, but it is an abomination. This is why committing adultery and fornication warranted the same penalty as someone who would have sex with an animal. It is an abomination.

I think sometimes that we get caught up in lesbianism and homosexuality and bestiality and transgender while at the same time we tolerate fornication and adultery right underneath our noses. Father does not see it any differently.

(Jeremiah 3:10) *"„And yet for all this her treacherous sister Judah hath not turned unto me with her whole heart, **but only in pretense**," saith the* LORD.*"*

There are people who are honoring YeHoVaH with their mouth, but their hearts are nowhere in it. They are going through the motions and doing all the right outward stuff. But YeHoVaH is looking at the heart and their heart is not even in what they are doing. So, they have this form of Godliness but they are not allowing the Almighty to bring about the repentance that is needed within to produce the power that comes from repentance. With repentance, the heart, the soul, the mind can walk in harmony and in unity with the Almighty. They were pretending.

(Jeremiah 3:11) *"YeHoVaH said to me, „Faithless Israel is **more righteous** than unfaithful Judah.""*

Why? Here is the thing about YeHoVaH. He says that if you are going to do it, then go do it. Be hot or be cold but do not come up in here like everything is fine when you know everything is not right. Do not come up in here telling me, "I love you, I love you, I love you" and you reject my commands. "If you love me, keep my commands." Do not go through the motion of religion.

This is why understanding how to research and study the Bible for yourself is so important. The churches and theology have taught us how to go through the motions. We get our praise and worship and we raise our hands and cry and fall down upon our face and cry "Abba" and "HalleluYah!" We put banners and signs upon the walls and we have the right Bibles and the right terminology. Then we turn around and say, "We do not have to keep God's law." We worship the one true God, but we do not have anything to do with those commands because that is for those Jewish people or Jesus Christ has done away with all of that.

That is pretending. That is what religion does.

Religion makes us pretenders, unless it is true religion. Father wants us to be either hot or cold. If you are going to commit adultery, go commit adultery. Now, I am not telling anybody to go commit adultery, but Yeshua said it like this: If you look upon a woman and lust in your heart, you have already committed adultery. What is in you is going to eventually come out.

And Father sees what is in us.

(Isaiah 50:1) *"Thus saith the LORD, „Where is the bill of your mother's divorcement, whom I have put away? or which of my creditors is it to whom I have sold you? Behold, for your iniquities have ye sold yourselves, and for your transgressions is your mother put away."*

He is speaking to Israel here.

The purpose of this New Covenant was to allow Israel to come back into relationship with YeHoVaH. The New Covenant was to be made with Israel and Judah and not with the Gentiles or the Western/Eastern Church. Notice I did not write "ekklesia" or "called out ones" with that "church." I want us to make a distinction between the "called out ones" and the Western/Eastern Church. The Western/Eastern Church are not the called-out ones.

The called-out ones are the community of believers that Messiah is building. He is not building a Western/Eastern Church. He is building a community of believers who keep the commands of YeHoVaH and who have faith in Yeshua. That is what he is building and that is what we are trying to help him build.

When Yeshua fulfilled this prophecy and established the New Covenant *(Matthew 26:26-29)* with his disciples who were of the House of Judah, He spoke of his sacrifice at Calvary. It would in due time involve the church/ekklesia (composed of Jew and Gentile). This was not just the House of Judah. It was the House of Israel.

Both Jew and Gentile were to come into relationship with YeHoVaH through faith in Messiah on the basis of the New Covenant. This New Covenant was made with Israel and Judah, but it also involved the church/ekklesia. I have already tried to establish that when we use the term "Jew" and "Gentile" from a New Testament perspective, it is really in most cases talking about Judah. But the overall meaning is all of Israel, not just Judah. In some places it is used as "Judean" — one who lives in the land of Judah or Judea.

Thus, our interpretation of *Jeremiah 31:31* includes these main points. These are good points to make note of.

- YeHoVaH (in Yeshua) was to make this New Covenant. It is the Father. Remember, Yeshua did nothing that the Father did not tell him to do. This New Covenant was not from Yeshua, it was <u>through</u> Yeshua.

- Yeshua made this covenant at his first coming through the work of the cross/execution stake.

- This covenant was to be a completely renewed arrangement between YeHoVaH and man. At first YeHoVaH took a people out of the earth for the purpose of bringing the entire creation to him. He used a people as an example just like he is using you and I as examples to provoke the world to righteousness. Unfortunately, the world around us in most cases is so depraved that it rejects anything that appears to be righteous. This is because the world has gotten to a place where it is calling good "evil" and evil "good."
- The covenant was to be made distinctly with the chosen nation (Israel and Judah).
- The covenant would eventually include those out of every nation who would believe in the blood of the Lamb and who would accept the terms of the Renewed Covenant.

Every covenant has terms. We looked at the covenants. There are the parties that the covenant is made between. There is the blood of the covenant. There are terms. There are conditions. There are unconditional covenants and conditional covenants. The unconditional covenant is that YeHoVaH is going to make the New Covenant regardless. The condition is whether we accept the terms of this New Covenant (or not).

What are the terms? **It is the law. It is now written in us.** That is important because if we understand it the way we should understand it, the tablets were placed inside the Ark of the Covenant. That is where the tablets were. What Moses wrote was not accessible to everybody. If people in the wilderness, any Hebrew person, any Israelite person, if anyone wanted to know what YeHoVaH said, they had to go to Moses, to the judges. Ultimately they had to go to the priests (the Sadducees, the Pharisees) because the common man did not have what we have today (which is a Bible in every house).

It did not work like that. Before the printing press, the Bible was hard to come by. And even when the printing press began to print books, only those who were well-off had access to them. This is how the Catholic Church was so effective in keeping the word of YeHoVaH from the common people.

You had to depend upon somebody to tell you what the Bible said. Regardless of what we think of King James, he said, "We are going to put an end to this foolishness. We are going to make the Bible accessible to all the common people so they can make decisions for themselves based upon what the Bible says." But even when the people were given access to the scriptures, they still looked to those who were clergy to interpret what the scriptures said. Many of the people could not even read (and that is still true today).

You hear people say, "I do not understand the Bible." The King James is confusing. It is hard to read the King James. They then get an NIV — the "Non-Inspired" Version. Everything outside of the King James is being looked upon as demonic. So now even the King James is being viewed by some groups as demonically inspired.

There is this attack that is coming straight from the gates of hell against the believers to cause people not to trust anything. Some will say, "You are adding to it because you tell people not to trust anything and to question everything." Yes, absolutely.

We should not be afraid to ask questions. What scares us are the answers. If you think you know something and you find out what you know is not really the truth, that is frightening. Some people do not want to know.

We have to accept the terms.

The Gentile Nations

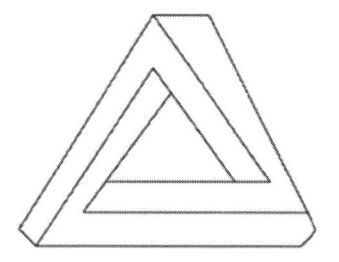

YOU REALLY NEED TO PAY CLOSE ATTENTION HERE.

(Matthew 12:17) *"That it might be fulfilled which was spoken by Esaias the prophet, saying,"*

Your King James Bible is going to say "Esaias." You can't look up Esaias. You won't find it. There is no book of Esaias. The King James (for some reason) calls Isaiah, "Esaias." You can look all day long in the table of contents, but you won't find him. He is not there; not under "Esaias."

Why would they do that? Why would they put Esaias for Isaiah? There is a bunch of dumb stuff in the King James. I am going to show you why I think they did it. They do not want you to go and see what Isaiah actually said. If you see what Isaiah actually said, it does not match what Matthew is saying. Matthew said it right. I think the translators mistranslated it.

(Matthew 12:18-21) *"Behold my servant, whom I have chosen; my beloved, in whom my soul is well pleased: I will put my spirit upon him, and he shall shew judgment to the Gentiles. He shall not strive, nor cry; neither shall any man hear his voice in the streets. A bruised reed shall he not break, and smoking flax shall he not quench, till he send forth judgment unto victory. And in his name shall the Gentiles trust."*

We see that the context is Messiah. Look at verse 21. Reading *Matthew* you would say, "That is the Gentiles who are going to believe in the name of Jesus." But what does Isaiah say? This is coming directly from *Isaiah 42:1-4* (BUT NOT VERBATIM). It deals with the Messiah's ministry to the Gentiles.

Let's look at them side-by-side in the King James:

Matthew 12:18-21	Isaiah 42:1-4
18 Behold my servant, whom I have chosen; my beloved, in whom my soul is well pleased: I will put my spirit upon him, and he shall shew judgment to the Gentiles.	1 Behold my servant, whom I uphold; mine elect, in whom my soul delighteth; I have put my spirit upon him: he shall bring forth judgment to the Gentiles.
19 He shall not strive, nor cry; neither shall any man hear his voice in the streets.	2 He shall not cry, nor lift up, nor cause his voice to be heard in the street.
20 A bruised reed shall he not break, and smoking flax shall he not quench, till he send forth judgment unto victory.	3 A bruised reed shall he not break, and the smoking flax shall he not quench: he shall bring forth judgment unto truth.
21 And in his <u>name</u> shall the Gentiles trust.	**4 He shall not fail nor be discouraged, till he have set judgment in the earth: and the isles shall wait for his <u>law.</u>**

Do you see any differences?

Look back at *Isaiah 42:4* in the NIV now:

*"He will not falter or be discouraged till he establishes justice on earth. **In his law** the islands will put their hope."*

Compare to (NIV):

(Matthew 12:21) *"And **in his name** shall the Gentiles trust."*

Notice what *Isaiah* is saying and what *Matthew* is saying. *Matthew* is saying that they are going to put their faith in his name. *Isaiah* says they are going to put their faith in his law.

Why would the translators change "law" to "name?" Most Christians are not going to read *Isaiah* because they can't find "Esaias." It is too much work.

Let's keep looking at *Isaiah 42:4* and now compare it with *Matthew 12:21*.

Look at them in the **Amplified**:

(Isaiah 42:4) *"He will not fail or become weak or be crushed and discouraged till he has established justice in the earth; and the islands and coastal regions shall wait hopefully for him and expect his direction and law."*

(Matthew 12:21) *"And in his name shall the Gentiles trust."*

The **New American Standard**

(Isaiah 42:4) *"He will not be disheartened or crushed Until he has established justice in the earth; and the coastlands will wait expectantly for his law."*

(Matthew 12:21) *"And in his name shall the Gentiles trust."*

The **New Living Translation**

(Isaiah 42:4) *"He will not stop until truth and righteousness prevail throughout the earth. Even distant lands beyond the sea will wait for his instruction."*

(Matthew 12:21) *"And in his name shall the Gentiles trust."*

The **Hebrew Roots Bible**

(Isaiah 42:4) *"He shall not fail nor be crushed until he has set justice in the earth; and the coasts shall wait for his Torah."*

(Matthew 12:21) *"And the nations will hope in his name."*

(Isaiah 42:1-4) *"Behold my servant; I will support him; my elect in whom my soul delights! I have put my Spirit on him; He shall bring forth justice to the nations. ²He shall not cry, nor lift up, nor cause his voice to be heard in the street. ³A bruised reed he shall not break, and a smoking wick he shall not quench; He shall bring forth justice to truth. ⁴He shall not fail nor be crushed until he has set justice in the earth; and the coasts shall wait for his <u>Torah</u>."*

The translators in the New Testament have taken the law out and put "his name" in instead. Why would they do that? How can you quote the scriptures for four verses verbatim up until the last verse and then change the last verse? But because it is in the New Testament, it makes sense. Gentiles should put their faith in his name. We do not have to believe in the law. All we have to do is believe in the name of Jesus Christ and we shall be saved. Whosoever calls upon his name, the name of Jesus, shall be saved. There is no other name under heaven whereby men shall be saved. The name of Jesus. That is all we need.

That is a blatant mistranslation.

This is why we have to compare scriptures. We have to compare Bibles. Anything that is written in the New Testament that is a quote from the Old Testament, we have to compare. You have to compare it because a little twist *changes everything*. And if you are already inclined to believe along those lines, I can tell you what the Father said. I will tell you what Yeshua said. The first thing out of people's mouths is that Paul said this. Paul said that.

I just told you what YeHoVaH said. I just told you what Yeshua said and you are going to argue with me using Paul? If Paul is saying something different than what YeHoVaH said and what Yeshua said, then who is wrong? Unless the translators have their finger in the mix and perverted what Paul said — which Peter said they would do.

I always have to look at what Paul wrote, because oftentimes as I have shared with people, Paul wrote letters, but he preached scripture. Paul preached the scriptures. There was no *Matthew, Mark, Luke* and *John*. There were no letters to the churches. There was no *Timothy* or *Titus*. Paul did not have any of those books, so he wasn't teaching from those books. They didn't exist. He preached from the Tanakh, from the prophets, from the writings and from the *Psalms*.

The translators for some reason removed his "law" and replaced his "name." As a result of doing that, people are now saying that this is what the gospel says. Matthew wrote this. I even looked in the Hebrew *Matthew* for this. I looked in every version I have at home with various translations of all of the Modern Hebrew, and the Besorah, and the Beshita. I am looking at all of these different versions. Some of them are only New Testament — the Aramaic. I was just looking at what they say, and they are all pretty much saying the same thing. They are not quoting *Isaiah*. They say, "Isaiah said this," but they are not saying what Isaiah said when it comes to this verse.

That says to me that some of these individuals are simply taking their version and inserting or using the same terminology instead of going back and seeing what *Isaiah* said and what is written. This is what the translators said, but this is what *Isaiah* said. If *Isaiah* says this and the translators said that and the translators are not saying what *Isaiah* said, even though they say it is from what *Isaiah* said, then somebody is wrong. I do not think it is *Isaiah*.

Not Gilligan's Isles

Do you see this word "isles" in Isaiah? There is also this word "law." This is the verse that is supposed to coincide with **Matthew 12:21**. *Isaiah* is saying something like that, but it is not in "his name." It is in "his law." The Gentiles shall wait for his law. The Gentiles shall put their trust in the law of God. This is what he is saying.

The word "isles" is first used when we talked about the tables of nations. This is where there is Japheth and this is the beginning of the isles of nations or the isles of the Gentiles.

*(**Genesis 10:5**) "By these were the isles of the Gentiles divided in their lands; every one after his tongue, after their families, in their nations."*

The first mention principle told us that the first time you see a word it generally carries that definition, that connotation, that understanding throughout the scripture. The first time we see the word "isles," it is associated with the Gentiles. This prophecy is spoken concerning the ethnic division of the Gentiles and not the chosen nation.

Gentiles were not in a covenant relationship with YeHoVaH. They were outside of the commonwealth of Israel and therefore were not entitled to the blessings of YeHoVaH. This is what Paul writes to us in *Ephesians 2*. They had no hope. They were outside, strangers, foreigners and alienated.

It was Yeshua who brought the Gentiles near. It was Yeshua through his blood and through his sacrifice of his life that gave access for the Gentiles to be grafted into the commonwealth of Israel. It is by his blood that Jew and Gentile, Hebrew and non-Hebrew, Israelites and all of the

nations come into covenant with the Father. No man can come to the Father except it be by Yeshua.

No matter whether you are native born, foreigners or strangers. If you do not come in through the blood, you do not get in. Everybody who comes in other than by Yeshua, the Bible says is a thief and a robber. They will be cast out into outer darkness. There is no way into the Kingdom of YeHoVaH while rejecting Yeshua. No way.

The prophet refers to a time when the Gentiles would come into blessing and trust in Messiah's law.

Two Streams of Prophecy

There are two main streams of prophecies in the Old Testament pertaining to the Gentiles. Read these sections to become familiar with the prophecies.

Prophecies of Judgment *(Isaiah 15-21; Jeremiah 46-51; Ezekiel 25-32)*

YeHoVaH mentions these Gentile nations by name.[12] If you have seen one, you have seen them all. A Gentile is a Gentile is a Gentile. It does not matter what region, what nation you come from. If you are not part of Israel, the only way to become part of Israel is through Messiah. This is what the Bible means when the gospel and salvation is of the Jews and not just for the Jews. Salvation came to the Jewish community

---

[12] You will find that throughout the Bible, North America, South America and Central America are not mentioned. I do not think Columbus had discovered them yet, but somehow people want to throw America into the prophets.

before it ever went into the Gentile community. Why? Because Father came to his own. Who were his own? The ones he had married — Israel. The one he had chosen out of all of the nations of the world. He chose the nation of Israel, which was a small nation and not even a great people. He did great things among them to show that he is all powerful.

He destroyed nations. Some he sent into war. A small group of people routed a whole bunch of people. In another case he just breathed. The way he dealt with Pharaoh in Egypt; they never had to lift a finger. You know as well as I do that according to the scriptures, the only way you get the spoils of war is if you go to war. Israel took the spoils and they did not lift a finger. Our Yah is powerful!

As Job said (and they are hard words to mutter especially when you are in dire straits):

(Job 13:15) "Though he slay me, yet will I put my trust in him."

"Though he slay me". This life that we live is so temporary, whether we live to be 80-years old, 90-years old or 100-years old. It is still a fleeting breath compared to eternity.

Prophecies of Blessings *(Isaiah 11:10; 42:1-4, 6; 49:6; 52:15; 55:5; 60:1-5: Zechariah 2:11; Malachi 1:11)*

These prophetic blessings actually mention Gentiles. The prophecies of blessing could only be fulfilled in Messiah. Outside of Messiah, they could only have judgment. The passage in *Matthew 12* is Messiah's confirmation that through him the Gentiles would be blessed.

Yeshua is the word that became flesh. He is the law. How can he abolish himself? He did not come to abolish himself. He came to bring fulfillment to that which the Father gave because the people had perverted it. The law had to become flesh. "Since you didn't know how to keep the law, he became flesh to walk it out for you and then I am out of here. What I did, you do."

Yeshua did not tell us to keep the Sabbath. He kept it!

He did not tell us we had to keep those "Jewish" feasts. He kept them!

He showed us by example. Be an example. Paul says, "Follow me as I follow Messiah." The things that were done in days of old were done for our example. Yeshua showed us by example how we were supposed to live. You have people trying to say that he never said it. No, he *lived* it.

This is what he did say: *"The things that I do, you shall do."* Well, if he kept the Sabbath, then you should keep the Sabbath. If he kept the feasts, then we are to keep them. Most people only want to take the miracles and the power of the Holy Spirit. Yeshua said "Follow me. Let me show you how to walk this walk. I am the living word. You want to learn what the word says? You want to learn how to keep the word, how to do the word, how to live the word? Watch me. I am going to show you. Once I am out of here, I am going to hold you accountable for the things that I showed you the things that I taught you and the things that I showed you as to my lifestyle."

The things that he began to do and teach, we have to do and teach what he did and what he taught; not just what he said. You have silly people out there saying, "Well, if he didn't confirm it." Show me one place where Yeshua said, "Keep the Sabbath." It is not there. He never said to keep the Sabbath. Well, no, he did not. He did not say, "*not* to keep it", either.

But he kept it.

What part of "Whatever I do, you shall do," do you not understand? I am not trying to be mean. But sometimes you have to say things in such a way, even though it may upset people — well, good. I am really trying to help you understand. Because for those of us whose eyes are open, our eyes have not always been open. We have to open eyes.

There are people with blinders on who are doing religious stuff. These people sound spiritual. They look spiritual. They are good examples of spirituality. These spiritual people reject the commands of YeHoVaH. Something is wrong with that. How can you be so passionate about God but passionately against what the Father said? You love the Father that much, but what he said is a curse?

Even Job had enough sense not to listen to his wife when she said, "Curse YeHoVaH and die." How can I curse the word? How can I curse the one who gives life? He is the sustainer of life. How can I take life from the life giver and reject the word that the life giver spoke? The words that He spoke *are* life. The **Torah is life. The law is holy. The law is righteous. The law is spiritual.**

How can I reject the law and keep the lawgiver? It doesn't make sense.

What if I come to live with you and not keep any of your house rules? I am just going to come into your house and I am going to live in your house. I am going to sleep in whatever bed I want, with whomever I want. I am going to eat what I want. I am going to lie around on your sofa and watch movies that you do not like. I am a terrible houseguest. The welcome mat is pulled out. You are in a room that I am not in, trying to figure out how to get me out of there.

That is YeHoVaH and Adam and Eve. "It is time for you to go. And just to make sure that you do not come back, I am putting in some guards."

The Church/Ekklesia

(Matthew 16:18) "And I say also unto thee, „That thou art Peter, and upon this rock I will build my church; and the gates of hell shall not prevail against it."

We are the only people that the gates of hell have no authority over. Why? Because we have been given authority over it. Now we just have to walk in that. If you do not walk in the authority that the Father has given you, then we will be victims just like Adam and Havah, Mr. and Mrs. Adam. We will allow the enemy to talk us out of our authority. Now he has authority over us, and in our lives, our homes, our marriages and among our children.

We are frustrated because we won't take authority. We won't walk in authority. That is not the devil's fault and it is not the world's fault. It is our fault. We see things perverted.

I am not trying to undermine authority, but we have to first start out on the right foundation before you can ever talk about exercising authority. Otherwise, you walk in a false authority, a false anointing, a false power and one where you demand authority while not having been given it.

The devil is a thief. He is the one who takes. He is the one who steals, kills and destroys, so **when we are trying to take authority we have not been given, that is a false authority.**

YeHoVaH says that the gates of hell are not going to prevail against his called-out ones. In using this term, Yeshua was not referring to the ethnic divisions of the chosen nation, nor to the Gentile nations. Rather he was referring to those who would be called out of every kindred, tongue, tribe and nation. These, the redeemed through faith in his blood, would constitute the third Ethnic Division known as the New Testament Church.

Unfortunately, I am not talking about the "church" on every corner. I am talking about the people who love YeHoVaH, who keep his commands and who have the testimony of Yeshua — faith in Messiah.

Class 63 Study Summary
Key Points

1. The first step to using the ethnic division principle is to determine whether the verse or passage under construction is relevant to any of the three main ethnic divisions (Israel, Gentiles, ekklesia).
2. Replacement theology says that prophecies given concerning Israel and Judah are relevant primarily to the church/ekklesia/called out ones. They take that which is prophesied to Israel or to Judah and attach them to the church as the "spiritual Israel." There is no such thing.
3. The New "Testament" really begins at Yeshua's death, so *Matthew, Mark, Luke* and *John* are really Old Testament books. Yeshua's death was at the end of the gospel records, not before.
4. There is a danger in exalting the chosen nation and natural birth above the church/ekklesia/called out ones and spiritual birth. Some people in the Messianic community do this. They say there are two classes: Jew and Gentile. That created first and second-class citizenship. This mindset was established in Judaism with the term "proselyte." This was someone not native-born but who had converted to Judaism.
5. Some people boast about the fact that they have "Jews" in their congregation. They talk about someone who was born a Jew as a "fulfilled" Jew, but this is a manmade idea. It is not biblical.
6. The ethnic division principle should be used in connection with the covenantal and election principles.
7. What Israel did as a nation in committing adultery was they began to worship idols.
8. Father does not see the sins of adultery, homosexuality, lesbianism, bestiality or transgender any differently. They are all the same sins to him and an abomination.
9. The ekklesia or called out ones are the community of believers that the Messiah is building.
10. The Renewed Covenant includes those out of every nation who believe in the blood of the Lamb and who accept the terms of the Renewed Covenant, which includes keeping the commandments of YeHoVaH.
11. The law is now written within us. That is part of the New or Renewed Covenant.
12. In the King James Bible, the prophet "Esaias" is actually Isaiah. We can wonder why it is spelled that way. It might be a mistranslation. Perhaps they did not want people to see what Isaiah actually said.
13. The difference between **Matthew 12:18-21** and **Isaiah 42:1-4** is evident when compared side by side. *Matthew* says they will put their faith in his name while *Isaiah* says they will put their faith in his law. This is an important distinction.
14. When we do the study we find that **Isaiah 42:4** is a blatant mistranslation from "law" to "his name." This is one example of why we have to search and compare scriptures.
15. There are two main streams of prophecy in the Old Testament pertaining to the Gentiles. They are prophecies of judgment and prophecies of blessings.
16. Yeshua showed us what to do. If he kept the Sabbath (he did), we should too. If he kept the laws and the feasts, we should too. The things that he said and did, we should say and do too.
17. The ekklesia are the only people that the gates of hell have no authority over. We have to walk in our authority, but we must start out on the right foundation before we can exercise that authority. Otherwise, we will walk in a false authority, a false anointing and a false power where we demand authority that we do not really have.

Review Exercise

1. There are two meanings to the word "Gentile." What are they and how do you explain the differences between them?

2. We looked at some of the differences in *Matthew 12:18-21* and *Isaiah 42:1-4* even though *Matthew* is supposed to be quoting from *Isaiah*. We assume that the translators injected some theological bias. In your own words, explain the differences between the two passages and its significance in the change of meaning. Imagine that you are explaining this to someone who says that "the law has been nailed to the cross."

3. We see two "genres" or streams of prophecy in the Bible that refer to Gentiles. Write a short paragraph about each.

4. We "elect" people to various offices. Think about that as you consider YeHoVaH's "elect." What parallels can you draw?

Rate the following statements by filling in the most appropriate number.

(1 = I do not agree 10 = I agree completely)

1. I can describe more in-depth what the scriptural idea of "Gentiles is."

   1. ○ 2. ○ 3. ○ 4. ○ 5. ○ 6. ○ 7. ○ 8. ○ 9. ○ 10. ○

2. I can compare the concepts of "covenant" and "election."

   1. ○ 2. ○ 3. ○ 4. ○ 5. ○ 6. ○ 7. ○ 8. ○ 9. ○ 10. ○

3. I can contrast a passage of the New Testament which is supposedly quoting from the Old.

   1. ○ 2. ○ 3. ○ 4. ○ 5. ○ 6. ○ 7. ○ 8. ○ 9. ○ 10. ○

My Journal

What I learned from this class:

_____
_____
_____
_____
_____
_____
_____
_____
_____
_____
_____
_____
_____
_____
_____
_____
_____

Discipleship Training Class 64

The Chronometrical Principle (part 1)

Objectives:

As a Discipleship student, at the end of this class you will be able to:

- Give an overview of the chronometrical principle
- Describe how three Hebrew words and four Greek words for time are used in scripture

The Chronometrical Principle

This is my favorite part of ministry because it allows me to share some things with you that will help you in your research and your study in how to eat, how to equip, how to prepare and how to share your faith with others (once you have learned the things that are important for you to learn).

If you will notice, people talk about stuff they understand. They talk about stuff they know. People who are big on sports, you can't shut them up. These guys may not know one verse of scripture. The moment you start talking Bible they don't have any conversation for you. **The more you are prepared in your subject matter, the easier it is to share with others.**

So, if you want to be able to share with others, you need to learn how to equip yourself. And part of what we are doing is equipping. We are helping you learn and understand the tools and the principles that are behind biblical interpretation or hermeneutics.

You may or may not be aware that we have all of our teachings on our web site at *ArthurBaileyMinistries.com*. Make sure you take advantage of that. We have the unique opportunity to share these teachings with you. We try to provide quality ministry all of the time. It is amazing when I look at where we started and the videos that we posted and the evolution of how we are constantly trying to provide the most quality teachings for you and your family.

The Chronometrical Principle

You have probably never heard of the –chronometrical principle. These are theological terms. These are terms that you will hear in Bible College and Seminary, but you won't hear them in churches or Bible studies. You won't hear them in congregations. You certainly may not hear them in Messianic or Hebrew Roots circles, but these are principles that are being applied by people as they are studying and researching the word.

The chronometrical principle is that principle by which the interpretation of a verse or passage is determined upon consideration of its chronometrical setting.

The word –chronometrical is taken from two Greek words:

–Chronos meaning –**time**.

–Metron meaning –**measure**.

So, in essence, it is the measurement of time.

In the words that I am going to be sharing with you, you will see these principles in the scriptures. You will actually see the words, even though you probably never looked up these words. When I first started, there was the Hebrew-Greek Key Word Study Bible. I did not know. After a long time, I would look up key words. But then one day it dawned on me that –man shall not live by bread alone, but by every word that proceeds out of the mouth of the Almighty.

So that principle, that understanding, that scripture helped me to understand that it was not just the key words that I needed to understand. I needed to understand every word, especially the words that have been taken from the Hebrew context and filtered through the Greek context, and filtered through the Latin and then filtered through to the English. There is a lot of filtering that is going on. I need to be able to look at the filters and see how the word has changed, even into our time today.

As we were looking at the last day of unleavened bread, we see the word –meat. Now, from an English perspective, meat is flesh. But from a King James perspective, oftentimes meat is grain and then meat is flesh. You see –meat in certain places. The assumption is that meat is flesh. Now, if you don't understand that in this case meat is grain, do you think you will get the proper understanding of what the verse is actually saying? No, you won't.

Note the following relevant words as defined by the dictionary.

Chronometry: The art of measuring time; the measuring of time by periods or divisions.

In a few lessons we will be getting into the aspect of the periods that most churches teach and the dispensations. Most Christians have heard of the term –dispensation. Some even consider themselves as dispensationalists. We are going to look at that, but this is laying the groundwork for the dispensational view of scripture. We are going to see that a lot of that is not necessarily correct or biblical.

But in order to understand the dispensational view, you have to understand chronometry and the chronometrical principle.

Chronometer: An instrument that measures time; specifically, a compact timekeeper of the highest possible accuracy.

Chronographer: One who writes concerning time or the events of time.

You have the chronometrical principle that involves chronometry. That is the art of measuring time. There is the chronometer (the instrument that measures it) and the chronographer, the one who writes concerning time.

The scriptures clearly reveal that YeHoVaH is the greatest chronographer of the ages. You are going to see that word –Ages in the Bible. It has meaning. –Ages is a chronometrical term.

YeHoVaH himself is eternal. –Eternal is a chronometrical term. When does it begin? When does eternal life begin? There are some who say that it begins when you die. I believe it begins (for me) the moment I came into faith. Eternal life begins. Those who believe in Yeshua shall never die.

YeHoVaH is not limited to time or by time. This is what Moses said;

(Psalm 90:2,4) *"...from everlasting to everlasting, Thou are YeHoVaH...For a thousand years in thy sight are but as yesterday when it is past, and as a watch in the night."*

(David did not write all of the *Psalms*.)

Man is subject to time, but YeHoVaH is the guardian of time and the designer of its ages. The writer to the *Hebrews* tells us that:

(Hebrews 11:3) *"...through faith we understand that the worlds* [Greek: –ages – translations vary in their handling of the word –aion] *were framed by the word of YeHoVaH..."*

Related Hebrew Words

The scriptural basis upon which this principle is built, is the usage of these words: age(s), time(s) and season(s). You hear people today, especially former Pentecostals. Spiritually filled people from a denominational perspective are saying, –This is a dry season for us, or –This is a tough season for me, or –We are in a season of change, or –We are in a season of… Everything is a season. That word has a place in the book.

Moedah

Ages, times and seasons — we need to understand the times and the seasons. Three Hebrew words are important to our study. The first is *mowadah*. You have seen this word. You have heard this word explained. All the way back in the book of *Genesis*, you will see this.

H4150 – **mow'ed, mo-ade"; or mo-ade"; or** (feminine) **moweadah,** *(2 Chronicles 8:13)* **mo-aw-daw"**; from H3259; properly, an appointment, i.e. a fixed time or season; specifically, a festival.

When we begin to look at the festival seasons (the feasts), we are talking about moedim or times and seasons. –An appointment; i.e. a fixed time or season; specifically, a festival ; translated: feasts.

(Leviticus 23:2, 4, 37, 44; Numbers 15:3; 29:39)

(Leviticus 23:2) "Speak unto the children of Israel, and say unto them, „Concerning the feasts of the LORD, which ye shall proclaim to be holy convocations, even these are my feasts.""

That's the word ***moedaw***.

(Leviticus 23:4) "These are the feasts of the LORD, even holy convocations, which ye shall proclaim in their seasons."

These are the ***moedim***.

We see these words also in *Numbers* (as referenced). So, when you see the word –feasts, when you look it up, it is going to be point to *moed,* which is the root.

Season(s)

Genesis 1:14; Exodus 13:10; Leviticus 23:4; Numbers 9:2, 3, 7; 28:2

In *Genesis* we see this word for the very first time.

(Genesis 1:14) *"And Elohim said, „Let there be lights in the firmament of the heaven to divide the day from the night; and let them be for signs, and for **seasons**, and for days, and years:""*

So, you see this word ‒season which is actually (if you look at it in the context) — YeHoVaH established the festival seasons at creation, long before he gave the command to Moshe to tell the children of Israel, ‒These are my feasts. He established the feasts at the very beginning of creation.

Time(s)

Genesis 17:21; 18:14; Exodus 23:15; 34:18; Psalm 102:13; Daniel 8:19; 11:27, 29, 35; Habakkuk 2:3.

In *Genesis 17,* the word **moed** is translated as ‒time for the first time. Let's also look in *Daniel*. The prophet Daniel shows us that:

(Daniel 8:19) *"And he said, „Behold, I will make thee know what shall be in the last end of the indignation: for **at the time appointed** the end shall be.""*

The end is going to come at the appointed time.

(Daniel 11:27) *"And both of these kings" hearts shall be to do mischief, and they shall speak lies at one table; but it shall not prosper: for yet the end shall be **at the time appointed**."*

We also see this word *moed*. You see, no matter what people say, no matter what people do; all mankind, all hearts, all minds, are in the hand of the Almighty.

This is why it is so important that we put our trust in him and not fear man. What can man do to us? If our ways please the Almighty, he makes even our enemies to be at peace with us.

Father has the heart of men in his hand, so we don't have to connive. We don't have to scheme. We don't have to manipulate. What we have to do is seek first the Kingdom of YeHoVaH and his righteousness. Live righteous and holy.

Stop trying to control other people. Stop trying to force other people to fit into your mold, to say things the way you say them or telling them that they are wrong. Father knows what is best. If we are focused on pleasing him, leave people alone. Share with them. Speak to them. Give them what we know. Then let the Father deal with them.

(Habakkuk 2:3) *"For the vision is yet for **an appointed time**, but at the end it shall speak, and not lie: though it tarry, wait for it; because it will surely come, it will not tarry."*

This is the wonderful thing. I am here in the city of North Carolina. If you told me I would be doing this five years ago — five years ago we were building a life and ministry in Grand Rapids, Michigan. We were putting our entire being, everything; just as we are putting everything into what we are doing now. We were doing this very thing in the city of Grand Rapids, Michigan. And the Father, through visions and through dreams and through prophetic utterances, told me that I would be doing some things. But I had no idea how that was going to happen with what was going on in the city of Grand Rapids and with what we were doing. But Father had to bring me out and bring me to Charlotte in order to accomplish what he spoke to me many years ago.

This is what *Habakkuk* is talking about. It is not about me trying to create a vision. It is about me following and understanding the vision he already has for us. Like the book of *Jeremiah*, it says that the Father knows the plans. He has a plan for every person. He knows that plan. I don't know the plan, but I know who knows the plan.

The goal is to get into his presence and let him reveal that plan like what *Habakkuk* has done.

(Habakkuk 2:1) *"I will stand upon my watch, and set me upon the tower, and will watch to see what he will say unto me, and what I shall answer when I am reproved."*

Now, if you look at the language, *Habakkuk* says, –I know that I am probably going to say something and Father is going to correct me. He is going to reprove me. I am going to have my pencil, my paper and I am going to be ready to write. I am going to respond. He is going to reprove me.

(Habakkuk 2:2) *"And the LORD answered me, and said, „Write the vision, and make it plain upon tables, that he may run that readeth it."* "

Write it down. Make it plain.

(Habakkuk 2:3) *"For the vision is yet for an appointed time, but at the end it shall speak, and not lie: though it tarry, wait for it; because it will surely come, it will not tarry."*

There are times when the Father will give us a vision. He will give us a dream. He will say, –Here it is, but it may not be for years that it manifests. He is saying here: –the appointed time. So, we see this word *moedim* translated as –time in the book of *Habakkuk*.

Eth

The next word is **eth**.

H6256 -„eth, ayth; from H5703; **time,** especially (adverb with preposition) now, when, et.' — + after, (al-) ways, certain, continually, evening, long (due) season, so (long) as (even-, evening-, noon-) tide, ((meal-)), what) time, when

We have all of these words for **eth**. The Old Testament Hebrew **eth** is –time translated:

Season(s)

Exodus 18:22, 26; Leviticus 26:4; Deuteronomy 11:14; 28:12; Psalms 1:3; 145:15; Jeremiah 5:24; Judges 10:14; 1 Chronicles 12:22; 29:30; Esther 1:13

Now you will see this word –season, but it is the word **eth**, not **moed**. Every time you see –season you can't assume that it is the same word when you look at the Hebrew. So, you must look at the context.

(Exodus 18:22) *"And let them judge the people at all seasons: and it shall be, that every great matter they shall bring unto thee, but every small matter they shall judge: so shall it be easier for thyself, and they shall bear the burden with thee."*

It is interesting here in this verse that they are going to judge people during the festivals. That is not what it is saying. There are four seasons in the year based upon winter, spring, summer and fall. Those are also considered seasons. The judges have to judge the people year-round. So, what it is saying is to let the judges judge the people at all seasons; not just at a certain time, not just at the feasts. This word is not *moed*, it is *eth*.

Moses is appointing elders. Elders are going to judge the people in all of the small matters all of the time. It is not a *moed*. It is a season. It is a time which includes all seasons in this particular context.

(Leviticus 26:4) *"Then I will give you rain **in due season**, and the land shall yield her increase, and the trees of the field shall yield their fruit."*

This is important because the word –due puts it into perspective. There are certain seasons when rain is supposed to come. If rain comes out of the due season, we have a problem. This is how meticulous the Father is. He says, –Listen, I am going to give you rain when it is supposed to rain and I am going to withhold the rain when it is not supposed to rain. Too much rain is a flood. Not enough rain is a drought. And being an agricultural people, you want rain when it is supposed to rain. You don't want rain when it is not supposed to rain.

For this word –**season**, the Father says in the right season. But this has nothing to do with the festivals. In the right season, in due season, I am going to give you rain.

Look up the other references to see how this word is used in all of them. The word *eth* is translated:

Time(s)

1 Chronicles 12:22; 28:30; Esther 1:13; 4:14; Job 24:1; Psalms 31:15; Ecclesiastes 3:1- 17; Daniel 11:35, 40; 12:1, 4, 9, 11; Zechariah 10:1

Let's go to *Job*.

(Job 24:1) *"Why, seeing times are not hidden from the Almighty, do they that know him not see his days?"*

We see here that the word is used in the form of *eth*. This word –time has absolutely nothing to do with seasons as much as *Job* is saying that Father sees all things all of the time. There is absolutely no time in history (past, present or future) that the Father does not see. Times are not hidden. There is absolutely no time that Father is not knowledgeable of what is going on in his creation.

We see these words –time appearing in these verses and we are talking about the chronometrical principle so that you will see these words and passages. Then we are going to show you how it is actually used in the Bible.

Yowm

The next word is *yowm*, –a day literally or figuratively (a space of time), translated as:

Day(s)

We see this word in ***Genesis 1:5; 5:1-8, Job 24:1; Isaiah 2:2; 13:6, 9; Jeremiah 23:20; Hosea 9:7; Joel 2:29, 31;*** and ***Malachi 4:5.***

(Genesis 1:5) *"And God called the light Day, and the darkness he called Night. And the evening and the morning were the first day."*

We then see later in chapter 5:

(Genesis 5:1-8) *"This is the book of the generations of Adam. In the day that God created man, in the likeness of God made he him;"*

² *"Male and female created he them; and blessed them, and called their name Adam, in the <u>day</u> when they were created."*

³ *"And Adam lived an hundred and thirty years, and begat a son in his own likeness, and after his image; and called his name Seth:"*

⁴ *"And <u>the days</u> of Adam after he had begotten Seth were eight hundred years: and he begat sons and daughters:"*

⁵ *"And <u>all the days</u> that Adam lived were nine hundred and thirty years: and he died."*

⁶ *"And Seth lived an hundred and five years, and begat Enos:"*

⁷ *"And Seth lived after he begat Enos eight hundred and seven years, and begat sons and daughters:"*

⁸ *"And <u>all the days</u> of Seth were nine hundred and twelve years: and he died."*

We see that this word here is a particular time, but it is translated as –day(s). During certain days Father did certain things, so literally or figuratively it is a space of time.

Time(s)

Genesis 4:3; Numbers 13:20; Deuteronomy 10:10; 20:19; Joshua 3:15; 11:18; 1 Samuel 14:18; 2 Kings 19:25; Psalms 27:5.

We are seeing the words –days, –times and –seasons as they relate to *moadaw*, *eth* and *yowm*. We have three different Hebrew words for the same English words. Do you see how you can mistranslate a scripture; assume you know the definition of a word when you interpret that word from an English perspective instead of the Hebrew in which it was written?

New Testament Greek

If that wasn't enough, we had three words for –days, –seasons and –time in the Hebrew. There are actually four in the Greek:

Aion   *Genea*   *Kairos*   *Kronos*

In some of the circles that I was in were some people who were big on those –kairos moments. That is the moment in time when the presence of the Almighty, the epiphany, the revelation, the illumination of something is a –kairos moment.

Aion

–An age; by extension, perpetuity of time; by implication, the world; an unbroken age, a segment of time, an era, a period of time viewed in relation to what takes place in it.

You are going to see that the scripture is broken down in time. There are people who break it down theologically and then there are the interpretations. When we begin to talk about these particular breaks where you go from Egypt to the wilderness to the land to exile, these are all periods of time where certain things happened in scripture.

When you look at scripture during those periods of time and you don't understand the chronometrical principle, you will just put things together. You will take things out of context. You will find that people will take a scripture that is in the context of a particular verse during a particular time. We are going to see some of this here. They will take the scripture out of the context of the time it was written in. They will put it into another time, spiritualize it and put a spin on it. The next thing you know, you have created a concept by taking a scripture out of context at a particular time when that scripture was written.

It happens all the time. That is why we have so much confusion, so many denominations, so many different doctrines and so many different approaches to the Bible. It is very hard to have conversations with people when you are using basic tools that everybody should have to work with because you can't fix everything on your car with a pair of pliers. There are people who take a –pair of pliers‖ approach to the scriptures.

For some vehicles you have to have metric tools. Even the American tools don't work. You can have a wonderful toolbox of American tools and go to work on a car and realize that you need metrics. You need torque wrenches. You need screwdrivers. You need different kinds of screwdrivers. You need extensions. There are so many things that you need in order to effectively work on a vehicle.

In any trade that you are in, you have to have the right tools. When we came to our current building to try to set up all of these wires, we found that the wire that you crimp a telephone wire to is not the same wire that you use to build a cable. It is certainly not the same wire you use to use some of these cameras with. So, there are certain tools.

There are people who are approaching the Bible but they don't have the proper tools. If you don't have the proper tools, some people will just take that hammer approach. –I'll just bang it and make it work. You'll hear somebody say, –Just give me a hammer. I am fed up with it.‖ No, you don't want to take a hammer approach to the scriptures. You have to be disciplined. That is the word and where discipleship comes in. It is the one who is disciplined in their approach to the things of YeHoVaH. You must be disciplined and discipled so that you can properly disciple and discipline others, not just with words, but by example.

We see that this word *aion* is translated as:

Age(s)

Ephesians 2:7; Colossians 1:26 and translated *"course"* in *Ephesians 2:2*

By the way, in order to get the proper translation, you have to have a Bible for which there are translation tools that you can use. This is why it is very difficult to study –the scriptures.‖ It is difficult to study some of these new Hebrew Roots Bibles, Messianic Bibles, even the Complete Jewish Bible and some of the others that people love to read from because there are no tools that are designed to research those. You can't do word searches or word studies.

*(Ephesians 2:2) "Wherein in time past ye walked according to the **course** of this world, according to the prince of the power of the air, the spirit that now worketh in the children of disobedience:"*

The course of this world is mentioned. Even in our generation, have you ever heard the term –generation gap? You will see this gap in how you dress. I know you have heard the term –old- fashioned. –You dress old-fashioned or you dress for a certain era, for a certain age. You are dating yourself. They used to wear that stuff in the '60s. –That's an '80s haircut.

Notice here that we have the word translated –**ages** :

*(Ephesians 2:7) "That in the **ages** to come he might shew the exceeding riches of his grace in his kindness toward us through Messiah Yeshua."*

We looked at *Ephesians 2:2* and saw –course. We see *aion* now in *2:7* and it is the word –**ages**. This is the age to come. The same word is –**course** five verses prior. Now, I don't know why they would use –**age** in one place and –**course** in another when it is the same Greek word. It seems like it should just be –**age**. It is *aion*. Every time you see it, it is *aion*. Instead, the translators decided to use different words.

*(Colossians 1:26) "Even the mystery which hath been hid from **ages** and from generations, but now is made manifest to his saints:"*

How many times have you ever bothered to look up the word –**age** as in the age in which we live?

Here the same word *aion* is translated:

–**Eternal** : *Ephesians 3:11; 1 Timothy 1:17.* We have –course, We have –age. Now here is –**eternal** from the same Greek word.

We are also going to see it translated as –**forever** : *Philippians 4:20; 1 Timothy 1:17.*

But all of those words from an English perspective have different meanings in our minds. An –**age** is not –**eternal**. It is either the present age, the past age or the future age. It is a –**course** of time. Now –**forever** and –**eternal** might have some significance. You can connect –**eternal** with –**forever**. Actually, –**forever** is not necessarily eternal in our minds, which is why we have to add –**and ever** so it is –**forever and ever.**

You have all of these words that are similar in a sense, but then you get to *aion* as –**world(s)** : *Matthew 13:39, 40, 49; 24:3; 1 Corinthians 10:11; Hebrews 1:2; 11:3.*

*(Matthew 13:39) "The enemy that sowed them is the devil; the harvest is the end of the **world**; and the reapers are the angels."*

He is giving an explanation of the parable of the seed. We see that the enemy that sowed those bad seeds was the devil. The harvest is the end of the world. You have heard people talk about that great end-time harvest. We see this word *aion* as world, course, age, eternal and forever.

Genea

Genea is –a generation; by implication, an age, a period of time (of limited duration). –During that generation or –the generation to come. We see how it talks about generational blessings; all of these blessings. You have generational curses. People like focusing on generational curses. I like focusing on the blessings, but it is to three and four generations or 1,000 generations. In *Exodus 20* it is dealing with those who love YeHoVaH and who keep the commands; showing mercy or love for a thousand generations.

But the sins of the Father pass down to the third and fourth generation of them that hate YeHoVaH. The difference, even in the book of *Exodus* and looking at the commands (the ten commands) is that you will see the distinction between loving YeHoVaH and hating YeHoVaH. Isn't that amazing?

Let's look at that for a moment. You hear a lot about the generational curses.

(Exodus 20:5) *"Thou shalt not bow down thyself to them, nor serve them: for I the LORD thy God am a jealous God, visiting the iniquity of the fathers upon the children unto the third and fourth generation of them that hate me;"*

That is the third and fourth generation, the iniquity of the Fathers, the lawlessness of the Father. What you see here is if a person does not obey Father's commands, that is what opens up ***Deuteronomy 28:15-66***, the curses of disobeying the commands. **When we don't keep his commands, we are showing contempt.**

Yeshua said, "If you love me, you will keep my commands."

Well, what if you don't keep his commands? Then what?

Loving YeHoVaH and hating YeHoVaH is as simple as keeping the commands.

This shows that you love him. Not keeping the commands shows that you hate him. People are not balling their fists up and saying –I hate you. No, you are not doing it that way. You are doing it by your actions. You will know a tree by its fruit. You will know a person by their actions. Regardless of what a person says, they can say they love YeHoVaH all they want. They can say they love God or they love the Lord all they want, but if you are not keeping his commands…

The Bible says that if you say that you love him and you don't keep his law, then you are a liar and the truth is not in you.

What is truth? His word is truth. What word? The word that was with YeHoVaH from the beginning, the word that became flesh.

His word is truth. So, if the truth is not in you, what he is saying is that his word (which is his commands) is not in you. This is what he is writing upon the hearts of people: the law that he wrote on tables of stones (which they broke). He is now going to write upon the hearts of individuals. You can either break them by not doing them or show that you have them written in your heart by keeping them.

"If you love me, keep my commandments. If you say that you love me and you don't keep my commands, then you are a liar."

So here in *Exodus* we see that he says, *"…visiting the iniquities on the children."* Let me tell you something. You can go to deliverance ministry all day long. You can have people spitting on you, coughing on you, casting out devils on you, have you spitting in a bucket, rolling on the floor, your eyes rolling back in your head and throwing up. But when you have done all of that and all of those demons have come out of you again, you still have to keep his commandments or they will come back. And they will see that hey, your house is swept and garnished. You –don't have to keep the law, but the demons will tell you that **it is the law that keeps YOU!**

It is the law that keeps them out. It is the commandments of YeHoVaH that shows who you are possessed by. You are either possessed by him or you are possessed by them. If he is in you, they can't dwell in you because he is light and in him there is no darkness. So, the darkness has to stay in the dark and you walk in the light. You walk in the light by showing that his word (which is light) is in you. He who is light dwells in you and his commandments live in you.

(Exodus 20:6) *"And shewing mercy unto thousands of them that love me, and keep my commandments."*

Do you see that? If you love YeHoVaH you show you love me because you keep my commandments. If you don't keep my commands, you are showing that you hate YeHoVaH. Therefore, these sins of the Father are going to pass down to the son. And if that Father doesn't keep the commands because his Father did not keep the commands, you will see that the sins of that Father are going to pass down to the son. That is the iniquity and the lawlessness.

Here is why it is important for us to walk in the commands in the presence of our children. This is why Father commanded Moses to command the people to teach the children the commands. It is because if they don't see the Father living out those commands, they are not going to live out the commands. Just because you as a Father and a Mother live out the commands, your children are going to decide whether they are going to follow the commands or not.

You have Adam and Eve (Mr. and Mrs. Adam) made in the express image of the Almighty. They have a child who is a murderer. They have a son, the first generation from them and one of them is a murderer. Who influenced him? He was not hanging out with the neighbor's children. He was not with a bad crowd. He *was* the bad crowd.

You have some people talking about how, –Oh, my baby's hanging out with the wrong crowd. No, you should be concerned about the children who are hanging out with your baby. As a parent sometimes, you have to protect your community from your child instead of trying to protect your child from the community.

I know that sounds hard, but some of you parents know what I am talking about.

So — showing mercy. I could never understand why the Father would incorporate that into the commands. If you have a child who won't listen to you and they disrespect you, you take that child down to the city gate and explain it to the elders. But who is going to do that? There are parents who would let their children run them ragged. They will do everything within their power. There are parents who have children living in their homes and they have to lock their doors while they go to sleep in their bedroom because they are afraid. That is a sad thing when you are afraid of the children or the people who live in your house. It is certainly not peaceful.

With some people we just have to put them out. They will have to fend for themselves.

I know that this is not what we are talking about, but when we ignore the commands of the Almighty, even though we may say that we are Torah-observant, that means you have to know where love and mercy and grace fit. But you also have to know where discipline fits because if you don't discipline your children, you don't love them. Their actions are going to show whether or not they have been disciplined. It will show by how they talk to you, by how they treat you. They will run all over you. They will take full advantage of you. They will expect you to do for them and not concern themselves about you, because after all, –they didn't ask to be here.

You have to really stand upon the word, not just in your mind, but in your heart. And oftentimes it is going to cause us to do some tough things. I know. I tried to get the mind and heart of the Almighty when he had to put his creation out of the garden that he meticulously prepared for them to live in.

That was heartbreaking. He told them, –The day you eat from that tree, you are going to die. Don't make me. And even in his mercy he clothed them. People talk about how that grace –came through Jesus. The mercy of YeHoVaH was apparent when he clothed individuals who had been given the death sentence. He did not give them the death sentence. It was their own actions that brought the death sentence. He says, –Listen, I have to put you out, but it is cold out there, so here are some clothes to keep you warm. But you have to go. You can't stay here.

Genea is translated –age(s) in *Ephesians*.

(Ephesians 3:5) *"Which in other **ages** was not made known unto the sons of men, as it is now revealed unto his holy apostles and prophets by the Spirit;"*

There were things that could not be seen by those who were not possessed by the Spirit. Therefore, there were individuals who yielded, who gave, who the Father allowed his Spirit to come upon. They would see things. They would prophesy. They would write. They would chronicle the words and visions, dreams and utterances that the Father would put in them.

Then there is us, we who have been given the Holy Spirit. The Holy Spirit shows us things. The Holy Spirit prepares us for things. We have to be willing to allow him to do that because he will show us things to come. He will show us how to avoid the traps and pitfalls in the world around us.

This word *genea* also appears a few verses later:

(Ephesians 3:21) *"Unto him be glory in the church by Christ Jesus throughout **all ages**, world without end. Amen."*

Then we see the word –generation(s) : *Luke 1:48, 50; Colossians 1:26.*

(Luke 1:48) *"For he hath regarded the low estate of his handmaiden: for, behold, from henceforth all **generations** shall call me blessed."*

That is all generations, everybody who reads this story. Just by reading it, they are going to call her –blessed.

Genea translates as –**nation** : *Philippians 2:15.*

Genea is a generation, ages. We see a period of time, now a nation (in the sense of a nation spanning a specific time period).

(Philippians 2:15) *"That ye may be blameless and harmless, the sons of God, without rebuke, in the midst of a crooked and perverse **nation**, among whom ye shine as lights in the world;"*

It is so easy sometimes to allow the world around us to influence us. How many times have we thought or said and even believed that if I were to walk according to the word, the world will walk upon me like a door mat? So, we find ourselves conforming. I constantly talk to my children. Even today I was just reminding them, –Listen, there is a way that seems right.

We feel that in order for people to understand us in the nation, in the world, in the age, in the time and place that we live, we don't want to be taken advantage of. We don't want people using us. Sometimes you have to (in their mind) be tough.

I was taking my son to the DMV. There was this young lady there with her mother. This was heart breaking. My son got out of my purview. We were in the DMV. He is there to get his permit. There are all of these people there. One minute I see that he is standing in line. I am looking for him and the young lady next to me says, –Are you looking for Aaron?   (My son.)
–He's over there. So, my son and her have made contact, eye contact. Her mother is sitting next to her.

So, I say to her, –You know Aaron? She says, –Yeah. I know Abel, too. She knows both of my sons. So, I am sitting here next to a stranger who knows the children in my household. So, I said,

–Oh, well, how is Aaron at school?

–Well, Aaron is cool.

–What about Abel?

–Well Abel is not there anymore. He graduated. He was kind of quiet.

And the Mother says, –Don't tell him anything. You have to go to school with those children. Don't tell him anything. Basically, she didn't want any trouble. She didn't want me going back home and asking my children about something that maybe she said. Where I grew up, parents were in their children's business. Today parents are telling their children, —Mind your own business. Don't be a snitch. You have to live with these people. Don't cause trouble. Try to get along. If you see something, act like you didn't see it. Don't tell the police anything. Don't tell anybody anything. Don't get involved.

That is the world literally violating the commands of YeHoVaH. That is because a false witness is not just somebody who says they saw something that they didn't see. A false witness is also somebody who says they didn't see something that they saw. –I don't want to be a snitch. You mean you don't want to be a witness. That is what you are saying. You don't want to be a witness. You don't want to be called to testify. –I am afraid of retribution. So, you don't want to be a witness.

You have parents who are teaching their children to be false witnesses by acting like they don't see something when they obviously see it. That is how this woman was preparing her daughter. She was ready to talk to me, but mama said, –Don't tell him anything because you have to go to school with those children.

I almost rebuked her, but I didn't know her. That was the day I was trying to be nice. I was trying to spread some joy and some sunshine. I was trying to encourage people and here this woman is begging for rebuke. But I let her go.

Genea is translated –time(s) in ***Acts 14:16; 15:21.***

(Acts 14:16) *"Who in times past suffered all nations to walk in their own ways."*

Father allowed people to do whatever they wanted to do. He is doing that today. He even gives people up to reprobate minds so that they may enjoy those things that are unseemly and not right. That is the compassion of the Father that says, –You keep up that life. It is obvious your mind is so seared and your conscious is so seared. This is what you will find.

One of the things that you may have heard of is Dr. Ben Carson. He has made some statements because he is moving out of neurosurgery into politics. He has made statements about homosexuals. And these guys come out there and say things and then they backpedal. The next thing you know they are apologizing to this group and that group because they said what they really felt. But now they suffer the backlash from it. They have to make things nice.

Listen, homosexuality is wrong. Lesbianism is wrong. But if we approach and condemn the homosexual, the lesbian, the person who has a relationship with animals, the Father has the same judgment for the nice person who is fornicating. He has the same judgment for the one who is committing adultery, the one you lie for and don't want their wife or their husband to ask you anything because you don't want to be the one to tell them. Father has the same issue toward people who live immoral lives, no matter what form of immorality they choose to live. Immorality is immorality is immorality.

Sometimes people can get so caught up in that immoral lifestyle that they become void of judgment. You talk to them. –I know, I know. But then at some point they say, –That's just the way I am and unless there is a miracle, I am not going to change. But it is another thing when you begin to say, –That's the way Father made me. There is a difference between –that's the way I am and –this is the way God made me. So now I am acceptable in his sight because he made me that way. I was born that way.

That is a reprobate. That person is void of judgment. The compassion, the mercy and the grace of the Almighty says, –Okay, that person is void of judgment. I am going to turn them over to a reprobate mind so at least they get to enjoy the little life they have because the day of judgment is going to come. And from that point on all the joy and the fun is gone. That's the mercy and the grace of the Father.

He is merciful. His mercy endures forever and ever throughout eternity.

Kairos

Kairos is an occasion; i.e. set or proper time; a measure of time; a fixed and definite time; a seasonable time; the right time; a period of time; a limited portion of time.

It is translated –**season(s)** : *Luke 4:13; 12:42; Acts 1:7; 14:17; 1 Thessalonians 5:1.*

(1 Thessalonians 5:1) *"But of the <u>times and the seasons</u>, brethren, ye have no need that I write unto you."*

You see this phrase –times and seasons. In some cases, it is the same word. It is like in –the time and time or in –the season and season. In English class we were taught to use words. I don't know how you were taught where you came from, but there are synonyms, which are words you use that basically say the same things. You don't just want to keep using the same word over and over, so you find a word that says the same thing just so it looks like you know more than two or three words. You have a repertoire of words to use to express what you are saying. You are saying the same thing using different words.

Kairos translates as –time(s) in *Mark 1:15; Luke 19:44; 21:24; Acts 3:18; Romans 5:6, 13:11; 2 Corinthians 6:2; Ephesians 1:10; 1 Thessalonians 2:17; 2 Thessalonians 2:6; 1 Timothy 4:1; 2 Timothy 3:1; Hebrews 9:10; 1 Peter 1:5, 11; Revelation 1:3; 11:18; 22:10.*

This word is used all throughout the Brit Chadasha.

Kronos

Kronos is defined as —a space in time (in general); a period of time; by implying delay. It is translated as –season(s) however in *Acts 19:22; 20:18; Revelation 6:11; 20:3.*

We just say *kairos* translated as **time** and as **season(s),** but we also see *kronos* as **season(s)**.

(Revelation 6:11) *"And white robes were given unto every one of them; and it was said unto them, that they should rest yet for a **little season**, until their fellow servants also and their brethren, that should be killed as they were, should be fulfilled."*

So, we see a rest for a little season.

We see the word *kronos* also translated as –space (as in space in time): *Acts 15:33; Revelation 2:21.*

Kronos also translates as –time(s) : *Acts 1:6-7; 3:21; 7:17; 17:30; Galatians 4:4; 1 Thessalonians 5:1; 1 Peter 1:20; Jude 18; Revelation 10:6.*

Kronos is used in different verses, but it is saying pretty much the same things: **times**, **seasons**, **space**.

Together these words support the concept that God has divided and arranged time into a series of successive times and seasons. We are going to look into that in the next lesson.

We know that there are spaces, times and seasons. The Bible is broken up into spaces, times and seasons. We have to understand when we are reading the Bible, what season it is in, what time frame it is in. This is why I tell people that if they are going to read a book, there are certain things that you want to know about the book. This helps you to understand the book.

Who wrote it? Who wrote the book will tell you a lot. When people want me to read something, I want to know who is the author of the book. Once I know the author of the book — usually on some of the books, they will give you a little outline of who the person is. But with the technology space and time that we are in you can also –*Google* them.

What I want to find out about this person is which theological perspective they are writing the book from. Everybody has a theological view. If it is a Baptist who wrote it, the book is going to be from a Baptist theology. If the person is Pentecostal, it is going to have a Pentecostal bent. Once I find this out, now I have a general idea of some of the things that may be said, so I should not be surprised when I read that theological perspective.

I read a book on keeping the Sabbath holy called, –Keeping the Sabbath Holy. Within the first paragraph of the book I see the words, –those of us who keep the Sunday Sabbath. So, everything in the book was written on the premise that Sunday was the Sabbath, but in the title it is, –Keeping the Sabbath Holy. Once you understand this, you understand that this was written by a Christian Reformed person.

When I began to explain and express the ideology of the biblical Sabbath, one of my reformed colleagues wanted me to read the book on keeping the Sabbath holy. I read the first paragraph and everything from the first paragraph and all 200+ pages start out on the premise that Sunday is the Sabbath.

Talk about a perverted book.

So theologically you can learn something by knowing the theology behind the person who is writing. You want to know who wrote the book when you read the Bible. There are certain books of the Bible that we still don't know who wrote them. I have to remind people sometimes because there is only a certain portion of this book that was actually written by the finger of the Almighty.

There is only a certain portion of this book that was written by the finger of YeHoVaH!

We know that to be the word. There are other portions of this book where we don't know who wrote it, so if I don't know who wrote it, that automatically creates doubt. Okay, I have to have a broad approach to this. But I think that many people have this love affair with this book and they believe that it was mysteriously and mythically given. You have seen the Michelangelo. It is like the Father took this King James Version and handed it down from heaven. That's the way some people approach it. They think that this book in its entirety in the King James Version was handed down from heaven by the Almighty. – If the King James was good enough for Moses, it is good enough for me.

This is why you need to know the times and the seasons. If you knew the times and the seasons, you would know that the King James Bible was not written in that time. That will save you some headaches right there. People would not make stupid statements like that and believe what they are saying.

So, you want to know who wrote the book. You want to know why. Why did they write this book? To whom was it written? When? These are valid questions. A good library is going to have a reference and that is where a good commentary comes in. A good commentary is going to tell you that this book was written possibly in this time and here is why.

Now you know that this was written between this time period and if you understand that, now you have chronology. You have the chronometrical principle at work. You know that this book was written during this time. –Okay, where was Israel? What was going on in the history of Israel during this time? What was their relationship with the Almighty like at this time?

That is going to help you understand the prophesies, the prophetic utterances and why they are being prophesied to in this manner. You need the historical data. You need the geographic data. You need the chronological data or the chronometrical data. You need this information in order to properly apply tools and to properly interpret the Bible so that you are not cutting and pasting, eisegeting, reading into the word and trying to make the Bible fit your theology.

Class 64 Study Summary
Key Points

1. The chronometrical principle is that principle by which the interpretation of a verse or passage of scripture is determined upon consideration of its chronometrical setting.
2. The word –chronometrical comes from two Greek words: –chronos meaning time and –metron meaning measure.
3. Chronometry is the art of measuring time. A chronometer is an instrument that measures time. A chronographer is someone who writes concerning time or the events of time.
4. There is a Hebrew word for ages, times and seasons. It is *mowed* and has various forms (i.e. *moade, moweadah, moedim, moed*). A moedim or moed is an appointed time or season.
5. When we put our trust in YeHoVaH, we do not have to fear man.
6. Our goal should be to get in the Father's presence and allow him to reveal his plan for us to us and then begin to walk in that plan.
7. The word –eth represents time as a specific or appointed time such as now, when, evening, tide, time when or a certain time. It can also mean seasons such as seasons of the year (winter, spring, summer, fall).
8. The word –yowm means a day literally or figuratively as a space of time.
9. We are to share with people and then leave them alone. The Father will deal with them.
10. There are three different Hebrew words for the same English words. This is how scripture can be mistranslated. For example, we have days, times and seasons as they relate to moadaw, eth and yowm. This is why it is important to search the scriptures and look up word definitions to get the exact meanings that have been lost in the translations.
11. The same problem occurs in the Greek language. Here we have four words in the Greek language for the same three English words: days, seasons and time. In the Greek they are Aion, Genea, Kairos and Kronos.
12. The Greek word Aion means an age by extension, perpetuity of time; unbroken age, segment.
13. You have to have the right tools in order to study and therefore fully appreciate the Bible.
14. Genea is a generation, by implication an age or period of time of limited duration or a nation.
15. Yeshua said, –If you love me you will keep my commandments. Loving YeHoVaH and hating YeHoVaH is as simple as keeping the commands or not keeping them.
16. The same laws that YeHoVaH wrote on the tablets of stone, he will write in the hearts of his people.
17. You can go to deliverance ministry all day long, but if you don't keep the commandments of YeHoVaH, there is nothing that will prevent evil spirits from returning. It is the law that keeps them out. It is the commandments of YeHoVaH that shows who possesses you.
18. The word –kairos is an occasion, a set or proper time, a measure of time or a fixed period.
19. The word –kronos is a space in time, a period of time (by implying delay) or a season.
20. God has divided and arranged time into a series of successive times and seasons.
21. There are certain books of the Bible that we still don't know who wrote them. Only a certain portion of the bible was actually written by the finger of the Almighty.
22. We need to know the times and seasons. This is important when understanding what was written, who wrote it and the overall chronology of time. This is so that we can properly interpret the Bible instead of taking what is written and trying to fit it into a theology.

Review Exercise

1. Complete this chart in order to sum up your understanding of how terms for the passage of time are utilized in the Bible:

Hebrew	Sum it up ...
Moedah	
Eth	
Yom (or *Yowm*)	
Greek	
Aion	
Genea	
Kairos	
Kronos	

2. Time is critical. For us it is one of the three crucial concepts (time, space, matter). How does an understanding of the biblical measurement of time enhance your understanding of scripture?

3. Many debates have centered around the biblical concepts involving time. Using the beginning tools that you now have in the chronometrical principle, how might you explain the terms used for time to someone who has an issue with time in the Bible?

_____
_____
_____
_____
_____

Rate the following statements by filling in the most appropriate number.

(1 = I do not agree 10 = I agree completely)

Objectives:

1. I can give an overview of the chronometrical principle.

   1. ○   2. ○   3. ○   4. ○   5. ○   6. ○   7. ○   8. ○   9. ○   10. ○

2. I can describe how three Hebrew words and four Greek words for time are used in scripture.

   1. ○   2. ○   3. ○   4. ○   5. ○   6. ○   7. ○   8. ○   9. ○   10. ○

My Journal

What I learned from this class:

Discipleship Training Class 65

The Chronometrical Principle (part 2)

Objectives:

As a Discipleship student, at the end of this class you will be able to:

- Define terms relating to time in the scripture
- Explain the theological division of Bible time into ages: past and present/future
- Define the validity of the "gap theory" of **Genesis 1:1-1:2**

Of all of the teaching that I do, I feel that these teachings are some of the most beneficial that you will encounter on your spiritual journey. Here you are literally able to learn principles. You can learn things that, unless you were to pay for a four-year Seminary or a Bible College degree, you would probably never hear. Even though you would not hear about the things that I am sharing with you, you would certainly see the results of these trainings that individuals who have gone through classes like this in Bible College and Seminary have had. You will hear certain key things in their messages.

As we are looking at these principles, you have probably been able to ascertain or recognize in sermons, things that you have heard. Even now as you are listening to messages, you are hearing the principles come out in the teachings. We are going to get further into something and I have an example that I want to share with you.

In the last lesson, we began looking at the chronometrical principle. We found that it is that principle by which the interpretation of a verse or passage is determined upon a consideration of its chronometrical setting. The word –chronometrical is taken from two Greek words: *chronos* meaning –time, and *metron* meaning –measure. It is the measurement of time. We looked at both Hebrew and Greek words dealing with this principle.

To review the Greek:

Aion: –an age; by extension, perpetuity of time; by implication, the world; an unbroken age, a segment of time, an era, a period of time viewed in relation to what takes place in it. You will hear scripture talking about the –end of the age or –the end of the world or –the worlds to come.

Genea: —A generation; by implication, an age, a period of time (of limited duration)

Kairos: –an occasion; i.e., set or proper time; a measure of time; a fixed and definite time; a seasonable time; the right time; a period of time; a limited portion of time

Kronos: —a space of time (in general); a period of time; by implying delay

Those words are associated with the chronometrical principle of scriptural interpretation. We looked at some of the ways those words were translated.

Together these words support the concept that YeHoVaH has divided and arranged time into a series of successive times and seasons.[13]

These ages can be divided as follows.

<u>**Past Ages**</u>

The Eternal Ages Past Age of Creation

Age of Recreation

Age of the Patriarchs-Promise; Adam-Abraham Age of the Chosen Nation-Law; Isaac/Israel-

Messiah

This is an all-inclusive term referring to all the ages of time prior to the New Testament. I have to share with you up front that these are all theological approaches to scripture interpretation. When you deal with theology, you have to understand that theology is based upon a system of beliefs by a particular denomination. So, theology is broken down. ***Theos*** is the Almighty. Theology is the study of. When we begin to look at the theological perspectives, we find that there is a Baptist theology. There is a Presbyterian theology. There is an Adventist theology. Theology is going to be boxed into the category of the approach of the denomination. The denomination is approaching the scripture from their theological perspective.

When you begin to add a theological perspective from a denominational point of view, then you are going to come to the conclusion of that denomination and what they believe, teach and practice and actually put upon their people to live in order to be a member in good standing.

When we think about this, the past ages from a theological standpoint are the ages of time prior to the New Testament. It is everything that happened from creation up until the New Testament period. It can also be used in a more limited sense to indicate any one of the ages prior to the cross.

You are going to see with these principles, that they can be manipulated. We will see that a little bit later.

*(**Hebrews 1:1**)* *"God, who at sundry times and in divers manners spake in time past unto the fathers by the prophets,"*

*(**Colossians 1:26**)* *"Even the mystery which hath been hid from ages and from generations, but now is made manifest to his saints:"*

The Eternal Ages Past — We see that YeHoVaH himself is eternal and unlimited as to time. He is the –I AM; having no beginning nor ending.

*(**Psalm 90:2**)* *"...from everlasting to everlasting, thou art YeHoVaH."*

---

[13] We will be looking at dispensationalism in a later lesson to try to understand why people believe what they believe about the times we live in. Why and where did they get the idea that there is a season and a time in which Father dealt with individuals on a dispensational point of view? Then they come up with dispensational theories that actually bring in these strange doctrines such as the Trinity and the rapture and all of those kinds of things. You are going to see how those came into being. These theological principles were implied or used to come up with those. There are downsides and also plus sides to understanding principles of biblical interpretation and how to use those principles properly.

So that is from eternity past to eternity future. How could an eternity be in the past, but it has no beginning? YeHoVaH has no beginning. If he has a beginning, no one knows when that beginning was. YeHoVaH was the beginning. He is the beginning.

(Revelation 1:8) *"I am Alpha and Omega, the beginning and the ending, saith the Lord,* ***which is, and which was, and which is to come, the Almighty.****"*

(Revelation 1:4) *"John to the seven churches which are in Asia: Grace be unto you, and peace, from him* ***which is, and which was, and which is to come****; and from the seven Spirits which are before his throne;"*

(Isaiah 41:4) *"Who hath wrought and done it, calling the generations from the beginning? I YeHoVaH,* ***the first, and with the last; I am He****."*

These verses encompass time past, time present and time future or eternity. You see the chronometrical principle of time past, time present and time future all expressed in these verses. The expressions –from everlasting and –which was both refer to YeHoVaH's existence in eternity past. He was in the beginning. He was the beginning. He is the beginning. Before him there was nothing or he was before nothing. It is interesting, I know.

The Age of Creation — Although scripture is somewhat silent concerning the creation of the angelic hosts and the universe of worlds, it does imply an age prior to creation of the earth as we know it, in which these were created. Understand that when we talk about these ages, we are talking about theology. We are talking about a theological approach to the Bible.

We don't know because we don't see the scriptures telling us when the angels were made. All we know is that they were there. They were always there. We see the seven days of creation as it pertains to the heavens and the earth, but we don't see a particular day where he made the angels or where Lucifer was created. The scripture is silent when it comes down to that.

We know that based upon certain scriptures that Lucifer (the serpent, the great dragon, HaSatan) was in the garden. We know that from *Revelation*, but we don't know when Lucifer was created. We know he was, but when? We don't know.

The Age of Creation implies an age prior to the creation of the earth as we know it. As we look at *Genesis*, we won't find that. We can look throughout the Bible and we still won't find it.

There are verses which hint to certain things, but nothing definite. And yet people want to have all of these heady theological conversations about angelic beings and sons of God and giants and all of these kinds of things. They create DVDs and teachings around it, but let me tell you something. The moment you go beyond what is written, you open yourself up to all manner of theology and the possibilities are even greater that you are going to go into error.

There are questions that people ask me. The reason why some people who are biblically astute and knowledgeable of scripture ask questions about the Bible is because they can't find the answers in the Bible. I think that if you can't find it and you are solid in your search, what makes you think I can find it? I am not trying to be smart or anything like that. I am just trying to be honest with people.

I think there are times when the pressure of the question creates this desire to try to answer the question. And because of that desire, we can go into –what ifs. We can go into theory. The moment you get into theory, you are creating things and pulling things out of mid-air and finding scripture to support your theory.

This is where people begin to eisegete. They begin to read into the Bible instead of exegeting (pulling out what is actually there). The moment you begin to read into it is the moment you go off course. There are a lot of people who go off course. And I try (as scripture tells us) not to go beyond what is written if the scripture is unclear on certain things (because the scripture is unclear). There is a difference between bringing clarity to a passage and trying to bring clarity to a theory from the Bible.

You can't use the Bible to justify a theory. You must stay within the context of scripture. The moment you take scripture out of context, you are now creating doctrine. Yeshua says that we have to beware of the doctrine of religion, the doctrine of denominations; which is the doctrine of the Pharisees, of the Sadducees; and then the doctrine of Herod, which is ultimately government.

Scripture is unclear on certain things and we might as well accept that.

(Genesis 1:1) *"In the beginning YeHoVaH created the heaven and the earth."*

(Colossians 1:16-17) *"For by him were all things created, that are in heaven, and that are in earth, visible and invisible, whether they be thrones, or dominions, or principalities, or powers: all things were created by him, and for him: And he is before all things, and by him all things consist."*

We see that he created the principalities, the powers and those things that are visible and those things that are invisible. We don't know when he created them, but we know that he did. He created everything pertaining to the earth and in the earth from *Genesis 1* to *Revelation*. We know that these are things that we can be pretty certain about. These are things where the scripture brings clarity. Through much study and pulling together the scriptures from *Genesis* to *Revelation*, we can look at the prophets and at the scripture from a chronological as well as a contextual principle.

We can see that there are certain things that the scripture is clear on. But there are certain things that it is unclear about.

We know that YeHoVaH made. He created all things. There is absolutely nothing created that he did not create.

(Revelation 4:11) *"Thou art worthy, O Lord, to receive glory and honour and power: for thou hast created all things, and for thy pleasure they are and were created."*

The heavenly hosts were created by the Almighty.

The Age of Recreation — Many Bible scholars assume that between verses 1 and 2 of *Genesis 1*, the fall of Satan took place; bringing about the chaotic condition spoken of in verse 2. You will hear things like the –gap theory. This is a theory which suggests that between ***Genesis 1:1*** and ***1:2*** the fall of Satan took place. There are some legitimate arguments for that and there are some solid arguments against it. That is why it is called a theory.

The idea is that yes, something went awry. The idea is that YeHoVaH who is light would not create things that are dark and chaotic. Would YeHoVaH an Elohim of order create something chaotic? This seems to suggest that something happened. But now trying to answer exactly what happened while not being there leads us into theories. We can argue these theories until Yeshua comes, but we cannot with any degree of 100% certainty say that our theories are correct. We have some pretty good arguments, but they don't necessarily mean that they are fact.

(Isaiah 45:18) *"For thus saith the* L<small>ORD</small> *that created the heavens; „God himself that formed the earth and made it; he hath established it, he created it not in vain, he formed it to be inhabited: I am the* L<small>ORD</small>*; and there is none else."*

This verse **implies** that when YeHoVaH created the heavens and the earth, he did not create the earth –without form and void, nor in a state of darkness. A person will take this verse and they will argue (based upon what *Isaiah* says) that it is impossible for YeHoVaH to have created the earth in a chaotic, dark state. This then suggests (and that is exactly what it does). It <u>suggests</u>.

Can I argue a suggestion as fact? Yet there are people out there who argue this as fact and who write books.

Look at the verse again in the Amplified:

(Isaiah 45:18 [Amplified]) *"For thus says the Lord who created the heavens, YeHoVaH himself who formed the earth and made it, who established it and created it not a worthless waste; He formed it to be inhabited: „I am the Lord, and there is no one else."*

The Amplified Bible here says that it was not created a worthless waste. He formed it to be inhabited. People will pull out these versions of the Bible and argue. And like I said, they are good arguments, but that doesn't mean that they are fact.

In connection with this, it is suggested that there was an indefinite period of time between the chaotic condition described in verse 2 and the events of the rest of the chapter.

I watch channels like the *History Channel*. And science is suggesting (based upon certain measurements) they have scientific measurements that have been done. They believe that the earth could be some billions of years old. People argue the existence of dinosaurs. Like many of you, I saw *Jurassic Park* a few times. They argue the existence of cave dwellers or cave men (Neanderthals). There is *Ice Age* and all of these theories that people argue scientifically. The question is, do science and the Bible contradict one another?

There are those who try to reconcile science and the Bible. In the process of doing all of these things, we are still left wondering. Based upon what the Bible teaches and what science teaches, based upon the Bible, we can justify 6,000 (years) and seven days of creation. If we look at the teaching that –a day is like a thousand years and a thousand years is as a day, we can surmise that based upon the history from Adam to Yeshua, we can say that there is going to be 7,000 years of history before the return.

There are all kinds of theories out there. If we are not careful, we begin to propagate theories that we can't prove. The moment you go out there on a limb, trying to get back is quite difficult. I suggest not going out there to begin with.

When you begin to talk about this indefinite period of time, you can get thousands of years or billions of years. You can even get (as some suggest), trillions of years between ***Genesis 1:1*** and ***1:2***. That's a lot of years to get between those verses.

The remainder of *Genesis 1* is actually a description of a period of recreation. By –recreation we mean –to create or form anew; to remake. There are words like –replenish that we find in *Genesis 1* that, as YeHoVaH commanded the man and the woman to replenish the earth, suggest that the earth had life forms before. It suggests that something chaotic took place where YeHoVaH destroyed the former things. Get into *Genesis 6* where you see that the flood comes. We see where YeHoVaH has the ability to completely wipe out life as we know it today with a single event and which he promised never to do by flood again. We know that it is possible that life existed on planet Earth and that it was destroyed and YeHoVaH started over with Adam and Eve. We know that it is possible, but can we prove it? Can we prove it from scripture?

That is where science comes in. I can't prove science. I am not a scientist. But when it comes down to arguing scripture, I have to stay within the framework of what scripture teaches and let the other people argue the other stuff.

Thus, YeHoVaH brings light out of darkness, order out of chaos, fruitfulness out of barrenness and life out of death; crowning this period with the creation of man, YeHoVaH's masterpiece. This age included the refashioning of the earth and the creation of man, a new creature, in the image of YeHoVaH.

The Age of the Patriarchs: Promise — From Adam to Abraham, there was a period of about 2,000 years. This –Age of the Fathers was bounded by Adam, the Father of the human race *(Genesis 5:1)* and Abraham, the Father of all of them who believe *(Romans 4:16-17)*.

This time period is substantiated by the genealogies given in *Genesis 5, 10* and *11* concerning the Godly Patriarchs. As noted in the covenantal principle, Adam, Noah and Abraham each received special covenantal promises. This distinguished this period as the age of promise. They were promised.

Abraham was the Father of many nations. There is the Abrahamic promise that was made. YeHoVaH promised Adam some things. They broke covenant with him. He promised that they were going to be removed from the garden if they did certain things and that the earth would be cursed as a result of what happened. He would have to work by the sweat of his brow. We know that Noah was promised that certain things were not going to happen. The rainbow is a sign of that promise.

We looked at the blood covenant. We saw circumcision. We see that there was a special covenantal promise that he would be the Father of many nations. There were promises that were associated with Abraham. There are promises that we enter into by entering into covenant with Abraham and his offspring Israel.

The Age of the Chosen Nation: Law — From Isaac to Yeshua there was another period of about 2,000 years. Here is where it gets tricky, especially with dispensationalists. If you had an opportunity to view an interview of David Cerullo by Michael Rood, David Cerullo was making some statements on the program. I kind of wished that I had taught this portion of our classes prior to David making those statements, because he kept using the phrase –the Age of the Church. Are you familiar with this? The –Age of the Church contrasted with the –Age of the Law.

Those are code words for dispensationalists. The Age of the Law was a particular age in which the law was in effect, meaning that when that age was over, the law was no longer in effect. Sometimes it grieves my spirit when I hear Messianics trying to sugar-coat the Torah as in, –It is YeHoVaH's instructions. They say things like, –We get to do, or –We are privileged because we get to do the commandments, or –We get to keep the law and celebrate the feasts. This seems to suggest that we are privileged because we get to do it, as if we don't have to do it.

You know people. If they think they don't have to do it, then why do it? This is especially so if you are taught by doing these things that you are –falling from grace. So, they put these spins on the truth to try and make it more palatable. Listen. Father doesn't care about your palate. He really doesn't because he is going to have the last word. You are either going to eat this word or that lake is going to eat you. It is that simple. I am not here to sugarcoat the law. The law is the law and we are under the law. Those who are not under the law are under the curse of the law.

The curse of the law is those curses that are associated with violating the law. The law is not cursed. For people to say that the law is cursed is to say that YeHoVaH gave the people he loved, the apple of his eye, a curse. Yeshua said clearly, —What Father is going to give his son a serpent if he asks for an egg? If we being evil know how to give good things to our children, how much more will our heavenly Father give the Holy Spirit to them that ask? Why would the Father give his people something that is cursed? It doesn't make sense.

We have these crazy people out there that are propagating this garbage.

When you hear words like –the Age of the Church, that is code. David was communicating code, but I don't think he knew any better because in one sense he was communicating this –age business. In another sense he was talking about the importance of keeping the feasts.

The feasts were in the Age of the Law, not in the Age of the Church (by people who talk about the – Church Age). The Church Age begins with Yeshua. Yeshua (according to that theology) delivered the church from the law and gave it a whole new day of worship — SUNday.

But you see, if you don't understand these principles, people will make statements that will fly right over your head. You are thinking that they are ministering to you, that they get it and that they understand it, but it is code for dispensationalism. It is code for people who are talking a theology, not a Bible.

You will not find the –Age of the Law in this book. That is theology. You will not find the –Age of the Church in this book. That is theology. That is dispensational theology that is trying to divide the Bible into sections, chapters and verses. Old Testament? That is theology and that theology is what causes the enmity between YeHoVaH and his people by putting religion in between him and us.

Now, we are dealing with religious terms and theological terms, not biblical terms. But if we understand these terms, we can now begin to see what people are saying to us a lot more clearly. We can hear what they are saying. Now we know how to say, –Hey, wait a minute. What do you mean by the _Age of the Church?' Please define that for me. What is the _Age of the Church?' What is the _Age of the Law?' I hear you saying it. I don't want to assume that you are saying what I think you are saying, so I want to give you an opportunity to clarify that for me. What are you saying? I want to make sure that I am hearing you correctly.

These are chronometrical principles you will never hear in worship in a Sunday Church or even in a Messianic community. You will never hear the term –chronometrical principle, but you will see the results of the chronometrical principle being applied with words like –the Age of the Law, –the Age of the Church or –dispensationalist.

They will use words in the Bible like the –Age to Come and the –Age Past. They will use those terms which are Greek words defined, or Greek words as English terms, when actually it is dealing with something else.

The –Age of the Sons was bounded by Isaac, the only begotten son of the Old Testament *(Hebrews 11:17)* and Yeshua, the only begotten Son of the New Testament. *(John 3:16)* YeHoVaH's promise to Abraham was centered in Isaac in that YeHoVaH said, *(Hebrews 11:18)* "…in Isaac shall thy seed be called." It was to be through the only begotten son that the chosen nation would come into existence.

(Hebrews 11:17-18) *"By faith Abraham, when he was tried, offered up Isaac: and he that had received the promises offered up his only begotten son, Of whom it was said, „That in Isaac shall thy seed be called:""*

This nation in its infancy was spoken of as YeHoVaH's son:

(Exodus 4:22-23) *"Israel is my son, even my firstborn."*

(Hosea 11:1) *"When Israel was a child, then I love him, and call my Son out of Egypt."*

(Exodus 4:22-23) *"And thou shalt say unto Pharaoh, „Thus saith the LORD, Israel is my son, **even my firstborn:** And I say unto thee, Let my son go, that he may serve me: and if thou refuse to let him go, behold, I will slay thy son, **even thy firstborn.**""*

Who is being referred to? It is referring to the sons of Israel. He was referring to Israel who was his son, his firstborn and from Israel came twelve sons which were also the tribes of Israel. Now Father is looking at Israel's offspring as one. What we see here is that YeHoVaH looked at Israel as one. This is what Yeshua was praying for the Messianic community; that we would be one.

(Hosea 11:1) *"When Israel was a child, then I loved him, and called my son out of Egypt."*

To this many membered son was given the law covenant with its tabernacle, priesthood, sacrifice, feasts and statutes, which were as –tutors and governors to bring this son into maturity.

With the failure of this son to fulfill the promises of YeHoVaH, the Father brought in his only begotten Son.

(Galatians 4:4-5) *"...made under the law, to redeem them that were under the law"*

It is at this point that theology takes liberty. By categorizing the Bible chronometrically, it can break the time into ages to fit its agenda. When you get into the book of *Galatians*, you are going to find that that is where a lot of arguments opposing the commandments are. There are a lot of arguments opposing the law.

When you begin to look at the chronometrical principle, you have to understand that this principle has already divided the book into ages. It has divided the Bible into chronological or measured time. Then it goes a step further. It divides the Bible into two large segments — the Old Testament and the New Testament; and at the New Testament, YeHoVaH started over.

It was not like he did with Noah where he destroyed everything. He started over with Yeshua and created this new community that was totally detached from the old community (other than those on Shavuot). Most Christians don't know that on the day of Pentecost there were Hebrews. These were Jewish people. These were individuals who were keeping the law. You have to understand this.

Yeshua said that the prerequisite to receiving the Holy Spirit was obedience to the law. As a matter of fact, let's look at this. You have a lot of counterfeits out there called Pentecostalism where people are now focusing on receiving the Holy Spirit apart from keeping the commands of the Almighty.

(John 14:15-16) *"If ye love me, keep my commandments. And I will pray the Father, and he shall give you another Comforter, that he may abide with you for ever;"*

"If you love me, keep my commandments — and I will pray."

When we look at the Holy Spirit coming upon the believers, the Jewish men who had come up to Pentecost, up to Shavuot at the appointed time (at the moedim) were law-abiding individuals that the Holy Spirit came upon.

When we look at Cornelius in *Acts 10,* the Bible lets us know that Cornelius was a just man who was zealous for the things of YeHoVaH. He gave alms to the poor. He was a righteous man. He loved the Jewish people. It gives every indication that Cornelius was a kosher-observant Italian who was seeking the God of Abraham, Isaac and Jacob. YeHoVaH disturbs Peter on a rooftop and tells him to go to Cornelius' house.

But the church doesn't want to look at these aspects. As a matter of fact, there is (as I would say) a stupid but brilliant explanation that helps to discount the law concerning Yeshua. It is that Yeshua had to come under the law in order to keep it fully to thereby do away with it.

So, Paul had to keep the law in order to reach those who were under the law to bring them out from under the law. Do you get this?

I tell you, theology takes a lot of liberty. If you don't see it, many of us have been hoodwinked, blinded by it, until we decided one day that we were going to search the Bible for ourselves.

Present/Future Ages

The term –Present Age is used to refer to the New Testament era. It is referred to in scripture as:

This world (age): *Matthew 13:22, 40; Luke 16:8; 20:34; Galatians 1:4; Titus 2:12*

The time of reformation: *Hebrews 9:10*

The time of restitution: *Acts 3:21*

The last days: *Acts 2:17; Hebrews 1:2*

The idea of the New Testament era or the term –New Testament does a major disservice to the people in this world. That is because there is the –Old Testament and there is the –New Testament. The New Testament begins where that page is between the –Old and the –New. It separates where Yeshua now comes onto the scene and puts a separation between the Old Testament and the New Testament.

Ironically you don't find the word –testament in the New Testament or in the Old Testament. You find the word –covenant. You see the liberty of translators who inserted words. You see how they put Easter in there and totally changed Passover to Easter. And you see that they created another religious holiday based upon one mention of a word. The majority of the world that confesses Jesus Christ as their Savior now celebrates Easter all because of a translation error or a translation propriety or translation liberty.

It is the same with the word –testament. The word –testament is not found in the Hebrew or the Greek, but it is found in the English. It comes from the word –*brit*. It comes from the word –covenant, meaning –to cut.

The New Testament is actually the New Covenant mentioned by *Jeremiah*. It is not a —New Testament. The idea of a New Testament refers to the books of the gospels and the letters that were written by the apostles. These were given the title –New Testament, but by whom?

By the translators.

With the New Testament separating the new from the old and based upon passages of the Bible to justify the division, they say that this was all the ‒will of the Father. And we bought it hook, line and sinker until we started searching the scriptures for ourselves as Bereans. We started asking questions. We see that the questions and the answers to those questions don't align themselves with what the Bible teaches.

This idea of a New Testament era is strictly a made-up term (theologically). But those theologians understand the language. When you begin to talk a certain language, only theologians understand. It is just like certain terms that only doctors understand or certain terms only chiropractors understand or lawyers understand. You don't go into a courtroom and try to represent yourself. The old expression that a person who represents themselves in a courtroom has a fool for a lawyer, is true.

You don't do surgery upon yourself. There are medical terms and legal terms that you have to look up in dictionaries. Then the definition of those words requires more dictionary search. The same thing applies to theology. There are code words in theological circles that theologians understand that go right over the laity's heads, like ‒Church Age. This word is not going to go over your head anymore.

When you hear people talking about the ‒Church Age, they are talking about people who are not under the law. When you hear people talking about the ‒Age of the Law, they are talking about a point in time when the law ‒ceased to exist. It was ‒done away with. It was fulfilled in Yeshua and we are ‒no longer required to keep it.

These individuals make these statements and you think they are talking right to you, but they are talking over your head. You think you are ‒gelling with them. And basically, you think they are agreeing with what you believe, when they are saying something totally different.

The Age of the Law theologically is a time period between Moses and Yeshua. At that point, the law ‒ceases. Therefore, you are ‒no longer under the law. That is what it teaches. It is hypocrisy. It is not biblical, but that is what is being taught in theological circles. You need to understand it so you will know how to properly confront it when those words are being thrown around by theologians who think they are talking in code.

The Present Age is referred to as ‒the time of Reformation. Now when you think about — Reformation for a Lutheran, the first thing they think of is Martin Luther and the Reformation period. There are all of these periods. The time of Reformation is referring to the Reformation (by theologians). That is why they called it ‒The Reformation. That is when the separation between the Jews and the church, the ‒spiritual Israel and replacement theology came about. All of these fancy words have hoodwinked people and gotten people like us at a period of time in our lives to get totally off course from this book into the theological broad way. We were serving YeHoVaH with all of our hearts or God, or the Lord. We were being zealous, but not according to knowledge.

The times of restitution — ‒Oh, we are in the last days. Yes, we are in the last days. There are people who propagate fear. They propagate this ideology that ‒Jesus is coming soon! And because Jesus is coming soon, you want to make sure that your life is in order (and that is true). He could come like a thief in the night. Yes, that is true.

‒Oh, but that good ol' gettin' up morning. Now we have people looking to the point where Jesus is going to come and deliver them from all of their bills. He is coming to deliver them from all of their heartaches. They are going to take eagle's wings and fly away to that great bye-and- bye in the sky. This is where a great majority of the church is right now with its dispensational and rapture theology. They are waiting for the day where the rest of the world is left behind and they don't have a clue where they are going. They are going to heaven. Well, where is heaven?

It is in the sky somewhere with streets of gold.

Remember, the Bible says that there is a new heaven and a new Jerusalem that is going to come down, so something is going to happen here on the earth. If we are going to heaven, some of us are going to come back, but that is another lesson.

This period of the Present/Future Age is also known theologically as the Messianic Age. That is this present age.

The Messianic Age — First Coming to Second Coming The Age to Come

The Eternal Ages Future

You will see all of these in the New Testament or Brit Chadasha, as some call it.

The Messianic Age — From the first coming of Messiah to his second coming is believed to be a period of approximately 2,000 years. This is the age in which Messiah is to perform his Messianic work.

From the first coming of Messiah to his second coming is to be around 2,000 years. It is like okay, now we are talking about 6,000 years because we know based upon time and the reckoning of time, that almost 2,000 years ago Yeshua was crucified. Now that the 2,000-year period is almost up, there is the expectation that he is going to come. This is the idea. The rapture is going to take place. When he comes, he is not going to touch down. He is going to come to a certain point. Those who are dead in Messiah are going to rise and those who are alive are going to join them. Then at a later point (1,000 years later) he is going to come and touch down.

There are all of these theories out there. I will tell you something. You can look at the scripture and you can support pre-tribulation, post-tribulation, pre-millennial, amillennial or post-millennial. You have all of these theories out there and you have denominations who swear and who are willing to die, even though they are adamantly opposed to one another. You have all of these belief systems out there. People are preaching it as if it is the gospel truth; although they oppose one another.

Which one of them is right? It all depends upon who you listen to.

This Messianic Age is supposed to be the age in which the Messiah is to perform his Messianic work. This work although one, involves two distinct phases. There are the first and second comings with the second being the ultimate completion of that which was begun in the first. This period is also referred to as the Age of the Holy Spirit. It is bounded by two great outpourings of the Spirit.

Pentecostals know it as the –former rain and the –latter rain. The latter rain is going to be greater than the former rain.

The New Testament clearly teaches that Messiah came as the fulfillment of the promises and as the ‑fulfiller and abolisher of the law. You see, this is where it gets tricky.

He is the fulfiller and the abolisher. Notice the theological switch here. The theologians will agree with you. We as Messianics love to point out **Matthew 5:17** when he says, ‑Think not that I have come to abolish the law or the prophets. I have not come to abolish or do away with, but to fulfill.

But what the Christians and the theologians who perpetuate a New Testament theology (the Age of the Church) say in their teaching and by practice is this. (This is why they don't keep the Sabbath or any of the feasts and festivals and any of the commands except the ones they choose to keep.) What they are teaching is that the Messiah came. Notice it says that the New Testament clearly teaches. It doesn't, but what theology clearly teaches is that Messiah came as the fulfillment of the promises and the fulfiller and the abolisher of the law.

Do you see that? This is what they say. This is what they are teaching in Seminary. This is what they are teaching in Bible Colleges. It is that the New Testament clearly teaches that Messiah came as the fulfillment of the promises and the fulfiller and abolisher of the law. He fulfilled the law and then he did away with it. He didn't do away with it until he fulfilled it.

No! **He did not abolish the law. He fulfilled the law.** But what they are saying is that he fulfilled the law. He perfected it and then he got rid of it because we didn't need it. This is why they don't keep it. This is why they don't practice it. This is why they teach you that you don't have to — because Yeshua did it all.

I hope you are getting this.

There is so much here that in times past we have been brainwashed by theology to believe that we do not have to keep the commands. Therefore, by practice we openly and belligerently violated and taught and preached that anybody who keeps the law has ‑fallen from grace.

So, he did this when by grace he instituted the New Covenant in his blood. Thus, he made provision for the outpouring of the Spirit and the formation of the church/ekklesia as his body. This is what they teach.

The chronometrical principle (like I said) is where the theologians and the interpreters begin to take liberty. They begin to insert words.

Testament or Covenant from a Greek or Hebrew perspective is interesting. ‑Testament doesn't have the full weight of ‑covenant, but it is a translatable word. So now instead of putting ‑covenant ‑ in some places, there is covenant. But in the places that matter, in order to perpetuate this New Testament belief, we insert the word ‑testament instead of covenant. If covenant was put there it would literally bring new meaning to the New Testament and it would literally be the ‑New Covenant.

Well, how can you call that portion of the Bible the ‑New Covenant? Now you also have to change the ‑old covenant to ‑testament so you have the Old Testament and the New Testament. Or you would have the ‑Old Covenant and the ‑New Testament, but that doesn't sound right. So, you change the ‑covenant to ‑testament and now you have two. You have the Old and the New Testaments.

This teaching says that when Yeshua by grace instituted the New Covenant in his blood, thus he made provision for the outpouring of the Spirit and the formation of the church/ekklesia as his body. This is partly true. Yeshua brought in grace. He instituted the New Covenant in his blood. **But he did not abolish the law.**

Messiah came at the end of the past ages and introduced the present Messianic Age. This is true. But when you begin to look at –past age and –Messianic Age, you see a break. If we use the scriptures and the words properly, you won't see it as a break. You will interpret it in the proper context.

(1 Corinthians 10:11) *"Now all these things happened unto them for examples: and they are written for our admonition, upon whom the ends of the world* [Greek--ages] *are come."*

The Greek word is –age, but the word in Hebrew deals with the end of the world.

(Hebrews 9:26) *"For then must he often have suffered since the foundation of the world: but now once in the end of the world hath he appeared to put away sin by the sacrifice of himself."*

The world as we know it is going to come to an end. *Revelation* makes it clear to us that there is going to be a new heaven and a new earth. And with that will be a new age. I know you don't like hearing the term –new age. As a matter of fact, we think terribly of –New Age. The word uses –age, but it is actually –world.

Then you have the New World Order. You have all of these words that have been taken and had a spin put onto them. So New Age and New World Order are all negative connotations.

It is during the Messianic Age that the mystery of the one body of Christ that is composed of Jew/Israel and Gentile is being revealed.

(Ephesians 3:4-6) *"Whereby, when ye read, ye may understand my knowledge in the mystery of Christ) Which in other ages was not made known unto the sons of men, as it is now revealed unto his holy apostles and prophets by the Spirit; That the Gentiles should be fellow heirs, and of the same body, and partakers of his promise in Christ by the gospel:"*

The scriptures reveal that this present age is to come to an end. This present world is to come to an end.

(Matthew 13:39, 40, 49) *"The harvest is the end of the world.* (Greek, –age) Yeshua is giving the explanation of the parable.

(Matthew 13:39, 40) *"The enemy that sowed them is the devil; the harvest is the end of the world; and the reapers are the angels. As therefore the tares are gathered and burned in the fire; so shall it be **in the end of this world**."*

(Matthew 13:49-50) *"So shall it be **at the end of the world**: the angels shall come forth, and sever the wicked from among the just, And shall cast them into the furnace of fire: there shall be wailing and gnashing of teeth."*

This is the end of the world.

(Matthew 24:3) *"And as he sat upon the mount of Olives, the disciples came unto him privately, saying, ,,Tell us, when shall these things be? and what shall be the sign of thy coming, and of **the end of the world?**"'* (Greek, –age)

This is the question that is asked. We know that there is a Hebrew gospel of *Matthew* and we have the Greek. There are those who want to argue the Greek when the Greek doesn't do justice to some passages of scripture, especially translating it from the Hebrew.

(Matthew 28:20) *"Teaching them to observe all things whatsoever I have commanded you: and, lo, I am with you always, even unto **the end of the world**.* [Greek, –age] *Amen."*

The Future Ages

This term is used to refer to the ages beyond the second coming of Messiah: those that are future to the present Messianic Age. The Bible does not give a full description of these future ages, but it does establish their reality by referring to them.

Again, remember that I told you earlier. Theologians take a lot of liberties with scripture in explaining it because their definition, their explanation is going to be based upon their theology. The scripture has to line up with their theology, not that the theology lines up with scripture. You form the theology, the belief system, based upon the scripture. Then you find the scripture to support a theological position.

We have to be very careful about that, even as Messianics/Hebrew Roots. It is so easy to eisegete or pull out to make the scriptures say what you want them to say in order to support your beliefs. You have to be careful with that. We have to be careful with that because you can take a belief system, you can take a belief position based upon your understanding at that time of scripture. Some people are unwilling to change even when Yeshua showed them that they should.

We have to be willing to make the changes that we need to make, especially when the Father by his Spirit shows us that we need to make those changes.

The Age to Come — This refers to the age immediately following the second coming of Christ. Many expositors speak of this as the Kingdom Age in its fullest earthly manifestation. However, there are sharp divisions of opinion concerning this future age. The scriptures do speak clearly of an age to come.

(Mark 10:30) *"...in the world* [Greek, –age] *to come eternal life."*

(Luke 20:34-36) *"And Jesus answering said unto them, „The children of this world* [Greek, –age] *marry, and are given in marriage: But they which shall be accounted worthy to obtain that world* [Greek, –age]*, and the resurrection from the dead, neither marry, nor are given in marriage: Neither can they die any more: for they are equal unto the angels; and are the children of God, being the children of the resurrection.""*

I am convinced that just as the Hebrew *Matthew* has somehow miraculously emerged over thousands of years, that we are going to see that *John* was not written in Greek. *Matthew* could not have been written in Greek. You are talking about Hebrew-speaking people penning their gospel in the Greek language? Just as the book of *Hebrews* was written in Greek?

Theology has pulled the wool over our eyes in a number of areas. I believe that knowledge is going to increase. A lot of the things that we believed (just as theologians have believed) will be exposed. As time moves on, more and more information is going to find its way to the surface. Things that have been locked up in vaults or buried are going to be unburied and unlocked.

We are going to see that this knowledge that is hidden to us right now is going to manifest. It may be in my lifetime or it may be after I am gone, but I will tell you right now. I find it very difficult to believe that Yeshua's disciples spoke Greek. I find that very difficult. I believe that they were Hebrew-speaking. I believe that they could communicate and that there were translators. I don't believe that *John* or *Matthew* or *Hebrews* or *Revelation* was written in Greek. I just find that hard to believe.

I may be proven wrong. People say I am wrong right now, but I believe that in time I will be proven right. It does not matter whether I am right or wrong. It is just that I think that when we begin to look at the scriptures from a Hebrew perspective, we are going to get more understanding and clarity than when we look at things from a Greek perspective. It is impossible for a Greek-minded or Western-minded person to really understand the Hebrew way, the commands, the God of the Hebrew people and Abraham, Isaac and Jacob. I just find it difficult.

As we continue to look at this word –age, we see that the children of this world marry. But they which shall be accounted worthy to obtain that world and the resurrection from the dead, neither marry nor are given in marriage.

(Luke 20:36) "*...neither can they die any more; for they are equal unto angels and are the children of God, being the children of the resurrection.*"

(Ephesians 1:21) "*...not only in this world,* [Greek, –age] *but also in that* **which is to come.**"

(Hebrews 6:5) "*...and the powers of the world* [Greek, –age] *to come.*"

The Eternal Ages Future — The eternal ages are referred to in scripture as:

- The Ages to Come *(Ephesians 2:7)*
- World without end *(Ephesians 3:21)*
- Forever and ever *(1 Timothy 1:17, 2 Timothy 4:18; Revelation 5:13, 14; 14:11; 20:10)*

The following scriptures speak of the endless ages to come:

(Ephesians 2:7) "*...that in the ages to come he might show the exceeding riches of his grace.*"

(Ephesians 3:21) "*Unto him be glory in the church/ekklesia by Messiah Yeshua throughout all ages, world without end. Amen.*"

The dominant thought in the scriptures concerning eternity future is the eternal bliss of the righteous and the eternal torment of the wicked.

Conclusions

According to the chronometrical principle, we see that YeHoVaH as the eternal administrator of time has ordained its successive ages. Therefore, he was also able to be the great chronographer of the ages; writing concerning them and their related events.

Thus, the literary method of chronography used in writing scripture gives rise to the chronometrical principle of interpreting scripture.

In the next lesson, we will get into how we are to use the chronometrical principle because it is important to understand how to use a principle that you have.

Class 65 Study Summary

Key Points

1. To review: <u>Aion</u> is an age by extension, perpetuity of time; by implication, the world; an unbroken age, a segment of time, era, period of time. <u>Genea</u> is a generation; by implication an age, period of time (of limited duration). <u>Kairos</u> is an occasion, set or proper time, measure of time, fixed and definite time, seasonable time; limited time. <u>Kronos</u> is a space of time in general; period of time; by implying delay.
2. Together these words support the concept that YeHoVaH has divided and arranged time into a series of successive times and seasons. These ages can be divided as follows:
   a. Eternal Ages Past (YeHoVaH, the I AM)
   b. Age of Creation (an implied age prior to the creation of the earth)
   c. Age of Recreation (between Genesis 1 and 2 and the fall of Satan)
   d. Age of the Patriarchs-Promise (Adam to Abraham, –Age of the Fathers)
   e. Age of the Chosen Nation-Law (Isaac/Israel to Messiah)
3. The past ages from a theological standpoint are the ages of time prior to the New Testament. It is everything that happened from creation up until the New Testament period.
4. The curse of the law is those curses that are associated with violating the law.
5. The –age of the church is code. David was talking about the importance of keeping the feasts. The feasts (according to theology) were in the age of the law, not in the age of the church. The –church age begins with Yeshua, according to manmade theology.
6. The –church of today says that Yeshua –Jesus delivered the church from the law and gave it a whole new day of worship. That day is Sunday (or Sun-day).
7. You will not find the –age of the law or the –age of the church in the Bible. That is theology.
8. People and their theology divide the Bible into different ages of time or dispensations. That is why we see the age of the law, the age of the church, the age of the sons, etc. What we have is the result of the chronometrical principle being applied. People categorize the Bible chronometrically to break time into ages to fit their agenda.
9. YeHoVaH looked at all of the tribes of Israel as one.
10. Yeshua said that the prerequisite to receiving the Holy Spirit was obedience to the law.
11. The term —present age is broken down into the New Testament era which consists of: a. this world; b. the time of reformation; c. the time of restitution; d. the last days
12. The New Testament is actually the New Covenant mentioned by *Jeremiah*. It is not a new –testament. The idea of a New Testament refers to the books of the gospels and the letters that were written by the apostles. These were given the title –New Testament by the translators. People separated the Tanakh from the gospels and letters written later and claimed this separation was the –will of the Father.
13. The Bible says there will be a new heaven and a new Jerusalem that will come down. Something is going to happen.
14. This period of the present/future age is theologically referred to as the Messianic Age.
15. Yeshua did not come to abolish the law. He fulfilled the law. By grace he instituted the New Covenant in his blood.
16. Theology has pulled the wool over people's eyes in many areas.
17. YeHoVaH is the eternal administrator of time and great chronographer of the ages.

Review Exercise

1. Complete this chart of biblical ages.

```
         PAST AGES          |          PRESENT / FUTURE AGES
                        ETERNITY
```

2. React to the statement in this lesson: –The moment you go beyond what is written, you open yourself up to all manner of theology and the possibilities are even greater that you are going to go into error.

3. What do you think about the fact that –there are certain things that scripture is clear on and certain things scripture is not clear about? Are you okay with ambiguity in the Bible?

4. We see that once you begin to form theories about the Bible, you have to support those theories.

    a. How would you go about identifying what someone is sharing with you as a theory?

b. How do you rally the tools you have studied in this course to bring clarity to –theoretical theology ?

_____
_____
_____
_____
_____
_____

Rate the following statements by filling in the most appropriate number.

(1 = I do not agree 10 = I agree completely)

Objectives:

1. I can define terms relating to time in the scripture.

   1.◯ 2.◯ 3.◯ 4.◯ 5.◯ 6.◯ 7.◯ 8.◯ 9.◯ 10.◯

2. I can explain the theological division of Bible time into ages: past and present/future.

   1.◯ 2.◯ 3.◯ 4.◯ 5.◯ 6.◯ 7.◯ 8.◯ 9.◯ 10.◯

3. I can define the validity of the –gap theory of *Genesis 1:1-1:2.*

   1.◯ 2.◯ 3.◯ 4.◯ 5.◯ 6.◯ 7.◯ 8.◯ 9.◯ 10.◯

My Journal

What I learned from this class:

_____
_____
_____
_____
_____
_____
_____
_____
_____
_____
_____

Please Continue Study

Coming Up Next :

THIRD SEMESTER

Second Quarter

Classes 66 - 79

Made in the USA
Columbia, SC
04 February 2025